THE SPEARS OF LACONIA

THE SPEARS
OF
LACONIA

BOOK 7 IN THE BABYLON SERIES

SAM SISAVATH

Published by Road to Babylon Media LLC
Visit www.roadtobabylon.com for news, updates, and announcements

Edited by Jennifer Jensen and Wendy Chan
Cover Art by Creative Paramita
Formatting by BB eBooks

ISBN-13: 978-0692538845
ISBN-10: 0692538844

BOOKS IN THE BABYLON SERIES
(READING ORDER)

Also by the Author

Sometimes you have to make a stand.

They've been relentlessly hounded ever since The Purge decimated the world, and every day since has been a struggle to stay one step ahead of the enemy.

Keo has returned, claiming to have information that can turn the tide of war against the ghouls. Lara wants nothing more than to strike back, but she has other problems: Will has yet to make contact, and a team she's sent on an important mission has gone off the radar.

Meanwhile, Texas becomes a battlefield as a new force rises to challenge the rule of the ghouls and their human collaborators. Led by a mysterious leader, this new threat has the firepower to cripple the enemy, but their cure might be worse than the disease.

Caught between two destructive forces, Lara, Keo, and their friends will have to make a choice—fall in line or forge their own path—before the decision is made for them.

A year after The Purge, any chance of victory will rest on the tips of the Spears, and those fearless enough to wield them…

BOOK ONE

REST YOUR WEARY HEAD

CHAPTER 1

FRANK

"YOU CAN'T WIN."

He ignored the voice. It had become easier with time, and like everything else about his new existence—this thing he called life after death *(Re-life?)*—it was about balancing acceptance with resistance, trying to hold onto the past while not neglecting the present. Because the here and now was where the danger lurked; it was also here that the answer to the future was within his grasp.

"You must know that by now. After all you've seen, all you've learned."

There was something odd about the voice these last few weeks, a guarded hesitation that hadn't been there when it first spoke to him in the early days. It wasn't fear—no, he wouldn't go that far—but it didn't sound nearly as certain as it once had been, either.

"She understood. Why did you think she came over? She opened the door, remember?"

Yes, he remembered. Kate had opened the door, dooming them. Almost.

Whatever happened to Kate?

Oh, that's right. He had killed her, that night outside the gas station. How long ago now? He couldn't remember at the moment, but it would come to him. It always did, eventually.

"Talk to me."

It was growing annoyed, the warning tone of a parent cajoling an uncooperative child while at the same time letting him know that it was losing patience. It wanted him to respond, because that was how it would track him. It had taken him a long time to learn how to erect the barrier inside his mind. But he had adapted. He always did.

Letters. An acronym. SE...*something.*

Memories came and went, sometimes garbled, other times clear as the crystal blue of her eyes, the glint of the sun against her blonde hair.

It helped to think of her. To concentrate on the smoothness of her skin. He longed to touch her again, to press against and taste her lips...

"Whatever it takes," he had said, *"whatever happens, you won't have to face another night alone."*

He'd said that to her, one of many unkept promises that haunted his nights and terrorized his days. He'd failed her then, but he could make up for it. He could save her; save everyone.

And all they had to do was find him.

Mabry.

He was the key. The beginning and the end. He was the voice in all their heads. In *his* head.

Mabry was the one constant. He was the eternal. Everywhere, and nowhere.

"I'll find you," Mabry said to him now inside his head. *"You can't run forever."*

He focused on the surrounding blackness, on the things that moved and thrived within the endless folds of darkness that he wouldn't have been able to see before. They were out there, swarms of them, clear as day—even though he had forgotten what day looked like, or the warmth of the sun against his skin.

They had been on his trail for months now, but their pursuit had increased in intensity in just the last few weeks. It was as if Mabry knew what he was trying to do. Was that possible? Were there holes in his barrier that he hadn't detected? Was Mabry burrowing around inside his mind this very second?

No. He couldn't afford this right now, because doubt was the enemy. He had to forge ahead, follow the original plan, because there was no victory without a plan…Z?

It came from somewhere in the recesses of his mind, deep, deep down in that place where pieces of his past slumbered, waiting to be resurrected.

Something about plans. Letters. A through Z…

He shook the jumbled thoughts away. It would come to him later.

Back to the present. Back to the now.

He could smell them all the way up here, the stench of their existence carried upward by the breeze that washed across all the rooftops from the ocean beyond the city limits. He could almost taste it, the bitter salt water against the tip of his tongue, sending strange sensations *(fear?)* through every inch of his body.

Their dark shapes vanished and reappeared out of office buildings, stores, and apartments. They were little more than tiny dots, like insignificant ants against the moonlit night. He had higher ground and could glimpse the entire city from up here. Safe on his perch, though he knew very well he would never be entirely safe. None of them were, so long as he was out there.

Mabry.

He was the key. The everything and the nothing, the beginning and the end; at once nowhere, and everywhere…

A soft *click* as the man came out of the rooftop access door and moved across the gravel floor toward him. The attempt at stealth was laudable, but he might as well be dropping firecrackers with every footstep. That, and the aroma of medical ointment over old wounds was impossible to ignore.

The rustling of a thick jacket as the man lay down on his stomach next to him and peered off the edge of the rooftop with a pair of night-vision binoculars. Mist formed in front of his partly covered face with every word, the taste of beef jerky still lingering on his lips even though the man probably couldn't smell it.

But *he* could smell it just fine, just as he could hear conversations multiple floors below or above him, or feel the rough or smooth texture of things without touching them. Everything was hyper-realized, all his senses razor sharp. They were the gifts that came with the curse, that made him more than what he was, though he would forego them all without hesitation if it meant he could be what he once was.

"Can you see them?" the man asked. "They were supposed to have arrived by now."

"No," he hissed.

He hated having to talk, hated the noise that came out with every single word. They were just another reminder of what he was. As a result, he tried to say as little as possible, which was difficult because communication with the man was necessary.

"*Can* you see that far?" the man asked.

"No."

"I thought you had super everything. I guess laser beams are out of the question, huh?"

He didn't bother to answer that one.

"You ever get cold?" the man asked.

"No."

"I guess you wouldn't. Being both hot and cold. How does that even work, anyway?"

"I don't know."

"You ever think about it?"

"No."

It was a lie. He often thought about what the transformation had done to him, but it always ended in frustration. He knew that it did things to him at a cellular level, but the details were beyond his understanding. He was a grunt before, and he was one now. Maybe she would know. Maybe he could ask her when he finally saw her again.

The man adjusted his position, his clothes scratching against the rooftop. "Looks like a party down there. How many?"

"Too many."

"How the hell do they keep finding us?"

"I don't know."

"You?"

"Maybe."

"Or us?"

"Maybe…"

The man pushed himself up into a sitting position, then opened a pouch along his cargo pants and took out an almost empty bag of beef jerky. He pulled out a stick and chewed *(too loud)* on it for a moment.

The stink of preserved meat made his nostrils twitch and reminded him that he no longer yearned for food as he once had. There was enough blood *(Mabry's)* flowing through him that he could survive for months, maybe even years. When he did thirst, it was easily satisfied with animal blood. Two cows in Louisiana, a pair of horses in Texas…

"You thought this through?" the man said after a while. "You're not who you once were, you know. What's to stop the Ranger from shooting first and listening to you never?"

"You'll convince them."

"I was afraid you'd say that." A brief pause, with only the man's soft breathing and calm heartbeat from under his clothes to fill the void. "Did you ever wonder that maybe it's better for her—for all of them—if they stayed away from Texas?"

"She has to know…"

"So you keep saying, but she's not the woman you remember." Another pause. "I'm just saying, this reunion might not work out the way you hope."

Another stick of jerky, followed by crunching and swallowing.

He looked down at the silhouetted forms racing back and forth below. They were free to roam and explore, to search every hole for him. But, like him, they would soon have to seek shelter, because the sun would be here.

How long had it been since he'd seen the sun? Months. It had been months, even though it felt like centuries.

"You miss it, don't you?" the man asked.

"Yes."

"You ever tempted to just say 'Fuck it,' and stepping into the light, so to speak?"

Tempted? Yes. It was worse in the early days, like an itch he couldn't scratch, a siren's call beckoning him to let it all go, to let *her* go. But he couldn't. He had failed to keep his promises, but he could still save her, even if it meant prolonging this miserable existence.

"Whatever it takes," he had said, *"whatever happens, you won't have to face another night alone."*

"No," he hissed.

"I don't believe you," the man said.

"Believe what you want."

"Gee, thanks, I'll do that."

Another *click* as the woman came out to join them. He had smelled her when she was still in the stairwell and heard her soft, careful footsteps from five floors down. Her heartbeat accelerated slightly under her winter clothing as she emerged into the open night, but he knew it wasn't the cold air—it was the sight of him.

It was why he wore the trench coat when he was around them, with the hoodie covering most of his face, only his eyes peering out from under the frayed brim. It seemed to work with the man, but then the man was an odd one. Weeks later, and the woman was still trying to get used to being around him.

"Did they show up yet?" she whispered to the man. He didn't know why she was whispering. Up here, the black eyes wouldn't be able to hear them anyway.

"Don't know," the man said.

"He can't see the ocean from here?"

"Apparently he can't see that far."

"Hunh."

"What I said."

"What about our other friends?"

"I don't think they're going anywhere anytime soon, but they're definitely tracking us."

"How?"

"Haven't figured that part out yet."

"Well, let me know when you do."

"That might take a while."

"Goes without saying."

The man snorted. "Anything going on downstairs?"

"I didn't hear anything. We locked all the doors, right?"

"I think so."

"You think so?"

"I'm pretty sure we did."

"You're always so comforting, Keo."

"I try."

The woman leaned over the edge, her short blonde hair moving against the breeze. "Jesus, look at them. If they find us in here..."

"That's it, positive thoughts," the man said.

She sighed. "We should have made a run for the beach. They don't like the water, right?"

"Definitely not."

"We should have made a run for the beach," she repeated.

"Lara and the *Trident* aren't here yet. We'd just end up waiting for them down there anyway. At least here we have a lot of floors between us and them."

The woman glanced over at him, brown eyes focusing as if she could make out his face behind the hoodie. "How many?" she asked.

"Too many," he hissed.

"Can you be more specific?"

"No."

"But you can see them down there."

"Yes."

"All of them?"

"Yes..."

The man chuckled. "Chatterbox, this guy."

THE MAN AND woman had names, but it was easier to think of them as just *the man* and *the woman*. They were somewhere on the twentieth floor above him, their voices reaching down through the vibrations that traveled along the steel and concrete and glass of the building. Though he couldn't hear every single word they spoke, he could hear just enough.

"…going to get us killed," the woman was saying.

"Relax," the man said.

"'Relax'?" She might have laughed, but that kind of nuance was lost on its way down the stairwell. "We're inside a building with a blue-eyed ghoul, Keo. And you want me to *relax?*"

"You don't have to be here. Tobias—"

"Screw Tobias."

"I thought you said there was nothing between the two of you?"

Silence. Then, two seconds later, the woman said, "You're an asshole."

The man laughed softly. "So that's a no?"

"I told you, there was never anything between us."

"All that time…"

"What about you?"

"What about me?"

"All that time alone, looking for us. Did you ever…?"

"No."

"I don't believe you. Even with that ugly scar, there are still plenty of desperate women out there."

"Ouch," he said.

This time he was sure she did laugh. "No offense."

"Oh sure, why should I take offense to that?"

The woman answered, but he had already gotten up and slipped out of the stairwell and into the darkened lobby before her words reached him. He sat inside the shadows, feeling at home among the forgotten relics of an old world.

A stubborn pool of moonlight managed to filter in through the glass walls across from him, the sidewalks and streets on the other side dull and gray. He wasn't worried about being exposed, because the black eyes had no special ability or heightened senses. But the creatures did have eyes and some measure of intelligence, enough that they could recognize the disturbances in their surroundings.

Dead, not stupid, someone once called them.

Who had said that? He couldn't remember, but it would come to him eventually. It always did, usually when he least expected it.

Flickers of movement as a dozen of the creatures emerged out of the darkness and moved up the sidewalk. He expected them to keep going past the building, because surely they hadn't left any clues to their presence outside, had they? He was sure of it, but then one of the black eyes stopped and cocked its head. He realized it was just glaring at its own reflection in the glass wall.

He was relieved, until the skeletal thing moved forward and grabbed the handle of one of the twin glass doors and tried pulling it instead of continuing on its way. The door didn't budge. Its black eyes looked confused for a moment, and then it tried pulling a few more times.

If it had stopped, that might have been the end of it, except the damn thing seemed suddenly determined to get inside. Its activity attracted the attention of the others, and a second—then a third—of the ghouls stopped and grabbed the other handle and began pulling at it, too.

But the doors held, just as he knew they would.

Two others *clacked* their way along the length of the glass wall and peered inside. He didn't move or react, because he knew they couldn't see him. Not through the darkness, with just the barest of moonlight to illuminate their search. One smashed a right arm that was little more than a stump into its section of the window, producing a dull *thud* and little else.

He watched the creatures give up and move on, one by one, until there were just two left behind, still fighting with the doors. They were gaunt things, almost like deformed children with pruned flesh. They abandoned the doors and moved along the walls, angling their bodies in an effort to spy on the darkened corners inside the lobby.

A sudden wave of sadness washed over him, and he wondered if *he* looked like these twisted and blackened remnants of what once was. Besides the blue eyes, what really made him stand out? There wasn't very much. The trench coat was just a façade, a vain attempt to hold onto a lie.

"You're not who you once were, you know," the man had said earlier on the rooftop. *"What's to stop the Ranger from shooting first and listening to you never?"*

The words stung because they were honest and true. He wasn't the man he once was. He wasn't a man at all.

He watched the creatures pressing themselves into the glass, smearing sections of it with thick, coagulated fluid that could be anything from blood to drool or pus. This was him now, and no amount of clothing would change that. How did he ever think he could convince her of anything? When they saw him, this was what they would see—a dark, blackened thing that had once been human, but was no longer.

"You're not who you once were, you know..."

Of course he knew. He'd always known, but he had managed to delude himself anyway, told one lie after another until he believed it, because he wanted so badly to save her, to make up for all the failures of the past. Because Mabry had to be stopped, and he knew how—

It fell from the sky and splattered against the concrete walkway, the loud *crunch* audible even from inside the lobby. A wave of thick black blood sprayed a nearby section of the glass wall in the aftermath.

Before he could recognize what it was—a black-eyed ghoul falling from above and obliterating itself against the pavement—another, then another, then *still another* fell like raindrops. They smashed into the sidewalk and road one by one, covering more sections of the outside wall in blood and flesh and pulverized bone—

Ghouls. Falling. *From above.*

The loud, unmistakable crash of breaking glass, followed by gleaming shards plummeting outside the building.

No, no. They were inside the building. *How did they get inside the building?*

He raced along the length of the shadowed back wall and slipped into the stairwell, and went up. He was almost floating in the air, his bare feet barely touching the cold concrete steps. He once considered wearing shoes because that would have added to the façade, but shoes were cumbersome and he had come to rely on his speed. More than once, it had been the difference between life and *(re)*death.

He was rounding the third floor when—

Bang! A gunshot from above, coming from the twentieth floor.

The taste of silver drenched his tongue all the way down here. Silver bullets. Either the man or the woman had fired. It didn't matter who, because they had just alerted the entire city to their location, and they wouldn't have done that unless they absolutely had to.

Sixth floor...

A short, startled scream. The woman.

Eighth floor...

The *pop-pop-pop* of automatic rifle fire began blasting through the building, and his skin rippled from head to toe as more silver was exposed to air.

Tenth floor...

He pushed harder as the shots came faster and louder. Every inch of him wanted to flee in the other direction, the growing proximity to silver nauseating. The metal wouldn't kill him unless it struck his brain, but it still hurt everywhere else. A lot.

He pushed on.

Fifteenth floor...

The man was shouting, telling the woman to run, run, *run*.

Sixteenth...

A constant stream of *pop-pop-pop* now. So much silver that he wanted to retch just to get it out of his system, but he couldn't remember how.

Twentieth!

A loud *bang!* as the stairwell door flew open and the woman stumbled into it back-first, fire spitting back into the floor from the barrel of her rifle. She heard him, spun around, the brown of her eyes widening—

Recognition flashed across her face, and she spun back to the open doorway and continued firing into it. "Hurry up!" she shouted. "It's here!"

"Fuck!" the man said as he stumbled into the stairwell, firing his entire magazine into the floor at full-auto. The man spun around, saw him, and shouted, "We're fucked, pal!"

"Go," he hissed.

"Go where?"

"Down."

"Down?"

"*Down!*" he shouted, grabbing the man by the jacket collar and jerking him down the steps. It took all of his self-control not to throw the man like a sack of useless flesh, because it would have been so, so easy.

The woman didn't need any encouragement; she raced down the steps, and they locked eyes for half a heartbeat as she passed him.

"Go," he hissed.

She went, reloading from a pouch around her waist as she did so.

"Come on!" the man shouted from below.

"Go!" he hissed.

The man gave him a confused look.

"We'll meet again!" he shouted.

The man might have nodded, but by then he had turned around to face the open door and the twentieth floor beyond.

They had broken through the windows—or, at least, the ones who had survived the climb up the side of the buildings. How many others hadn't made it up and were still falling, splattering one by one against the sidewalks below? The survivors were now crawling over their dead and toward him.

"*There you are,*" the familiar voice said inside his head.

He grabbed the first black-eyed ghoul that reached him around the neck and smashed it into the wall, its frail bones crumbling under its skin like twigs. He felt no satisfaction in hearing the *crack* of its limbs, the *snap* of its neck. There might have even been some strange surge of sadness, but he passed that off to Mabry invading his mind, trying to slow him down with his words.

"I told you I'd find you again."

He used the flopping creature as a weapon, hitting one, two, *three* more of the monsters as he pushed into the floor, leaving the stairwell behind. The taste of silver lingering in the air—still embedded in the twisted bodies of dead ghouls on the floor—threatened to overwhelm him, but he thought of the alternative and kept going.

"There is no safety. No sanctuary."

He waded through the throng of flesh and bone and squealing things, striking and pushing and punching and kicking what he could. They were like children, grabbing at his legs and trying to cling to his arms. Bony fingers clutched at his elbows and knees and snaked around his throat in an attempt to impede his progress.

"Nowhere that I can't find you again and again and again."

They had stopped trying to reach the stairwell behind him, their pursuit of the man and woman forgotten because he was their singular purpose, their goal. Mabry's voice rushed through his head as it did theirs, because his blood flowed through all their veins. What they saw, he saw. What he commanded, they did.

"Embrace what you are. What you've become."

He grabbed another one by the throat and began using it as a battering ram. He smashed skull into skull, leaping over grasping arms, and snapped limbs as he landed. A chest caved under him and covered him in black liquid from head to toe. His vision began to darken as fluids that weren't his own splashed his eyes.

"You have so much potential. We could do so much together in the years to come…"

Bony fingers continued scraping against the brick and mortar outside the building, signaling that more of them were coming. Too many. Always too many. Hands appeared out of the darkness and grappled onto the windowsills, pulling up rail-thin creatures with accusing black eyes.

"The decades to come..."

Blood gushed around him, splattering every part of his moving form in thick chunks. Theirs. His. He couldn't tell the difference anymore.

"...the centuries..."

His vision had all but disappeared, forcing him to glimpse the far wall across the floor through a black fog that was quickly darkening further and further still.

"You can't save her. You can barely save yourself."

He wanted to give in, to let Mabry's voice wash over him. Every ounce of his being longed to embrace the everything, and the nothing. It would be so easy; all he had to do was stop moving, stop snapping the necks of the weak things pushing against him. All he had to do was stop punching his fists through their skulls and caving in their already shrunken chests. They screamed soundless words as he tossed them aside and kicked them across the room.

"Give in," Mabry said, his voice soothing, comforting.

And still they came, an unrelenting tide of shriveled dark flesh and dead black eyes. They filled the floor, scrambling over cubicles, the stampede of bare feet *tap-tap-tapping* against the bloodied tiles.

"Come home."

He dropped the shattered bones he'd been using as weapons and leaped. Outstretched fingers brushed against his legs and arms, every one of them inches from finding purchase, just before he smashed into the top half of one of the windows and burst out into the night air.

The kiss of the wind, cool against his flesh, made him gasp with surprise.

It had been a while since he actually felt the weather; it was always a constant balance of cold and heat, the incongruity fighting for dominance over him. Inside him. Outside him. Everywhere. It was easier not to feel at all.

But it was different this time. Tonight. Because he was flying, and the building across the street appeared, rushing toward him in a blur.

How far?

Close.

How did it get so close?

Then a figure flickered against a long stretch of glass curtain wall, a bright pool of moonlight peeking out from behind the clouds above him at last, highlighting a bony creature of black skin and gleaming blue eyes, the dirty and torn fabrics of a faded brown trench coat fluttering behind it like some kind of cape.

For a second—just a split second—he remembered how to smile, before shattering glass filled his eardrums and pain stabbed through him like a thousand spears.

Pain. Overwhelming, glorious pain.

"Pain lets you know you're still alive," someone had once said.

He couldn't remember who had said it, but it would come to him eventually, like it always did.

CHAPTER 2

GABY

IT WAS PITCH dark and she could barely make out Nate's outline on the bench next to her, though she could hear his soft breathing just fine. And there was his scent, which she had become familiar with over the last few weeks. It would have almost been romantic if they weren't squeezed into the back of a van parked out in the open along a curb in a Texas town that was, at this very moment, infested with ghouls.

Across from them Danny was whispering, small clouds forming around his outline with every word.

"…he stops at a Wallbys pharmacy and runs up to the counter and says, out of breath, 'Mister, mister, you got any condoms?' The pharmacist smiles knowingly and grabs a pack and rings it up. 'Who's the lucky girl?' he asks. 'Girl?' the guy says. 'There's no girl.' The pharmacist looks confused, then realizes, 'Ah! It's the twenty-first century!' 'Lucky guy, I mean,' the pharmacist corrects himself. To which the guy flashes an embarrassed grin and says, 'It's just me, I'm afraid.' 'But what do you need the condoms for, then?' the pharmacist asks. 'Well, I believe in safe sex,' the guy answers."

"I don't get it," Nate whispered.

"Because he believes in safe sex," Danny said.

"I still don't get it."

"No?"

Nate shook his head. Or, at least, Gaby saw the shape of his head moving slightly left then right as he did his very best to move as little as possible.

Danny looked over at her, blue eyes barely visible in the suffocating darkness. "You get it?"

Gaby smiled back at him. "I got it."

"That's my girl. What say we ditch this buzzkill? He's really bringing me down."

"He'll come around."

"Yeah, I'll come around," Nate said. Then, softly, "As soon as you get funnier."

"I heard that," Danny said.

"You were supposed to."

Nate's head was turned in her direction, and they exchanged a smile. They were close enough that she was reasonably certain he could see her response. Of course, it was so dark in the back of the van with the grime covering up the front windshield to their right and the two smaller back windows behind them, that it was entirely possible she was wrong. It didn't help that all three of them had taken up positions in the darkest parts of the vehicle.

A van. They were riding out the night in a van. She would have preferred a stronger hideout. Anything, in fact, but a vehicle in the middle of an open street. Not that they'd had any choice. Fleeing Hellion with daylight running out hadn't helped; neither had all the movements inside the buildings they'd checked. It seemed as if there was a ghoul inside every single one of them.

So it was a van or nothing. She just hoped it was enough to avoid—

Whump! as something landed on the rooftop above her. That was quickly followed by the *tap-tap* of bare feet moving from the back of the van toward the front. Slowly, as if it had all the time *(night)* in the world.

Gaby slowly—oh so slowly—extended one finger and flicked off the safety on the M4 rifle in front of her. The soft *click!* sounded so much louder inside the close confines of the vehicle, though she passed that off as her imagination playing tricks with her.

Probably.

She slipped her left hand around the pistol grip underneath the carbine's barrel and tightened it, feeling the leather fingerless gloves constricting against the cold object. Next to her, just a few inches down the bench, Nate's breathing picked up slightly. Not a lot, but enough that she noticed. She couldn't tell what Danny was doing across from them, but his head looked slightly tilted up toward the ceiling, so he had heard the creature landing and moving around up there as well.

There was a *clicking* sound in her right ear, followed by Danny's voice, whispering through the earbud connected to the radio clipped to her hip. "Just one. We'll sit still as mice and let them pass us by. No muss, no fuss, you can keep your virgin daughters, Gus."

She uncurled her fingers from around the pistol grip and moved it a bit to the left, found the Push-To-Talk switch, and *clicked* it with as much deliberate speed as she could muster. "Roger that."

She glanced over at one of the two back windows—one-by-one foot glass panes covered in a thick film of dirt and time and the elements. Without anything brighter than the moon outside, there was no chance of seeing out, and vice versa. She flexed her fingers to keep the blood circulating, because the last thing she needed right now was to go numb—

Whump! as the creature leaped off the roof and there was just the silence again.

Close one.

They waited to hear more sounds of ghouls outside. The creatures traveled in groups, and where there was one, there were usually more. Sometimes a lot more.

One minute became two, then three…

…five…

Click, then Danny's voice in her right ear. "Well, that was a close one. Now, as I was saying, why don't we dump the Natester here? He's just dragging us down, what with his inability to understand a perfectly serviceable joke and that stupid haircut."

"Hey," Nate said.

"No thanks, I already ate," Danny said. "Also, I'm not a horse, though I've been confused with an ass once or twice…"

WILDEN, TEXAS, WAS 240 square miles of unincorporated land and sat peacefully under the morning sun. To look at it from a distance, as they had while rushing by it on State Highway 105, thankful to just be alive after the mess in Hellion, she hadn't thought there was anything worth salvaging. The hour or so they had spent looking had proven her correct. Not that they'd actually gone into most of the buildings; there were plenty of signs that they were occupied, and had been for the better part of a year.

The town was dead in more ways than one, but there was nothing wrong with the embracing warmth of morning. She spent a moment basking in the rays of sunlight, thankful to be in Texas. The state was never known for its cold winters, but the temperature dropped enough at night that she was glad for the extra thermal clothing they had on under their vests, and there was enough of a constant breeze in the daylight that she remained comfortable without having to add or remove layers.

Last night's impromptu refuge was parked on the curb of FM 163, a long stretch of two-lane road (with a very generous middle) flanked by the occasional houses, and surrounded by vast farmland. In another few years, the grass would overtake the man-made structures and there wouldn't be much of Wilden left for passersby to see. In time this place would be forgotten, and maybe them with it.

That's it, happy thoughts in the morning. Way to go, girl.

The van *creaked* up and down behind her as Danny climbed out. He stretched, making way too much noise, then rubbed his eyes before taking a long drink of water from a refilled bottle.

"Are we there yet?" he asked.

Gaby pulled a map out of one of the pockets along her stripped-down assault vest and held it up to the sunlight. "We should be there within the day. You said the road gets bumpy when we're closer?"

"Sure, bumpy, as long as your definition of 'bumpy' is 'potholes from hell.' Then yup, it definitely gets a little bumpy."

"I guess we should add better suspension to the list of things to look out for," Nate said, appearing from the front of the van. The sight of his absurd Mohawk never failed to make her smile, and a part of her thought that was why he insisted on keeping it.

Nate wore the same rig as Danny and her—vest over long-sleeve thermal clothing, loose cargo pants to hold more than just the essentials, and all-purpose boots. They had brought along pump-action shotguns to complement their M4s, with the rest of their load devoted to ammo, though they had less now than when they had started off. She hoped they wouldn't need the remaining rounds, but someone once told her to always hope for the best and prepare for the worst, a mantra she'd found immensely useful these days.

Danny reached back into the van, pulled out his tactical pack, and swung it on. "Sounds about right. Start looking around for Grave Digger, kids."

"Grave Digger?" Gaby said.

"The monster truck?"

She shook her head.

"It's famous," Danny said. "Like, world famous and shit. It crushes cars and opponents' spirits. Like me."

Gaby and Nate exchanged a blank look.

"Ugh, kids," Danny grunted. "Get off my lawn."

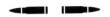

"HOW MUCH OF the sweet stuff we got left, kid?" Danny asked as he climbed out of the Dodge.

He had spent the last ten or so minutes inside, talking on the ham radio with the *Trident,* letting them know the three of them were still in one piece and that the "expedition," as Lara called it, was still on track.

Gaby stood up in the truck bed, where she had been counting the remaining red fuel cans hidden underneath a heavy tarp. "Six left, five gallons per. So thirty in all. Should get us to Starch, but I don't know about getting back." She made a face. "Your math was off, Danny. We spent way too much fuel getting just this far."

"Miss Candy always did say I sucked at math. It probably didn't help we got bogged down in Hell Town."

"Hellion."

"Same difference."

"So how are we getting back?"

"We'll find a way. Ranger motto: 'Always be prepared.'"

"Isn't that the Boy Scouts' motto?"

"That's just what we let them think." Danny put his hands on his hips and glanced around at their surroundings. "Could have definitely picked a better place. This must be what they mean when they say two-horse town. Minus the horses."

"Could be worse."

"How's that?"

"We could be dead."

"Sure, there's *that.*"

She smirked. "What did Lara say?"

"They had to detour south temporarily, but they'll be back in time to pick us up when we're ready. In the meantime, we're to proceed as planned."

"Why are they heading south?"

"Keo."

She smiled. "Good to know he's still kicking around out there."

"The guy's like a cockroach. When you least expect it, he pops up and poops on your food."

"Ugh. Thanks for the visual."

"You're welcome."

"How's everyone else?"

"They're on a luxury yacht, kid. Don't waste your time worrying about them. Spend it worrying about me. And your boyfriend with the funky haircut."

She jumped down from the Dodge and looked around at the vehicles inside the parking lot of Wilden Middle School. Mostly trucks, and they had been sitting in the sun for the last year. All the evidence pointed to the town's residents converging here when The Purge hit—not that it had saved them. Even though they hadn't gone into the building, Gaby already knew what they would find if they did.

Leaving the Dodge here, half a mile from the van where they had spent the night, was a calculated move. Mixed in with the old cars it was easy to miss, unless the ghouls spent a lot of time counting vehicles. Could they even count? The creatures weren't stupid or mindless; far from it, even if they appeared to be at times—especially when there were so many of them that they looked like a singular entity coming at you. There was a basic, almost primal intelligence to them that had allowed them to survive and thrive. They were *"dead, not stupid,"* as Will liked to say. Not stupid, no, but they could be fooled.

"Where'd your boyfriend run off to?" Danny asked.

"Looking for our ride."

"Still?"

"It's only been thirty minutes, Danny."

"Feels like thirty-one."

"What about these vehicles?"

Danny shook his head, then pointed. "That one's too small, that one's too big, and that one's way too pink. Why would you paint your car pink in Hickstown, USA?"

"To be daring?"

"Stupid is more like it."

She sighed. "We should have stayed clear of Hellion, Danny. Then the truck would still be in one piece and we wouldn't need to look for a replacement."

"We should have done a lot of things. For instance, dating a guy without a Mohawk. Personally, that would have been at the top of my list."

"Nate has his moments."

"Is one of them the Mohawk?"

"One of many," she smiled.

Her (and Danny's) right ear *clicked,* and they heard Nate's voice. "Found one."

"Speak of the devil, and he shall radio in," Danny said.

Gaby ignored him and pressed her Push-to-Talk switch, said into her throat mic, "Where are you?"

"About a mile from your spot," Nate said. "Past the VFW building. Got a couple of hogs here, too, in case you're interested."

"Yum," Danny said.

"Not those kinds of hogs. Motorcycles."

"Well, that's disappointing."

"What's the replacement truck look like?" Gaby asked.

"Burnt orange, large tires, and a gun rack in the back," Nate said.

"I think I'm in love," Danny said. "Stay there; we'll come to you."

"Roger that."

Danny grinned wryly at her. "I guess he's not useless, after all."

"Told you."

"Yeah, yeah."

She circled around the truck, passing a pair of bullet holes in the side, a broken taillight, and craters in the tailgate that hadn't been there when they had found the Dodge back at Port Arthur. All of the damage had occurred as they passed a town called Hellion about thirty miles down the state highway.

Definitely should have steered clear of the place. Even the name sounds like trouble.

She tried to think of the bright side—they had made it out of there alive, for one—as she climbed into the driver seat, the door *creaking* badly as she pulled it closed. Danny slid in next to her, his boots *crunching* broken glass on the floor. Most of those shards came from his shattered door window, though plenty had fallen loose from the spiderwebbed front windshield.

Gaby turned the key and the ten-year-old Dodge struggled to

turn over, and for a brief moment she envisioned the two of them carrying the six remaining five-gallon cans over to Nate's position. And of course they'd have to take the car battery with them. All of that, while walking under the morning sun—

Vroom! as the car finally turned over.

"We're on our way now," Danny said, his voice echoing inside her ear and inside the cab. "You said burnt orange?"

"Yup," Nate answered. "My dad had something like it back in Louisiana. Except his was white."

"That's all very fascinating, Natepoleon, but I didn't ask for your life story," Danny said.

"Cut him a break, Danny," Gaby said.

"Oh, relax. I'm just busting his balls so you can ride in and massage them for him."

"Ugh," she said.

"Yeah, I think I just threw up a little bit in my mouth, too," Danny sighed.

NATE HAD FOUND a Ford F-150 truck in the parking lot of a feed store further up FM 163. The morning was crisp and cool enough that Gaby was glad she couldn't smell whatever was being stored in a pair of red barns behind the main building. If there was anything in there besides ghouls, anyway.

The truck still looked relatively new and Nate was sitting on the hood, shotgun slung over his back and M4 in his lap, waiting for them. He was beaming as she pulled off the road, turned around, and then backed up until she was parked parallel to the Ford.

"What do you think?" Nate asked, hopping down.

"Not bad, for an idiot with a Mohawk," Danny said.

"Lay off the hair. Chicks dig it." He smiled at her. "Right?"

"Eh," Gaby said, climbing into the back of their truck.

Danny began transporting their equipment from the Dodge over to the Ford, including switching the battery over, while she lowered one of the gas cans down to Nate, who poured it into the F-150's gas tank. It took thirty minutes before they could pile into the new truck, ready to leave Wilden behind.

Gaby settled in behind the wheel and adjusted her driver-side mirror, then rolled down the window. She put the car in gear and maneuvered out of the parking lot and back onto the road, heading west. Danny occupied the front passenger seat, while Nate sat in the back with their supplies. They had brought enough to get to Starch and back, and a little bit more just in case they ran into trouble.

Another one of your lessons, Will. 'Just in case.'

"Starch?" she asked.

"Starch," Danny nodded.

He unfolded a map in his lap, though she didn't know why. From here, it was as simple as locating the state highway and driving until they ran into US 59, after which it was a straight shot up to Starch. She had eyeballed her own map so many times she was sure she could reach their destination by memory.

"Are we still sure it's going to be there when we show up?" Nate asked from the backseat.

"It's an underground bunker," Danny said. "It's not going to dig itself up and fly off."

"I'm more concerned about what's inside it. Who's to say someone else didn't stumble across it after you left? It's been, what, a year since you guys abandoned it?"

"Give or take."

"Yeah, so, what if all of this is for nothing?"

Danny folded the map back up and put it away. "Then you've just been on the best field trip of your life. You're welcome."

Nate grunted, and Gaby smiled.

"Should have brought marshmallows," Nate said.

"That's the spirit," Danny said. He leaned around in his seat and smiled back at Nate. "Wanna hear a joke?"

"Do I have a choice?"

"Old man is sitting in the park one day," Danny said, as if Nate hadn't said anything, "waiting for someone to play chess with him.

This super hot woman in a red dress walks by and the old coot shouts at her, 'Hey, hot thing, you wanna play chess?' The woman stops and looks at him, puts her hands on her hips, and says—"

Danny stopped in mid-sentence.

"What?" Nate said. "What did the woman say?"

"Shhh," Danny said, holding up his hand.

Nate went quiet.

"Stop the car," Danny snapped.

Gaby stepped on the brake, but Danny had already unbuckled his seat belt and jumped out of the F-150 before she had come to a complete stop. She glanced back at Nate and saw him looking after Danny's figure as he raced from the front to the back.

Nate turned back to her. "What the hell?"

She shook her head and threw open her car door, Nate doing the same behind her. She hadn't taken a complete step out of the truck when she heard it. Or maybe she felt it first. It could have very well been both simultaneously.

The country road actually seemed to be vibrating as it appeared, and it was impossible to miss its gray belly against the clear morning sky.

A plane.

Not just any plane, but a *warplane.*

It blasted overhead, the sound unlike anything she remembered—until she realized it had been almost a year since she'd seen a plane in the sky, much less been close enough that her teeth chattered slightly as it went by. By the time she had turned her head, it was already behind her and getting smaller. If the pilot had seen her or Nate, or Danny at the back of the F-150, it hadn't shown it by stopping or turning.

She unslung her rifle on instinct and flicked off the safety, belatedly realizing how dumb the move was. What exactly did she think she was going to do against *that?* Shoot it?

The plane was fast, but her perception of its initial speed was off because it had been such a long time since she had seen planes in the air. All this time, they had wondered what had happened to the U.S.

Air Force. Or the Army. Hell, all those weeks on the ocean without a single sign of the U.S. Navy had been disheartening for everyone, so much so that they simply stopped talking about it one day because the conversation always became so depressing.

And she was definitely looking at some kind of military plane. Even a civilian like her, who had never been anywhere close to a warplane, could make out the very distinctive shapes of bombs under the craft's fixed wings. Or were those missiles of some type?

"Shit," Nate said. "Is that what I think it is?"

"Warthog," Danny said, walking back to them.

"I've never seen one of those live before."

"Warthog?" Gaby said.

"A-10 Thunderbolt," Danny said. "I haven't seen one since Afghanistan. Word of advice: If you hear something that sounds like Godzilla blowing a massive fart, run and hide while you still can, though the chances are it's already too late."

The plane had kept going until she could barely make out its shape in the distance. Gaby wasn't entirely sure what she was feeling at the moment. Maybe elation at the sight of the aircraft, quickly followed by massive disappointment that it had kept going as if she, Nate, and Danny didn't exist at all.

"You think it saw us?" she asked.

"Definitely," Danny said. "We're the only things moving down here for miles. The pilot'd have to be blind not to see us, and last time I checked, Uncle Sam doesn't let blind folks fly his warplanes."

"Uncle Sam," Nate said, looking at Danny. "You don't think…?"

"That the U.S. government's back in play?" Danny shrugged. "I'll be honest with you kids. I don't know if I want that to be true or not."

"Why not?" Gaby asked.

"Because it's been a year since everything went tits up, and the Uncle Sam that shows up now isn't going to be the one I remembered. Or necessarily want."

Gaby pulled out her map and laid it on the truck's warm hood, the engine still churning underneath the paper. She glanced down at it, then in the direction the plane had gone.

"Where's it headed?" Nate asked. "Starch?"

"If it keeps going in that direction and turns right," Gaby said. "But why would it be headed there? No one knows we're out here." She looked back at Danny. "Right?"

He nodded. "Last time I checked."

"So what's it doing out here?" Nate asked, looking in the direction of the plane.

Danny opened his mouth to answer, but he hadn't gotten a word out when they heard something that sounded like a mechanical roar in the distance. It was a long string of noises, so distinctive and loud that even though it had clearly originated miles away, they could still hear it as if it were right in front of them.

Broooooooooooorrrrttttttttt!

"Danny," Gaby said, breathless. "What the hell is that?"

"The Warthog," Danny said, looking off into the distance. "That thing I said about Godzilla farting? That wasn't a joke. That's it right there. That's the sound of an A-10 raining death and destruction with 30mm Gatling guns."

The pavement under her trembled as another long string of *broooooooooooorrrrttttttttt!* filled the sky, like the bellowing of a great beast that had finally awakened after a long slumber.

CHAPTER 3

LARA

"LARA."

Will was back. *Finally.* After all the days and weeks of fearing the worst and almost giving up, he was finally here and calling her name, just as she knew he would if she waited long enough. It was all about faith, after all; not so much in things working out, but in Will keeping his promise because she knew he would if there was even an ounce of strength left in his body.

Thank God you're back. You had me worried there for a moment.

"Lara, you there?"

No. It wasn't Will. It was familiar, but it *wasn't Will.*

She opened her eyes and blinked against the bright sunlight pouring through an open window. She had rolled into the rays' path, somehow moving from one side of the bed to the other during the night without realizing it.

"Lara."

She glanced at the two-way portable radio sitting atop the nightstand.

"Lara," Blaine's familiar gruff voice said through the radio. "You awake yet? There's something you need to see."

She leaned over, picking up the radio and pressing the transmit lever. "What is it?"

"It's a body."

"Did you say a *body?*"

"Yeah. Showed up along with this morning's currents."

"I'll be right there."

She threw the covers off and stumbled out of bed with the radio in one hand. A cool breeze from the window kept her from (mostly) having to smell yesterday's clothing, still clinging to her. Falling asleep fully dressed was nothing new; if anyone ever noticed, no one said anything.

"Has Keo made contact yet?" she said into the radio while standing between the bed and the small bathroom on the other side of the captain's cabin.

"Haven't heard a peep from him since yesterday," Blaine said. "Bad sign?"

"It's still early."

In the bathroom, she splashed her face with cold water from the sink, then gave herself a quick glance in the mirror. Puffy eyes. Dry hair. Pale and slightly cracked lips to complement dangerously tanned skin. Even the blue of her eyes looked duller than usual.

The boat was quiet around her, like it always was early in the morning. Even more so these days with Danny, Gaby, and Nate gone.

Because I sent them out there. Would you have done the same thing, Will?

She wiped her face with a towel and left the cabin. She found Blaine at his post inside the bridge, standing behind the helm even though the *Trident* was anchored in place.

Lara shivered a bit despite her thermal clothing, the December air ventilating from the open sky roof much chillier than the breeze inside her cabin. Fortunately there was always plenty of sun up here in this part of the boat. Blaine, who practically lived on the Upper Deck these days, didn't seem to mind or even feel the lower temperature.

"Showed up a few hours ago," Blaine said. "I wasn't sure what it was at first, but the waves kept bringing it closer."

Lara picked up a pair of binoculars from the dashboard and

peered through it. She had to take a couple of steps to one side to see past the holes that dotted the windshield, the result of stray buckshot. One of these days they'd get around to replacing the glass, but that day was still far off.

"See it?" Blaine asked.

It was hard to miss even from a distance, because it was the only black thing in the clear blue Gulf of Mexico waters for miles around. The body was wearing some kind of black uniform. Now where had she seen that before?

"Collaborator?" she asked. "I can't make out the pattern of the uniform from here."

"Could be."

"Danny said the ones in Texas wear black. That looks black to me." She lowered the binoculars. "How far are we from the coast-line?"

"Still twenty miles out. But it didn't come from Sunport."

"Are you sure?"

"Pretty sure. It's been steadily drifting westward—from the east."

"Farther out to sea?"

"Uh huh."

"Could be part of a long-range boat patrol. Maybe it capsized. What was the weather like last night?"

"Like this morning, but just a bit windier." He paused for a moment, maybe replaying last night's conditions in his head to be sure. "Even if Mother Nature did that, it doesn't explain what it's doing this far out."

Blaine's voice was calm, as if seeing a uniformed body floating all the way out here, with no obvious point of origin, happened every day. It didn't, but after all she—*they*—had been through, this wasn't even at the top of their WTF list.

She watched the corpse drift nearer, completely at the mercy of the waves that kept it afloat. If the *Trident* hadn't been anchored, it might have washed right past them. It certainly would have last night in the dark. If she had learned one thing since being out here, it was that the vastness of the ocean was not to be underestimated.

"If there was a collaborator boat out here last night, they might have been communicating through the radio," she said. "Did you hear anything?"

"Not a peep."

"You were up here all night?"

"Maddie relieved me after midnight."

She stared at the blackened body in silence for a moment, its presence triggering alarm bells. They had done everything possible to avoid running across civilization since Song Island, opting instead to keep their heads down. Sending Danny, Gaby, and Nate back out there hadn't been easy. It had cost her a lot of sleepless nights, and she wasn't the only one suffering.

"Speaking of the radio," Blaine said, "not a peep from the expedition yet."

She glanced down at her watch: 7:45 A.M. "They'll radio in when they're awake."

"You think they're still asleep?"

"Time works differently out there." She unclipped her radio and pressed the transmit lever. "Maddie."

"What's up?" Maddie answered.

"You see it?"

"Hard to miss. That's a uniform, right?"

"Looks like it. Grab Benny and bring it in."

"Sweet," Maddie said. "A can of SPAM for breakfast, and I get to fish a body out of the water. Best morning *evah*."

LARA STOOD AT the back of the Lower Deck, bracing against the bite of a hard wind and trying not to catch the cold that Elise and Vera had come down with a few days ago, a condition that kept the girls mostly confined to their rooms on the Main Deck. She watched Maddie deftly maneuver the inflatable boat toward them, with Benny sitting at the stern and the body they had fished out of the water just a black, indistinguishable lump around his legs. The tender was nineteen feet long, and it bounced against the active waves.

"Ah, the smell of rotting corpses in the morning," a voice said. "Now this is the life."

"Don't exaggerate; it's just one corpse," Lara said.

"Po-tay-to, po-tah-to," Carly said, walking up next to her.

Her friend shaded her eyes and peered at the approaching boat. Carly's hair had turned a darker shade of red since they had begun living on the yacht, and, like everyone else, she had developed a noticeable tan.

"By the way, when was the last time you changed clothes?" Carly asked.

Lara sighed. "Don't start with me."

"I'm just saying. As our fearless leader, you should at least comport yourself in a more scent-friendly manner."

"'Comport'?"

"What, didn't I use it correctly?"

"Eh," she shrugged.

"Give me a break; I didn't have any fancy educumacallit," Carly said. Then, "Speaking of illiterate ne'er-do-wells, when are we picking up Keo?"

Lara smiled. "He hasn't radioed in yet."

"That's not good."

"That seems to be the consensus."

"But you don't think so?"

"I don't want to jump to conclusions. He said they had a good place to stay last night. He could have just run into some trouble making his way to the beach this morning. Maybe a dead battery or something minor like that. The small things have a way of ballooning into big deals these days."

"I guess he deserves the benefit of the doubt, being that he sort of saved our bacon a few times and all."

"He said he's been taking a lot of precautions since Galveston."

"Undead trouble?"

"Them, too."

"That's K-pop for ya. Guy knows how to get himself into trouble, doesn't he?"

"He's not the only one."

She owed Keo. They all did, but her in particular. In the first few weeks after Song Island, there were times when she hadn't thought she would be able to keep it together, keep everyone together. Danny's condition, Will's absence, and the chaos of the gun battle had all made her doubt every decision she made. If Keo hadn't been there...

You would have liked him, Will.

"You think it's a good idea bringing it onboard?" Carly asked, squinting her eyes at the tender as it drew closer to the *Trident*'s aft. "What if it has diseases or something? The kids are already sick."

"We'll keep it away from the others, find out what we can, then toss it back into the ocean when we're done."

"Tough boat," Carly chuckled. Then, turning around, "You kids have fun. I'm going to the bridge to wait for Danny to call in."

"THAT'S A SHARK," Zoe said, pointing at what was left of the man's right leg—a stump that ended at the knee. "The missing fingers are fish nibbles. And these two—" she pointed first at the man's cheek, then his neck "—are your department."

"Gunshot wounds," Lara said, looking down at the two small holes barely visible against the rest of the man's bloated flesh, which was pretty much every part of him that wasn't covered up by clothing.

The man wore some kind of urban assault vest, and water still drained from his empty ammo pouches long after they brought him on deck. A tactical gun belt with an empty holster sagged against his waist and thigh, the Velcro starting to lose its effectiveness after being drowned in the ocean for so long. There were two hollow slits where his eyes used to be, though he still had most of his left ear and the bridge part of his nose. There was a knee guard on his remaining leg and his black cargo pants were shredded, the tears revealing glistening pale skin on the other side.

"He's not dressed like a collaborator," Maddie said. "No patches or name tags."

"Looks like a commando or something," Benny said.

Maddie and Benny had deposited the body on the slick swimming pool area at the back of the yacht. Zoe was crouched next to it now, holding a rag against her mouth and nose. Lara wished she had been that forward thinking. The body was bloated and had been in the water long enough that the face was deformed and fleshy and looked as if it would melt off if she so much as touched it. Zoe did all of her prodding with a pair of surgical gloves.

"How long do you think it's been in the water, doc?" Maddie asked.

Zoe stood up, pulled the rag back, and took a breath of fresh air. "Hard to tell. The cold water probably kept it together longer than normal, and there's still gas in the body, which resulted in floating, so if I had to guess…" She thought about it for a moment. "Anywhere from a few days to a week?"

"Why didn't the sharks finish it off?" Benny asked.

"Contrary to what you see on TV, humans aren't very high on a shark's menu. There are a lot more manageable and easier-to-digest prey in the ocean. Imagine trying to eat a whole cow when there are burgers all around you."

"Which still leaves us with a lot of questions," Maddie said. "What happened to the poor sap, who was he, and where did he come from?"

"Well, Sunport's the closest city," Benny said.

"It didn't come from Sunport," Maddie said. "Blaine said it was moving with the currents from farther out."

"It couldn't have come from very far," Zoe said. "When he was shot, he sank, then the gas raised him back up to the surface and the waves finally brought him to us."

"A ship, maybe?" Maddie said. "We always wondered who else was out here besides us. I mean, it's a big ocean. There's got to be more people, right? Before us, there was Gage and his friends."

"Maybe it's the Navy," Benny said. He sounded almost hopeful. "He really does look like some kind of commando. Maybe the U.S. Navy is still out there somewhere."

"For some reason, he doesn't look military to me," Maddie said.

"Then maybe he's from those Bengal Islands that Keo talked about. He said there were a lot of people there."

"The clothes he's wearing, the gunshots..." Maddie shook her head. "It had to have been one hell of a gunfight."

"I still think it's the military," Benny said. "Blaine and I talked about it a lot, about what happened to all the Navy ships that were caught out here when everything went down. The aircraft carriers, battleships and destroyers, all those guys. They had to have gone somewhere."

"It's been a year," Maddie said. "If they're still out there, we would have heard from them by now, don't you think?"

"What about the one in Colorado?" Zoe asked. "Carly said there was a colonel hiding in a mountain somewhere."

"Beecher," Maddie nodded. "We made contact with him on the radio."

"What did he say about the rest of the military?"

"He knew as much as we did. Which wasn't very much."

There was a moment of silence until the others looked over at her. Maybe they finally realized she hadn't said anything in a while.

"What's the next play, boss?" Maddie asked. "It might be worth it to find out where this guy came from."

"Maybe not," Zoe said. "People with guns, wearing combat gear, running around out here shooting each other?" The doctor shook her head. "I'm not sure those are the kinds of people we'd necessarily want to cross paths with. Not now. Not after Song Island."

"Doc's got a good point," Benny said.

They were still looking at her, waiting for her to say something. *What would Will do?*

"Can you learn anything else from him?" she finally asked Zoe.

The older woman shook her head. "I don't see the point. We

know how he died. GSWs. Anything else he can tell us would be in his pockets."

"Already went through them," Maddie said. "Empty."

"All right," Lara said. "Throw him back into the ocean. Wherever he came from, however he got here, or what happened to him, let the Gulf keep his secrets. We have other things to worry about."

SHE WAS IN the captain's cabin, looking at the same old heavily annotated map of the Gulf of Mexico spread out on a table, that she had been using since they boarded the *Trident* back on Song Island. She had circled Sunport, twenty miles in front of them at the moment, and Port Arthur, where Danny, Gaby, and Nate had made land a few days ago. If it hadn't been Keo who had called, she would never have strayed far from Port Arthur. Just the idea of leaving the expedition behind to come south made her feel sick to her stomach.

This better be important, Keo.

If he was even still alive out there. The last time she had talked to him, he had given her the impression he and his companions were barely a step ahead of their pursuers. What if they had finally run out of luck?

She glanced at her watch. She didn't know what she was expecting, but the silence from Keo nagged at her. Unlike Danny, who had already radioed in from some town called Wilden an hour ago, it was all quiet from the Keo front. The man was unpredictable and prone to rash decisions, but then again a lot of those questionable choices he'd made had been in her favor, so maybe she should be grateful—

A knock on the cabin door interrupted her thoughts.

"Come in," she said.

Bonnie stepped inside in loose-fitting cargo pants and an olive thermal sweater, looking more like a soldier than even Benny or Blaine. Lara was still amazed by the transformation Bonnie had gone through since they first met on Song Island. Then again, she could probably say the same thing about all of them, including herself, though the others didn't quite look at home with an M4 slung over their backs and a gun belt hanging off their hips. Bonnie did, and even managed to pull off the short haircut.

"What's up?" she asked.

"I heard Keo still hasn't called yet," Bonnie said.

"Not yet."

"You think he's okay?"

"I don't know."

Bonnie walked over and leaned against the table, then stared down at the map even though Lara could tell it wasn't her chicken scratch notes that were on the ex-model's mind at the moment.

"What is it, Bonnie?" she asked.

"Carrie's worried about him," Bonnie said.

"Keo can handle himself. I'm more worried about the others."

"The—what do you call it?"

"Expedition."

"Right. The expedition. Are they okay?"

"Alive and well. I talked to Danny earlier."

"Good. That's good."

"How's everyone doing? I know I haven't been moving through the decks as much as before."

"Everyone's good, doing their part. Don't worry about us. You already have a lot on your mind."

"So no secret meetings about overthrowing my rule?"

Bonnie chuckled. "Not since two weeks ago. You're safe for at least another few days."

"Good to hear." She walked over to her small fridge in the corner and came back with two cold water bottles, handing one to Bonnie. "So why did you really come here?"

"That obvious, huh?"

Lara shrugged.

"It's Gage," Bonnie said.

Of course it would be Gage. She knew the man would come back to haunt her eventually. She had been dreading it, but at the same time knowing it was inevitable, that the sooner she dealt with it the easier she would be able to sleep at night.

Or, at least, that's what she told herself.

"What about him?" Lara asked.

"After Carrie asked me to come see you about Keo, she told me that when she took Gage his breakfast this morning, she left his room with a bad feeling."

"What did she say exactly?"

Bonnie paused for a moment. Then, "She couldn't put it into words, just that he didn't seem right. Like he was waiting for her to make a mistake. She left as soon as she could, but she hasn't been able to shake it."

She sighed.

Gage. The *Trident*'s former captain.

What would Will do?

"He's been down there for a while," Bonnie continued. "Long enough that I think he's figured out by now we don't need him to run the yacht anymore."

She nodded, remembering the look on the man's face when she took him off the bridge and gave the helm to Blaine. *He knows,* she remembered thinking at the time. *His usefulness has come to an end, and he knows.*

"What are you doing to do?" Bonnie asked. There was a slight wavering in her voice, as if she was afraid to hear the answer.

"I'll take care of it," Lara said.

CHAPTER 4

KEO

ANOTHER FINE MESS you've got yourself into. Shoulda taken the easy way out when you had the chance, pal. And you had a lot of chances, didn't you?

Live and learn…maybe.

He expected ghouls in the shadows, but the floor was empty when he took his first tentative step outside the janitor's closet at the end of the hallway, silver bullet-loaded M4 in front of him and one eye fixed behind the weapon's red dot sight. The trigger felt good against his finger, and the warmth of morning sunlight was like a comforting embrace. The pain in his leg—the result of a bullet hole—had resurfaced thanks to last night's mad dash; running for your life, apparently, didn't contribute to the healing process.

Jordan moved quietly behind him, watching his six. They weren't quite moving in stacking formation, but he could feel the fabric of her sweaty clothes every time she turned too quickly to sweep an open door or one of the (too many) hallways to their left and right. He was doing the same, watching and listening for signs of something to shoot, watching for things that didn't belong, and doing his very best to shut out her persistent haggard breathing.

It took much longer to reach the stairwell than he would have liked. Either the floor had widened sometime last night, or they were moving very, very slowly. The feel of sunlight through the *(Still intact, so that's a good sign)* windows to their right made him breathe just a little bit easier with every step.

The tiled floor showed signs of the dirt they had tracked in here last night and the cubicles they had run past still looked in one piece this morning. More importantly, he couldn't smell them in the air. Even a floor this large wouldn't have been able to hide the creatures' stench, especially if there was more than one of them around, and there had definitely been more than one of them around last night.

So far, so good.

Keo couldn't help it and grinned to himself.

Famous last words there, pal.

They remained silent (or at least they didn't talk, but it was hard to stay completely quiet; their boots' soles squeaked every so often against the dust-caked floor) during the trek until they finally arrived at the stairwell door.

Keo glanced back at Jordan, standing behind him pulling security. She looked over her shoulder, saw him, and nodded. Just a week of running around out here with her and they were already working like an (almost) well-oiled machine. In another month, he'd probably know what her sweat tasted like.

He turned back and pressed one ear against the warm stairwell door.

Five seconds…

Ten…

Nothing.

There was just stillness on the other side.

He looked back at Jordan, and she mouthed, *"Anything?"*

He shook his head before turning back around to the door. This time he put one hand on the doorknob, finding courage in the streams of sunlight splashing all the way across the floor and over half the door. It was surprisingly warm inside the building at the moment, but that could have just been thanks to his thick winter clothing.

"Go," Ol' Blue Eyes had hissed at him last night inside the stairwell.

THE SPEARS OF LACONIA

"Go where?" Keo had responded.

"Down!" he had shouted.

And that was where he and Jordan had gone. They went down the stairs, expecting ghouls to appear from below at any moment. He kept waiting and waiting, but black eyes and the terrifying noise of stampeding bare feet never filled the enclosed space around them. There were only his and Jordan's labored breathing and their pounding boots all the way down to—

The third floor. He didn't know why he had chosen it. Maybe he didn't trust his luck to last for thirty more feet. Or maybe he instinctively knew there wasn't anything good waiting for them in the lobby. Certainly no escape from the building. If there were already ghouls inside, then there would be even more outside. A hell of a lot more. Every single creature that had been sniffing their trail for the last week ever since Santa Marie Island would be converging on the single building as soon as Jordan fired that first shot.

"We'll meet again!" the blue-eyed ghoul had shouted. Or hissed. Though Keo sometimes thought the creature was making an effort to sound more human—

A nervous tap on his shoulder.

He glanced back at Jordan, who gave him a quizzical look.

"Ready?" he mouthed.

She retreated a few steps to give him room, then aimed her M4 at the door. Finally, she nodded. Keo took a long, solid breath, then made sure the sun was still splashing across the door. You could never be too careful when it came to sunlight these days.

Now.

He pulled the door open and swung it all the way to the side while he took three quick steps backward.

In the five seconds it took the door to fully open, hit the spring doorstop on the wall, and swing back in the other direction, a dozen ghouls piled inside the enclosed space in front of him had untangled their elongated limbs. He wasn't sure if he saw surprise in their black eyes or heard squeals of delight, but he definitely smelled the acidic burn of vaporizing flesh as the sun hit them.

He fired into the door anyway—it was mostly just instinct, the need to shoot when presented with a target—and put a three-round burst into the center mass of the writhing blob of flesh. A round hit bone and ricocheted into another creature trying to come unglued from the mass around it. Ghouls shrieked as spilt black blood turn gray, then white, and limbs *clattered* to the hard concrete landing. The frontal half of a head vanished before his eyes—

The door closed back up with a solid *click!*

"Jesus Christ," Jordan breathed next to him.

"Yeah," Keo said. He wrinkled his nose at the stinging smell in the air and began breathing through his mouth. "I guess we're not going in there."

"Our supplies, they're on the twentieth floor, Keo."

"Uh huh."

"The radio's up there, too."

"I know."

"It took us forever to find that thing."

"Don't remind me."

"Goddammit," Jordan said, and pursed her lips in frustration.

They took another couple of steps back from the door, just far enough to escape the gagging stench in the air, but still close enough to hear the movements from the other side. The sudden shift from deathly stillness to frantic activity seemed to be coming not just from in front of them, but also from below and above them, as if the entire building had come alive.

Despite the comforting feel of the sun against his back, Keo shivered unwittingly anyway. He never liked being this close to the undead things, and he didn't think he would ever get used to it. He *hoped* he never got used to it, because the day that happened would also mean he was no longer operating at full readiness, and that was dangerous.

"Come on," he said, and led her away.

They walked silently through two rows of cubicles, drawn irresistibly to the sunlight pouring in through the glass curtain wall on the other side of the floor.

"I guess it was too much to expect them to all follow Frank out of the building," Keo said.

"'Frank'?" Jordan said.

"Ol' Blue Eyes."

"You gave him a name? When did that happen?"

"Guy saved my life twice. The least I could do was call him something other than 'it'."

"Why Frank?"

"You know, because of what he is...*was.*"

Jordan looked blankly at him.

"Mary Shelley?" Keo said.

"Oh." Then, "Not quite human anymore, but not quite...the other thing, either." She flashed him an approving smile. "Clever. I didn't know you had it in you."

He shrugged. "It comes and goes."

"Frank," Jordan repeated. "I could think of worse names, I guess. It's definitely better than Keo."

"Now you're just trying to hurt my feelings."

"You're a tough guy, you can take it."

"Still, everyone's got their limits, Jordan."

She snorted, then glanced up at the ceiling. "What did he say to you last night? When we were on the twentieth floor?"

"*We'll meet again.*"

"*We'll meet again'?*"

"Uh huh."

"That sounds..." She shivered instead of finishing.

"Yeah," Keo said. "Still freaks me out a little, thinking about that promise."

They finally reached the other side of the floor, where the windows were still in place, the creatures having somehow climbed all the way up to the twentieth floor while bypassing the rest. He guessed the brick-and-mortar walls outside had just enough handholds for things that didn't care about falling. He remembered the surreal sight of them last night, plummeting out of the sky, arms and legs flailing, as he and Jordan raced through the floor in search of someplace to hide.

"You think he's dead?" Jordan asked.

"I don't know. He's survived before. T18, the island…"

"There were a hell of a lot more of them here last night, Keo."

"He has a knack for surviving. It wouldn't surprise me if he found a way out of here while we were hiding in the janitor's closet."

Keo pressed against a section of the dust-covered window and peered down at the sidewalks and streets below. Downtown Sunport was as quiet and still this morning as when they had reached its city limits yesterday evening.

He could see bones on the ground below—arms and legs, most of them still attached to the skeletal remains of ghouls that hadn't been able to crawl their way out of the path of the rising sun after free-falling down the side of the building last night. The fall might not have killed them, but it had pulverized and shattered limbs, making escape difficult.

Jordan was staring back at the stairwell door across the floor. "How are we getting down?"

"We'll improvise," he said, and began backpedaling.

"What—" Jordan said, before realizing what he was doing, and hurried backward after him. "Geez, would it kill you to give me a heads up?"

"Heads up," he said.

She smirked. "Jackass."

Keo stopped about ten meters from the wall and stitched one of the windows with a three-round burst. He stopped firing and they listened to glass falling and shattering against the sidewalk below, the sound echoing across the city for a few seconds afterward. Cold wind flooded inside through the newly made hole, and Keo welcomed the fresh air into his lungs.

"Now what?" Jordan asked.

"Ladies first," he said.

THREE FLOORS WERE better than twenty and were easily manageable once they pulled apart curtains from some of the offices and tied them together into a makeshift rope. He lowered Jordan down first, then followed.

The sidewalk was covered in bones, and the still-strong smell of vaporized blood and flesh stung his nostrils while he was coming down. It was worse once he reached the pavement, and he had to pull his shirt over his nose to stave off most of the stench. Jordan had already done likewise while waiting for him.

"How would we know if he made it or not?" she asked, her voice muffled through her shirt.

Keo walked into the middle of the street, maneuvering around a pair of stalled vehicles, including one with a caved-in roof from when a creature had fallen down on top of it, and looked up. He found the twentieth floor easily enough, thanks to the line of broken windows stretching from one end of the building to the other.

He tried to put himself in Frank's shoes *(bare feet?)*. Frank wasn't limited by what a human body could do. Keo had seen that for himself three times now. The guy could take a beating, and the things he did defied the laws of physics. Hell, it defied the laws of *nature*.

The last time Keo had seen him, Frank was on the twentieth floor. Keo hadn't understood what he was doing until he was squeezed into the janitor's closet with Jordan, listening and waiting for an attack that never came.

It was Frank; it had always been Frank. They wanted him and Frank knew that, which was why he hadn't followed them down. He gave the creatures what they wanted instead of leading them to Keo and Jordan. Himself.

That's three times now you've saved my life.

Dammit. How do you even begin to repay someone who has saved your life not one, two, but *three* times? Keo wasn't entirely sure he was looking forward to finding out the answer to that question.

"What are you looking at?" Jordan said behind him.

Keo eyeballed the twentieth floor, then turned and looked at the building facing it from across the street. The opposite structure was almost entirely all black marble but shorter at just fifteen stories.

Then he saw it and couldn't help but grin.

"What?" Jordan said. "What are you grinning at like an idiot?"

"He fell short," Keo said.

"Who?"

"Frank." Keo pointed at a lone broken window on the fourteenth floor of the black marble building. "He was aiming for the rooftop but he had too far of a jump, and his trajectory dipped before he reached it. He's fast—and shit, can he jump—but apparently even he has his limitations."

Jordan stared at the single broken window on the fourteenth floor of the building across the street. "Are you saying he leapt from our building to that one? Keo, that's—"

"Impossible?" Keo smiled. "Jordan, we've been walking around with a blue-eyed ghoul for the last week, trying to stay one step ahead of collaborators and undead things. 'Impossible' shouldn't even be in our vocabulary anymore."

KEO WASN'T SURPRISED to find ghouls inside the lobby of the marble building. He could see them moving around in the shadowed parts through the windows, and he spent just as much time wondering how many were inside as he did ignoring the lingering smell of dead things in the streets around him.

"So I guess that's out of the question," Jordan said, standing next to him.

"Guess so."

"What now?"

"How are you for ammo?"

She tapped the ammo pouches around her waist, then sighed.

"That much, huh?" he said.

"One more for the M4, and two for the Glock. You?"

"Same."

She sneaked a look over her shoulder, back at the taller building they'd just climbed down from. "Our supplies are still up there, along with the radio."

"The operative phrase being 'up there.'"

"Maybe we can climb. Those things did."

"And a lot of them went splat."

"Good point." She returned her gaze to the lobby in front of them. "You think he's in there somewhere?"

"I don't know. He had all night to fight his way out. He might not even be in the city anymore."

"You really believe that?"

He didn't answer right away.

"Keo?"

"I don't know," he finally said. "How many were at Santa Marie Island? Two hundred tops? Last night was an entire city's worth. That's…a lot."

"This thing, the one he calls Mabry," Jordan said quietly, as if afraid the creature might hear her if she said the name too loudly. "It's behind this. It wants him."

Keo nodded. He didn't like saying the name any more than she did. Hell, he didn't even want to think it. The fact that Frank was uncomfortable saying the name out loud said it all.

If it can scare him…

He looked down the street, past the stalled vehicles and year-old trash left unattended by a city that had once been crowded with people. He could almost sniff the ocean water from here.

"They might be out there," Jordan said. "Your friends."

"Only one way to find out."

"Maybe we'll get lucky and find a working vehicle, so we won't have to walk the entire way."

Keo chuckled as they started up the street.

"What?" Jordan said. "One of us has to stay positive."

"You're doing a good job of it."

"Oh, shut up. It's your fault I'm here in the first place."

"Hey, you didn't have to tag along."

"Right, like I had much of a choice after T18 and Santa Marie Island."

"There was always Tobias."

She sighed. "You're right. I should have left with Tobias…"

SUNPORT, TEXAS, WAS an oil-based industry town, which meant groupings of oil refineries dotted the landscape as Keo and Jordan left the downtown area behind and took FM 1495 toward the beach. They had been walking ever since Santa Marie Island, picking their way south along the coastline. It had been a real pain in the ass with his gimpy leg, but eventually the wound became numbed enough on day three (or was it day four?) that he could walk without grimacing.

The sight (and sounds) of so many collaborators along the roads had slowed their progress, and traveling by night hadn't been a good idea since the world ended. But just because he was used to walking didn't mean he wouldn't trade it all for a working vehicle at the first opportunity.

Once past the Sunport city limits, they found themselves flanked by heavy industry to their left and almost entirely undeveloped land to their right, with small streams snaking around wetlands. Although they'd passed plenty of homes and subdivisions on their way into town, there was very little of that out here. It took a while, but eventually Keo managed to steal glimpses of sunlight dancing off the surface of water in the distance.

The Gulf of Mexico awaited. And, if he was lucky, the *Trident* was anchored somewhere out there, close enough that they would be able to see him. Because, of course, he'd been very lucky these last few days.

Riiiiiight.

The highway gave way to small roads and the occasional motels, while palm trees replaced power poles. They slowed when they reached a two-story blue building advertising seafood and beach rental supplies that had a couple of trucks in the parking lot. They checked both vehicles but came up empty.

They cautiously entered the building—a combo restaurant and general store—and checked every shadowy corner and crevice, and under every table and counter. There was no familiar smell of ghoul occupancy, but you couldn't always count on that kind of tell. They found rotting food in the kitchen but struck gold with a 12-count case of unopened water bottles in a back closet. Keo scrounged up a faded gym bag from one of the pantries that he then stuffed with eight of the bottles while Jordan found plastic bags and carried the remaining four in them.

Assured they weren't going to die of thirst—which would have sucked, with all that undrinkable ocean saltwater mocking them—they continued to the beach. It took another two hours before Keo finally saw welcoming white sand. He was surprised to see cars parked on the dunes, but otherwise no signs of another living soul for miles. Keo ended up wasting about half a minute watching a crab navigating around the points of his boots.

"Food," Jordan smiled.

"Give him a break; the guy's just trying to get home."

"When did you get so soft?"

He sighed. "I've been asking myself that question for a while now."

When the crab was finally on its way, Keo slumped down on the sand and sighed with relief. The long walk from Sunport hadn't done his healing wounds any favors, but he was an old hand at pushing through lingering pain. He unlaced his boots, pulled off his socks and stuck both feet into the warm, mushy beach floor. There were no palm trees in any direction, which was odd because they had passed rows of them on the road over.

Jordan sat down next to him and began massaging her toes. She opened one of the warm water bottles and finished it off before flinging it toward a trash barrel nearby, but the wind caught it before it even had a chance to hit its mark.

"Don't mess with Texas," Keo said.

"Huh?" she said.

"Isn't that the state motto?"

"Texas can sue me."

"I hear tort reform's a big thing down here."

The beach stretched for miles to both sides of them, with the only buildings he could see sprinkled in the distance to his left. Their right was almost entirely barren except for a couple of abandoned vehicles parked dangerously close to the water. If he just stared forward, he could almost fool himself into thinking that civilization didn't exist at all out here.

Keo leaned back on his elbows and soaked in the sun, watching the endless waves of ocean foam attempting to reach up the beach about thirty meters in front of him. Blue skies hovered over the Gulf of Mexico, and there were few clouds to obscure the scenery. It was a hell of a sight, and he wouldn't have minded a house out here for summer vacations.

"What do you think those trucks were doing out here?" Jordan said after a while.

"Sightseeing?"

"You think it's worth taking the time to search them?"

"Be my guest."

"Maybe later."

Keo closed his eyes and listened to her breathing softly next to him. Jordan was sticky with sweat, but he thought she smelled just fine against the fresh ocean breeze.

"I can't help but notice that I don't see a luxury yacht anchored anywhere out there," Jordan said. "How about you? You see a boat out there, Keo? Maybe it's me. My parents had cataracts. Maybe I'm getting them, too."

He smiled to himself. "I don't see them."

"So we're screwed."

"Even if they're out there, we couldn't see them anyway. We agreed they'd anchor twenty miles out to stay out of view. I was supposed to radio them when we reached the beach so they could swing by and pick us up."

"Ah," she said, almost wistfully, "the best-laid plans and blah

blah blah."

"It's not all bad."

"No?"

"We're the only two souls on a beach, staring at a glorious sky and listening to waves crashing. I could think of worse places to be right now."

"I can't tell if you're serious."

"I am."

"Why?"

"Why what?"

"Why are you serious? This last week could have been for nothing, especially if Frank's dead."

Keo sat up and brushed sand off his elbows. "Jordan…"

"What?"

He reached into the gym bag and took out two bottles of water, opening them and handing one to her. "Salute," he said, holding up his.

She rolled her eyes but smiled anyway and bumped his bottle with hers. "A tall glass and some ice would be nice."

"How about a bottle of red wine while we're at it?"

"Cabernet?"

"Of course."

"Now you're talking."

He took a long drink before lying back down. He buried the bottle halfway into the sand next to him, then closed his eyes again. The warmth of the sun against his face was like a soothing pair of massaging hands, and Keo let himself embrace it. If he was going to die out here, right now, he could think of worse ways to go.

"Hey," Jordan said after a while.

He didn't open his eyes, but said, "Hmm?"

"What do you think Gillian's doing right now, back in T18?"

Fucking Jay, he thought, and said, "I don't know. Why?"

"I was just wondering."

"Jordan…"

"What?"

"Shut up and enjoy the beach," he said, letting his body sink deeper into the soft sand underneath him.

After a while, all he could hear was the *sloshing* waves in front of him and the soft, comforting sound of Jordan's breathing next to him.

CHAPTER 5

GABY

IT WAS A small town on the outskirts of Cleveland, Texas, hidden away from prying eyes, or anyone who might have been traveling along US59. Once upon a time it'd had a name, but it had since been given a letter and a number and been resettled with survivors—men, women, and children who had accepted that the world was no longer a safe place, that surviving was better than fighting.

The A-10, or Warthog, as Danny called it, had been thorough. If it had left survivors behind, she couldn't see them from the hillside where she was crouched alongside Danny and Nate. The buildings that once lined an unnamed main street had been reduced to rubble, the result of the 30mm cannon she had heard belching out something that sounded like a creature from a monster movie. What the plane's Gatling gun hadn't obliterated, the air-to-surface missiles underneath its wings had taken care of. There were four large craters spread across the length of the resettlement from south to north, and thick plumes of smoke hovered above it like storm clouds.

Gaby thought about those old World War II documentaries her dad used to love watching, remembered marveling at the unreal sight of cities buried under the remains of buildings that once stood so proud. Despite all that property damage, she never saw the bodies, or the real carnage. Maybe her dad never allowed her to see the grisly footage or it had been edited out. The raw details had always remained hidden, but she couldn't ignore them now.

She could see the bodies from the hillside—or, at least, parts of them. The arms and legs of victims jutting unceremoniously out of rubble as shredded clothing clung to jagged piles of brick and mortar. Skeletal shells of what used to be buildings somehow managed to remain upright, though it was difficult to tell what they used to be. Pockets of fire dotted the landscape, as if marking where the town began and ended. The air was thick with sulfur and she found herself breathing through her mouth to keep from gagging, despite the fact she was still far enough away that she shouldn't have been affected by the smell.

Next to her, Nate and Danny had gone very quiet and still. Except for the occasional wind howling through the carcass of buildings below them, there was almost no other noise except for her shallow breathing and slightly accelerated heartbeat.

"We should go," Nate said. He sounded almost breathless. "We shouldn't be here. We shouldn't be seeing this."

"He's got a point," Danny said. "That hog might come back. Or it might have friends."

"Christ, how much armament does one of those things carry, anyway?"

"Depends on its objective. There's a reason it was so goddamn effective in the Stan."

Gaby stood up. She didn't know what she was going to do until it was already too late to stop. Her joints popped as she moved, but she ignored them and gripped the M4 tightly in front of her.

"Gaby, wait," Nate said.

"There might be survivors," she said, and hurried down the hill.

"There's nothing down there, Gaby. Not anymore."

She kept going, her boots fighting for purchase against the sloping hillside, until Nate's voice was lost against the scraping noises. Or maybe she had just effectively shut him out as she hopped the last few feet; it helped that her heartbeat had gone from slightly raised to hammering out of control against her chest.

"THERE MIGHT BE survivors," she had said, knowing what a terrible lie that was even as the words tumbled out of her mouth.

Reaching the beginning of the town just confirmed it. Nothing could have survived what she was looking at. The gun runs, as Danny called them, had been incredibly efficient. The Warthogs were effective at their jobs, he said, which was why they were so good at providing close-quarter air support. That was their specialty, after all.

She stepped around the craters that pockmarked the main street that ran through town, the curvatures of the unnatural holes still darkened with wet blood. The 30mm rounds that hadn't landed on the buildings had instead dug gaping holes in the pavements and reduced the sidewalks into disorganized slabs. A sea of broken glass and small concrete chunks *crunched* under her boots with every step. Gaby held a handkerchief over her mouth to keep out the choking sting of smoke and blood.

The bodies were almost all hidden under the remains of buildings, charred wooden frames, and structural steel beams. The sight of an exposed belly, the pregnant mother's head missing, inside what used to be a bakery, almost made her retch. She kept moving, pushing on, resisting the urge to look back at the body, telling herself the woman (and the child inside her) would still be dead if she looked a second or third time.

Her eyes stung and she fought back tears, too afraid of what would come out if she failed to suppress the emotions. The prospect of Danny and Nate seeing her break down was enough, and she pushed on. She couldn't allow the men to see her be reduced to the Gaby from a year ago, the little girl who had to rely on Matt and Josh to keep her safe. That girl was long, long gone.

"Gaby." Nate's voice from behind her. "Wait up."

She started to turn back when something emerged from behind a dead horse in front of her. Gaby tensed, raising the M4. She stopped when she saw bristling brown and white hair as a cat darted across the street. Its coat of fur was singed black, and there were parts of the animal that had been burned off, exposing flaring red skin underneath.

"What the hell was that?" Nate said.

"Cat," she said.

"Jesus, I thought it was a giant rat or something."

Gaby looked after the animal for a moment before turning back to the horse. Or at the figure trapped underneath it…still moving.

"I got a live one!" she shouted, before jogging forward with her carbine at the ready.

The earbud in her right ear *clicked*, and she heard Nate's voice: "Danny, we got survivors."

"How many?" Danny asked through the earbud.

"Just one so far," Nate said.

"Be careful. It could be a trap."

"Will do."

But it wasn't a trap, Gaby found, when she stopped next to the horse and its rider, a woman in a North Face jacket open to reveal a black uniform underneath. There was a patch of Texas on the jacket's right shoulder and a name tag that read "Morris." One half of her face was covered in blood, the wetness matting short black hair to her skin, and she was busy trying to push the horse off her. Even if the dead animal were still alive to obey—there was a hole from a large caliber round in the belly of Morris's mount—Gaby doubted the woman would have found freedom to her liking: There was a large pool of blood under her, which she might not even have noticed yet.

The soldier finally gave up and instead locked eyes with Gaby. Then she sighed and lay back, letting both hands drop to her sides. She hadn't tried reaching for her holstered weapon, which was the only reason Gaby hadn't shot her yet. Pieces of an M4 rifle were sprinkled liberally among what looked like the remains of a wooden toy train set.

The air around them was thick with a red, black, and white cloud coming from a nearby apartment building. Gaby was glad for the handkerchief over her mouth, something the soldier didn't have.

Then again, choking on pulverized concrete and brick was the least of the injured woman's concerns at the moment.

"Gaby?" Nate said as he jogged over to her.

"She's injured," Gaby said.

Nate peered down at Morris, holding his own piece of cloth to his mouth.

"What are you looking at?" the woman said.

Nate pulled back. "She's not going to make it."

"Says you," Morris said.

"I got her," Gaby said. "Keep looking for other survivors."

Nate nodded and walked off.

"Mohawk boy's not wrong; I can't move," Morris said, turning dull brown eyes back to Gaby. She sounded surprisingly nonchalant, as if they were old friends wasting away a lazy Sunday. "I think my legs are broken. I can't feel anything down there."

"What happened?" Gaby asked.

Morris blinked up at her, trying to see through blood that had covered up a part of her right eye. "You don't know?"

Gaby shook her head. "Why did it attack you?"

"I would tell you if I knew, but I don't. Did I mention my legs are probably broken?"

Gaby nodded. She waited for the woman to continue, but Morris looked like she had lost interest in the conversation. She let her head loll to one side and stared down the street at nothing in particular. The only sound, other than Gaby's still quickening heartbeat, was Nate's boots moving among the ruins on the other side of the street.

"Four hundred people," Morris said quietly.

"Four hundred?" Gaby repeated.

Morris nodded. Or tilted her head slightly up, then down, in something that resembled a nodding motion.

"Here?" Gaby said. "In this place?"

"Four hundred people," Morris said again. Her lips quivered, as if she was going to say something else, but instead she just closed her eyes…and stopped breathing.

Gaby stared at the woman in silence for a moment. A part of her thought Morris might be playacting, but that wasn't true because ten, then fifteen seconds later, and Morris's chest still hadn't moved again.

"What did she say?" Nate asked, coming back over.

"Four hundred," Gaby said.

"Four hundred?"

Gaby slung her rifle and looked around them at the toppled buildings, at the visible body parts. "They were inside when the plane hit."

"Someone probably ordered them into the buildings," Nate said. "They would have been able to hear it coming for miles." He shook his head. "They would have been better off making a run for it; they were sitting ducks inside those buildings." He wiped at some soot underneath his chin. "She said 400?"

Gaby nodded.

"Christ," Nate said. "This isn't right. Whoever did this—whoever ordered this…" He shook his head again. "This isn't right."

She didn't know how to reply, didn't know if anything she said would be even remotely enough, so she turned around and maneuvered past Morris and her mount instead.

"Come on," she said, "there might be more survivors up the street."

Nate followed, their boots *crunching* broken glass and concrete chunks as they stepped through puddles of blood.

And they hadn't even hit the halfway mark through town yet…

"When it finished with the town, it did an extra gun run along a country road that runs parallel to a creek," Danny said. "There are more bodies out there."

"Survivors?" Nate asked.

"Maybe a half dozen vehicles made it through."

"Thank God."

Danny glanced down at his watch. "We should avoid the state highway from now on. Skip around using the smaller roads until we hit US59, then pick our way north to Starch. It'll take longer, but better late than dead."

"How many?" Gaby asked.

"How many what?"

"How many got caught out there? That didn't get away?"

"It doesn't matter."

"Yes, it does."

Danny didn't answer her.

"How many, Danny?" she pressed.

"It doesn't matter, Gaby," he said again. For a brief moment, he reminded her so much of Will, who could end a conversation with just a few words and the right inflection in his voice. "Let's get going," Danny continued. "I want to be in Starch by noon. Nate, it's your turn at the reins."

Nate nodded and slipped into the truck behind the steering wheel while she took a moment to look back one last time at the town. The clouds of black and gray smoke still loitered above it, as if they would never leave. From a distance, the carnage looked almost poetic, but she knew better; there was nothing artful about the bloodbath below those dull colors.

"Gaby," Danny said behind her. "We gotta go."

She turned around and climbed into the backseat as Nate fired up the engine, then maneuvered across the empty lanes toward the feeder road exit to get them off the highway. Danny was right: What had earlier been clear sailing to Starch—there was no such thing as traffic out here, far from the nearest big city—was now a wide-open potential kill zone.

Gaby leaned back against her seat, feeling impossibly drained by the long walk from one end of the destroyed town to the other. She closed her eyes and placed her cheek against the door, the interior of the truck swamped by the cold weather. In front of her, Nate's Mohawk battled against the breeze, a sight that made her smile despite everything she had seen the last few hours.

"They don't miss," Danny had said as they approached the town, all the while listening to the series of chaotic explosions that were so loud even the road had trembled under their truck. "The Avengers are straight-on Gatling guns; they're right in front of the cockpit so the pilots have to see exactly what they're shooting at. And they hardly ever miss."

"Four hundred…"

Gaby replayed Morris's words in her head, heard again the anger and something that sounded almost like disbelief in the woman's voice. She saw again the sadness and regret in Morris's eyes as she stared off, as if she could see something down the street that wasn't just ruins and body parts and blood. Four hundred people, except for however many had been in those "half dozen" vehicles that had managed to escape along the creek.

She opened her eyes when Nate said from the front seat, "What are we dealing with here?"

"I don't have a clue," Danny said.

"That Warthog. Where would something like that come from?"

"There are three Air Force bases in Texas that I know of for certain, probably more I haven't heard of or been to. That A-10 could have come from any number of places. It's not like Uncle Sam's still around to keep them under lock and key. Frankly, I'm surprised this is the first time we've seen one of those things since Happy Times went bye-bye."

"So why didn't you and Will ever go looking for one? Or hell, maybe something more up-to-date, like an Apache?"

"Can you fly an Apache, kid?"

"Well, no…"

"Yeah, neither could we. There could be a fleet of AC-130s sitting around just waiting for us, and we wouldn't be able to do a damn thing with them 'cause we don't know our cockpits from our cockheads. Why do you think a commercial pilot makes more money than the guy who digs ditches?"

"Sorry, stupid question."

"There are no stupid questions, just stupid people that ask

them."

Nate grunted before slowing down the F-150 and turning, taking them even further away from the highway. They were headed north now and soon would have to turn back west so they wouldn't pass Starch by completely. The longer route, but the safer one, especially with that Warthog still up there, somewhere…

"Those people back there," Nate was saying. "They didn't deserve that. Even if they were collaborating with the ghouls."

"No one deserves that," Danny said.

"What are you going to tell Lara?"

"Hell if I know."

"*Are* you going to tell her?"

Danny didn't answer right away. Gaby found herself waiting anxiously for the answer, too.

"I don't know," Danny finally said. "I'll decide when we contact them again, hopefully from the warmth and comfort of Harold Campbell's facility this time."

Gaby didn't have the strength to join their conversation, and instead closed her eyes again and leaned tighter against the door. Winter was already here, but in Texas it was sometimes difficult to tell. Christmas was somewhere over the horizon, and with it another New Year's Eve where no one would be celebrating, or singing *Auld Lang Syne*. Maybe the cold would help wash away the smell of smoke and blood that still clung to her hair and skin and every inch of her clothing. God, she needed a bath in the worst—

"Fuck, shit!" Danny shouted from the front seat.

Her eyes flew open and she sat up straight, was about to say something when she saw it—sunlight reflecting off the gray of its wings as it streaked toward them from the other side of the small feeder road.

"Out!" Danny shouted. *"Get the fuck out and find cover now!"*

She wasn't even certain if the truck was still moving or if it had stopped when Danny threw open his passenger side door and leaped out. She reached for her own door handle with one hand, the other grabbing her rifle leaning against the seat. The door was opening and she was almost out when she remembered her pack and all the equipment—

"Gaby!" Danny's voice, from the other side of the vehicle, booming in her ears. "Move your ass!"

She moved her ass, flinging the door wide open and throwing the rest of her out, one hand clutching her rifle.

Never lose your rifle. Never lose your rifle!

She stumbled and fell, saw the highway floor rushing up at a million miles an hour, and had to stick out both hands to stop her fall. She lost her grip on the M4 in the process and cursed herself *(What would Will say?)* when the road began trembling as if it was getting ready to split open.

She couldn't help herself and turned her head and looked up, wondering idly if the Warthog streaking toward them right now was the same one that had laid waste to Morris's town—

"Gaby!" Nate's voice, piercing through her idiotic thoughts, as he snatched her up from the road with one strong hand.

Gaby fumbled with her footing, groping the air for her carbine lying just out of her reach on the road.

No, no, no! Never lose your rifle! Never lose your rifle!

Before she could break free from Nate's grip to retrieve her weapon—he was much stronger than she remembered, his arms clutching to her in a viselike grip—they were both falling backward off the road and into a ditch.

She was flailing through empty air, trying to get her bearings, when she heard the terrible *brooooooooooorrrrttttttttt* of the A-10 as its primary weapon, the 30mm cannon, started spinning—

She landed in the bottom of the ditch, eating a mouthful of grass and dirt as she did so. Before she could spit out the earthly contents, the road behind her came apart and her bones shook violently. The Warthog swooped over them and she looked up, somehow seeing past the blades of grass covering her face.

The sight was almost magnificent—a gray metal eagle, its fixed wings spread wide and proud, flying much lower than any plane should. She expected to see bombs or missiles, but there weren't any.

Then she remembered: Of course it wasn't carrying any spare armaments, because it had spent everything on the town. On those poor people.

"Four hundred…"

"Gaby, move it!" Nate shouted, pulling her up from the ditch floor.

She struggled to do just that, hating herself for reverting back to the eighteen-year-old girl she thought she had buried a year ago under Will and Danny's tutelage. The refined Gaby, who had survived Dunbar and the farmhouse and the assault on Song Island, was nowhere to be found as she stumbled into the cold side of the ditch to keep herself upright.

Standing now, she could see the remains of the F-150 in front of her. It was a flaming wreck in the middle of the cratered road, its twisted metal frame little more than a barely recognizable shell of its former self.

No, no, she thought, because everything was in there. The gas cans, the supplies, the boxes of silver ammo…

Crack! as a piece of dirt and grass spit into the air less than a foot in front of her face as a bullet chopped into the ground.

Gaby looked up the road as sunlight gleamed off the hood of a black truck racing toward them. Erratic figures clung to the back, one of them aiming at her behind a rifle resting on the roof of the cab.

No, not one truck. *Two.*

Then the ground began shaking again as the Warthog swooped over them one more time, the wake of its passing nearly throwing her off her already wobbly feet. Nate, next to her, had to grab onto the ditch wall to keep upright. Her first instincts were to duck, as if that would save her from the plane's weapons.

The A-10 hadn't gone very far before it started turning. The sight of it, getting ready to come back for yet another pass, did something unexplainable to her. Gaby felt rising anger at the plane's presence, the arrogance of the man—and she thought it *had* to be a man—inside the cockpit at this very moment.

She reached down and drew her Glock.

"Don't!" Nate said, grabbing her wrist.

"What?" It was the only thing she could think of to say, just before he snatched the gun out of her hand and threw it up to the burning road.

Nate did the same thing to his sidearm before throwing both arms into the air, shouting, "Don't shoot! Don't shoot!" He looked over at her, saw the flash of anger on her face, and said, "Trust me, you gotta trust me."

She did trust him, but she was also angry. Not just with him, but with everything that had happened. The town, the bodies, Morris, and that *goddamn plane* as it swooped by over them one more time.

But he was right. Nate was right. The Warthog. The two trucks. The men with assault rifles in the back of them.

Slowly, very slowly, the anger fizzled, and she turned around and mimicked Nate, raising both arms into the air just as the first truck—a dirt-caked GMC—stopped above them. The second vehicle—a slightly more beat-up white Silverado—squealed to a stop next to it. Men in tan military-style uniforms leaped out and swarmed them, rifles bouncing dangerously in their hands.

"Get up here!" one of the men shouted.

"Keep your hands up!" another one said, spittle flying out of his lips. "Keep them fucking up!"

Gaby and Nate climbed up, keeping their hands raised as high as they could make them. It was difficult to navigate the sloping side of the ditch without the use of their hands, but they both managed it anyway, though she had to use her elbows for leverage.

When she and Nate were back on the road, the men circled them, weapons pointed at their faces. They looked wild, almost out of control, and she realized at that moment just how close she had come to being killed if Nate hadn't wrestled the gun from her.

She looked back at the men, searching for all the things she was used to seeing on collaborators, like Morris back in town. Instead, she saw bright red collars with a white circle in the middle, surrounded by sharp lines that were clearly supposed to represent sun rays.

The emblem stood out against the pale drab of their fatigues, as did the all-white patch of the state of Texas over their right breasts with their names stenciled in the center.

Gaby's eyes were pulled back to an AK-47 pointed in her face. The man behind it was in his late twenties, tall, and he stared back at her even as his forefinger moved dangerously (nervously?) back and forth against the trigger.

I don't want to die. God, I don't want to die.

She heard voices and looked across the road, past the flaming ball that used to be their F-150, and saw Danny, hands raised, being patted down by another soldier while the man's comrades kept the ex-Ranger under their guns.

Danny must have sensed her, because he looked over and nodded, as if to say, *"We'll be okay."*

She wanted to believe him, even as one of the men grabbed and twisted her arms painfully behind her back. She let out a small grunt as someone else ran his hands over her ribcage, then turned her pockets inside out. Two others were doing the same to Nate next to her. Their captors couldn't have been rougher if they tried.

Above them, the Warthog swooped low as it passed them by, the rush of icy cold air against her face a stark reminder of what had happened to the town behind them and the hell they had involuntarily walked right into.

We should have stayed out of Texas. God, why did we ever come back?

Will would never have let us come back here...

CHAPTER 6

LARA

"THIS IS BULLSHIT," Gage said. "I did everything you asked. I even taught the Mexican how to drive the damn boat. I answered every question he and that midget had. I did *everything* you asked."

The 'midget'? Oh, he means Maddie.

She fully expected this reaction from Gage but wasn't quite prepared for the emotion behind it. If she closed her eyes and didn't know who he was, or what he had done, she could almost believe he was being unjustly treated. Almost.

But of course she knew exactly who the man was; more importantly, what he had been prepared to do at Song Island if Keo hadn't boarded the *Trident* and taken it over. She knew all of that, and yet she couldn't help but ask herself for the twentieth time since she stepped inside the room:

What would Will do?

The problem with that was she knew exactly what Will would have done, and none of it included locking Gage inside a cabin on the lower decks of the yacht away from the rest of the population. Will also wouldn't have fed Gage twice a day and let him out to see the sun every other day. Will wouldn't have done any of those things, because once Gage's usefulness came to an end, so did the man's reason for being.

But she wasn't Will, and she would never be. One of these days she'd know once and for all if that was a good thing or a bad thing.

For now, it was just her inside a slightly too-dark room, trying not to gag on the musky stench that lingered over everything despite the open portside window. The cabin was big enough for two people, with a single cot in a corner and its own small toilet and sink. It probably had better amenities than Gage had given his past victims.

"You know that, right?" Gage was saying. "I did everything you asked of me. You wouldn't have gotten off Song Island if it wasn't for me. Who kept this boat running after that? Me, Lara. I did. *Me.*"

What exactly did he expect her to say? She knew what he had done, which was precisely the problem. She knew what he had done after Song Island, but she also knew, if not all the gory details, of what he had done before they ever met him.

Gage was not a good man. He was a killer, a thief, a liar, and an opportunist. Which was why she couldn't allow him to mingle with the rest of the crew and wouldn't let him go near the kids. That was also why he spent his days down here eating alone, watching the ocean from his window, and counting down the hours until either Bonnie or Benny came down to take him up for his hour-long alone time in the sunlight above deck.

"Where's my reward?" Gage asked. "Where's the gratitude? I deserve something, don't I?"

"There is no reward," she said.

"You promised me."

"I didn't promise you anything, except that you'd keep living. And you have."

She wasn't sure if that deflated him or if it just made him angrier. Gage stood across the room from her, watching her back with an intensity that probably should have intimidated her. He shouldn't have wasted his time; she'd faced worse things in her life since The Purge, and she'd survived them all. Gage was, after all, only human.

His eyes eventually fell to her right hand, hanging loosely at her side, next to the holstered Glock. She didn't have her rifle because she rarely carried it around these days. She should have been hesitant to stand this close to him, with only eight (nine?) feet of space separating them. They were near enough that she could smell the odor emanating from his skin. Bonnie had told her that Gage rarely bathed in the ocean when he was above deck, and they theorized that he was afraid they'd drive off and leave him floating in the ocean. She had to admit, she'd thought about doing just that—or something like it—on more than one occasion.

Bonnie's heavy, booted footsteps echoed from the open door behind her. The ex-model was somewhere further up the corridor, close enough that Lara knew she could hear everything being said. They always had at least one person outside Gage's door, just in case.

You taught me that, Will. Just in case...'

"So, what now?" Gage asked. "You're just going to throw me away? Like trash? *I did everything you asked.*"

The answer should have come easily. She had spent more than one sleepless night thinking about it, and each time the outcome was the same: She couldn't trust Gage. The man standing in front of her might be wearing shabby and stained clothes, and smelling slightly of urine and a lot of sweat, but she could see it in his eyes. Gage had been thinking about this moment, too, imagining what he would do when it finally came. She wondered if he ever managed to convince himself things might work out in his favor, or if he always knew this was the inevitable conclusion.

He had to know, didn't he? Maybe...

"Well?" he said, sounding annoyed by her silence. "What happens to me now, Lara?"

"Now you leave," she said.

"Leave? Just like that?"

"I'm going to give you one of the inflatable boats and enough fuel to reach land, if you drive straight toward it. What you do when you get there is up to you."

"A boat and some fuel?" He tilted his head slightly to one side, as if he could divine her true intentions if he found the right angle. "That's it?"

"And some food and water to last a few days. After that, you're on your own."

"What about weapons?"

"No weapons."

"You can't do that to me."

"This isn't a negotiation. I'm telling you what's going to happen, and you're going to accept it because there is no Door B or Door C. There is just this door." She glanced at her watch. "Your boat will be ready in one hour. Make the most of the time you have left and pack up."

"I need *guns!*"

She shook her head, amazed at how calm she was. Her voice hadn't risen noticeably and her body, along with the hand hovering beside the Glock, remained perfectly steady. She wouldn't have thought any of this was possible as she walked the length of the boat and climbed down to the lower deck, then moved through the engine room and toward his cabin. She remembered the look on Bonnie's face as she walked past the other woman, who could barely look her in the eyes. Like everyone, Bonnie had been dreading this moment, too.

But for whatever reason, Lara didn't feel the sudden surge of adrenaline or pangs of guilt. There was just...calmness, because she knew exactly why she was doing this and why there were no other options. It just had to be done.

"No guns," she said. "At least not from us. What you find out there is up to you. All I'm giving you is a boat, fuel, and some food and water."

"You can't do this..."

"It's happening."

"No..."

"You don't have a choice."

"Don't I?" he said, peering at her, his head still cocked at an odd angle.

"No," she said. "You can take what I give you and make the best of it, or you can take your chances." She finally moved her hand, placing her palm over the butt of her sidearm. "It's up to you."

He didn't say anything and simply glared at her for a few seconds. He didn't move, though she thought he wanted to. Desperately wanted to.

But he didn't move.

"I'll send Bonnie back down here to get you in one hour," she said. "Be ready."

She turned to leave.

"Lara," he said.

She ignored him and continued walking to the door. "One hour."

"*Lara!*" he shouted, the sound of her name like a knife.

That time she stopped and turned back around *just in time to see him lunging at her.*

Oh, goddammit, she thought, realizing just how badly she had read the situation. She wasn't prepared for this. Not when she thought it was all over.

Gage had lost a lot of weight since she first met him, and although he still limped noticeably on one leg despite the brace, it didn't seem to slow him down one bit at the moment. She wasn't ready for his speed or the bloodshot eyes coming right at her. He didn't so much as cross the small space between them as he launched himself, his body like a living spring that had been coiled, waiting to explode in this one single moment.

And there was something else—a streak of sunlight shining through the open window, reflecting across the flat surface of an object, long and sharp, in his right hand, his fingers gripped tightly around its cloth-covered base. Some kind of knife, maybe a piece of metal he had pried loose somewhere. Whatever it was, he had been hiding it on him when she entered, but he was showing it to her now as he streaked across the room *right at her.*

Lara lifted her left arm instinctively, not even realizing what she was doing until the shiv sliced into her flesh. There should have been pain—a lot of it, given how forceful Gage had struck, the blow's impact magnified by his forward momentum—except there was just a stinging sensation, as if her body didn't truly grasp what was happening and her mind couldn't interpret the true meaning behind the stream of blood arcing through the air.

She lost her balance even as she was backpedaling and stumbled out the open door and into the hallway beyond. He was still coming, face contorted into an expression that was part anger and part triumph. He didn't so much as follow her out as he stalked after her, (her) blood flitting off the object in his right hand with his every step.

She was still off balance and stumbling blindly backward, trying desperately to exert some control over her legs, when her back slammed into the smooth metal wall of the hallway outside the room. There was pain that time, but also surprise at how much distance she had covered in such a short time between when Gage struck and now. The breath rushed out of her as she stabbed her right hand down to her hip, found the familiar grip of the Glock, and jerked the weapon up just as Gage raised his right hand and brought it back down a heartbeat later, aiming from right to left—

Bang!

The gunshot was like an explosion inside the close confines of steel and concrete that made up the lower deck. The *Trident*'s engine was still shut off, so there was nothing to dampen the noise; it was still echoing in her head like a jackhammer seconds later.

Gage seemed to take one, then two, hesitant steps backward, his slashing right hand frozen in the air as if he had simply forgotten how or why it was up there in the first place. His fingers were so tightly clenched around the knife's handle that they were almost as white as his paling face. Blood gushed from his stomach as he attempted to stanch it with his left hand, sticky wetness slipping through his fingers.

"You—" he said, looking back at her.

She shot him again, this time in the chest, before he could finish what he was about to say. The second gunshot sounded curiously softer than the first, which didn't make a lot of sense, but then maybe her racing heartbeat, so loud that both her ears seemed to be thrumming, had something to do with that.

Gage fell back through the open cabin door and slammed into the floor with a heavy *thump!*, followed a split second later by the clattering of the knife at his booted feet.

The heavy pounding of footsteps came from another part of the boat, then someone was shouting her name.

She was still trying to figure out what was happening, or how she had ended up sitting in a pool of blood, when a voice gasped, "Jesus, Lara, Jesus," followed by a sharp squawking noise and someone shouting Zoe's name.

◄━━ ━━►

"SO THAT WAS your brilliant plan?" Carly asked. "You were going to West him? Girl, you should have talked to me about it first. I would have advised you to just shoot the fucker and throw him overboard. No muss, no fuss."

Lara looked up quizzically at her friend. She found it hard to focus on her face for some reason, so had to settle for Carly's bright red hair as a marker.

"What?" Carly said.

"'West him'?" Lara said, her voice hoarse. "What does that even mean?"

"You remember West, don't you? Yee-haw? You smashed his head in with a radio when he snuck into your room with a gun back at the hotel?"

"Oh."

West. Jesus, she had forgotten all about West. He had come to Song Island with Bonnie and the others. There had been another man with him, but for the life of her, Lara couldn't recall his name at the moment.

"You really did forget," Carly was saying. "Is this one of Danny and Will's famous compartmentalization thingies?"

"No, I just forgot about him."

"Really."

THE SPEARS OF LACONIA   75

She nodded.

"I wonder what happened to him," Carly said. "You think he ever made it after you and Danny sent him out into the world with just his boxers and a pair of socks?"

"I don't know. I don't really care, either."

"Fair enough. He and his buddy did try to gut Blaine."

She glanced around the room. She was glad to see harsh sunlight coming in through a window to one side *(Still daylight)*. Considering the unspectacular decorations along the walls and the slightly hard bed she was lying on at the moment, they had taken her back to her cabin.

"He used a piece of his cot, in case you were wondering," Carly said. "One of the frames, according to Maddie. He must have spent days sharpening that thing. I guess when you're down there with just that hole to look out of, you need to find ways to fill your time. Like making shanks. What an asshole."

Lara looked down at her left hand, then lifted it as much as she could. It was covered in gauze, and the complete absence of pain was a surprise. In fact, she didn't feel much of anything at all. A combination of painkillers and...something.

"What did Zoe give me?" she asked.

Carly shrugged. "Beats the hell out of me. You're the third-year medical student; you tell me."

"That was a long time ago. Feels like another lifetime..."

"Anyway, you bled all over the place. Freaked all of us out. Imagine what we'd do without you to boss us around."

Lara managed a weak smile. "You would have gotten by."

"I don't know about that."

There was something on Carly's face, a seriousness that Lara rarely saw, and it made her wonder just how close to death's door she had been outside of Gage's cabin. She remembered pain, a lot of screaming, and wetness...

"I'm okay," Lara said.

"No, you're not," Carly said, "but you will be. We'll see to that. So you need to get some rest and we'll do our best to keep this floating barge running in the meantime. I know it's hard to believe, but we're not all dopes. Well, not completely."

"Danny?"

"Still nothing from that idiot. But he's got four more hours until nightfall, so I'm delaying panic time until then."

"What about Keo?"

"Also nada." She frowned. "That's worrying, right? It's noon, Lara. He should have radioed in by now. We did come all the way down here just to pick his sorry ass up."

She nodded. Or thought she did. Maybe a slight up and down motion.

"Blaine wants to go look for him," Carly continued. "Or at least go closer to the coast, in case he lost his radio but is waiting for us on the beach or something."

"No," she said.

"Why not?"

"If we're close enough to the beach to see him, then someone can see us, too."

"Oh. Good point. I guess that's why you get paid the big bucks."

"Something like that. Besides, Keo can take care of himself." She forced herself to focus on Carly's face. "Tell Blaine not to expose us unnecessarily, understand?"

Carly nodded. "You're the boss, boss."

Lara saw something else on her friend's face. It was something that had been there for a long time now, and that she had seen on the others' faces as well. She knew this moment would come—had, in fact, expected it much earlier.

"What's on your mind?" she asked.

Carly looked hesitant, like someone preparing to pick her way through a minefield. "Maybe it's time we finally talk about why we're still hanging around the Gulf of Mexico, why you keep delaying going to the Bengal Islands."

Will...

"We need to talk about it sooner or later," Carly continued.

Will... I waited for you. I waited days and weeks for you.

Goddamn you. You promised me. You promised *me.*

"But it can wait until you're better," Carly said. "Zoe and I will look in on you through the day, make sure you don't try to sneak off on us. I don't think we can afford to lose you, too."

The way we lost Will…

Carly turned to go.

"Carly…" she said when Carly was at the door. "When Danny and the others come back, we'll go."

"Are you sure?" Carly asked.

She nodded. Or tried to.

Carly pursed her lips into a sympathetic smile. "I'll let the others know."

"What about Gage?" she asked.

"We tossed him overboard. Gage being a piece of shit human being and all, we thought it was about time he contributed to the world by feeding the fishes."

"Good," she said, closing her eyes.

Will's voice echoing inside her head, the way it had ever since that last night on Song Island:

"Whatever happens, keep moving forward. Don't stop to look back. Keep moving forward, because that's how we survive."

IT WAS DARK outside her window when she opened her eyes a second time. Alarm bells immediately went off and didn't stop until she could hear the low howl of the wind outside, the gentle slapping of water against the *Trident's* hull.

Safe. Still safe.

There was a wall clock, but she didn't bother looking for it in the semidarkness. There was enough moonlight that she could make out the foot of her bed and a small figure huddled in the corner under a blanket.

It took her a moment to piece together Elise's round face, the girl's head resting against the armchair, long hair draped across her oval-shaped face. She thought about calling to Elise, telling the girl to go back to the room she shared with Vera, where she wouldn't have to twist herself into a pretzel to fit into a chair. But she saw the way Elise was sleeping, as peaceful as she had ever seen the girl, and decided against it.

Lara was already on her back, so she didn't have to do very much to look up at the shadows dancing across the ceiling. Instead of making her nervous, they soothed her nerves, and she didn't move for the longest time. The drugs Zoe had given her prevented her from fully concentrating on any one thing, including all the rambling thoughts inside her head, for which she was grateful for.

A soft *thoom* from somewhere in the distance made her glance toward the door. She only heard it because everything else was so quiet. If she thought the nights on Song Island could be deathly still, out here among the waves it was even more pronounced.

There it was again: *thoom*.

A low rumbling, almost like thunder, coming from a distance. Except there were no hints of raindrops pelting the roof above her. The *Trident* had had to move through two rainstorms in the last month, and she knew what rain sounded and felt like; this wasn't it.

She climbed out of bed, relieved Zoe hadn't connected her to any of the field equipment she had set up to take care of their walking wounded. Danny had been Zoe's first and *(Thank God)* only customer so far. Someone had put her into one of her cotton jogging pants and sweatshirts, which explained why her body was so warm despite the open window.

Lara padded across the room, thankful her injury was confined to her left arm. How long had she been asleep? It was hard to gauge time by the darkness, especially with her head still swimming around in a medication-infused fog.

She passed Elise's sleeping form, the girl completely oblivious—

Thoom.

Definitely not thunder. Or rain. It wasn't loud or ferocious enough to be gunshots on the boat. Or nearby, which would have meant a second boat. And they were still out in the ocean. Or were they? Had Blaine moved them closer to shore?

"Blaine wants to go look for him," Carly had said, referring to Keo.

The door opened before she even reached for it, and Bonnie's tall frame blocked her path into the hallway. The other woman looked shocked to see Lara standing there, her left arm bent at the elbow, held tight against her chest.

"You heard it, too?" Bonnie asked.

Lara nodded. "What was it?"

"Explosions."

"Explosions?"

"From the beach. From Sunport."

Keo.

"Where's everyone?" she asked.

Bonnie held up her radio. "On the bridge."

They turned right and went up the darkened hallway. Why was it so dark? Usually there were one or two LED lights set on dim along the corridors.

Next to her, Bonnie looked like she wanted to wrap an arm around Lara's waist to keep her upright, but Lara was moving just fine. That was the good news. The bad news was that she was starting to feel a slight tingle coming from her left arm, a clear indication the pain meds were losing their effectiveness.

"Can you walk okay?" Bonnie asked.

"I'm fine. What happened to the lights?"

"Blaine switched them off."

"Why?"

"He didn't say."

Lara could hear voices—Blaine's and someone else's—from the other side of the open bridge door in front of them.

"Did Keo radio in yet?" she asked.

"I don't think so," Bonnie said. "But you'll have to ask Blaine. That's his and Carly's department."

The other voice belonged to Carly, and she was standing with Blaine in front of the console, looking out the wraparound wind-shield. They stood in complete darkness, with only streams of moonlight and the occasional blinking dashboard buttons to see with. Blaine was peering behind a pair of binoculars, and though she couldn't actually make out the Texas coastline outside, she couldn't shake the feeling they were much closer than they had been earlier today.

Carly glanced over her shoulder. "Hey, what are you doing up?"

"We've moved," Lara said.

"I moved us closer to shore," Blaine said. "Don't worry; I switched off the lights before I got close enough to be spotted."

She nodded, relieved. "What's going on?"

"I'm betting my nonexistent week's salary on World War III," Carly said.

There was another *thoom!* in the distance, and like the previous ones, this came from the Texas shoreline, exactly where Sunport would be. As she peered out the windshield at the darkened world, a stream of red and orange flames appeared as if from a dragon's mouth and slashed from left to right, before seeming to diffuse and disappear, leaving behind small pockets of fire that seemed to be...*moving around?*

There was another *thoom!* This one was so loud, she swore she could feel the impact causing the boat to shake slightly under her bare feet, but that couldn't have been possible given their distance...could it?

"You need to see this," Blaine said, and handed her his binoculars.

She stepped closer toward the windshield and looked through the lens.

The binocular had night vision, which allowed her to see further than she could have with the naked eye. They were still too far away for her to make out every single detail, but she had no problems picking up the objects moving around in the fields beyond the beach. They looked to be on fire.

There was another *thoom!* and for just a split second, the explosion lit up what looked like a vehicle surrounded by hordes of ghouls.

"Is that...?" she said.

"It's a tank," Blaine said, barely able to contain his excitement. "It's a fucking U.S. Army tank."

CHAPTER 7

GABY

IT SEEMED TO take forever to get to wherever they were going, with Gaby blindfolded and lying in the back of a moving truck the entire time. Her legs were bound at the ankles, her arms twisted painfully behind her back. Nate and Danny were somewhere to her right, their familiar scents a welcome distraction from the constant bumps in the road. At least they hadn't gagged her, thank God.

She could also sniff the other two in the back of the truck with them.

Soldiers. More soldiers.

But not the same ones from Louisiana or the ones in black uniforms they had encountered in Hellion when they first made their way inland a few days ago. No, these were different men. Different loyalties. And different agendas.

"What happened?" she had asked Morris.

"You don't know?" Morris had replied, blinking up at her through a layer of blood.

No, she didn't know, and neither had Morris. Because these men weren't collaborators, and neither was the pilot that had laid waste to Morris's town. These men were something else completely. Something more...dangerous.

Her captors hadn't said a word since she, Danny, and Nate were unceremoniously tossed into the back of the truck, and every now and then she could hear the Warthog in the background. Or, at least, she thought it was the same warplane that had destroyed their vehicle. The possibility that there could be more than one of them out there made her shiver involuntarily.

Every now and then, voices managed to rise over the clatter of the moving truck. Muffled sounds, men talking through radios.

One of the soldiers said into the wind, "Three, all still kicking."

"Collaborators?" a male voice asked.

"Doesn't look like it," the man said. He was somewhere to her right, probably sitting on the wheel housing.

"What do they look like?" the voice asked.

"I dunno. Civilians. No uniforms, but they were packing serious heat. Probably had more in the truck before Cole wasted it. We haven't asked them any questions yet."

"Okay, make sure they're still breathing when you get back."

"Roger that," the man said.

Gaby waited to hear more, but there was just the continuous *thump-thump* of the truck's tires going up and down the unpaved road under them. Each time they hit a hole or had to go over a bump, Gaby's head lifted slightly, only to slam back down against the cold (and dirty) truck bed. She tried to time the rise and falls but could never get it right and gave up after half a dozen failed attempts.

They must have been moving through a wooded area, because the temperature dropped noticeably despite the combined sweating of her, Nate, Danny, and their two guards. High tree canopies, enough to block out the sun in this part of the countryside, embraced her in cool shadows.

She did her best to keep track of time, but it was difficult without her eyes. Besides, her ears were filled with nothing but the *thump-thump* of the tires. It could have been a few hours or less than that since they were captured. The warmth of the sun against one side of her face kept her calm, the usual dread of incoming nightfall staved off momentarily. She hadn't realized how much living on the *Trident* this last month had dulled her survival instincts until she set foot back on land earlier this week. That mess in Hellion was proof of that.

We got soft…and this is what happens when you get soft.

She was angry at herself, at how she had handled the ambush on the road, and how close to dying she had been in that ditch if it hadn't been for Nate's fast thinking. She despised the feeling of helplessness, something she had tried to beat out of her ever since losing Josh to the collaborators and realized the only person she could afford to depend on was herself.

You would have been so disappointed in me, Will. At least you weren't here to see me screw up so badly.

She was still trying to come to terms with her failures when the vehicle began to noticeably slow down. A little later, the sharp squeal and slightly burning aroma of well-worn tires braking wafted into her realm of smell.

Footsteps as the two men in the back maneuvered around her, Danny, and Nate on their way to the back. The loud *clank!* of the tailgate being unlatched, followed by the *bang!* as it slammed down. A stream of voices, vehicles in motion, the extra body odor of a lot of people perspiring in the sun despite the cool air, and the *clicks* and *clacks* of…what was that? Metal? Trinkets?

Bullets. She was listening to the sound of bullets being moved around in crates. Not just that, but they were making them, too. The evidence was in the thick taste of smelting metal in the air. The question was: Were they making silver bullets?

Rough hands grabbed her by the shoulders and spun her around before they began dragging her backward like a slab of meat. Then there was just empty air and for a moment she thought she was going to fall, but the same pair of hands maintained their grip and turned her around again.

"Feet down," a gruff voice said. Not the same man she had heard earlier on the radio.

Gaby lowered her feet, touching nothing for the longest time until—there, solid ground. Dirt, not concrete.

The same pair of hands pulled her slightly forward, off the open tailgate, and stood her up. "Don't move and you won't fall," the man said.

She stood still and listened to more *clinking* and *clacking* going on all around her. There were a lot of people squeezed into a small area, and every single one of them seemed to be in constant motion.

A man next to her grunted, then a familiar voice said, "Are we there yet?"

Danny.

She almost smiled, but didn't. There was no telling who was watching and how they would react.

"Where are we?" someone else said. *Nate.*

"Shut up," the voice from the radio said. "You'll speak when spoken to. Got it?"

"Can you run that by me again?" Danny said.

The *whump!* of something hitting flesh.

Danny's voice again, but this time sounding like he had his teeth clenched in pain, "So that's a no?"

"Smartass," the gruff voice said. Then, "Where does he want them?"

"He's in the hangar," another voice said. "Take them over."

"On foot?"

"We need the truck for transportation. Besides, you need to lose some weight anyway. The walk'll do you good."

"Fuck you."

The other voice laughed.

A hand grabbed Gaby's right arm and held her steady as someone else cut the zip tie around her ankles. The same hand then pushed her forward. She took that as a sign they wanted her to walk, so she did. Hopefully she didn't run into something, like one of the many vehicles moving around her.

Her escort walked slightly behind her. A woman. Gaby could tell even with blindfolds on, because there was no mistaking the sudden difference in bodily smell between the guys who had brought her here and the one who taken over.

"This would be easier if I could see," Gaby said, picking her way over uneven dirt floor, the rising heat of the sun beating down on her.

"No talking," her escort said. Gaby was right; it was a woman.

"You have a name?" she asked anyway.

There was no response.

"Are we at an airport?" Gaby asked.

Still no response.

"Not the most talkative bunch," Danny said somewhere to her right.

"You okay?" Nate said from her left.

"I'm fine, dear; don't worry about me," Danny said.

"Gaby," Nate said.

She smiled before realizing he couldn't see through his own blindfold. "I'm okay. You?"

"Trying not to trip. And a little sore all over."

"That's what she said," Danny said.

"Shut up and keep walking straight," Gaby's female escort snapped. She was sure the woman wasn't alone, though her companions were keeping their distance.

After about thirty seconds of walking silently across what felt like an open field, the woman finally said, "How did you know?" just as Gaby felt the ground under her switch from soft dirt to hard concrete.

"Know what?" Gaby said.

"That we're at an airfield."

"Someone said to take us to the hangar."

"Ah."

"What's going on? Are you guys making bullets?"

The woman didn't answer.

"I thought we were talking," Gaby said.

"You thought wrong," the woman said.

"That's what they used to call me in college," Danny chimed in. "Thought Wrong Danny. Wanna know why?"

"No," the woman said.

"Sure you do."

"I have a gun that says I don't."

"Well, since it's my personal motto that the gun is always right, I'll save the explanation for later."

"You do that," their guard said.

They walked on for another five minutes, until the loud chatter of people, machines, and vehicles began to fade behind them. She wasn't sure how far the paved ground went, but it seemed to stretch on endlessly. She was trying to remember how far they had walked when the ground began to vibrate and a loud rush of air hit her with such surprising force she started to fall over, and would have, if a pair of hands didn't grab her from behind first.

"Easy there," the woman said.

Gaby found her footing again and turned her head in a vain attempt to follow the object's trajectory. "What was that?"

"One of the Warthogs coming in for a landing. It's on the other side of the runway, but they pack quite a punch."

Jesus, did she just say 'one of the Warthogs'? Gaby thought, before saying out loud, trying to keep her voice as steady as possible, "How many of them do you have?"

"Need to know, Erin," a familiar male gruff voice said from behind them.

"I'm not an idiot, Louis," the woman, Erin, said. Then, with a push against Gaby's back that seemed to indicate the friendly chatter was over, "We're almost there. Keep straight."

BRIGHT SUNLIGHT FLOODED the wide hangar through a series of high windows along all four sides. The arched roof looked overly tall, though the fact she'd just had her blindfolds removed for the first time in a long time might have had a little something to do with her inability to properly judge dimensions at the moment.

Catwalks extended from the bottom of the structure all the way to the windows, ending in platforms that looked big enough for a dozen or so men to keep an eye out on the surrounding area. There were metal bars over the windows, which, like the walkways, appeared to have been tacked on very recently. They definitely didn't look as if they were part of the building's original blueprints.

The floor was coated in some kind of shiny material that reflected her face, along with everyone else standing around her, including Danny to her right and Nate to her left. She didn't know if they were flanking her on purpose, or if that was just how they had been escorted inside. Not that she minded. She liked having them there at her sides, though she would never say it out loud.

They had been led across an airfield and into a hangar, but there were no planes inside. Instead, the cavernous space had been converted into some kind of storage warehouse, with a small army of people in tan uniforms loading a pair of green Army trucks with plastic moving boxes, wooden crates, and metal containers. A woman with a long ponytail *(That's definitely not Army regulation)* handed luggage over to a man crouched at the back of one of the trucks, and Gaby heard more of the *clicks* and *clacks* of loose items moving around inside.

There were just as many sneakers as there were combat boots squeaking against the glossy floor as the flurry of people went about their business. More boxes, along with garbage bags and just about anything that could have been used as containers, lined the far wall of the building, waiting to be loaded. Duct tape, ropes, and strips of cloth hid the contents, though one of the boxes was slightly see-through, and Gaby was trying to peek at the objects on the other side—

A loud *crash!* made her look away.

One of the soldiers in the trucks had missed a handoff, and a gray plastic box had broken against the floor. Candleholders, pens, and silverware were rolling around. They were all silver. Every single one of them.

They're making silver bullets, which means they know about the silver.

There was no panic—no angry voices or barking orders—and people got to work gathering up the spilled items and putting them back into other containers. More than a few of them, she noticed, looked too young to be wearing military uniforms of any sort.

A boy who couldn't have been more than fifteen, his tan pants hanging loosely off a slim waist, picked up a crate from the far wall and grunted his way over to a truck. The teenager's shirt collar was green and featured the same white sun emblem that was on the collars of the men who had captured her on the road. Those men, she remembered, had red collars. Like the other workers inside the warehouse at the moment, the boy wasn't armed.

When one of the trucks had filled up, someone slammed the tailgate closed. The truck roared to life, then drove out of the hangar. As soon as it was out, another Army truck began backing into position.

Gaby took the opportunity to look behind her at a steady stream of vehicles moving like busy bees around the airfield. She couldn't see the entirety of the place from her angle, but what she could see told her she was dealing with a very organized group of people who clearly knew what they were doing.

The presence of the sun eased her mind a bit, but she badly wished she knew the exact time. Besides taking their weapons, radios, and gun belts, their captors had also taken their watches. She hated not knowing how many hours she had before nightfall, especially out here. Things were so much simpler back on the *Trident*, where nightfall didn't arrive with the same kind of crawling dread.

She turned back around when a voice said, "Did you find any uniforms on them?"

A lone figure broke off from the group of people in front of her. He had been there this entire time, she realized, with his back to them as he shuffled items between the back of the building and the trucks. The man pulled off work gloves and wiped sweat from his face with the back of his hand as he walked over. He wore the same tan uniform as the others, along with the Texas patch over his right breast, and the only thing that stood out about him was the black collar with the white sun emblem in the center.

Red, green, and now black.

The man was in his late fifties and stood eye-to-eye with Danny, but there was something imposing about him that had nothing to do with his height or size. It was in the way he carried himself, the stern, almost paternal look in his eyes. His name tag read: "Mercer."

"No, sir," the gruff voice answered from somewhere behind her. "We searched the truck. Or what was left of it. Cole got a little trigger-happy and blasted the thing before we could take them into custody."

Mercer nodded, then looked at all three of them one at a time. He casually put his gloves into his back pocket before finally asking, "Who's in charge?"

"I guess that would be me," Danny said.

"What's your name, son?"

"Danny, but my mother calls me Daniel. You can call me that, too, but I'll have to insist on at least fifteen years of child-rearing first."

The older man trained soft brown eyes on Danny. Anyone else might have turned weak in the knees under that gaze, but most people weren't Danny, who had survived too many things the last few months—and the years before the world ended—to be affected. Even so, Gaby thought Danny might have actually just…stood a bit straighter?

Mercer finally turned those same calm eyes on her before moving on to Nate a few seconds later. He must not have found anything interesting about them, because he ended up back on Danny. "What unit were you in, son?"

"Seventy-fifth Ranger Regiment, Third Battalion out of Fort Benning," Danny said.

"Fort Benning is an excellent producer of Rangers."

"They did the best they could with what they had."

"And your friends?"

"She's Gaby, and he's Nathaniel."

"Just Nate," Nate said.

Mercer didn't acknowledge either her or Nate. He saw them, but he didn't *see* them. She didn't know whether she should feel a little annoyed, or glad. Did she really want Mercer to "see" her? Maybe not...

Around them, the activity continued, even as another truck backed inside, the *beep-beep-beep* of its warning signal loud in the confines of the hangar. The piles of items at the back wall were already much smaller than the last time she looked.

"You were at T29," Mercer was saying.

"T29?" Danny said.

"The town we attacked earlier today. What were you doing there?"

"Four hundred..." Morris had said. Gaby thought she could still taste the smoke and blood on the tip of her tongue.

"Saw your hog swooping in for the kill and decided to go see what all the fuss was about," Danny said. "That's the full extent of us being there."

"You killed them," Gaby said. She didn't realize she had spoken until the words blurted out, drawing Mercer's eyes to her. There was something about those eyes that made her want to take a step back, and it took all of her willpower to remain perfectly still. Maybe the rising anger and the still-fresh memories of Morris's town helped. "There were 400 people in that town. Men, women, and children."

"And pregnant women," Nate said. "You murdered pregnant women, for God's sake."

"It's war," Mercer said. "People die in wars."

"There were *pregnant women* in that town!" Nate shouted, his words booming in the hangar, so loud that they even managed to pierce through the *beep-beep-beep* of another Army truck backing inside.

The soldiers working behind Mercer stopped and looked over. A few of them even glanced at Mercer for some kind of response.

Mercer didn't respond right away, and instead stared back at Nate as if waiting for his fury to burn out. Gaby thought he was going to have a long wait, because she had never seen Nate so angry before—his face was almost red and his nostrils flared, and suddenly that Mohawk looked threatening instead of funny.

"Collateral damage," Mercer said finally.

"That's it?" Nate said. "That's all you have to say?"

"That's all that needs to be said." And just like that, he dismissed Nate and focused on Danny. "Let's talk, soldier."

"Why not? Not like I have a hot date or anything," Danny said.

The older man walked off and Danny turned and followed, but not before giving her a slight nod that she would have missed entirely if she hadn't been looking for it.

"Be cool," that nod said.

Mercer had climbed into the front passenger seat of a Jeep waiting outside the hangar. Danny took a seat in the back as the vehicle drove off through some kind of private airfield with a small cluster of administrative buildings all the way on the other side. That was also where most of the vehicles and people not in the hangar were congregated, and where, she guessed, they had been dropped off earlier.

"Sonofabitch," Nate said next to her, gritting his teeth.

Gaby took his hand and squeezed. He looked over and pursed his lips, but she could still see the anger on his face. It was the very first time she had ever seen him so angry and though it probably shouldn't have, it made her like him even more.

"Come on," Erin said, turning and leading them through the hangar.

While blindfolded, Gaby had thought Erin was in her thirties based entirely on her voice, but she was actually younger—late twenties, and tall. Gaby was used to being one of the taller girls in most rooms, but Erin towered over her at about five-ten, with long dark hair in a ponytail and light hazel eyes. She had a slightly Eurasian look about her, but her accent was all Texan.

The soldier with the gruff voice, Louis, followed behind them. He was in his thirties, balding, and squat. He had a rifle slung over his back and always kept a good distance, as if afraid she or Nate would try something. Maybe she might have done exactly that before she saw all the manpower Mercer had assembled around them.

They were led to an office in the back right corner. It was the only room in the entire structure and two more soldiers stood guard with M4 rifles. Like Erin and Louis, they had red collars on top of their uniforms. That, she realized, was what distinguished them from the worker bees in the place.

Red collars for the warriors and green for support? Was that how it worked? Then what were the ones with black collars, like Mercer? Maybe those were the commanders, the ones who called the shots. That would also make them the ones who were, ultimately, the most responsible for butchering the 400 people in Morris's town.

Erin walked on ahead of them to one of the two open windows, looked in, and said, "All the way to the back." She waited for whoever was inside to obey, then walked to the door and opened it. There was no lock, but Gaby guessed they didn't really need it with the two guards outside.

"What happens now?" Gaby asked.

"Once he decides what to do with you, you'll be the first to know," Erin said. "Until then, you're to sit tight."

"Once who decides?" Nate asked.

"Mercer," Erin said.

"Is he your commanding officer?"

"Something like that."

"Need to know, Erin, shit," Louis said.

Erin took out a box cutter from her pocket and sliced the zip ties from around Gaby's and Nate's wrists.

"Thanks," Gaby said.

Erin ignored her, said, "Inside."

Nate locked eyes with Gaby, and though most of his anger had diffused during the walk over here, she could still see the spark of fury in his eyes. For a moment she thought he was going to do something stupid, just like she had almost done back on the road. She wanted to tell him not to, because even if they could get by Erin and Louis and the two guards, there was still Danny somewhere out there with Mercer, not to mention the literal army of soldiers between them.

But Nate didn't try anything, and Gaby gratefully gave him a pursed smile as they entered the office together, side by side. Erin closed the door behind them, and one of the soldiers standing guard appeared on the other side of the closest window and glanced in. He didn't look especially threatening, but the M4 in his hands was another matter.

It took a few seconds to notice the stink of too many people jammed into one room, though the smell would have probably been ten times worse if the windows weren't open. There were five of them and they were huddled against the back wall a second ago, but were now spreading out again in order to give themselves—and each other—some leg room. There used to be furniture inside the office, including a large desk in the center, but they had all been removed, leaving behind just dust outlines.

"Fresh meat," a voice chuckled from across the room.

Gaby tracked the source to a short man sitting in a corner, legs splayed in front of him as if he owned the space. He had black hair and dark eyes, and there was absolutely nothing trustworthy about him that she could find in the second or two their eyes locked. The man, like his companions, wore identical black uniforms with a patch of the state of Texas on their shoulders.

Collaborators.

The short man eyeballed Gaby up and down before breaking out into a grin. "And here I thought I'd seen the last of you. Small world."

He looked familiar, even underneath the grime and speckles of dry blood that clung to his face, but she couldn't quite place him.

She focused on his name tag instead.

It said: "Mason."

CHAPTER 8

KEO

AFTER TWO HOURS of sitting and lying on the sand, drinking warm water, and looking out at the endless expanse of ocean while waiting for something to show up, Jordan finally said, "I don't think they're out there."

"The problem is, they could be here already," Keo said, "and we wouldn't know it. They won't risk coming this close to shore in the daytime. Lara's too smart for that."

"We should have gone up for the radio."

"We should have done a lot of things. Story of my life."

"Sounds like a fun life."

"It has its moments." He blinked up at the sun. "I'm hungry."

"Ditto."

They got up, brushed the sand off their clothes, and headed up the beach in the direction of the row of houses they'd seen from a distance. Closer, they found a half dozen homes clustered around the same general area, partitioned off from the beach by rickety four-foot fences that wouldn't have kept out the family of crabs Keo'd had to walk around while licking his lips at the prospect of crab meat later that night.

Finally, something good to look forward to.

He expected to find luxury beachfront properties, but the houses were old and covered in peeling paint, and he had a difficult time imagining them looking any better just a year ago when there were still owners around to maintain them. The buildings had no uniform designs but did share tall foundation stilts and wooden stairs that snaked up to second floors. In case the beach flooded, he guessed, though the idea of being trapped in one of these when the Gulf of Mexico decided to come ashore left him a little nervous.

Sun-bleached grass covered a wide field on the other side of the fence, the weeds going all the way up to their knees as they moved through them. A mangy dog that had been sleeping in the shade heard them coming and jogged off, looking annoyed by the human presence.

"Must be your smell," Jordan said.

"Must be," he said, "because we both know you smell like lilacs and roses."

"You sweet talker, you."

"Either that, or my nose is all stuffy."

"Then you had to go and ruin it."

"It's what I do."

"Try to do a little less of it."

"And suppress my natural charms? Perish the thought."

She smirked. "Try anyway."

They checked out a wide squat house with a gray roof, accessing the second floor by creaking wooden stairs along its side. Keo was afraid the staircase might break under him as they ascended, but it remained improbably in one piece all the way to the unlocked front door.

He peeked inside at the empty living room. The windows were sans curtains, leaving a healthy amount of sunlight to splash across the dust-covered furniture. Everything was bright and gray and brown, and he didn't have to sniff the air to know there wasn't anything worth finding inside, including anything of the undead variety.

"Maybe check the kitchen just in case?" Jordan said.

"Sure, why not. Maybe we'll find a carton of ice cream inside the fridge, too."

"Wouldn't that be nice?"

They went inside and checked the kitchen and found it just as empty as he had expected. He opened the fridge only after pinching his nose and sucking in a large breath, and closed the door exactly three seconds later after giving it a cursory look.

"Anything?" Jordan asked, coming out of a back hallway.

He shook his head and sucked in a fresh breath of air. "You?"

"I don't think they were home when it happened. I didn't see any traces of blood or signs of a struggle."

"Told you. Waste of time."

"Yeah, yeah," she said, and headed back to the door.

They walked a short distance from the house with the gray roof to one next door with orange paint. This one looked more promising, with newer construction, and the steps up to the second floor didn't creak nearly as much. The door, when he tried it, was locked, which was a good sign. A quick glance at the closed windows to his right got him an eyeful of cotton curtains.

"Looks good," he said.

"Remember, I get first stab at the carton of ice cream," she said.

"Yes, ma'am."

He slung his M4 and drew his Glock, then looked over at Jordan. She had kept her M4 in front of her and was already in position to assault the door before he had ever said anything.

He must have smiled to himself, because Jordan said, "What are you looking all goofy for?"

"Goofy?"

"It must be those ugly scars on your face. Reminds me of this guy I used to know in middle school. Goofy Larry."

"Sounds like a great guy."

"He was, if it wasn't for the smell."

Keo sniffed himself. "I'll take a bath in the ocean later."

"Promises, promises," she said. Then, "Open the door, Romeo, and let's get this show on the road before I die of old age."

He took a step back and gave the doorknob a hard look. It

wasn't anything elaborate, just a round metallic silver *(But not real silver, natch)* knob with a keyhole in the center.

"Maybe we should try knocking first?" Jordan said. "You know, in case there's someone already inside."

"You think?"

"It'd be the right thing to—"

Crash! as Keo kicked the door at the spot just underneath the doorknob before she could finish.

The door swung open, the doorknob and lock hanging off the doorframe.

Jordan sighed. "Dick."

He grinned, then took a step forward and inside, raising the Glock to chest level. He swept left, then right, before forward again. Jordan followed, leaving just enough room for him to turn, if necessary. The house had been sealed off for so long that the lack of ventilation hit Keo first. It would have been stuffy and hot if the outside weather weren't so chilly, especially this close to the ocean.

He moved through the living room, passing leather brown furniture, and maneuvered around a glass coffee table with old copies of *Sports Illustrated* and *Cosmopolitan* in two separate stacks. His and hers, he presumed. The interior looked more inviting than its exterior, a chandelier dangling from the ceiling and framed photos all around of a couple, but no kids. Fishing poles lined one wall, and an array of sports caps took up space on another. A generous layer of dust covered everything, and Keo fought back a sneeze as he made a beeline for the kitchen in the back.

Jordan had positioned herself in front of the back hallway to his right and was aiming her M4 into the darkness. He was thankful their weapons were loaded with silver ammo, even more grateful he had convinced Jordan to waste a couple of days to raid homes and hammer out some silver bullets along the way. Too bad everything, including all that hard-to-find bullet-making material, was lost somewhere in downtown Sunport at the moment.

If it wasn't for shitty luck…

"Let's clear the hallway first," he said.

He moved in front of her, and Jordan slung her rifle and drew her Glock. Keo took out a small Maglite from his pocket and flicked it on, then proceeded into the darkened hallway, the bright LED beam moving from wall to floor to ceiling and back again.

"I don't smell anything," Jordan said from behind him.

He nodded. She didn't mean she couldn't smell "anything," because they could smell plenty. What she meant was she couldn't smell *them*, because the creatures always gave off an identifiable stench when they were inside a place, especially one that was this lacking in proper ventilation.

There were three doors in the back of the hallway, leading to two bedrooms and a bathroom at the end, but none of them had anything worth finding. Like the first house, there were no obvious signs of a struggle or old, browning blood. Which begged the question: Where the hell were Sunport's beachside residents when The Purge hit?

When they finished clearing the closets and anything else with a door, Keo left Jordan in the house to look for something useful while he went back outside and made his way down to the first floor. The building rested on stilts like all the other homes, but unlike the gray house next door or the white one on the other side, this one had something that looked like a storage shack underneath it. There was a door in front with a large padlock, but it was wood, and Keo easily got around it by prying the hasp free with his Ka-Bar.

Inside, he found an old couch underneath a heavy blue tarp and camping equipment scattered along a shelf in the back. More promising were three five-gallon water bottles and unmarked brown boxes on the higher shelves, probably in case the room flooded. A dirt-covered bag contained a pile of old, size-small T-shirts. Keo took down and opened one of the boxes and smiled at the unmarked silver cans inside. He held one can up and shook it, heard water sloshing around inside. Canned goods. His luck was finally looking up.

He grabbed one of the boxes and turned to leave when he heard a *creak* underneath him. It was very slight, and he might have not even triggered it if he hadn't been holding the extra weight.

He stepped back and looked down at an old rug with fraying edges. At one point it had been covered in green, red, and brown patterns, but it was mostly just brown now. Keo put the box down and pulled back the fabric, then peered through the flurry of erupted dust at a wooden door. There was no lock, but he did spot a small rectangular hole near one end, just big enough for a couple of fingers to slip through.

Keo took out the Maglite and shined it through the hole, spying dirt sprinkled across a floor on the other end, but no signs of obsidian eyes or black flesh. Even so, he leaned forward and sniffed the air around the rectangular opening just to be sure.

Nothing. Well, just dirt, but nothing undead.

He drew his Glock anyway (*Just in case, as the folks on the* Trident *would say*), then put the flashlight between his teeth and bit down to keep it in place. He slipped the fingers of his left hand into the opening and yanked as hard as he could.

The door swung open, revealing a rectangular shaped gray underground space; the parts of the four walls that weren't covered in clumps of damp earth looked like cinderblocks. Some kind of extra underground (hidden?) storage area, though it resembled more of a coffin when viewed from above. At the moment it was empty, and he wondered how tight a fit it would be for, say, two people.

Keo holstered the Glock, kicked the trapdoor closed, and picked up the box and left.

"IF THE TRIDENT doesn't show up, I know where we're staying tonight," Keo said, dumping the box of canned goods on the kitchen counter.

Jordan was standing next to the sink, pouring warm water over her head to wash off the dirt and sand she'd accumulated. Her short hair had grown out noticeably since T18, but it would still be a while before she had the long ponytail he remembered from their time at

Earl's cabin. She had made a pretty big mess, but then it wasn't like the owners would be complaining anytime soon.

"Downstairs?" Jordan said, running a towel she'd found in the bathroom through her wet hair.

"Uh huh. Looks pretty comfortable."

She flashed him a disbelieving look while water poured down her face and onto the sink.

"Mostly," he added.

"How big is it?"

"Big enough for two people to be cozy."

"Cozy, huh?"

"You don't like cozy?"

"I didn't know we were at the cozy stage."

"No?"

She gave him a long look, as if she was seriously considering his question. Finally, she shrugged. "What's in the box?"

"Food."

"Sweet."

He took out one of the cans and tossed it to her. "Enjoy."

"You shouldn't have," she said, and tied the towel around her head like a bun, then opened one of the drawers and rummaged around before producing a spoon. "Can't find a can opener. You still have your Swiss spork, or did you lose everything with your pack, too?"

"That's why you should always keep the essentials on your person at all times, Jordan."

"Thanks, Dad. Do you still have it or not?"

He fished out his combo spork/can opener. The utensil was just over six inches long, made of strong titanium, with a spork at the front and can opener teeth at the end. A scork, officially, but the name bothered him for some reason he couldn't explain, so he stuck with 'spork.'

He took out another can and opened it, then showed the contents to her.

Jordan wrinkled her nose at the smell. "Disgusting."

"Really? How long were you running around out there in the woods with Tobias?"

"Not long enough to think kidney beans are even remotely good eatin'."

Keo finished prying off the lid, then tossed the utensil to her. Jordan had a little more trouble opening hers, but when she finally managed to cut open half the lid, she peered in at the contents and beamed across the kitchen at him.

"Good?" he asked.

"SpaghettiOs. Beats kidney beans."

"You do know kidney beans aren't actually beans made of kidneys, right?"

"I'm not an idiot."

He laughed. "Just wanted to make sure." He pulled out another can. "Let's see what else is in here."

"I call dibs on the first fruit."

"I don't think that's how this works."

"I got the spork," she smiled, holding it up.

KEO WAS HOPING for some variety, but they had to settle for two more cans of kidney beans and SpaghettiOs. They left the rest unopened so they wouldn't waste them, even though there were still a dozen more inside, and those extra boxes downstairs. As much as she had favored the SpaghettiOs at first, Jordan asked him to switch cans halfway through their second helping.

They sat on the floor next to the couch in the living room as they ate. The position allowed them to see the front door and the windows to their left but not be seen in return by anyone peering in. Keo had closed the door, and though he couldn't use the lock anymore, an armchair pushed against it solved that problem.

He was looking at a framed photo of the home's owners, a man in his forties with a bushy beard and a woman the same age, though about fifty pounds lighter. They appeared happy, but then he had seen a lot of photos since the end of the world, and without fail they all seemed happy. Smiling at the camera was a façade from back when things still made sense; there wasn't a whole lot to smile about these days.

After a while, he glanced down at his watch: 3:19 P.M. Less than two hours before sundown, because it got dark early in Texas in the winter.

"You think they're really out there?" Jordan asked between spoonfuls of beans. Unlike earlier, when her stomach was growling as she ate, she was mostly just going through the motions now, filling up her belly because her body demanded the nutrients, and because the open cans would just be wasted if they didn't eat them now.

"Who?" he said.

"Your friends on the yacht."

"I hope so."

"But you don't know for sure."

"Nope."

"That's not very encouraging."

"Nope."

"Have you tried calling them on your cell?"

"I did, but their line's always busy, keeps going to voice mail. Plus, I think I'm out of my roaming zone."

"That's how they getcha. Roaming charges."

"Tell me about it."

She forced down another spoonful of beans. "You guys slept together?"

The question caught him by surprise, and it took Keo a few seconds to process it. Jordan, meanwhile, looked amused by his reaction.

"Who? Me and Lara?" he finally said.

"No, you and the Queen of England."

He shook his head. "No."

"Never?"

"Never."

"What is she, ugly or something?"

He chuckled. "No."

"Fat?"

"No, nothing like that. She's actually very attractive. And, um, thin, I guess."

"You're not sure."

"I mean, she's reasonably attractive physically."

"Well, reasonably attractive is good." He sighed and she chuckled. "I'm just busting your balls, Keo."

"The reason it never happened was...it just never happened, that's all."

"You guys were on that boat together for more than a month, and nothing ever happened?"

"We weren't the only ones onboard."

"Still..."

"It never occurred to me to sleep with her. Besides, she was vulnerable back then, after Song Island."

"Waiting for her boyfriend..."

"Yeah." He paused for a moment, then said, "I can't decide if you think so highly of me that you think everyone I'm around will immediately want to jump my bones, or if you think so little of me that I'd go after a woman who just lost her boyfriend."

Jordan grinned to herself, clearly still amused. "Can't it be both?"

"I don't see how."

"Okay, it's probably a little more of the former."

"Ah."

"Or is it a little more of the latter?" She shrugged. "I'll let you know when I figure it out."

"Very kind of you."

She went back to forcing herself to scoop up another spoonful of beans and swallow them down. After a while, she said, "Have I told you how much I enjoy these heart-to-heart moments of ours?"

"Is that right?"

"Not really, no."

"Ah," he said.

THE PLAN WAS to stay on the second floor and then move to the storage building downstairs when it got dark, but they didn't get that far, because around 4:30 P.M., Keo felt the floor under him trembling. It was very slight, and he might not have even noticed it if both he and Jordan hadn't stopped eating and talking and were just sitting quietly and listening to the soft buzz of insects outside the house.

"What the hell was that?" Jordan said, springing to her feet and snatching up her rifle.

Keo did the same thing, looking toward the window. "Stay here."

"The hell I am."

"Jordan—"

"What do I look like, a damsel in distress?"

He didn't bother arguing with her (after a week on the road with Jordan, he knew better), and hurried across the room to the window and peeked out from behind the curtains. The front of the house faced the beach, which of course was the point of owning real estate out here. Right now the beach was just as empty as when he had checked it thirty minutes ago, with the only sound coming from the waves crashing against the sand. The Gulf of Mexico was serene, with a warm orange glow creeping across the horizon.

Jordan looked out the other window next to his for a moment, then said, "Anything?"

He shook his head. "You?"

"Bupkis."

Keo put his hand against the wall and held his breath.

There, the same vibration he had felt earlier, as if a large machine was slowly cranking up but still far from reaching its full potential. It was a familiar sensation, but he couldn't quite place it at the moment.

"What is it?" Jordan asked.

He shook his head, then went to the door and pushed the armchair out of the way. He opened it a crack and looked out. He took a second to eyeball the house with the gray roof next door, then the one with the white paint. No movements came from either building, but now instead of just feeling the vibrations, he thought he could hear it, too.

Whatever it was, it was getting closer.

He slipped outside and crouched his way to the banister that overlooked the vast field of grass behind the house. More homes on stilts, each one as old and weathered as the one he was hiding behind at the moment. Beyond that, in the industrial area of Sunport, were large domed structures blinking in the distance like marbles.

Keo hugged the exterior wall, using it as a shield, and leaned out and looked to his left, back toward the road he and Jordan had taken earlier to reach the beach. Rays of sunlight glinted off the top of a vehicle as it rumbled up the highway in their direction, and Keo only had to see it for a second to know what it was.

Fuck me.

It was tan colored and moving on fourteen wheels (seven on each side) housed inside caterpillar tracks and was still about 200 meters up the road. He would have felt that sixty-ton monster moving from miles away. It helped, of course, that there wasn't anything except the waves of the ocean behind him to steal its thunder.

Keo recognized the vehicle even without the benefit of binoculars. The turret on top was turning slowly, and there was something odd about the machine gun mounts, but he was too far away to know for sure.

Footsteps behind him, just before Jordan whispered, breathless, "Jesus, is that a tank?"

He nodded. "It's an M1 Abrams."

"Fuck me."

"What I said."

There was writing along the armor tiles above the wheels of the tank as well as across the long cannon jutting out of the front like a baseball bat. He had absolutely no chance of reading what those letters spelled out from his position. That, and the angle was all wrong, which he guessed was a good thing. That meant the tank's occupants probably couldn't see him, either.

"Where is it going?" Jordan asked.

"Looks like the beach."

"What's at the beach?"

"Sun and sand."

"Wiseass."

He smiled to himself.

"You don't think…?" she started to say.

"What?"

"That the U.S. Army is up and running again?"

She sounded almost hopeful, and he felt bad when he said, "Soldiers aren't really soldiers anymore, remember? There's nothing to stop another Steve or Jack from adding a tank to their arsenal. God knows they don't seem to have any problems finding gasoline."

"But where would you find something like that?"

"There must be hundreds of war machines sitting unattended on all the Army bases around the country. Texas alone probably has two or three of them. Guns, ammo…and tanks."

She nodded reluctantly, and he felt oddly guilty about being the one to dash her hopes, especially since there was so little of it around these days to begin with.

"Doesn't mean I'm right," he added. "Who knows what's been going on out there? Even a lumbering, inefficient dinosaur like the U.S. government could have finally gotten its shit together after a year, right?"

"What are you, North Korea's spokesman?"

"There's no leader quite like the Dear Leader."

The growing rumble of the tank's tracks and the increased vibrations along the house drew their attention back to the road.

The Abrams was deceptively swift for a vehicle of its size and was capable of forty-five miles per hour on smooth pavement, and wherever it had come from, it was pretty clear the crew had fuel to burn…just like every other collaborator he had ever run across.

"Come on," Keo said, and turned around.

Jordan followed him down the stairs and they moved around the first floor, sticking to the walls of the storage shack. Down here, with the shade of the second floor above them and the overgrown grass all around, they were less exposed.

"This changes everything, doesn't it?" Jordan said.

"Maybe."

"You don't think so?"

"It depends on who they are."

"Any ideas?"

"A few."

"Any of them good for us?"

"Nope."

She sighed. "Figures."

They leaned around a corner to watch the tank as it halted about twenty meters from where the road and beach met. The turret moved again, this time in a full 360-degrees—slowly, taking in the entire area around it as if it had all the time in the world. And maybe it did, especially inside its armored shell.

Apparently satisfied there was no ambush waiting for them, there was a loud *clang!* as a hatch opened, and a head wearing a sports cap poked outside just before a man in a sweat-drenched wife beater and cargo pants climbed out.

"How many people does something like that hold?" Jordan asked.

"You just really need a driver, but Abrams are designed for a four-man crew. Theoretically, you could put in a few more, but it'd be a tight squeeze."

"You know a lot about tanks."

"Just enough to know not to be standing on the wrong side of one."

"Sounds like a good policy for any vehicle," she said.

The man jumped off the vehicle and landed on the road, then began stretching while a second figure appeared out of the same hatch behind him. The second man hopped down, too. He was wearing some kind of tan-colored military uniform with the shirt buttons undone. Keo glimpsed red collars around his neck and some kind of round white emblem on them. The man poured water over his head and whipped it back and forth, spraying the guy in the wife beater, who shouted out a curse and jumped away.

A third figure appeared above the first two, but he remained on top of the turret, scanning the surrounding area with binoculars.

Keo dropped to the ground and was about to tell Jordan to do the same, but she was already flat on her stomach next to him. Her chin was pressed against the dirt, head slightly tilted, and both palms in the dirt. He couldn't help but smile.

"Can he see us?" she whispered.

"I think the high grass will cover us."

"What if they decide to search the houses?"

"Then I guess we'll have to kill them."

"They have a tank."

"They can't search a house while inside the tank."

Keo turned over onto his back and laid the M4 next to him, then put his hands on his chest and stared up at the sky.

Sunlight was fading. The orange glow he had seen in the horizon earlier had reached them and was now spreading across Sunport. It was so quiet, with only the nearby waves and Jordan's soft breathing next to him, that he thought about closing his eyes and catching a nap.

He wouldn't have minded staying here forever, if he could. If he conserved his supplies, the canned goods and bottled waters could be stretched out, and who knows what were in the other houses? Even if Lara never showed up, and if Frank's mortality proved to be more human than blue-eyed ghoul, he could see himself wasting the next few months of his life out here, on this long stretch of beach. And there were those fishing poles in the house above him. Fish for lunch, crab for dinner. Why not?

No, it wouldn't be such a bad life at all. Why keep fighting if he didn't have to? Maybe all those people in T18 and the other towns had the right idea. Gillian understood. She had chosen predictability over running around out here, constantly afraid for her life.

Gillian.

Dammit. He still remembered the feel of her belly, the shock of discovering she was pregnant, that he had been too late. Then there was Jay. The asshole had to be a good guy, too. *Not* an asshole, as it turned out.

If it wasn't for shitty luck…

"Again?" Jordan whispered next to him.

"Hmm?"

"You're thinking about her again."

"Who?"

"You know who."

"How do you know?"

"You're like a book, Keo. Don't ever play poker with me."

"Thanks for the warning."

She looked back in the direction of the tank. "Any more thoughts on what they're doing down here?"

"Lots," he lied. "But most of them are probably wrong."

"So what do you suggest we do in the meantime?"

"Lie back and see what happens."

"Really. That's your big plan?"

"For now." He glanced down at his watch. "It'll be night soon."

"It's always night soon," Jordan said. "Remember when you were afraid of the dark, but then you grew up and realized there was nothing to be afraid of? The good ol' days."

"Yeah," he said.

The good ol' days. Oh, he remembered them, all right. Back when his biggest goal in life was to see the world and make a few bucks, even if he had to kill a few people along the way for the privilege.

The good ol' days. Like when he thought Gillian was still waiting for him.

If it wasn't for shitty luck…

CHAPTER 9

GABY

"SMALL WORLD," MASON said.

Gaby didn't have to go very far in her memory banks to remember the last time she had seen the man. L15. The collaborator town in Louisiana where Josh had taken her after the pawnshop. Mason had been there, in charge while Josh was away.

"You know this guy?" Nate asked.

They sat shoulder-to-shoulder on the floor, with the door to their right and the windows to their left. She had no desire to mix with the collaborators in the room; as a result, they sat staring across at each other.

"L15," Gaby said. "He was there at the same time as me."

She stared forward, holding Mason's brooding dark beady eyes, and at the same time ignoring the other four men in the room with them. It might have been two against five, but she was going to let them know—all of them, but especially Mason—that there were no cowering damsels in distress among them at the moment.

"The one with Josh?" Nate said.

She nodded.

"Sorry about your boyfriend," Mason said. "Never made it off the island, from what I heard. Kid had a lot of potential, but he bit off more than he could chew. I tried to warn him, but he got it into his head he was something special. That's when you know a fall's coming—when they think they're too big. You can never be too big, especially these days."

She didn't reply. If Mason thought talking about Josh was going to elicit some kind of emotion from her, he was mistaken. She hadn't erased Josh from her memory—she couldn't, even if she wanted to, which she didn't because he was a part of her and would always be— but she had learned to push him into the background and focus on what was still important, like Lara, the girls on the *Trident,* her job, and Nate.

"Do yourself a favor and shut the hell up," Nate said to Mason.

"Just trying to be friendly," Mason said.

"You can stop now."

"You the new guy, huh?" He looked back at Gaby. "*Tsk tsk.* The kid isn't even cold yet, and you've already moved on? Where's the loyalty?"

"Hey, asshole," Nate said. When Mason glanced back at him, "Keep talking, and we're going to find out if my fist can fit down your throat."

Mason chuckled. "I'm shaking."

"You should be."

"What's with the Mohawk?"

"What's with the blood on your face? You make a habit of getting your ass kicked? Keep it up, and it's going to happen again."

Mason smirked, then exchanged a brief look with the other collaborators in the room, as if to say, *'Listen to this guy.'* But he didn't say anything again, which told her he wasn't taking Nate's threats nearly as lightly as he had made it seem.

With seven people stuffed inside what was essentially an enclosed space of about fifteen-by-fifteen feet, it should have been uncomfortable, except it wasn't, thanks to the two open windows. There was enough light inside the hangar to see with, and the sounds of Mercer's people working and engines coming and going made for a constant soundtrack behind them.

Now that Mason wasn't running his mouth, she spent the next

few seconds observing the collaborators in front of her. Mason's hair was damp with sweat and his clothes were dirty, with spots of dried blood stretching all the way down to one side of his neck. There might have been blood on his clothes, too, but the fabric was too dark for her to be sure. The others looked as disheveled and beaten as Mason, and apparently even more tired, because none of them had said a word.

Then, just when she thought she was going to be able to enjoy the peace and quiet, Mason said, "Like what you see?"

"Keep it up," Nate said. "You just keep it up, shorty."

Mason ignored him and focused on her. "We've been looking for you, you know. After Song Island. They had us searching every building along the coast. What do you think I'm doing back in Texas? It ain't because I miss it."

Gaby didn't answer him, but she stared back, almost daring him to keep talking. Will had drilled it into her during all those months of training: the importance of intel. Here was Mason, volunteering information she didn't have but that might come in handy one day— or maybe sooner. She remained silent and let him keep talking.

"I liked him, the kid," Mason was saying. "He could be a little annoying at times, but smart as a whip. Hated to hear what happened to him. Were you there? Did the kid go down like a champ?"

Josh died to save me, and I'll always love him for it, she thought, but didn't say it out loud, because this man didn't deserve to know about Josh's fate.

"I bet he did," Mason said anyway. "He talked about you all the time. Gaby this, Gaby that. Hell, after the first month, I think I could have written a book about the life and times of Gaby. Little Miss Perfect. Personally, I don't see what the big fuss is about. Mind you, not that I'd kick you out of bed."

"Mister," Nate said, his voice rising noticeably, "I'm going to tell you one more time—"

"Or you'll do what?" Mason said.

Nate started to get up, but Gaby grabbed his arm. "He's not worth it."

"That's right; listen to blondie," Mason snorted before miming a whip snapping in the air.

A couple of the men sitting around him chuckled, but the rest remained quiet. Mason might have been "whipping" for Nate's benefit, but it was his men that looked as if they'd had all the fight whipped out of them. The blood on Mason was old, and they were clearly still wearing the same (smelly) uniforms since their capture. How long had they been here? A day? A week? Longer? If Mercer's red-collared soldiers had treated her, Nate, and Danny like pieces of meat when they were captured, she couldn't imagine what they had done to these collaborators, who as far as she knew, were the real targets.

Like Morris. Like the people back in T29.

Gaby fixed Mason with a hard stare. "Did you ever think this was how it would all end?"

"How's that?" Mason said.

"Here, in this small room, wearing that uniform you thought would be your salvation."

The man seemed to actually put some thought into her question. She had no doubts that Mason was every bit the opportunist she'd always seen him as: a conniving asshole who did whatever was necessary to get by, even if it meant selling out the human race. And for a while, it had worked out very well for him. Mercer's people had changed that. They had changed everything, for everyone.

Finally, Mason shrugged. "It could have been worse. I could have spent the last year running for my life like the two of you. If this is it, you won't get any complaints from me."

"I don't believe that," Gaby said.

"No?"

"I think you'll complain to the very end. Guys like you always do."

"'Guys like me'? Sweetheart, you don't know anything about guys like me."

"I know everything there is to know. You think you're complicated?" She gave him a pitying smile. "You're so simple, it's embarrassing."

"Is that right? Why don't you share this great insight with the rest of the class."

"I would, but I'd just be wasting my breath. Maybe one day, if you're really nice, I might tell you."

"Hope springs eternal, they say."

"Not for you."

Mason might have had a clever comeback, but before he could offer it, a voice from one of the open windows said, "Move to the back, now."

She glanced up at Erin's familiar face looking in at them.

Gaby and Nate stood up. Mason, across from her, stretched up next to a collaborator who towered over him like a giant. The sight was absurd, but Gaby didn't have time to enjoy it before she had to move to the back of the room with everyone else.

The door opened behind them and Danny stepped inside. "Miss me?"

"You okay?" she asked.

"Hey, that's my line."

"Sorry."

"I'll let it go just this time, but only because of the clearly shitty company you've been keeping while I was away."

Erin closed the door behind him, and Gaby and Nate walked back over to the other side and they sat down together.

Three against five now. I like those odds.

"Is it just me, or is Erin kind of hot?" Danny said.

"She's okay," Nate said, then sneaked a look in Gaby's direction for some reason.

Men, she thought.

"You kids been getting into trouble while I was away?" Danny asked.

"Nothing we couldn't handle," Nate said.

"Glad to hear it." He held up one of his wrists. "Got my watch back."

"Aren't you special," Gaby said.

"I know, right?"

"Why'd they give it back to you?" Nate asked.

"I told you, I'm special. Pay attention."

"Did you find out where we are exactly?" Gaby asked.

"Some podunk town called Larkin."

"We're way off course."

"Would appear so."

"What did he want to talk to you about?" Nate asked. "Mercer?"

"Mostly, our differing approaches to fighting the ghouls," Danny said. "His is to strike, while I lean more toward hiding. Like every other officer I've ever met, Mercer doesn't seem to have any problems sending other people's boys and girls to go die for him."

"How do you know he's an officer?"

"I can smell them from a mile away."

"But did he actually say he was an officer?" Gaby said. "You know as well as I do that anyone can call themselves anything these days," she added, looking across the room at Mason.

The short man didn't respond and pretended to look at one of the open windows to her left instead.

"Oh, he's a fancy pants, all right," Danny said. "Or was, anyway. These days, he's the Everyman leading the charge. We both know it's bullshit, but as you saw out there, it seems to be working gangbusters with the masses."

"So what else did he say?"

"The takeaway is that he thinks the only way to beat the ghouls is by destroying their food supply. One way or another."

Food supply? she thought, but it didn't take very long for her to understand. *Oh.*

"The towns," Nate said.

"Specifically, the people in them, yeah," Danny nodded.

"You said 'one way or another.' What does that mean?"

"He's keeping that one to himself."

"There were 400 people in T29, Danny," Gaby said.

"I mentioned that. He may or may not have gotten a boner when he found out how many people his Warthog killed this morning."

"Jesus Christ," Nate said.

"What I said. Minus the whole using the Lord's name in vain part."

Gaby didn't know how to respond to any of this. Nate didn't, either, and the three of them sat very quietly against the wall and listened to a truck *beep-beep-beeping* its way into the hangar outside the room. One of the guards standing outside coughed just before a loud *clang!* as a tailgate slammed open.

"What did he want with you?" Nate asked. "He knew you were a Ranger. I got the feeling my ROTC credentials didn't measure up, or Gaby's."

"He wanted me to enlist," Danny said. "Told me I had two choices: either get with the program or get out of the way. Or, and I quote, 'You're either with us, or you're against us.'"

"And what did you say?" Gaby asked.

"That I'd think about it. He wants an answer in two hours."

"That's why he gave you back your watch," Nate said.

"You're sharp, kid. I should call you Sharp Nate from now on."

"No thanks."

"Your loss."

"What happens in two hours?" Gaby asked.

"They're getting the hell out of Dodge," Danny said. "I can be on one of those trucks with them when they do, or left behind with the dead weight. That's what he calls everyone inside this room, by the by."

"I've been called worse," Nate said.

"I bet you have."

"So they're just going to leave us behind when they go?"

Danny glanced over at her and hiked a thumb in Nate's direction. "Captain Optimism, this guy. Thinks they're just going to let us walk out of here."

THEY STOOD IN front of the windows, watching a small handful of people still loading up the only truck inside the hangar. Mercer's people had done such a good job clearing out the place that she didn't realize how large the building was until now. With the drastic drawback of people and vehicles, she could now hear every squeaking footstep and *clang* from the back of the transport.

"Being the thinker that I am, I've pieced together this plan of theirs," Danny was saying, standing between her and Nate. "Mercer didn't confirm or deny, on account of him not fully trusting me yet. Or at all."

"Shocker," Nate said.

"I know, right? I have a very trustworthy face. Anyway, they've been bombing towns around this part of the state all morning and all day. We had the misfortune of running across one of their strafing runs. Before that, they were gathering intelligence. Probably months of preparation, all for the big payoff—which was today. The patience and planning is actually pretty damn impressive, the whole indiscriminately killing civilians part notwithstanding."

"Earlier, Erin let slip that they had more than one plane," Gaby said. "Did Mercer say how many?"

"Numbers have nothing to do with it. There are more planes out there than there are guys that can fly them. Mercer only has a few pilots in his stable, which really puts a damper on how far he can extend his areas of operation. That's why the one we saw take out T29 didn't buzz very far afterward. Mercer's using it as his eye in the sky, watching out for a counterattack."

"The collaborators," Gaby said.

Danny nodded. "They have no choice. Can't just sit there taking hit after hit, not when your bloodsucking masters' food supply is being bled out." He peeked back at Mason and the others on the other side of the room. "It's inevitable, and Mercer knows it."

"He's drawing them in, isn't he?" Nate asked.

"Uh huh. I got the impression today's running just as smoothly as he'd planned," Danny said, returning his gaze back out the window. "They've been here for a while now, quietly setting all this up. Until today, they've been raiding the surrounding towns for silver and weapons. That's what's in all those boxes they're transporting. Aunt Sally's expensive cutlery and Uncle Bailey's all-silver retirement pen. Mercer's taking them somewhere else, because this place isn't going to be very useful after tonight."

"What's going to happen tonight?" she asked, almost afraid to know the answer.

"This airfield isn't designed to keep people out. To keep any *thing* out."

She didn't have to ask him what any *"thing"* was. She knew, and so did Nate.

They were silent again, watching as a couple of teenagers in tan uniforms dragged a heavy cedar trunk across the hangar floor, then lifted it with a lot of effort into the Army truck. The two leaned against the vehicle for a moment, passing around a single canteen that they both drank from. Neither one of them looked older than sixteen.

"I don't see where we have any choice," Nate finally said. "We play along for now, leave this place with them, then figure a way out of it later."

He looked over at Gaby, as if for confirmation. She nodded, because he was right. There was no other choice. It was either go along with Mercer now or stay here, and she had a feeling their captors weren't going to give them back their weapons when they said good-bye.

"He's right, Danny," she said.

"That's not going to work, either," Danny said.

She stared at him. "What aren't you telling us?"

"Remember *Indecent Proposal* with Demi Moore?"

Gaby and Nate exchanged a look.

"No?" Danny said.

"I don't think Nate and I even know who Demi Moore is," Gaby said.

"Damn, I'm old," Danny said. Then, "Long story short: He asked me to the prom, but he didn't say anything about you two tagging along."

"He just wanted you."

"I told you. Special."

"Well, crap," Nate said.

"Uh huh," Danny nodded somberly.

Gaby exchanged another look with Nate. This time it was he who nodded back at her, and she couldn't help but smile. It was amazing how they could know what each other was thinking with just a look. Did she ever use to have this kind of connection with Josh? Or Lara, or any of the others? Maybe this was what it was like to be Danny and Will. One look, and they knew exactly what the other was thinking.

"You should go, Danny," Gaby said. "There's no reason for you to stay behind, too. Once you're able, find a way back home. Nate and I will be right behind you as soon as we can."

"I figured we might be a day or two late," Nate nodded, playing along. "But we'll all be back eating fish together by the end of the week."

Danny glanced at Nate, then at her.

She nodded and pursed her lips into a smile, hoping it was at least a little bit convincing. "We'll be fine. Look at this place; nothing's getting through these walls. We'll ride out the night, then follow you home."

"Absolutely," Nate said. "Who knows? We might even beat you back to Port Arthur. You never know."

Danny rolled his eyes at them. "Give me a break. I was born at night, but not last night. I'm not going anywhere without you two dummies."

"Danny, don't be stupid," she said.

"Have you been talking to Carly again?"

She sighed and shook her head. "Danny, you have to go. We'll be on your heels by morning."

"Not gonna happen, so save your breath. Both Lara and Carly would kick my ass, and that's not the kind of threesome I had in mind." He glanced down at his watch. "Besides, if they were going to kill us, they would have done it already. They want to keep us alive."

"Why?" she asked.

"I guess we'll find out tonight," Danny said. He glanced back at Mason and the collaborators again. "You've been awfully quiet. Got something to say?"

"You should have taken the deal," Mason said. "I would have."

"See, that's the difference between you and me. I'm not an asshole."

"I'm a survivor."

"No, you're an asshole. If I have to say it a third time, you're going to find out what a Danny Knuckle Sandwich tastes like. Hint: It's knuckle-licious."

Mason snorted but looked away.

"Good boy," Danny said, and turned back to the window. "Speaking of knuckle sandwiches…"

A Jeep had parked outside the hangar and Erin, in the front passenger seat, climbed out. She walked through the building, past the half dozen people still loading up the final truck, and stopped on the other side of the window to look in at them.

"He wants your answer," she said to Danny.

"The conditions still stand?" Danny asked.

"I'm afraid so." Her eyes met Gaby's gaze for just a moment before returning to Danny. "What should I tell him?"

"We're like the Three Musketeers," Danny said. "One cake for all, cake for everyone. Or something. I'm not very good with sayings."

Erin gave him a confused look.

"Thanks, but no thanks," Danny said.

The woman nodded. "Good luck," she said, and turned to leave.

"Erin," Gaby said.

The older woman stopped and looked back at her.

"Do you know what's happening out there?" Gaby asked. "What your planes are doing? They're slaughtering civilians. Men, women, and children. There were pregnant women in those towns. There were over 400 people in T29 alone."

Gaby was hoping for some kind of sign, an indication that all of this was new to Erin, but it wasn't there.

She knows. Jesus, she knows.

Erin looked at Danny again. "If you change your mind in the next hour, tell the guards."

"Not gonna happen," Danny said.

"How do you live with yourself?" Nate asked her.

Erin ignored him and turned around and walked back to the waiting Jeep. Gaby wasn't sure, but she thought Erin was walking faster than she really had to.

"She knows," Nate said quietly.

"They all know," Danny said. "But they're committed. Heart, soul, and ammo."

"What's going to happen tonight?" Gaby asked.

Danny glanced down at his watch. "I guess we'll find out soon enough."

"I was hoping for a better answer."

"And I was hoping for a cheeseburger and some French fries the size of my wrists," Danny said, "but we can't always get what we want, kid."

CHAPTER 10

FRANK

"WHY DO YOU fight?"

It was followed by a laugh, or something that might have been a laugh. It was hard to tell nuance when his mind was filled with so many voices, so many thoughts, like trying to listen to a city of people talking all at once.

"There is no victory waiting for you at the end of this."

A sigh of frustration, like a father growing impatient with a child. Maybe that wasn't so far from the truth. He was like a child, at least according to Mabry. They all were; he and the millions and billions out there that flowed from Mabry's blood.

"They'll never accept you. She will never accept you. Can you blame her? You're not the man you once were. You're not even a man anymore."

He didn't answer, because it was a trick. Like all the other times, the voice just wanted him to respond so he would reveal himself. Mabry knew he was connected, listening in, because there was no detaching himself from them. Oh, he could erect walls and build other mental defenses, but he could never, ever become separated. That was the strength of the brood, after all—the oneness.

"You're just making this difficult on yourself. Why can't see you see that?"

Push it away, into the back of his mind, where the voice became smaller. He couldn't shut it out, but he could ignore it to some degree, send it to the outer edges of his consciousness where it was still audible but less demanding. Instead, he focused on the here and now, on remaining perfectly still and quiet, and allowing his body to heal.

He slept just beyond the reach of sunlight, though he could feel the heat even down here. Rays like knives, stabbing down at him, poking and prodding, always looking to connect, to slash and rend until he was just bones. Useless bleach-white bones.

There had been too many hands, too many feet, and too many teeth. They had hurt him, pushed him to the brink, but he had survived their onslaught the only way he knew how—by fighting, by clawing, by willing himself through the drowning sea. He didn't know any other way but to fight.

It didn't used to take this long to heal, but then he had never been hurt like this before. These days, the wounds closed a little slower, the breaks mended more deliberately, and the blood took longer to replenish. One of these days, he wouldn't be able to heal at all, to regenerate all his losses, but that day was still far off.

His eyes snapped open, the dirt like sandpaper against his eyeballs. Something was happening. Something was…approaching.

A foot of earth separated him from sunlight. The heat called to him, even stronger than Mabry's voice inside his head. As he lay there, resting in a tomb of his own making, the damp soil around him trembled as if coming alive. The walls shook, as did the patch of ground under and over him.

Had they found him? Had one of his defenses failed without him knowing it? Did Mabry know where he was and had sent his forces?

No, that was impossible. It was still daylight. He could feel it, like a lover calling to him. And he wanted to give in, wanted to embrace it like he once had, but knowing he couldn't because doing so—

No, not ghouls.

Something else. Something…bigger.

It emerged from the city on wheels, close enough to his resting place that he could smell its leaked fluids as it lumbered. But it wasn't flesh and bone. No. This was an animal made of metal. Hard, grinding metal.

He knew instantly what it was. Sometimes it was difficult to remember details from his past life, but this wasn't one of those moments. He easily dug out the information from when he still wore a uniform, carried guns, climbed mountains, and took lives.

A tank. It was a tank.

THE GROUND SHOOK, passing from the many particles of dirt that sheathed him. It came from a distance—from where the waves crashed against sand, beyond the city, and where the tank had gone.

Nightfall. He knew without having to see the darkness. The shift in temperature against his skin, the cold that seeped through the earth and folded over him on all sides like a blanket, were evidence enough.

Earlier, he had felt the multiple tremors as they emerged from their nests, growing in intensity as they neared his position. There were hundreds. *Thousands.* They passed overhead, oblivious to his presence. It wasn't him they were after. No. It was the machine. The thing that had appeared earlier. The tank.

They were summoned, called forth by the blue eyes. *"Take it,"* the blue eyes said. *"Peel them from their metal skin."*

Another crack of thunder.

No, not thunder. A gun firing.

A cannon.

The tank.

The squeal of black-eyed creatures erupted inside his mind, surging across the connection that bonded him to the brood, to Mabry and the others. Their deaths were like sledgehammers, pounding against the sides of his skull. What he felt, Mabry could surely feel, too. Even more so.

He almost smiled against the dirt at the thought of Mabry hurting, feeling every death, every shriek of pain. If he concentrated enough, he could almost smell the sting of burning flesh as the black eyes vanished against the blast.

And yet they continued climbing out of the darkness and flowed like an unstoppable tide toward the beach. They were wary of the water, but the enemy had stopped just beyond the tides. Even so, the taste of ocean water lingered against their senses, terrorizing them with their possibilities.

"Take it," the voices said. *"They've already done too much damage. Stop them now. Here. Show them this world is ours."*

The voices belonged to the blue eyes. The ones leading the charge—directing the attack. They stood back, willing the black eyes forward like every officer he had ever known. Safe from the grinder and brave in their safety. He despised them, but was also cautious around them. They could sense him, just as he could them. He had to walk lightly, skirt around the edge, and never reveal himself.

It had begun while he was asleep, healing the cuts and gashes along his arms and legs and face. His concentration, his mental wall, always slipped when he was at his weakest, like he was at the moment. But Mabry hadn't found him yet. No, this wasn't about him. The creatures had not come here for him. They had come for the men inside the tank.

"They did it," the voices said. *"They're trying to take our food from us. We'll show them they should have stayed hidden."*

Another *boom*, followed by more screams of pain inside his head. The tank fired again and again, and each time the ground shook as if threatening to come apart. The continuous howls of black eyes accompanied the smell of singed flesh, and clouds of pulverized bone turned the darkness gray. He saw and sniffed the carnage through the senses of the creatures that were converging on the beach, driven forward by the relentless voices in their heads.

"Forward," the voices commanded. *"Take the machine! Take it now!"*

Amid the chaos, he became aware of a new sound. No, not new, but old. A strange noise he hadn't heard in some time. Music. It was music coming from the tank. From…speakers?

A house came apart, its foundations splintering against a stray cannon round, the smell of burning wood and disintegrating concrete, along with brick and mortar pluming in the air. Black eyes raced through them, unhindered by the wanton destruction.

Then something else. A new smell filling his senses. Not just wood burning, but searing flesh accompanying the cries of pain.

Fire. There was sustained fire among the explosions.

And yet they persisted, assaulting the armored shell of the machine from all sides and flailing against its unyielding skin. They clung onto the moving cannon, hoping to slow it down, their skeletal forms trembling as it let loose and split open another house. The ground shattered as the walls tumbled down and the ceiling collapsed inward, swallowing up a pair of black eyes that had been perched on the roof.

Now was the time, while the black eyes were obsessed with the tank. They were relentless, pouring unlimited numbers against it. He couldn't see the ground anymore, just a mass of squirming black flesh oozing toward the tan vehicle as it swiveled and fired, swiveled and fired. And all the while, the loud music blared from its speakers, like some unholy noise from the pits of hell designed to drive men mad.

He detached his mind from his body and drifted freely through the layers of soft earth and grabbed the first consciousness that appeared. The creature was weak like all the rest, and he took control of its mind without any effort. They were just husks, vessels for Mabry and the blue eyes to command at will. It had taken him a lot of trial and error, but he was always good at adapting, finding an opening, and exploiting it.

He pushed the creature aside, into the back of its own mind where it could still see and hear and smell but was little more than a voyeur now. Then he moved its legs, from walking to running, then full-on sprinting toward the beach.

Faster. Faster!

There, the war machine. It was still moving, its gun firing, walls of flame stabbing from its armored shell. Black eyes roared as fire engulfed them, eating flesh from bones and vaporizing the precious blood. *Mabry's blood.* They fell, disappearing among the fields of scorched grass. Smoke rose from buildings, walls of loose ground filling the air with every thunderous explosion.

He stood under darkness, a lone figure at the edge of the battle-field, and watched the horde of black eyes throwing themselves forward, drawn irresistibly to the squatting thing that refused to fall, or stop, or go silent. All this, while music blared from speakers attached to it, jumbled words filling the night sky, only occasionally broken by the bone-rattling *boom* of cannon fire.

He remained in the background so the blue eyes wouldn't sense him. They were preoccupied trying to find some way, some hidden angle or slit, to pry open the mechanical beast. They commanded the swarm to crawl over the spinning turret, howling with frustration and pain as blankets of fire enveloped their soldiers one by one by one...

"Take it!" the voices shouted.

But the machine would not be taken, and it continued to turn even as a few hundred living things clung to it. Its gears grinded on even as the sprockets and crevices became clogged with burnt flesh and bone and spraying blood. They pounded against the metal with balled fists, fingers attempting in vain to pull open heavy doors that wouldn't budge. The ground groaned under the combined weight, threatening to sink them all.

And the voices screamed: *"Tear it apart! Inch by inch! Tear it apart!"*

A stream of flames licked across the blackness, torching swaying grass and thickets of flesh in its path. Then the *boom* of the main cannon, shattering eardrums and destroying everything in its path.

The pointlessness of the scene, the pure carnage and death and destruction, depressed him, but he knew it wasn't really him, because he didn't care for these things. The pangs of sadness came from the creature he had shoved aside; its fear and fury were seeping into him. Husk though it may be, the creature still *felt*, at least inside its own mind.

He backed away from the field as more endless numbers of black eyes streamed past him, charging into the breach, obeying the command of the blue eyes.

"More!" they shouted. *"More!"* even as another two dozen disappeared in a hail of fire and earth.

He retreated, leaving the battlefield behind, when a brightly lit building flashed across his mind's eye. It was there and gone before he could fully grasp what he had seen.

A building? Where? Lights? And why were the ghouls moving toward it?

There was something else happening at another place, at the exact same time. The ghouls were busy fighting on two fronts tonight, and the blue eyes were at both places to direct the attacks, their voices slight echoes in the back of his mind because of distance.

He abandoned the vessel he was occupying and let himself float along the stream that joined the brood, finding himself moving further and further away from the beach. Houses, basements, empty cities and rooftops flashed by eyes that didn't belong to him. Tens of thousands of disjointed voices scrambled through his mind, but he pushed through them and searched for—

There, the same building he had seen earlier.

He focused on it, using the lights emanating from the structure as a beacon. Closer now, he began hiding within the consciousness of random black eyes, jumping between skins, hearing and seeing and feeling what they did, before moving on to the next one, and still the next one. Gathering intelligence, processing what he could, and never staying still for too long.

It had been difficult in the beginning, spying on the brood while remaining unseen. So many trials and errors and near misses. Mabry had almost caught him a half dozen times, but it was the blue eyes that were the most dangerous. There were too many of them, and they knew what he was doing. The black eyes were easier; they were just empty bodies to be taken, the way Mabry had done over the years, the centuries...

But he had learned and adapted, because that was what he did. He adapted and didn't perish. Was that one of his sayings? Or someone else's? It didn't matter. It would come to him eventually. It always did.

He detached himself from another one of the creatures and weaved through the endless pair of eyes and ears, seeing and hearing glimpses of what he needed, but always moving forward, getting closer toward the building with the lights, because it was important. The blue eyes were there for a reason.

"The building," the voices said inside his mind. *"Take the building."*

There, at last.

It was just as brightly lit as when he had first glimpsed it the first time. No longer just a flash of light in the distance, but clear as day. He understood now why the blue eyes were so unsure of themselves.

It shouldn't be here, and it shouldn't have been this bright. Not here, not now, surrounded by black eyes watching from within the darkened woods that surrounded the place. Someone had made a mistake. Or had they?

The confusion seeped through every one of the creatures, including the one he was hiding within at the moment.

"Something's wrong," the voices said. *"Something's not right…"*

He jumped bodies until he finally found a black eye moving across an airfield toward the well-lit building. Men in uniforms with masked faces—*collaborators*—watched him pass. He could smell fear clinging to their pores.

He wasn't alone. Far from it. Black eyes streamed out of the trees around him and stampeded through overgrown fields of grass, then across smooth, paved roads. The stinging scent of jet fuel filled his nostrils, along with the lingering sweat of human bodies that had slaved in the area not long ago.

"The building," the voices said in unison inside his head. *"They're in the building."*

He bounded across open space with his brethren, the hesitation giving way to confidence, their strength swelling with their numbers. It was why Mabry had waited so long, why they took the cities first.

"They've miscalculated," the voices said, the confusion from earlier replaced by resounding confidence. *"We'll take them alive. Learn their locations. Then we'll show them why they should have stayed hidden."*

Closer now, he spied normal eyes flitting across high windows along the walls of the building. The bright lights continued to pave his way, multiple sirens calling to him and the thousands of others to the left and right and behind him.

He ran faster, willing the skinny legs under him to move faster.

Faster and faster and *faster!*

"Take it," the voices shouted. *"Take it!"*

Then something strange happened. The ground under him quaked, and the trees burst into flames. The screams of black eyes filled his mind, the smell of scorched flesh blanketing the air, and he stumbled and fell and was swallowed by the earth as it was torn asunder—

He retreated through the legion of ghouls, jumping from one to another, seeking safety as the crack of thunder—no, explosions— screamed across the night sky, wild wind threatening to engulf him in their wake. The taste of metal crackled inside the creature's mouth, what jagged teeth it had left chattering in the aftermath.

There, a lone black-eyed ghoul had somehow managed to reach the outskirts of the blasts. It was almost at the building and was leaping when he forced himself into its mind. The creature struggled for an instant—just an instant—and he peered out through its eyes even as—

He was falling!

He reached out and snatched onto one of the metal bars fastened over a window and hung on. Figures were moving on the other side, scrambling around a metal catwalk.

One of them stopped and turned.

They locked eyes for an instant before the man raised two curious eyebrows, light blue eyes looking back out at him, short and damp sandy blond hair matted to his forehead.

Danny.

BOOK TWO

EASY PEASY COMPANY

CHAPTER 11

GABY

AFTER WATCHING MERCER'S people working like assembly line robots for the better part of the day, the sudden absence of all activity inside the hangar was unnatural, like the prelude to something bad. Really, really bad.

"How screwed are we?" Nate asked. "From one to ten?"

"Around fifteen," Danny said.

"I said one to ten."

"Ten. And five more."

Nate sighed and looked to Gaby for help. She managed a smile, if just barely.

The mood had gotten noticeably gloomier since Erin came back to the office, opened the door, then said to them, "The first one who steps outside before we close the hangar doors gets shot. Don't test me."

No one tested her, but they did stand at the open windows—her, Nate, and Danny, with Mason and the other four crowding behind them—and watched Erin and the two that had been guarding the office climb into the back of the Ford truck waiting outside. The soldiers then crouched and took aim at them while two others swung the heavy doors closed with a loud *bang!* The sound of locks snapping into place, followed by heavy chains sliding into position, left no doubt what was happening and that any semblance of optimism she might have had was all for naught because *they were being locked inside the hangar.*

They scrambled out of the office like escaped prisoners when they heard the vehicle fading into the background, Mason and his men making the door before she, Nate, or Danny could.

"Get it open!" Mason shouted.

Gaby could have told them it wasn't going to work. That was the point of holding them back, after all. But she didn't bother and instead watched the uniformed men sweating against the large twin doors, grunting like wild animals. They seemed to get louder with every passing second that the doors didn't budge.

"Spread out," Mason said when they finally gave up on the front doors. "Look for another way out of here. Cover every inch. We don't wanna still be here when night falls, boys! Not in this condition!"

One of the men found a back door, but it also wouldn't open for him. He started kicking it, then threw his shoulder into the steel frame, and when that didn't work, he began pacing in front of it like a cornered animal. Two others, including the biggest among them ("Lucas" was written on his name tag) joined the first and tried their luck. Lucas had to be over six-eight, with a massive frame and a neck that was probably bigger than one of her thighs, and while his hands made the door lever look like a toy, he only ended up breaking the latch loose. There was clearly something even stronger than Lucas on the other side.

Mason had been watching them straining and cursing, and when Lucas tossed the broken off lever away with disgust, he said, "Look for something we can use to pry the doors open. Find *anything.*"

"Never say die," Danny said, watching Mason's people racing around the hangar. "You almost gotta respect them."

She, Danny, and Nate didn't bother joining in the collaborators' search because they knew better. They had watched Mercer's people clean out everything in the place before leaving. They had left absolutely nothing behind. Well, that wasn't entirely true. They had left *them* behind. The question was: Why?

"Come on; let's see what we can see," Danny said, and began jogging up one of the catwalks that led to the windows over the front doors. He reached the top and looked out, then rasped his knuckles on the glass.

"No go?" she asked.

"Thicker than Nate's head and twice as bright."

"Hey, I kick ass on standardized tests," Nate said.

"But it's the burglar bars on the other side that's the problem," Danny continued.

"What's out there?" Mason called from below.

"I'm not your fucking secretary," Danny said back down.

Mason smirked before hurrying over, then climbed up the other catwalk across from them. A couple of his men followed. They left the other two below, including Lucas, still trying in vain to open the single back door, though that had become more difficult now without the lever.

The platform she was moving on wasn't nearly as long or wide as it had looked from below; the whole thing was about four feet wide and just long enough to cover both high windows. There were eight windows in all inside the hangar—four up front, two in the back, and finally one more on each side.

"They planned this out," Nate was saying.

"What?" she said.

"This," he said, gesturing at the catwalks. "There's no telling how long they've been using this place, collecting the silver from the surrounding towns, getting it ready for today."

"I got the feeling Mercer had FOBs all across the state," Danny said.

"FOB?" she asked.

"Forward operating bases," Nate said. "It would explain going through the effort to put the bars outside and the catwalks. Just in case they were discovered." He shook his head. "A lot of planning went into today. A lot…"

"If you want, I'll let Mercer know you want to be best buds with him," Danny said. "Share dips and chips over Sunday football and all that good All-American whoopee do."

"I'm just saying, the level of planning..." Nate said, but let the rest trail off.

Four hundred dead men, women, and children, she thought, the smell of smoke and blood still fresh in her mind and, she swore, on her clothes. Where there was numbness when she walked across T29, there was now anger. At Mercer, at Erin, at all the people following him.

She turned back to the window and looked past the burglar bars. Mercer's people had abandoned the airfield, leaving behind a few vehicles parked outside the cluster of administrative buildings across the field from them. The shift from activity to stillness was startling, and she kept waiting for someone to come outside, but no one did.

Gaby refocused on the empty landing strip that stretched beyond her peripheral vision, on the buildings at the end, and then beyond them at the insurmountable walls of trees that surrounded the place. It reminded her of the airport outside her own small town, one of those places you wouldn't even know existed unless you were from the area. Most of the planes that landed here were probably small private aircraft. She thought she could see still-wet fuel stains along the pavement, but that could just be the dwindling sunlight playing tricks with her eyes.

"Gaby, look," Nate said.

She followed his gaze upward. The sky. It was darkening.

"How long do we have?" she asked.

"An hour, give or take," Danny said.

"How long is give or take?"

"Thirty minutes-ish."

"You said this was part of the plan, that Mercer always intended to leave someone behind in here."

Danny nodded. "He didn't spill all the details, but that's what I gathered, yeah."

"Christ," Nate said next to her. His voice had dropped noticeably, though it wouldn't have taken much for Mason and the others to hear, given the echoey nature of the hangar. "They used the airfield as an FOB, but they always intended to abandon it after today. It wouldn't have taken much to track the hog and whatever else he's got running or flying around out there back to this place."

"We're bait," Gaby said.

"Well, they were," Danny said, nodding across at Mason and his two comrades. "We just got unlucky."

"What are the chances this entire airfield is booby-trapped?" Nate asked.

"Lots and lots."

"I was afraid you'd say that."

"Shouldn't have asked, then."

"I can't seem to learn that lesson," Nate sighed.

She looked across at Mason as he peered out the windows. If he'd heard them talking, he was doing a good job not reacting to it. One of the collaborators on the platform with him had punched the windowpane so hard that it cracked (but didn't break) and left his hand a bloody mess.

Idiot, she thought, watching the man struggle to stanch the bleeding with his shirt.

The collaborator was doing a piss-poor job of it, and she wondered how long it would take him to bleed to death when she heard a noise that hadn't been there before. With everyone moving around, talking, and Mason's people raising hell against unyielding metal, she had missed the low rumbling until now. It vibrated along the length of the hangar and traveled across her hand that was pressed against the windowsill.

"Guys, listen," she said.

Nate and Danny went very still and listened.

"What is that, some kind of generator?" Nate asked.

"I think so," she nodded. "It's coming from outside."

They looked through the windows again, this time searching closer to the building instead of scanning the fields surrounding it. Whatever it was, it had to be close enough that the tremors could be felt. And Nate was right; it did sound like a generator. But why would Mercer's people leave something like that behind? A generator, and especially the gas running it, was worth its weight in gold these days.

"It has to be nearby," she said.

"Can't see it," Nate said, standing up on tiptoe and trying to look down directly below them. "You?"

"No."

"Why would they leave a generator behind?"

"I don't know." She glanced at Danny. "What's going to happen when night falls?"

"Bad things, would be my guess," Danny said.

"You should have left with them."

He sighed. "Don't rub it in."

"Carly's going to be so pissed when she finds out what you did."

"Don't worry; whenever she gets mad at me, I just double down on the oral sex."

"I shouldn't be hearing this."

"TMI?"

"Just a little bit," Gaby said, managing to smile back at him.

"Sonofabitch," Nate said.

She looked over. "What?"

"Lights," he said, pointing up. "They've been above us this entire time."

Gaby leaned against the window and looked up. She hadn't seen them before because there was still too much light outside, but now that it had gotten darker, they were harder to miss.

There were LED floodlights positioned above their windows. Not just theirs, but Mason's and the ones behind them as well, though those were harder to spot from their platform.

"The generator," she said. "That must be what it's for."

"They're going to use us as bait, all right," Nate said. "We're going to be the only building lit up like a Christmas tree for miles out here. If Mason's pals didn't already know we're here, they're not going to be able to miss us come nightfall."

"Like moths to the flame," Danny said quietly. "I hate it when

I'm right."

———— ————

GABY DIDN'T KNOW what the hangar's twin doors were made of, but it was apparently strong enough material that kicking them only produced dull *thudding* sounds, though that didn't stop the collaborators from raining blow after blow against them anyway. When all that effort left two of them limping, they turned their attention to the rest of the building. Lucas, meanwhile, hadn't given up trying to break his way through the back door. He had made some impressive dents, but for the most part, the door remained unimpressed.

She stayed on the platform next to the front windows with Nate and Danny and watched Mason directing his soldiers below them. In between the constant banging, the wails of frustration, the slight hum of the generator outside, and Mason urging the others to attack harder and faster, was the distinctive *tick-tick-tick* of Danny's watch. Like a time bomb, letting her know that the end was coming.

"Like moths to the flame," Danny had said, because in less than an hour the entire airfield would be submerged in darkness…except for their building. If the collaborators and their ghoul allies had an ounce of brain, they would have traced the attacks back here. She wouldn't be surprised if they were already out there, biding their time. Surely they could already see the lights. And they could afford to wait for nightfall, too. Unlike her, Danny, and Nate.

Mason, hands on his hips, glanced up at them. "You wanna come down here and do your part?"

"And what part would that be?" Danny asked. "The kicking or the crying? I'm not very good at either."

"Whatever strikes your fancy, smartass."

"I'm familiar with the ass part, but not so much the first. Just ask my girlfriend. But you boys go right ahead and keep at it." Then he pointed and said, "I can see a little crack over there. Try ramming that thick skull of yours, maybe that'll do the trick."

Mason grunted, while around him the others had stopped to

rest. Even Lucas seemed to have given up on the back door. He was bent slightly over, sweat dripping from his face.

"Shut it down, boys," Mason said. "It's going to be dark soon; might as well save your strength for tomorrow."

The others gave him a confused look.

"If we can't get out, nothing can get in, either," Mason continued. Then he glanced up at her and Danny. "Of course, if people in the right uniforms show up tonight, that's another story."

"You willing to bet your life on your friends not shooting on sight?" Danny asked. "After the day they've had out there?"

"I guess we'll find out."

"I guess so."

One of the collaborators had walked over to stand next to Mason. The man was wiping at sweat along his forehead with the back of his hand, and she recognized him as the idiot who had gashed his fist on the window earlier. His right hand was swaddled in a piece of his shirt and she noticed he had a bit of a paunch, because apparently they ate pretty well in the towns.

The man had dark eyes, and they zeroed in on her. "Why don't you come on down here, little girl," he said. "When our friends show up, I'll put in a good word for you. Of course, you'll have to be nice to me first."

"Patterson, shut up," Mason said.

"Fuck off," Patterson snapped back.

Apparently someone's not as in charge as he thinks, Gaby thought, staring back at Patterson. If the man expected her to be flustered by his comments, he was mistaken. She'd faced worse, and she would survive him, too.

Nate, leaning against the railing next to her, tensed at Patterson's comments, but before she could calm him, Mason spoke first.

"Don't pay any attention to him," Mason was saying, smiling at her with something that she could almost believe was actual sympathy. "He hasn't gotten laid in a while, that's all."

"Man, I'm getting really sick of your mouth," Patterson said, whirling on Mason. The fingers of his left hand clenched into a balled fist. She wondered if he was left-handed or if that was because he had ruined his right on the window earlier. "You're not in charge anymore. You stopped calling the shots when you got us caught."

"Is that right?" Mason said, turning to face Patterson.

Patterson wasn't exactly a tall man. She guessed he was five-ten, though face-to-face (*chin to forehead?*) with the five-three Mason, he might as well be a giant. She felt almost sorry for Mason. Almost.

"You fucking little midget," Patterson said, spittle flying out of his mouth. Gaby wondered how long he had been keeping *that* in. "I'm sick of listening to you telling us what to do. In fact, I'm sick of your face."

"Hey, you know how difficult it is to find moisturizer out here?"

Patterson wasn't deterred. "I don't even know who put you in charge. As far as I can tell, you're just a little runt from Louisiana."

"I'm from Texas, chum. I just happened to be in Louisiana until a few weeks ago."

"Who gives a shit. I didn't ask for your résumé."

Mason chuckled. "What exactly are you're trying to say, Patterson?"

The other three hadn't butted in. They stood back and watched, maybe just a little bit curious to see what would happen next. She got the impression that, like Patterson, they didn't particularly care very much for Mason's leadership abilities, either.

Patterson leaned in until his face was a mere half a foot from Mason's, lording his height over the smaller man. "What I'm trying to say is, you need to shut the fuck up and let us do what we have to do."

"Which would be?"

Patterson's eyes shot back up to her. "I've been watching that piece of ass all day. You can have her friends. You like guys, right, Mason?" He didn't wait for Mason to answer and glanced over at Lucas and the other two. "What about you guys? You with me? Lucas?"

The other two turned to Lucas, as if seeking permission. Maybe because Lucas could break all of them against his knees like twigs, if he wanted to. But the big man didn't say anything, and Gaby couldn't have begun to guess what was going through his head at this very moment.

Patterson apparently had just as much trouble, because he said, "Lucas, come on. You with me? We can do this. You and me. You can have the girl first. I'm not against sloppy seconds."

Next to her, Nate tensed even further, and she heard Danny whisper softly, "Don't. It'll be over soon."

She looked over at Danny, but he was staring at Mason. She didn't know why she was so calm despite what they were saying about doing to her, as if she wasn't there listening to all of it. Maybe it was because in order to get to her, they had to come up the catwalk. She had higher ground and Nate at her side. Even better, she had Danny. The Gaby from a year ago would have been terrified, but she hadn't been that Gaby in a long time now.

Three against five. I still like those odds.

"Come on, Lucas," Patterson was saying, sounding dangerously close to pleading. "You and me, man. You with me, or what?"

"Son," Mason said, directing everything—his eyes, his words, his full attention—at Patterson as if no one else existed inside the hangar, "you need to shut it down now, before it's too late."

"Son?" Patterson looked back at Mason. "I'm not your son, ass—" Patterson said, but he never got to finish.

Mason moved so fast Gaby had trouble following him. One moment he was standing face-to-face with Patterson, then a second later the taller man was on the slick hangar floor as a thick arc of blood sprayed through the air. Mason had what looked like a small knife clenched in his right fist, and it took her a few seconds to realize it was a small, rusted over piece of metal barely longer than her forefinger. Blood dripped from the object in Mason's hand as he stood over Patterson's twitching form.

Patterson wasn't dead, though he might have wished he were. His legs moved in jerky motions as he clutched his neck, bright red squirts of blood forcing their way between his fingers. Mason must have struck an artery, which would explain the large amount of blood pumping out of Patterson at the moment.

Mason seemed to sigh—or, at least, he made a loud show of it—before looking back at the remaining three collaborators. "Anyone else want to undermine my authority?"

"Nah," Lucas said.

The other two didn't say anything, and their eyes remained fixed on Patterson's thrashing form.

"Now then," Mason said, slipping the makeshift knife into one of his pockets, then settling his dark beady eyes on Nate, Gaby, and Danny on the platform above him. "I suggest we all calm the fuck down and enjoy the show. What do you think, soldier boy?"

"I think your leadership style leaves a lot to be desired," Danny said.

Mason grinned. "It gets the job done."

"Patterson would disagree."

"Yeah, well…" Mason looked down at Patterson, whose wide-open eyes stared back up accusingly at him. "I think he was originally from Oklahoma, and I never really had much use for Sooners."

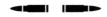

IT SHOULD HAVE been dark inside the hangar, but the combination of very bright *(too bright)* LED floodlights outside the windows and moonlight were enough for them to see each other with. She had no trouble seeing Patterson resting where he had fallen, almost directly below them. His eyes were still wide open, but there were no signs of life behind them.

She sneaked a glance at Mason and one of the collaborators leaning against their windows. Despite everything Mason had said about "people in the right uniforms" showing up, she could see the doubt on his face and in the anxious way he peered outside.

If Mason was concerned, Danny was the exact opposite. He was leaning against the window on the other side of Nate with something that almost looked like a ghost of a smile on his lips. The sight of it confused and annoyed her.

"What is it?" she asked.

He looked over. "Hmm?"

"You're smiling like an idiot."

"Was I?"

"Yeah."

He shrugged. "I was just trying to remember how many times Willie boy and me have been in situations just like this one."

"How many times?"

"Too many to count. In the Stan, during Harris County SWAT, then later, when things really got weird…" That smile again. "We always got through it, though. He'd come up with a plan and I'd carry it out to perfection, if I do say so myself. That's what they used to call me in college, you know. Perfection Danny."

"The two of you ever been in a situation this bad?" Nate asked.

"Worse," Danny said.

"Worse?" Nate said doubtfully.

"We had a bad habit of getting up creeks without paddles. The shit we got into, and got out of…" He shook his head, smiling at the darkness outside.

It was the first time she could recall Danny talking about Will like he would never come back. In the weeks after Song Island, after Danny had recovered from his wound, she had kept a close watch on him. They all did—her, Carly, Lara, even Maddie and Blaine. In so many ways, the fact that Lara had the rest of them to worry about allowed her to better deal with Will's absence. Danny, on the other hand, had to wake up to hear the bad news.

Now, as she watched Danny staring out the window, as quiet and thoughtful as she had ever seen him, she couldn't imagine what was going through his mind at the moment. They had never really talked about the loss of Will, but she knew it weighed heavily on him. Not just the huge empty space Will had left behind, but all the responsibilities Danny had had to take up as a result of it.

She didn't expect Danny to start spilling his guts now, and he didn't disappoint her. Instead of pushing him to do something he would never do, she looked out the window at the encroaching darkness, at the undecipherable walls of trees that surrounded the entire airfield.

Christ, it was dark out there, and getting darker with every passing minute.

Clanging metal as Mason rushed down the catwalk, leaving the other collaborator behind on the platform. Mason disappeared into the office with Lucas and the fourth man. She could hear them talking quietly inside, making plans.

"What are they talking about in there?" Nate asked, looking back at the office on the other side of the building.

"Nothing good," she said.

"We better keep an eye on them. Him, too," Nate said, nodding at the lone collaborator on the platform across from them.

If the man heard them, he didn't react to it.

She nodded, when something suddenly moved in the corner of her right eye, and she turned back to the window and peered past the bars toward the small group of darkened buildings across the airfield.

"Danny," she hissed.

Danny glanced over. "What?"

"Movement," she said, taking a step to her left until she was no longer exposed in front of the window.

Danny did the same on his side. "Where?"

"The buildings."

"Ghouls?" Nate asked, hugging the wall behind her.

"I don't think so. They didn't move like ghouls."

"Mason's BFFs," Danny said, narrowing his eyes. "They're in the fields. Stealthy bastards must have been picking their way toward us for the last few minutes under the cover of darkness."

"How many?" Nate asked.

Danny looked over at her. "A dozen?"

"Sounds right," she nodded.

Nate looked back down at the office, where Mason and the others were still inside. He turned back to her and was about to say something when the collaborator Mason had left behind on the platform across from them bellowed out, "Mason! We got company!"

Mason, Lucas, and the fourth man rushed outside, but only Mason ran up the catwalk stairs, his boots *clanging* loudly.

She turned back around to her window and focused on the grassy fields that flanked the long landing strip. There were a dozen figures that she could see, some crouching, others lying on their stomachs, their black uniforms making them nearly invisible.

"You see that?" Danny said.

"What?" Nate said.

"They're wearing gas masks."

She saw it: moonlight glinting off the lens of a gas mask covering one of the men's faces. She could only see the one man because he had raised himself up to his knees and was aiming a rifle at the hangar.

It had been a while since she had run across collaborators in gas masks, and the sight of the kneeling man outside made her shiver slightly. She would never forget Mercy Hospital in Louisiana as long as she lived, because it was where she had killed her first man. She didn't remember what the man looked like, only the shape of the breathing apparatus covering his face and the dark shape of his eyes behind the clear lens. In some ways, the fact that she couldn't see all of his face when she killed him made it easier to deal with. The lack of detail meant the nightmares were less vivid.

"Looks like your time's about up," Mason said from across the hangar. He was grinning stupidly at them. "Those are our boys out there. Better hope—"

Crack! as a bullet drilled through the windowpane half an inch above Mason's head and *pinged!* off the back wall before ricocheting and embedding into the smooth floor a mere two feet from Patterson's dead body.

"Fuck me!" Mason shouted as he ducked on the platform.

The other collaborator mirrored Mason's action, throwing his arms over his head as if that would protect him from a bullet. Luckily they were both under the windowsill, so the shooter couldn't see them.

Gaby and Nate remained where they were, hidden from view next to their window.

Danny, similarly unexposed, was chuckling. "Looks like they didn't get your memo, Mason. You didn't send it by carrier pigeon, did you? Birds are so unreliable these days."

"Shit!" Mason said to no one in particular. He scooted along the platform before sliding up against the wall, where he could stay out of view.

"The fuck they shot at us for?" the other man asked as he did the same thing, sliding up along the side of the other window.

"Why don't you go out there and ask them, Hendricks," Mason said.

The man named Hendricks seemed to think about it before leaning slightly toward the window and shouting out, "Hey, don't shoot—"

Crack! as a second bullet drilled through the windowpane a foot from Hendricks's face and *pinged!* off the back of the hangar before burying itself into the floor like the first shot.

Hendricks jerked his head away from the window and shouted, "Fuck!"

Lucas and the fourth man were hugging the wall below them, apparently unsure whether to stay where they were or to make a run for the back office. She would have stayed in the safety of the room because ricocheting bullets didn't care what uniforms you were wearing, or if you wore one at all.

"I don't think they know their friends are in here," Nate said, grinning at her.

"Either that, or they don't care," she said.

"My guess is they're not taking any chances," Danny said. Then, louder so Mason and the others could hear, "In fact, if I were them, I'd take this hangar out from a distance. Safer that way. Hey, Mason, you boys carrying RPGs these days?"

Mason glared over at him but didn't answer.

Gaby peered out the window again, keeping as far back as possible while still seeing out—somewhat, anyway. Her angle was limited and she was very aware of how brightly lit her window was at this very moment, giving the shooters clear-as-day targets to aim at.

"See anything?" Nate asked behind her.

She shook her head. "Not a whole lot."

"Can't see shit on this side, either," Danny said.

She couldn't see forward, where she had spotted the collaborator in the gas mask, but she could see off to the side just fine. The problem was the endless wall of trees that stared back at her. There was nothing out there—

Oh God, she thought, and said breathlessly, "Danny, the trees. *The trees.*"

She didn't need lights or night vision to see them as they poured out of the woods surrounding the airfield; there were so many that she swore the building around her was trembling against the stampede of bare feet.

"How many?" Nate whispered behind her.

"Too many," she whispered back.

"What's out there?" Mason shouted over to them. "What are you seeing?"

She didn't answer him. Neither did Danny.

Their lack of response only made Mason angrier, and he shouted again, "Hey, fucktards, what's out there?"

Gaby was braced against the wall when it started to shudder, the vibrations causing her body to move with it. It wasn't like when she felt the creatures coming out of the trees. No, this was stronger, more intense. Before she could properly register it, the entire hangar was rumbling as if it was going to come apart at the seams—

Danny whirled away from the window and screamed at them, *"Down! Get the fuck down!"*

She dropped to the platform on instinct, just as pieces of the windows began to spiderweb, and she heard the sound that she knew would haunt her nightmares for as long as she lived, however long that might be.

It came from above, like a great beast unleashing its rage upon the world.

Brooooooooooorrrrrttttttttt!

CHAPTER 12

KEO

WELL, I'VE HAD better nights.

And that was before the tankers fired up the music. They were blaring heavy metal, and the drums and guitars were just loud enough to drown out the soothing waves of the ocean just beyond the beach.

I've had a lot better nights.

After the speakers came to life, the cannon fire began. Again and again and again. Each time it let loose, the ground shook. He waited for them to run out of shells. Surely they didn't have a full load, did they?

But that wasn't all they had on them. He remembered glimpsing the gun turrets from a distance and knowing they had been modified, but not how or why. In his wildest dreams, he wouldn't have guessed someone would come up with the bright idea to rig a flamethrower to a sixty-ton war machine. It was a tad overkill, if someone were to ask him.

The unmistakable whiff of burning flesh made its way through the trapdoor above him soon after the cannon fire began. At first, he thought it might have been barbecue cooking. Well, he wasn't too far off the mark; it just wasn't the kind of searing meat he usually preferred. It simultaneously sounded, felt, and smelled like the world was having one big party and coming to a glorious, bloody end.

Keo had been to a lot of bad places, seen a lot of bad things, and had even done some of them (okay, maybe most of them), but he had to admit, what was happening above him now was entirely new. Then again, it could just be his present circumstance making things look much worse than they really were.

Yeah, let's go with that.

"Jesus, how many times have they fired that thing?" Jordan said next to him.

"I don't know," he said.

"Guess."

"Do I have to?"

"It'll help pass the time."

"How so?"

"Just guess."

On cue, another *thoom!* rang out, and the enclosed space trembled. Keo imagined a slew of ghouls disintegrating against the explosion somewhere out there. Closer to home, a piece of dirt that had been clinging to a section of the wall for God knew how long fell loose and landed on his hand. He flicked it away.

"What was that?" Jordan asked, alarmed.

"Nothing; just a piece of dirt."

"Stop that. I have enough dirt on this side and under my ass, I don't need some of yours, too."

"Sorry."

They were in the *(coffin)* rectangular space under the storage building that he had discovered earlier. It wasn't nearly as roomy as he had promised Jordan, though there was enough space for both of them to lie down, even if they couldn't twitch their arms or legs, or blow at a piece of dirt without it landing on one other.

Not that Keo minded too much. If he had to be sealed off from the world in a literal hole in the ground with anyone, at least Jordan smelled better than most. Not that she had done anything special, but women, even ones covered in dirt and grime as she was at the moment, with a week's worth of sweat to boot, was still preferable to the best-smelling guy he'd ever had the misfortune to lie down next to. Besides, it felt good to give his legs a long rest.

As far as he could tell, the house above them was still standing, though he couldn't say the same for the others around it. The possibility of losing the building wasn't the problem; it was being trapped under its pile of rubble that made him nervous. Keo had come to accept the possibility of death in a variety of ways, and buried alive was far, far down the list.

Shoulda made a run for it. Hell, shoulda done a lot of things, pal.

"Well?" Jordan said.

"Well what?"

"I asked you a question. How many times have they fired that thing? About twenty?"

"Ten?"

"Can't be…"

"Around ten."

"It has to be more."

"Maybe."

"Are you even trying?"

"Of course."

She sighed, her breath warm against his left ear. He could feel her body heat, hear the soft rustling of clothes as she moved her legs and arms from time to time. She got more restless each time the tank fired and a cloud of dust shook loose from the oak door a foot from their faces. The floor under them was cold and wet and hard, like sleeping on the world's worst, most painful mattress.

"What the hell is that, anyway?" she asked.

"What?"

"That music…"

"'War Pigs.'"

"What did you call me?"

He grinned. "It's a song called 'War Pigs' by Black Sabbath."

"Oh." Then, "I didn't know you were into heavy metal."

"I'm not, but I knew this guy who was. Got himself killed in Mogadishu a few years back. RPG pierced the car we were riding in and gutted him."

"Gutted him? I thought rockets were supposed to explode."

"This one didn't. It sliced through the door and got him in the stomach. Missed the client by a foot. The poor bastard was muttering 'God' for three straight days after that. After a while, *I* wanted to kill him."

"That must have been awful."

"Why? He lived."

"No, I meant your friend."

"Oh. Yeah. It was pretty ugly."

"Were you good friends?"

"Nah. Truth is, I didn't really like him that much."

"Why not?"

"His taste in music sucked."

"Oh sure, why not hate a guy because you disagree with his taste in music."

"Glad you approve."

She made a sound that might have been a snort. "So these people you used to work for…"

"What about them?"

"They have a name?"

"Yes."

When he didn't elaborate, she said, "What was it?"

"You wouldn't know them. They don't show up in the Yellow Pages."

She chuckled.

"What?" he said.

"Phone books. I remember when everyone had one. Then the Internet happened. I guess we're going to have to go back to phone books now, huh?"

"We're going to need working phones first."

"Yeah, there's that. Well, one problem at a time."

Another *thoom!*, and the ground around them shook again, the shockwave lingering a bit longer this time. He listened to another house toppling somewhere in the background.

Shit, they're landing closer and closer.

"What exactly are they doing out there?" Jordan asked, sounding simultaneously angry and scared.

"Making a hell of a mess, would be my guess."

"What if it really is the U.S. Army? What if they're finally fighting back?"

"What they're doing up there isn't fighting back."

"I don't understand…"

"There's no point in blowing up a beach full of ghouls," he said. "If you wanted to kill the bastards, you could go around firebombing buildings and taking out all the places they use as nests during the day. Break a lot of windows, bust down all the doors you can find— all that fun vandalism stuff we used to do back when we were kids."

"Speak for yourself."

"Okay, that I used to do when I was a kid. Eventually, you'd have to accept that there's no point in killing them."

"I can't believe you're saying that. The more we kill, the less of them there are."

"You really think so?"

"The question is, why don't you?"

"Because there are millions of them out there, Jordan. Maybe billions. You can kill a hundred of them, even thousands a day, and you wouldn't make a dent. It also won't get you any closer to winning this war. You'd just get every blue eyes in the area sicced on you. Ones like Frank, except less friendly. Anyone running around out there shelling beaches doesn't understand what they're facing."

"Which is?"

"That we're living behind enemy lines. The entire planet's occupied territory. The last thing you want to be doing out there is drawing attention to yourself if you don't have to."

He expected an argument, but she was very quiet for a long time.

"I forget that you've been out there longer and seen more than I have," she said finally. "Even when I was at T18, then running around in the woods with Tobias, I was never really *out* there. What else do you know?"

"Just that the ones behind all this had it planned out from the very beginning. Frank said as much. He said he could hear them talking, hear voices of the ones in charge. They knew what they were doing from day one. The blood farms, the hospitals, the military response..."

"Did he say what happened to the Army? What about the Navy?"

"He said they weren't around anymore."

"That's it?"

"We didn't really get into details. He's mostly a man of few words. Anyway, if they were still out there, don't you think they would have shown themselves by now?"

"Yeah, there's that..."

"Besides, I learned long ago not to put your faith in Uncle Sam's boys. They're overrated and will only disappoint you in the end."

"Sounds personal. Daddy issues?"

"Maybe a tad."

"Anyway, when did you guys have these conversations? And where was I during them?"

"Usually asleep."

"You could have woken me. Maybe I had some questions for him, too."

He chuckled.

"What's so funny?" she asked.

"The thought of you and Frank, talking. You don't know, do you?"

"Know what?"

"Maybe you don't know."

"What are you talking about?"

"How you are around him. You're...stiff."

"Stiff?"

"Tense."

"I didn't..." She stopped short, then said, "Do you think he noticed?"

Oh, he noticed all right, Keo thought, but said, "Probably not."

Jordan went silent after that. He couldn't see her face, so he didn't know if she was replaying all those nights when they were with Frank and how she had acted (unknowingly, as it turned out) around him. Or maybe she was doing what he was doing and trying to time the aftershocks after each cannon impact and grimacing when they sounded just a little bit closer than the last time.

"Are you missing T18 yet?" he asked.

She sighed. "Maybe a little bit. Why?"

"Sometimes I think the people in the towns are the smart ones. At least they get to sleep in their own beds, with a stomach full of food, and not just kidney beans."

"I thought you like kidney beans."

"I don't like them that much."

Another bout of silence, with just Ozzy Osbourne somewhere on the other side of the trapdoor. The speakers must have taken a hit, because Ozzy's voice had become strained and at times incomprehensible.

"So, Black Sabbath, huh?" Jordan said after a while.

"Yup. Black Sabbath."

"They must have that damn song on an endless loop."

"Sounds like it."

"Speakers."

"Uh huh."

"These tanks come with speakers?"

"Probably custom add-ons."

"It's not bad. The song. Not sure I'd like to listen to it 500 times in a row, but hey, whatever floats their boat." She paused for a moment, then, "What happens if they hit the house above us?"

"Probably nothing good."

"Can you be a little more specific?"

"It'll fall down and bury us. We'd survive for a few days while trying to open the door, but eventually we'd give up when it won't budge because of all the rubble on top of it."

"Sounds like fun."

"Then we'd both die of thirst in a few days. Unless you start eating me, or I start eating you. We could probably live off each other's meat and blood for a few extra days or weeks, if you can keep it all down."

"Very vivid; thanks."

"You're welcome."

Another *thoom!*

Keo squeezed his eyes shut against a particularly thick cloud of dust floating down over his face from the door above them. He coughed, and so did Jordan next to him.

"That one was pretty close," she said.

"Uh huh."

"The closest one yet."

"Yup."

"Not good."

"Nope."

"What are the chances we can make the beach if we climb out right now?"

"Depends…"

"On?"

"How many of the bloodsuckers are around the house right now that will notice us when we poke our heads out."

"How many, you think?"

"A few hundred?"

"Sounds manageable."

"Or maybe a few thousand."

"That, not so much." She sighed. "You wanna risk it?"

"No."

"Yeah, me neither."

The cannon fire, the smell of burning flesh, and Ozzy's waning voice filled the temporary silence inside the room. He tried to pick out the crashing ocean waves in the background, but it was a lost cause through the thick walls. At least they had their thermal clothing, which kept the cool temperature at bay. The only real issue at the moment was the chances of being buried alive down here.

Don't think about it. If you don't think about it, it won't happen.

Yeah, that's it. Let's go with that.

"Keo," Jordan whispered.

"What?"

"Is that smell what I think it is?"

"Yeah."

"Ugh."

"Yeah."

"If you say 'yeah' one more time, I'm going to punch you in the balls."

"Sounds painful," he said.

"I don't know what Gillian sees in you."

"Must be my charming personality."

"What personality?"

"Man, you're really going for the low blows tonight, aren't you?"

She chuckled, just as the tank loosed another round, the resulting *thoom!* causing his teeth to chatter for a few seconds afterward.

"That was a close one," Jordan said.

"The one before that was closer."

"Was it?"

"Uh huh."

"Not good."

"Nope."

"I'm going to die down here, aren't I?"

"Think positive."

"The power of positive thinking?"

"Something like that."

"Hey, Keo," she said.

"What?"

"Did you ever think you were going to die under someone's storage shed?"

He thought about it for a moment. "Definitely not under someone's storage shed."

"You must have lived one hell of a life before all of this."

"It was a wild ride, yeah."

"Can I confess something?"

"Go for it."

"Maybe it's a good thing we never met until now."

"Why's that?"

"Because I would have totally fallen for you. I mean, head over heels. Sex on floors, and all that good stuff."

"Nice."

She laughed. "But then you'd break my heart, and I'd spend the next few years screwing every guy I meet in an attempt to forget you."

"We wouldn't want that."

"Yeah. It's a good thing we didn't meet before all of this."

"Yeah," he said wistfully. "It's a good thing…"

CHAPTER 13

GABY

THE EARTH EXPLODED, splitting open up and down the airfield, and then it started spitting dirt and concrete and flesh and bone against the hangar. The windows shattered against the concussive force, a few thousand pieces spraying inward in the hundreds of seconds afterward, the continuous *pek-pek-pek* of glass falling like machine-gun fire.

Gaby looked up in time to see Hendricks, the collaborator on the platform across the front doors from her, making the mistake of staying upright as the chaos began. He was still staring, slack-jawed, when a massive chunk of the landing strip smashed through the window, snapping the iron bars as if they were candy. Hendricks realized his mistake too late, and the piece of concrete pummeled him as he attempted to turn and flee. He sailed across the room and fell, landing in a grotesque pile not far from Patterson's body.

Mason, on the same platform as Hendricks, proved to be smarter. He was already pressed into the metal grates when Hendricks was struck. The collaborator glanced up and they locked eyes for a moment, and he might have actually even grinned at her.

She mouthed back a curse when another series of explosions tore through the world and the entire building *thrummed* in the aftermath of what sounded like a dozen bombs going off at once.

The glass on the other side of the hangar shattered, pelting Lucas and the other collaborator as they made a run for the office in the back. Lucas caught a flying shard the size of Gaby's arm in the thigh, the sharp, bloody point jutting out the front. The big man roared, so loud that she could actually hear him over the end of the world.

Gaby watched Lucas grab the chunk of glass sticking out behind him, and she wanted to shout at him to *Stop, you idiot, you're only going to make it worse,* but she didn't. Not that Lucas would have heard her over the maelstrom of destruction outside the hangar walls anyway. Lucas somehow managed to get a firm grip with both hands despite having to twist around at the waist, and began pulling. Blood gushed and Lucas let out another monstrous roar, but this time it was entirely lost against the nightmarish *brooooooooooorrrrttttttttt* of an A-10 unleashing death from above.

She stared at Lucas, unable to look away, when hands grabbed her right arm and a familiar voice shouted very close to her ear, "Come on; we gotta get down from here before this whole building collapses!"

It was Danny, dragging her up to her feet, having to do almost all the work because she was still stunned by the sight of Lucas stumbling around below her, obscenely spraying blood onto the floor. She finally came to her senses and struggled to her feet even as Danny began pulling her toward the catwalk.

"Nate!" she shouted.

Nate was picking himself up behind her, grabbing at the railing for support as another massive explosion *boomed!* through the fields outside. "Go!" he shouted. "I'm right behind you!"

She turned and followed Danny as he hopped down the steps two, then three at a time. She thought she was going to trip at least a dozen times on the way down, but somehow—miraculously—managed to maintain her balance all the way—

Brooooooooooorrrrttttttttt.

Her whole body shivered at the sound, as if the devil itself was touching her on the shoulders. It was indescribable, at once terroriz-ing and innocuous. But she knew it was far from innocent. She had seen what a Thunderbolt's cannon could do.

T29. Four hundred souls.

"Go go go!" Nate shouted from behind her, the *clang-clang-clang* of his boots breaking through her useless thoughts.

As the last few catwalk steps rushed up at her, a piece of the room disappeared, and something fast and large hit the floor in front of her and dug a gaping hole as it burrowed deep. A stray round, she realized, from an A-10's 30mm cannon. Even as she processed that information, a second and third round punched through one of the thick front doors as if it were little more than papier-mâché. Seeing it do that, with so little effort, made her grimace at what it could do to the human body.

She jumped the last few feet and landed in a crouch next to Patterson's body, her boots splashing in a pool of his drying blood. A few hours ago that might have made her queasy, but at the moment all she could think about was, *Run run run!*

Danny was already racing across the hangar toward the office at the far end. She wanted to ask him what was the point, because those walls weren't going to stand up against the Warthog's main gun if it decided to strafe them again. Certainly it wouldn't do a hell lot of good if the building itself came tumbling down—

"Help me!" someone shrieked, and Gaby spun around in time to see Lucas leaning against the back wall, one meaty hand clutching his thigh. Small streams of blood poured between his fingers and his face was impossibly pale.

"Gaby!" Nate, coming up fast behind her, grabbed her arm. *"Go go go!"*

He pulled her toward the office, but she couldn't stop looking back at Lucas. The other collaborator who had been with him had disappeared, was maybe lost somewhere in the rubble—

A thunderous *boom!*, just before Lucas disappeared as a piece of the building crashed down from above, burying the big man in a few hundred pieces of what used to be the roof. Cold air swamped inside, but she was too busy being terrified to feel it at the moment.

"Gaby, come on!" Nate shouted, pulling her forward.

It won't do any good, she thought. *The office won't do any good. Why can't you guys see that?* But she was too busy stumbling, trying to keep up with Nate as he pulled her toward the office by the hand as if she were a lost child.

Danny was already at the door, holding it open with one hand. "Come on, lovebirds! Suck face later!"

She was halfway to Danny when a flurry of movement made her glance to her right just as Mason nearly cannonballed down the catwalk stairs, clinging to the railing as the building trembled with every explosion—

Brooooooooooorrrrrtttttttt!

The sound caused Gaby's legs to weaken, and she wobbled as she lunged through the open office door and kept going. Her forward momentum carried her all the way to the far wall, and she had to stick out both hands to keep from smashing into the ugly peeling paint.

Nate crashed against the wallpaper beside her, his blue eyes seeking hers out immediately. "You okay?"

She nodded silently, too afraid of what might come out if she tried opening her mouth to speak. Her legs were still shaking, her arms trembling, and for some reason her teeth were chattering, even though she knew it wasn't from the cold pouring into the building through the large gaping holes all over the hangar.

"Fuck!" someone shouted at the same time a black form slid along the floor and slammed into the wall next to her in a heap. *Mason.*

Gaby ignored him and looked back at Danny as he slammed the door shut *(Yeah, that's going to do it, Danny, that's going to keep the building from falling on top of us)*, then hurried over to the windows and pushed one, then the other down.

Danny even took the extra few seconds to flick the locks on both windows into place before stepping back. "Just in case," he said, grinning at her and Nate.

She managed to smile back, even though she didn't know how or why.

Danny flattened his back against the wall to her right at the same time they heard another plane (Or was it the same one? How many did Mercer have flying around out there tonight?) slashing by above them, even louder now that there was a giant hole (Holes?) in the roof.

Brooooooooooorrrrttttttttt!

Pieces of the office ceiling tore free and fell around her feet just as the hangar let out a groan that seemed to be coming from every inch of its foundation.

She became aware of something moving outside the windows and glanced over in time to see the last of Mason's collaborators—the same one who had been with Lucas—running toward them, even as different sections of the roof continued to collapse around him. The man reached out a hand toward the windows—toward *her*—just before he was sucked under a cascade of beams and shiny metal. A cloud of dust flooded against the windows, covering the glass in sheets of metallic gray.

Gaby wished she could have said she felt sorry for him, but that would have been a lie. He was the enemy; had been, for the last year or so of her life after The Purge. After losing so much—Will, Josh—and with so much more at risk, she didn't have the strength to care what happened to a man whose name she didn't even know.

She looked up and saw the night sky, visible through the jagged opening where a large part of the roof used to be. It was a clear night with barely any clouds, and there was plenty of moonlight to see with. She marveled at the sight, feeling strangely calm, when the belly of a plane appeared and disappeared half a heartbeat later, and she braced herself for what she knew would come next.

Brooooooooooorrrrttttttttt.

My God, that sound. *That sound!*

"Well, this isn't going well," Danny said, his voice slightly more haggard than she was used to hearing even in all the previous life-and-death situations they had found themselves in.

A hand—Nate's—wrapped around hers. She was startled by the sudden contact, but the warmth of his fingers, squeezing her numbed (and cold) ones, was a welcoming feeling. His face was covered in sweat and dirt and blood, and she thought about asking where the blood came from, but he looked okay, or at least unharmed, and his smile was convincing enough that she didn't.

They slid down the wall and sat on the floor, Danny doing the same to her right. Mason had scurried over to his own corner, his eyes darting to the ceiling as it continued to creak and groan against the continued onslaught outside. Maybe like her, he was waiting for it to break apart and come crashing down and put an end to everything. Maybe, she thought, that might be for the best...

"Danny," Nate said. "I saw parachutes. Outside, when one of the Warthogs made its pass."

Danny wiped at a small trickle of blood dripping from his hairline before cleaning his palm on his pants. "Cluster bombs. The A-10s are dropping them like leaking piñatas out there."

"Where the hell would they get something like that?"

"Probably secured them the same time they did the planes. Why not, right? Everything's just sitting around in hangars like this one. But, you know, still in one piece."

Gaby listened to them while focusing on the windows across the room. Even with the thick layer of crushed cement caking the glass panes, she could see enough to know the walls were still standing. A large swath of moonlight lit up the beams and bent steel sheets that had come tumbling down. Somewhere underneath all that was Lucas and the other guy. A part of her accepted that they both had it coming; they were sellouts to the human race, after all. And yet, there was the lingering old Gaby who felt sorry for them, who hoped they hadn't suffered at the very end—

Something fell out of the sky and bounced against a section of the fallen roof, then slipped and slid almost comically, bony arms and legs flailing out of control, before finally landing in a pile on the floor. There was so much moonlight that she had no problem at all seeing its pruned black skin and domed head as it straightened up and turned, sensing their presence. Sensing *her* presence.

The creature's twin dark orbs focused in on her, and it had been so long since she had come face to face with one of the creatures that Gaby had forgotten how unnatural they looked, how emaciated and deformed. This one, in particular, gave the impression of a little child standing on rail-thin legs, its flesh like oily film wrapped around protruding bones.

Gaby scrambled to her feet at the same time as Nate and Danny. She didn't have to say anything—they had seen the thing falling out of the sky like some sick gift from the heavens, too. She didn't know about Mason, somewhere in his own corner of the office, and she didn't particularly care.

Danny rushed forward first and had gotten halfway when the creature smashed itself into the other side of the window. It had used its head like a battering ram, and the glass cracked but somehow managed to remain intact. Everything would have been fine if the ghoul had stopped then, but of course it didn't, and even as Danny hesitated after the initial strike, the creature struck again and again and *again*.

"Danny!" she shouted, just before one of the windows shattered and glass sprayed inside the room.

Danny was almost at the window when he stopped and darted left to avoid the flying shards. The creature shoved itself through the opening and landed in a pile of limbs, pieces of glass jutting from its domed head like spikes.

Closer and without the window to limit her vision of it, the creature looked smaller, even unthreatening. That was, until it opened its mouth, showing off caverns of crooked sharp brown-and-yellow teeth. Thick clumps of saliva dripped from the corners of its mouth as it moved—*straight toward her*.

"Hey, ugly!" Danny shouted.

The thing froze in place, appearing more confused than afraid (Was it still even capable of fear?), and turned in Danny's direction. It hadn't gotten its head completely around when Danny struck it in its hollowed chest with a piece of the window frame that had come loose during the creature's entry. The wood was weak and it *cracked* into kindling on impact, but it did manage to send the bloodsucker sprawling to the floor. The blow and fall dislodged one of the pieces of glass jutting from its head, though that still left plenty more fragments in place.

Gaby had no illusions the ghoul would stay down for longer than a few seconds, and she was proven right. It quickly untangled its limbs like a snake and was already rising when she saw more black shapes falling out of the sky behind it. They dropped seemingly from nowhere, crashing into the piles of rubble before finally flopping to the floor on the other side of the office windows.

"Well, this ain't good," Danny said.

"What now?" Nate shouted from behind them.

"Get back."

"And then?" she asked.

"I dunno. Make it up as we go, I guess."

"Good plan," Nate said.

"You got a better idea? I'm all ears," Danny said.

"Not right now."

"All right, then."

Somewhere behind her, Mason had stood up in his own private little corner, his makeshift knife clenched tightly in one hand and his eyes glued on the broken windows even as the ghouls stood up and moved toward the office. She wondered if Mason knew for certain that his uniform wouldn't save him, or if he was erring on the side of caution by hanging back to see what would happen next.

Two of the creatures were attempting to squirm through the broken window, slicing themselves on the jagged glass, but of course that didn't slow them down for even a second. Thick black blood sprayed the walls and floor, but they didn't stop until they had flopped inside, leaving space for the other two to follow them in. They hadn't bothered with the door or with the other unbroken window.

Path of least resistance, she thought, before saying, "Danny?"

He glanced back at her and grinned again. He was still clutching the window frame, though it was mostly a handful of skinny twigs now. Gaby didn't know why, but she grinned back at him. Was this what it was like for him and Will in all those times they found themselves fighting for their lives? An exchange of stupid jokes and cocky grins? Because they expected to survive, even if they didn't know how exactly?

Except she didn't really feel as if everything was going to be okay this time, because something very important was missing: *Will.*

"Think of something," Nate said.

"Thinking!" Danny shouted back.

"Think faster!"

"That doesn't help!"

She heard a gasp *(Oh God, was that me?)* when one of the creatures lunged at them. Its bones *clacked* as it moved, clearly with some difficulty. She didn't have to look far to see why: one of its legs was damaged, maybe from the fall into the hangar.

Before she could react, Danny had moved in front of her and was choking up on the remains of his weapon when something she had never seen before or thought would ever happen in her lifetime, did.

Something blindsided the attacking creature and sent it sprawling to the floor. It slid across the room before finally crashing into the side wall. It was locked with something, before she realized that that "something" was another ghoul. *They were fighting.*

She couldn't tell the ghouls apart—they all looked the same, little more than thin layers of black skin and dangerously sharp bones—and there was a moment when the world seemed to stop except for the two creatures struggling on the floor. Gaby stared because she didn't know what else to do. Nate and Danny looked just as perplexed next to her, as were the other three ghouls already inside the office with them.

Jesus, what's happening?

One of the creatures had managed to get the upper hand and was straddling the other one. It wrapped bony fingers around the other's throat, pinning it to the floor. Then, with its other hand, it jerked the ghoul's arm from its socket with a sickening *crunch.*

"Oh, Christ," Nate said, sounding as if he might vomit.

But Nate didn't, though his voice did have an unforeseen effect: it snapped the other three ghouls out of their stupor, and their eyes abandoned the two struggling on the floor to refocus on her, Nate, and Danny. One of them opened its mouth, and bloody saliva dripped to the floor.

"Eyes forward, kids!" Danny said.

"Mason, the knife!" Nate shouted.

She looked back at Mason, standing in the corner with his "knife" held in front of him like a sword and not the finger-sized weapon that it really was. If he understood what Nate wanted, he didn't respond.

"Mason, give me your fucking knife if you're not going to use it!" Nate shouted.

"Forget him!" Danny said. "Stick together!"

The ghouls moved almost as one toward them, but they hadn't taken more than a few steps when something hit a creature in the head. It took Gaby half a second to realize it was *an arm*. Someone— no, some *thing*—was using a ghoul arm like a baseball bat—

The same creature that had broadsided the first one and knocked it to the floor. It was up and swinging the arm, striking down the first ghoul before turning its attention on the other two. Bones broke and flesh *twumped!*, and another one of the ghouls fell to the floor. The third one spun and lunged at its attacker and the two of them spilled into a corner next to the window, vanishing into a part of the office where moonlight couldn't reach, though she could just barely make out limbs flailing in the darkness.

She was still trying to come to grips with what had happened when one of the fallen ghouls started to get back up.

No, no, no!

She ran right at it—heard Nate shout her name—and kicked out and caught the creature in the head as it was picking itself from the floor. Despite wearing heavy combat boots, her leg shook with the impact as the monster lifted up into the air as if levitating—and for a moment she thought its head might pop loose like in the cartoons— before it fell back down to earth a few feet away.

Instead of giving it time to pick itself up again, Gaby lunged forward and stomped down on its head with her boot, hearing rather than feeling the skull underneath *crunching*. Thick gobs of black coagulated blood splashed the floor and parts of her pant legs. The stench of tainted blood filled her nostrils as she took a step back, but she pushed it away and kicked the creature in the chest, sending it skidding across the office, where it crumpled against the wall under the windows.

She turned, her chest heaving, looking for Nate and Danny in the semidarkness of the office. For some reason, it seemed to have gotten harder to see in the last few seconds despite the plentiful moonlight coming freely through the now mostly-roofless hangar, bright streams of light reflecting off metal beams and steel sheets strewn around them.

She finally located Nate in the back. He hadn't moved and was staring at her with his mouth slightly agape.

A flash of movement, and she whirled around, ready to fight, only to see Danny shoving the remains of his window frame into another one of the creature's eyes before grabbing it by one leg and swinging it into the wall, again and again and again, leaving bloody patches against the wallpaper each time. Finally, when there didn't seem to be any blood left in the skinny thing, he flung it across the room with a loud, tired grunt.

Danny stumbled back, out of breath, and watched as the remains of the ghoul tried to get back up. "Oh, fuck me. That didn't really work, did it?"

Because they don't die, remember? It doesn't matter if you cut off their limbs or their heads. They don't die. As long as there's blood flowing through them, they don't die.

"Any suggestions?" Danny asked.

She was too busy watching the creature she had fought pick itself up from the floor, even though it didn't have a head anymore, to answer him. There was just a big lump hanging off long, stringy neck muscles like an unused hoodie, clumps of blood *slurping* free with every movement.

Danny's ghoul had given up trying to stand, and despite a crushed skull, it began crawling toward him, spindly arms dragging its remains forward one pull at a time. Two broken legs, twisted into impossible angles, twitched behind it.

"Jesus, I think I'm going to throw up," Nate said behind them. But like the last time, he didn't.

"Back, back," Danny said.

She backpedaled, the ghoul blood sticking to one of her boots making a *clumping* sound with every step. She winced each time, but managed to keep moving, when—

There was a ringing *crack!* from the darkened corner next to the window where the two ghouls had disappeared earlier.

She turned, as did Nate and Danny, and even Mason still hiding in his corner somewhere to her right. The collaborator stuck the knife out in front of him, as if that would be enough to ward off any ghoul that decided to zero in on him.

The creature stepped out of the shadows, blood dripping from gashes along its cheeks and body. There was a hole the size of her fist in its chest, where a steady flow of black liquid trickled out. She couldn't tell if it was the same one that had, for whatever reason, attacked the others. One emaciated thing was the same as another. *Right?*

The ghoul looked back at her for a moment, as if those obsidian eyes were trying to remember her, to carve her image into its mind. (If it even had a mind anymore.)

"Dead, not stupid," Will always said.

She looked down and saw that the creature was holding the other ghoul's head in its hand, its fingers digging into the empty eye sockets.

She didn't know how long she and the creature stared at one another. A second might have passed, or maybe a minute, before Nate's voice pulled her back from the other side of the planet.

"Gaby, be careful," Nate said, stepping between her and the ghoul.

"What the hell's it doing now?" Danny said, but he hadn't gotten "now" out when the ghoul looked away from her and threw the head it had been holding out the window.

Then it disappeared back into the corner before returning a few seconds later, dragging the headless ghoul it had been struggling with out with it. They watched it toss the twitching body out the window, knocking loose blood-smeared glass shards that had managed to cling to the frames.

The other two ghouls that were slowly, pitifully making their way across the office had stopped for a brief moment and turned to look at the creature that had attacked them. Or maybe "look" wasn't the right word, because you needed eyes to look, and heads that were still in one piece, didn't you?

The third ghoul ignored the other two, finding nothing that resembled a threat from them apparently, and walked to the window and climbed out, then began crawling up the side of the rubble.

"What the fuck," a voice said behind them.

She looked back at Mason, staring after the creature.

"It's got the right idea," Danny said, looking back at the other two ghouls that had begun, once again, to gradually slink their way toward them one painfully slow inch at a time. Whatever dangers they might have presented a few minutes ago had evaporated into something pathetic and sad.

"Yeah," she said, the single word coming out of her as almost a breathless whisper.

Danny moved first, and Gaby followed.

"Guys?" Nate said behind them.

They went after the ghoul that had managed to rise back up on its mangled legs first. The creature reached for her, but she ducked its clawing hands and grabbed it around the top half of its arms while Danny took the other side. They carried it toward the window and threw it out before they even reached their destination. Their aim was off by a few inches, and the ghoul crashed into one side of the window but managed to collapse outside in a hail of bones and bleeding flesh anyway.

"One down," Danny said.

When she glanced back, Nate was moving around a crawling ghoul. It was trying to grope at his legs, but he kept sidestepping it. He could have moved in slow motion and the creature wouldn't have been able to get him, it was that slow.

"Legs," Danny said.

They grabbed the thing by its legs, keeping away from its impossibly sharp-looking fingers, and dragged it to the window. The creature reeked from every pore, and she had to breathe through her mouth. From the look on his face, Nate was again on the verge of vomiting. The thing weighed almost nothing, like a mannequin. This time, they threw it through the window without hitting the frames.

"Last one," Danny said.

It was trying to crawl out of the corner. It had no choice, because it was missing one of its arms and its legs were both broken. But there was nothing wrong with its eyes, and they shifted from Nate to Gaby and back again. Nate was closer so it zeroed in on him, not that it was going to reach him anytime soon.

She walked calmly over and grabbed it by a leg, Nate taking the other one, and they dragged the creature toward the window. It flailed with its remaining arm and somehow managed to turn over onto its back. If she looked hard enough, she could almost see something that might have been anger behind its hollowed eyes.

"I got it," Nate said, and Gaby let go when they reached the window.

Nate lifted it off the floor by one leg, as if it were a bag of flour, and flung it through the window. It landed with a *crunch* outside among the other three. They were all still "alive" out there, trying to crawl back to the windows, inch by inch, irresistibly drawn to her, Nate, and Danny.

No, not them, but to the *blood* in their veins.

"Should we...?" Nate said.

"What?" Danny said.

"Go out there and stop them?"

"There's no point," Danny said. "The sun will be out long before they reach us."

Gaby suddenly remembered they weren't alone in the office and glanced over at Mason. He had sat back down in the corner, blood-smeared arms hanging off his bent knees. She couldn't see the knife anywhere, but she didn't believe for a second that he didn't have it hidden somewhere on him, within easy reach. He looked shell-shocked, and she wondered if she had the same expression on her face.

"What?" he said, his eyes meeting hers.

"You saw it," she said. "What the other one did."

He didn't say anything and seemed to be waiting for her to continue. When she didn't, he said, "And?"

"Why?"

"Why?" he repeated.

"Yeah, why?" Danny said.

"How the fuck should I know," Mason said.

"Because you're one of them, asshole," Nate said.

"Fuck you, kid. I've never seen that before in my life."

"Never?" Danny said doubtfully.

"I've seen a lot of things, but…" He shook his head. "What I just saw… What that thing just did… I've never seen that before. You can believe it or not, I don't really give a shit."

Gaby stared at him. Mason was an opportunist, a liar, and a killer, but she believed every word he had just said.

"Where'd you get the shank?" Danny asked.

"Wouldn't you like to know," Mason said.

"Better keep an eye on it, short stack; someone might take it from you before the night's out."

"You're welcome to try."

Danny smirked and turned back to the windows. She did, too, and watched the creatures as they continued their interminably slow crawl toward the office. They were bleeding from multiple wounds and stumps as they moved, but that was difficult to see against their black skin. It was easier to make out the gray dust clinging to their gaping wounds and fresh, thick pools of blood that dotted the remains of the hangar floor.

"Hear that?" Danny asked.

"What?" Nate said. "I don't hear anything."

"Exactly."

She hadn't noticed it until now, but it was deathly silent outside the building and in the airfield around them. She couldn't remember when it had happened. She kept waiting to hear the sound of warplanes coming back, followed by the sight of gray metal flashing above them, but there was just the clear moonlit night sky visible through the large hole in the roof.

"It's stopped," she said. "Outside. It's stopped."

Danny nodded. "Hard to believe, but as bad as it was in here, someone just got royally fucked out there."

"You're right, that is hard to believe," Nate said.

Gaby looked over at Mason again and caught him staring back at her.

"Truce," he said.

"Go fuck yourself," she said.

Mason laughed. It was a loud roaring laugh, as if he had been keeping it in forever and only now got the chance to finally unleash it. Either that, or the man had lost his marbles. After the events of the night, she wouldn't have blamed him for going off the deep end. She still wasn't entirely sure she had seen what she had seen, either— except Danny and Nate had witnessed it, too, so it had to have been real.

Didn't it?

CHAPTER 14

FRANK

HE WAS BETWEEN vessels when Mabry discovered his presence among the hordes fleeing the airfield. He knew it was only a matter of time; he couldn't hope to hide forever among the throng, especially after exposing himself inside the hangar.

"She always did say you were a fast learner."

There was something that sounded dangerously like pride in the voice, but it might have just been another trick. He pushed it aside and continued on when hands suddenly seized his arms and wrestled him to the ground. Fingers tightened around his ankles and wrists, and a pair of black eyes glared down at him.

"There you are," the creature said inside his head.

It didn't come from the ghoul—this frail thing straddling his waist as the others held him down. No, it came from somewhere else. *Mabry.* He was inside the creature's body, using it as a ventriloquist would his puppet, like he had done back in the hangar when he saved Danny and Gaby.

"I told you, you couldn't hide forever."

He let go of the physical body and slid back into the river of fractured thoughts and chaotic memories. He had learned to project his mind long ago, but it was easy to lose his way if he wasn't careful. Distance still eluded him, and the farther he traveled, the harder it was to maintain control.

He leapfrogged from one consciousness to another, letting himself be carried with the flow instead of fighting it. So many images, so many sounds, so many jumbled thoughts that, once upon a time, were capable of so much more. Those days were long gone, usurped by this new existence. They were just shells of what they used to be, suits to be worn and discarded. He didn't feel pity for them because they were beyond caring.

"Where are you going?"

The voice pecked away at the edges of his mind, prodding and always trying to lure him back into the open. He didn't bite and concentrated on the mission at hand.

They were out there somewhere—the men who had dropped the bombs and left behind the explosions. Men with warplanes. A new player. Maybe a new ally...

"You're grasping at straws."

He could feel them getting closer. The blue eyes. It forced him to keep moving, grabbing and abandoning bodies at will now, trying to stay one step ahead of them. The first time had been difficult, but everything became easier with practice—

Flames licked at his face and charred bodies blocked his path. His vision was flooded with severed limbs and decapitated heads and sheets of flesh stripped from bones.

Death from above, as a gray metal beast split the air above him, leaving behind fire and splatters of thick black clumps of blood that covered the trees and ground, making for treacherous footing. The creature he was wearing was missing an arm, but there was nothing wrong with its legs.

He pursued the warplane along with the rest of the brood. It would have to come down sooner or later, and when it did, he would find out who was behind this. He couldn't let go now, or he might never be able to find his way back here. He pushed on through the sea of destruction, determined to reach the other side.

"Where is he?" the voices asked. *"He's close by. Find him—*There!*"*

They were converging, skating burning brushes, when he released the ghoul and surfed the currents and found another one—

Where? How far had he gone this time? He'd discovered the limitations of what he could do during his many trial runs. The farther he projected himself, the more control he surrendered. Mabry didn't have this problem, which was how he could be everywhere and nowhere at once.

He was still somewhere in the woods, the feel of heat licking at his skin, causing an involuntary whimper to escape his scarred lips. The creature put up a futile attempt at resistance, but he pushed it down and turned around and darted even further into the woods, hoping to skirt around the blue eyes. They were out there, searching, trying to locate him again.

The crackling of burning trees filled his nostrils, and flames stabbed at him from the sides. Every one of the creature's senses was overwhelmed by the thick, putrid aroma of searing flesh, including its own. He skipped over warm patches of blood and *crunched* bones as all around him, ghouls fled the fire. The scream of the machines shredding the night sky, raining down death and destruction at will.

A tree tumbled, crushing two flailing forms underneath its gnarled trunk. He jumped and followed the others through the scorching fire, the familiar sensation of pain reminding him of what he used to be, even as heat enclosed around his feet, ripping at skin, and traveled up his legs.

He released, returning into the ocean of voices and jumbled thoughts. What once was, what little remained. A surprising burst of sadness for all that they'd lost, all they could never get back. All *he* could never retrieve.

And Mabry's voice, calling to him, always.

"It's time to give up this rebellion. It's time to embrace who you are. All you have to do is stop running. Stop fighting. You can't win. You never could."

There, a ghoul perched on a tree, watching as two of its brethren were engulfed in fire, their screams flooding its mind. He seized it, then made the creature stand up and jump down, then turn, directing it toward the edge of the burning woods. Figures fled to the left and right of him, others already moving much, much farther up ahead.

And still so many more behind him.

A heavy *thrumming* in the air and the ground shook, and he glanced up while in mid-jump as the shimmering gray metal object, made almost shiny by the fire below it, sliced through the air high above the tree canopies. The warplane had a name, but it escaped him at the moment. An animal of some sort.

The plane loosed its cargo and the earth cracked open, the trees collapsing in waves. The sound of hundreds of ghouls screaming in pain all at the same time overwhelmed his mind, and he lost his footing. He went headfirst into some brush and came out the other side, his joints *clacking* as he struggled to rise.

Too much. It was too much. He couldn't fight it, couldn't push it aside—

A wall of flames embraced him, the pain almost instantly unbearable, and he had no choice but to—

IT WAS GONE. No matter how hard he tried, he couldn't pick his way through the voices a second time and find the ones pursuing the plane. The problem was distance and control. The farther he projected, the less he had. It was a problem Mabry didn't have. But then, he wasn't Mabry. None of them were. There was only one, and there would only always be the one.

He opened his eyes to earth and darkness. Home. At least for tonight.

The silence beyond his makeshift tomb was broken only occasionally by the surf meeting the beach in the distance, bringing with it the smell of ocean water, at once reassuring and terrifying. The madness in the fields behind him was over; the blue eyes had sounded the retreat. The war machine had ceased its cannon fire, and there was just the blessed serenity of undisturbed night again.

How long before sunrise? He wasn't sure, but there was enough time to do what he needed to do, even if his body was still weak. He shouldn't have been tired, but he was. It wasn't a physical pain—not the kind that left his muscles sore and tendons tight and flesh beat up. It was a mental fatigue, a strain that was hard to account for but was there, present in the throbbing against his skull and the blurring in his vision. Jumping between bodies was always draining, and this time he had stayed longer than he usually did, or wanted.

It was a risk, but it couldn't be helped. Danny and Gaby needed him. There had been two others in the hangar with them. Men whose faces were familiar, but their names eluded him at the moment. They were back there, in the part of his memory where he kept the things that didn't matter, that he could afford to forget.

Danny and Gaby mattered, though. What were they doing out there? They had almost died. Would have, if he hadn't intervened.

What were they doing out there?

But there were no answers to be found down here in the darkness, so he dug and crawled, and pulled and pushed, until he was free. He straightened and gratefully let the darkness embrace him. He was somewhere between the buildings and the water, in a patch of unspectacular ground with nothing to mark his current presence or eventual leave.

He slid through the wind, the torn fabric of the trench coat the only sound as he raced across the outskirts of the city, leaving the taunting scent of the ocean far behind. Topography was difficult to gauge when he was wearing bodies, but he had glimpsed enough of the burning woods to get a general direction. Somewhere out there, the plane would have to eventually come back down.

THEY WERE OUT at night, like they always were, and he avoided them by using the shadows. There were shadows within shadows, if you knew where to look. With patience and experience, he had learned to anticipate the shifting of the darkness, always managing to stay one step ahead of the black eyes.

He moved further inland, always aware of the gradual rise in temperature against his skin, the promise of sunrise like a hand from the past reaching out to take hold of him. So he ran faster, aware that he was abandoning Keo and the woman, and leaving behind his need to see *her* again.

But he had to, because out there, somewhere, was an army. And if he could find it, take control of it, wield it against Mabry...

"You're grasping at straws," Mabry had said.

Maybe, maybe...

He didn't get tired easily these days, so he was able to slip and dodge and dart through buildings, alleyways, and wide-open fields. He bided his time when he needed to and called forth speed when it served him. He lost count of how many empty houses he had passed, the endless empty stretches of roads covered by never-ending clusters of vehicles. He would have avoided the cities entirely if he could, but that required too much time, and he had little to waste.

The sounds of the warplanes from the past echoed inside his head as he ran. Another time, another place. A lot of sand and blood and fire...

He pulled himself back to the present as a horde of black eyes stampeded across a flat and empty field. There, the red walls and angled roofs of a barn. The front alley doors were sealed tight, so he ignored them and jumped instead, grabbing the awning and swinging himself up and over and through an open loft door.

He landed in old bales of hay and watched the creatures racing by under the moonlight. A few hundred, which could only mean a search party. How many more were out there right now, scouring the land for him? Did Mabry know he was nearby? Had he allowed the walls in his mind to slip—

Click!

A small figure, partially shrouded in shadows, stood between two molding bales of hay. Fragile hands trembled as they held onto a silver-chromed revolver that was pointed at him, pale lips parting and closing involuntarily, a small heartbeat rapidly increasing every half second as she exposed herself.

He looked past the dirty pants and sweater and recognized a stick-thin form underneath. Malnourished, the stink of urine and fecal matter oozing from every inch of her, making her nearly impossible to distinguish from the natural decay of the barn.

A second figure, smaller than the first, peeked out from the back. A boy, shaggy hair covered in dirt and straws; like the older one, he had the stink of the building all over him. The two of them were a sorry sight, and he felt something that might have been pity even as the silver that made up the weapon tickled the back of his brain.

"Shoot it!" the boy whispered.

"Shhh!" the girl said. "Stay back like I told you!"

But the boy didn't go back. Instead, he clutched a rusted steak knife almost as big as his entire arm in both hands. The sharp edge was dull but the metal gleamed in the darkness anyway, dangerous enough for a normal human being, but not to him at the moment. Not at this distance, anyway.

The girl cocked her head, staring at him from across the loft, trying to get a good look at him through the remains of the hoodie over his head. She had dark brown eyes, and they were drawn irresistibly to the pulsating blue of his own. He looked away, back out the doors as the last of the ghouls disappeared into the moonlight.

Crunch-crunch as the girl took a step, then another one, toward him. Perhaps to get a better look at his face, or to make an easier shot. Sweat trailed down her temple despite the cold night air. She wasn't wearing shoes, and he smelled fresh packed dirt around her toes. The small, barely noticeable squeeze as her finger tightened, tightened against the trigger.

Could she make the shot? Unlikely, given how badly she was shaking, but all it would take was one lucky round. Of course, he could avoid it easily. All he had to do was snap her neck—

No. Not that way.

He stared back at the girl. "Don't," he hissed.

Confusion swept across her dirty face. Long, stringy brown hair drooped over her eyes, and the gun continued to tremble slightly in her hands.

In the back, the boy leaned out of the shadows, dull knife ready.

"They'll hear you," he said to the girl, "and come back. Do you understand?"

Her eyes darted to the loft opening, then back to him. Did she believe him? Maybe. Was that why she and the boy were hiding? Had they seen the ghouls streaming across the fields earlier, even before he did? Or was this their home? Did they live here in the barn?

"Understand?" he asked.

Finally, she nodded, and he sensed hesitation as the gun lowered. Not much, just half an inch, but it was enough. Even better, her finger eased back on the trigger.

"Good," he said.

"What *are* you, mister?" the girl asked, cocking her head, still trying to get a better look at him under the hoodie.

When he didn't respond, the girl said, "Mister? Are you…?"

"Hide," he said.

"Emmy?" the little boy whispered from the back of the loft. "What's happening?"

"Shhh!" Emmy snapped back at him.

She was turned around facing the boy when he leaped outside, landed on the ground, and ran off. He didn't look back. He didn't want to, but he couldn't stop the girl's voice from echoing over and over inside his head.

"What are *you, mister?"* she had asked.

He slipped into a patch of woods and skirted around a pair of dead cities, racing against the night, trying to outdistance the coming morning. Never tiring, never sweating, never slowing down.

Out there, somewhere, someone was bringing the war to Mabry's doorsteps. Someone who wasn't afraid, who had a plan. Someone with planes and bombs, and maybe even an army at his disposal.

He pushed through the brush and emerged out onto the side of a highway next to a town still filled with the smell of death and destruction, of gunpowder and explosive residue. The streets were once filled with bodies, but they had been taken away; the ones buried under rubble had also been dug up.

He ran across the remains of homes and buildings, and all the while, the girl's voice echoed in his head:

"What are you, mister?"

HE SMELLED THE sweat under their clothes before he even heard or saw them: two soldiers perched in a pair of trees wearing black clothing and black paint over their faces. Almost invisible against the night. Almost. They cradled weapons attached with long suppressors in case they needed to fire them.

And something else. He had detected a trace of it earlier, but wasn't sure. Now, closer, he was certain.

Silver bullets.

Their weapons' magazines were loaded with silver bullets. He tasted the bitter metal against the tip of his tongue and swallowed it down, then made no sounds as he moved under them. They never saw him—never heard or smelled or felt him. The woods hid his presence, the heat and cold emanating from his pores indistinguishable against the chilly air.

He picked up the familiar scent of fresh gasoline that he had been tracking for the last hour. They had abandoned the roads and picked their way here, where he found the barely day-old tire tracks in the ground. The vehicles were hidden now, their engines cold and undetectable against the pulse of the night. They had picked wisely, hiding in a part of the world that humans had abandoned years ago and the black eyes had stopped searching months earlier.

Except it was nearly impossible for his heightened senses to ignore the combined heat radiating from their bodies. They were pressed against each other, finding strength and comfort in accidental contacts, the quickening heartbeats of so many people crammed into a couple of old abandoned buildings like jackhammers.

He sniffed the men on the rooftops. Multiple snipers, gripping recently oiled machine guns. A couple were dozing off, but more than enough were still awake, jacked up with the help of chemicals.

Again, the metallic taste of silver bullets bit against his tongue.

They had so much silver. Not just on them, but also inside the buildings, in the crates piled in the backs of their vehicles. They were well-organized, well-prepared. Was he really looking at an army?

"You're grasping at straws," Mabry had said.

Maybe, maybe…

He looked back into the woods. He could still smell them, the two brave souls watching the perimeter behind him.

Maybe they would have some answers.

THE OLDER OF the two men almost managed to pull the trigger in time. Almost. There was a second of hesitation—which was all he needed to grab the younger man's weapon—and he pulled, sending the soldier flailing to the ground below.

Before the older man could lift his rifle to fire, he leaped across the open space and smashed the man's head into the tree trunk. The resulting *crunch!* caused him a second of remorse, but he pushed it aside as the body disappeared into a bush below.

He leaped down soundlessly and stalked toward the first man, who was scrambling for his holstered sidearm but finding it slippery. There was no suppressor on the gun, but the man either didn't notice or was too frightened to think of the consequences.

He batted the gun away just as the man managed to lift it, and the weapon disappeared into the grass. He'd heard the *crack* as the soldier's wrist broke, and before the man could open his mouth to scream, he placed a hand over it. Pale gray eyes flew wide, but pain or not, the man had enough remaining sense of self-preservation to reach down with his other hand for the handle of his sheathed knife.

The silver coating on the blade made his skin crawl, but he ignored it and grabbed the soldier's hand as he lifted the knife and twisted—not too hard this time, just enough to force the man to let go of the weapon. The figure underneath him thrashed, terror washing over his painted face. Unlike the girl at the loft, the soldier could see him clearly for what he was—the icy blue of his eyes under the hoodie, the impossible cold and heat that oozed from every pore of his flesh.

"Shhh," he hissed, putting one finger to his lips.

The soldier went still, the horror in his eyes giving way to confusion.

"Don't scream," he hissed.

The smell of urine leaked through the man's thermal clothing, but the soldier might not even realized what he had done.

"Scream, and you'll die," he hissed. "Scream, and the others will die. You'll bring death on them. The others, like me, in the woods around you. Do you understand?"

The soldier was no fool and he understood, going perfectly still as a result. But the gray eyes continued to stare, unable to pull away from the dark face hiding underneath the frayed fabric of the hoodie.

He removed his hand.

"What *are* you?" the soldier said, the three words coming out in a breathless whisper that formed clouds of mist between them.

"Shhh," he said, staring back at the man under him. "This might hurt a little, but I have to know."

"Know what?" the soldier said, fear flickering back across his face.

"Everything," he said, placing one hand on the soldier's forehead and leaning in closer.

MERCER.

The man's name was Mercer. He was responsible for the ambush at the airfield, a single day that was months in the planning.

Images of warplanes streaking across the sky and over clear blue waters. An endless expanse of ocean that made his skin quiver at the sight. People cheering. Children in overalls…fishing?

"You're with us, or you're against us."

Men in uniforms training for hours, days, weeks, and months. Firing hundreds—thousands?—of bullets. That's okay, because bullets are plentiful. You can always make more—or pick them up.

A voice on the radio resulting in a new kind of bullet. *Silver bullets.*

Where did they get all the silver?

Everywhere. From homes. Buildings. Piles of silver being smelted down.

Someone spray painting a white sun emblem onto the side of a vehicle. A tan-colored tank.

No. *Tanks.*

Another place, another time. A new mission. Watching bombs being attached to fixed wings. Then those same bombs dropping in the distance. The ground rumbling. Burning trees. Excited reports of hundreds dead over the radio. Thousands?

"You're with us, or you're against us."

A city on the ocean. Another one underground. Gray walls and mazes of metal pipes, yellow tubing, and machinery.

Civilians. Soldiers. Uniforms. Guns. Ammo.

Flocks of birds? Bird soup...

Pull back, pull back...

Mercer. Concentrate on Mercer.

There. Fifties. Imposing, but just a man. A very dangerous man in control of an army.

"You're with us, or you're against us."

More images of people, places, and things, but none of them involving Mercer. He had to know more about Mercer. Can he be trusted? Does he pose any danger to *her?*

No, no. He'd lost his way.

Find it. Have to find it again.

There...

A boy on his tenth birthday blowing out a candle in a backyard as people cheered. *(No.)* A brand new bike falling, a boy crying. *(No!)* A nervous first kiss in the back of a car. *(Pull back! Pull back!)*

No, too far back. He'd lost his way.

No, no, no...

BLOOD TRICKLED OUT of the soldier's nose, somehow finding its way to the corners of his mouth. Gray eyes stared accusingly up at him, the blackened face frozen in a mask of shock, confusion, and pain.

He stood up from the lifeless body and stared for a moment. A flash of guilt, and then it was gone. He wasn't sure if that should have disturbed him. He had felt the same way—and passed it over just as quickly—with the older man in the tree. He couldn't help but think he should have been more disturbed by how easily he killed them.

Shouldn't he?

He might have lingered on the conflicting emotions if not for the encroaching sunrise against his back. It wouldn't be long now. Maybe an hour. Maybe less. He could already feel the heat pressing against his skin, urging him to move on, to forget about the dead.

He fled through the woods, replaying the soldier's memories in his head. The man hadn't been privy to much, but he had known enough. Snippets of important things, events, and speeches that he had been around to see and hear.

"You're with us, or you're against us."

Mercer's words, a clear signal that today was just the beginning, that the worst was yet to come.

He had sought out an army, hoping to find allies to use against Mabry. But all he had found instead was...what, exactly? Another enemy? Or something worse? *Was* there something worse than Mabry?

Maybe. One way or another, the answer would come.

It always did, eventually.

CHAPTER 15

KEO

BLEACHED WHITE BONES *crunched* under his boots, and the acidic smell of burnt flesh lingered in the early morning sun, threatening to suffocate him if he so much as let down his guard. It was only bearable because of the size small T-shirt he had found in the storage shed covering the lower half of his face, and though that made breathing difficult, it was preferable to the alternative.

He was making steady progress toward the M1 Abrams tank that had, sometime during the chaos, ended up in the fields about 200 meters from where it had started on the road. He wouldn't be surprised if the thing had simply run out of fuel, given how active it had been last night.

It sat unmoving under the bright sun now, jagged pieces of white bones wedged between its tracked wheels, bony fingers clutched around sections of the 120mm cannon and limbs jutting out along the crevices of the turret. A couple of ghouls had managed to wedge themselves into the loader's armor gun shield, for all the good that had done.

Further visual evidence of last night's carnage could be found all across the fields around him. The craters of 120mm impacts dotted the landscape, and the crumpled heaps of destroyed homes made him question if he had emerged out of the storage box into a landfill instead of a beachside neighborhood. Miraculously, the house with the red roof that he and Jordan had hidden underneath had been spared. Maybe his luck was looking up after all.

Let's not get too ahead of ourselves, pal.

He stepped through the carcass of a white house with Trex decking, then wound his way through the remains of the living room and out the back, into a crater about a meter deep, before climbing back up among blackened grass. The tank was frozen about fifty meters in front of him, sunlight glinting off its desert tan hide and the shattered remains of bones draped over it.

He slipped out from behind the leftovers of another house and jogged across charred grass, doing his best to skip around as many skeletal remains as possible, though he might as well be trying to avoid the ground for all the good that did. It was impossible not to *crunch* or *snap* an arm or a limb or a deformed skull as he made his way toward his objective. After a while, he just gave up trying. If the tankers heard him coming through all that armor, then so be it.

Forty meters to the Abrams, and Keo was finally able to make out the words "Eat Me" along the length of the 120mm cannon, while "Get Off Me Bro" was spray painted across the armor tiles that covered the track wheels. A white circle with triangle-shaped objects coming out of it was prominently displayed at the front of the tank. After a second glance, he concluded the emblem was supposed to be a sun, and the "triangles" its rays. He had seen a lot of U.S. Army insignias, and that was definitely not one of them.

Thirty meters later, Keo was able to identify some kind of modified flamethrower welded in place of a machine gun inside the loader's gun shield on top of the turret. An M240 was mounted on the second station, but he didn't remember machine gun fire from last night. He could, though, recall in great detail the thick smell of barbecuing meat.

Keo changed up his approach and began moving sideways so he could take the remaining distance from the rear. He felt a flood of relief not having that smoothbore cannon pointing right at him—or anywhere close to him, for that matter. He knew it was stupid;

chances were, they had blown all their load last night. Still, the sight of that thing staring right at him...

With just five meters left to go, Keo was feeling good about making it to the tank undiscovered. That was, until the loud grinding of metal filled the air. He dived to the ground and rolled to his right until he was covered in the shadow of the M1's turret. Keo pulled down the shirt and took in a deep breath, his first unhindered one since he had stepped out of the storage shack. Thank God for the constant waves of fresh air coming from the ocean nearby, otherwise he might have choked on the stench.

There were impossibly white skeletal remains all around him, a shattered skull directly two inches from his head, and his rifle was resting on a pile of white and gray ash. He did his very best to ignore something pricking at his legs through the fabric of his pants. Probably a broken hand, or fingers...

A loud *clang!*, followed by a figure with a shaved head raising himself out of the commander's hatch of the tank. The man was wearing a tan shirt and pants, and the same sun emblem was embroidered across a red collar, but nothing to indicate rank. The shirt had a white patch of the Lone Star State in the front, with scribbling inside it, but Keo was at the wrong angle to read the letters. It was a military uniform of some sort, but not one he was familiar with. But then, BDUs came in all shapes and sizes, and maybe this was a new variation for a new world?

The possibility that Jordan might have been right, that maybe he was looking at remnants of the U.S. Army, made him question what he was doing out in the fields hiding from them. The last thing he wanted was to start popping U.S. soldiers.

Keo took his hand off the M4, then reached down and drew the Glock. His fingers brushed against something sharp hidden among the grass, and something else was poking at his stomach and had been for the last few seconds, but he managed to ignore it, too, even though he had a pretty good idea what it was.

The soldier *(?)* had climbed out of the tank and was stretching. When he was done, he opened a canteen and took a long drink from it while glancing around at the fields. "Jesus Christ," the man said. He tossed the canteen back into the open hatch, then dug out a white silk handkerchief and pressed it against his mouth.

Keo heard a second voice, this one coming from inside the tank, but he couldn't make out the words.

"We made a hell of a mess," the man standing on top of the Abrams said, his voice muffled by the cloth. "Got a whole fuck lot of them, boys." He lowered the handkerchief and let out a satisfied sigh. "Who's got mop-up duty—" the man continued, but he stopped in mid-sentence because he had been turning when he said it, and—

Keo pushed himself up from the ground at the same time the man's eyes locked onto him. He got his knees under him, then held out his left hand, the palm outward, while his right kept the Glock pointed down at the ground.

"Wait," Keo said.

The man stared at him, mouth partially agape. His right hand was holding the cloth, and while he wore a gun belt, the sidearm was on his right side, which meant he was right-handed.

"Don't—" Keo said, when the man dropped the handkerchief and reached for his holstered weapon.

Keo shot the man in the chest.

The soldier fell, slamming into the turret before sliding off it, the white silk cloth fluttering in the air after him.

Keo jumped up to his feet and ran toward the Abrams, thinking, *Fuck, fuck, fuck* with every step.

"What if it really is the U.S. Army? What if they're finally fighting back?" Jordan had said last night.

Then I'm screwed, Jordan, Keo thought as he grabbed the closest handhold on the vehicle, his feet searching for anything to use as a stepping stone, finding them, then flinging himself up and over the turret.

He made the top of the tank just as a head poked out of the same commander's hatch. The man had short spiky hair and was whirling around, the back of his head initially facing Keo. When the soldier finally completed his turn, the man's eyes widened at the sight of Keo perched behind him. Keo might have held his fire, except the soldier had a gun in his hand and was swinging it around.

*Sonofa*bitch, Keo thought, and shot the tanker between the eyes. The man's head snapped back before it dropped and slid through the hatch.

Keo scrambled over the turret and reached the opening and looked through it, seeing a third figure below. The man had one hand cradling his dead comrade and the other stretching up with a Sig Sauer. Keo jerked his head back as the man fired—a thunderous *boom!* as the gunshot exploded in the confines of the tank—and the round *zipped* past his head, so close he swore he could feel the trail blazed by the bullet.

Instead of leaning back toward the hatch, Keo held out his hand, gun pointed down, and fired two times into the Abrams. Before he even knew if he had hit his target or not, Keo lunged forward and jumped through the round door feetfirst and—

—landed with a wet *thud* against the stomach of the man with the spiky hair, his momentum sending both him and the tanker with the Sig Sauer sprawling across the metal floor. Keo didn't have to shoot the third man again because he was already dead—there was a single hole in his chest.

Keo lost his balance as soon as he touched down somewhere in the turret basket and hit his ass on cold, hard metal. Thankfully he was facing the right direction and immediately saw the fourth soldier up front, reclining back in the driver seat underneath the main gun. The man was turning his head and reaching for his sidearm, still in its holster draped over his seat, at the same time.

"Think about it!" Keo shouted, his voice thundering inside the vehicle.

The man did and stopped moving altogether. While his body was frozen in mid-turn, his eyes were free to dart to his two dead comrades before returning to Keo. He was covered in sweat despite wearing only a white undershirt and khaki shorts, similar dress to the third man Keo had shot. A pile of tan-colored uniforms hung from handholds around them.

"Shit," the guy said.

"Yeah," Keo said.

"U.S. ARMY?" KEO asked.

The soldier, who said his name was Gregson, shook his head.

"Collaborator?"

"Hell no," Gregson said, looking almost insulted.

"Guess not," Jordan said.

She stood next to Keo, holding another T-shirt from the storage shed over her mouth. Keo hadn't needed his since hauling Gregson out of the tank. He wasn't entirely sure what that said about his sense of smell that he could "get used" to his current environment.

Gregson sat on the ground with his back against the wheels of the Abrams. He had looked older when Keo first saw him inside the cramped space of the tank, but under the morning sun he was a man in his mid-twenties, with light blue eyes and dirty brown hair. His arms, covered in sleeves of tattoos, were draped over his knees. If he ever had any thoughts about escaping, he let it go when he saw the uniformed body on the ground with the hole in its chest.

"So if you're not U.S. Army and you're not collaborators, who are you?" Keo asked.

Gregson didn't answer right away, as if he was trying to decide whether or not he should say anything to them. Keo could have told him that only delusional idiots tried to withstand interrogation. Sooner or later, you broke. Everyone did. Which was precisely why his old organization never bothered to rescue captured operatives.

"The way I see it, we're on the same side," Keo continued.

That elicited a snort from Gregson. "Was that before or after you killed my friends?"

"I had no choice. You should thank me for having the self-control not to shoot you back there."

Gregson seemed to think about that before finally saying, "I guess."

"So, let's start at the beginning. Who are you, and what were you doing running around out here last night, shooting up the beach?"

"I was following orders."

"Whose?"

"Mercer's."

"Never heard of him." He turned to Jordan: "You?"

She shook her head. "Doesn't ring a bell."

"So, who's Mercer?" Keo asked Gregson.

"He's a great man," Gregson said. "That's all you need to know."

"And this great man told you to come down here and empty 120mm shells on an innocent beach?"

"Not exactly."

"So what, exactly?"

Gregson hesitated.

Keo sighed and drew his sidearm. "I've tried to do this the easy way, but you're just wasting my time now."

"I thought you said we were on the same side," Gregson said quickly.

"Not if you keep making me ask twice. I *hate* having to ask twice."

"All right."

"All right?"

"Yeah, all right." Then, after Keo had holstered his sidearm: "We overshot our mark yesterday, ended up having to fight it out with those collaborator assholes. Then we saw the beach and thought, what the hell. We couldn't link back up with our forces anyway, so we figured we'd go out with a bang. Worst-case scenario, we were prepared to drive right into the ocean a la *Thelma and Louise.*"

"I don't know what that is," Keo said.

"The movie?"

Keo shook his head.

"I've heard of it," Jordan said.

"Good?" Keo asked.

She shrugged. "It was an oldie. I liked the car, though."

"I guess that's all that counts," he chuckled before turning back to Gregson. "Where are the rest of your forces?"

"Sorry, can't do," Gregson smiled back. "Need-to-know, and you don't need to know. Shoot me if you want, but I'm not telling you shit about that."

"Tough guy."

"When it comes to that? Fuck yeah, tough enough."

Keo nodded. He believed the man. "So what were you doing out here yesterday? Can't hurt to tell us that, right?"

Gregson thought about that for a moment too, before nodding. "We were doing our part."

"Which was what, exactly?"

"Take out one of the towns."

"The collaborator towns?"

"What other kinds are there?"

Keo exchanged a glance with Jordan, and he could tell she was thinking the exact same thing: *Gillian. T18.*

He turned back to Gregson. "What do you mean, 'take out' one of the towns?"

"What do you think I meant?" Gregson said. He reached back and banged on the tank. "This thing's designed to do one thing, and it ain't making pies."

"You shelled it? The town?"

"We flattened the fuck out of it, yeah."

"And the people in it?" Jordan asked.

Gregson shrugged.

"What the hell does that mean?" she said, a noticeable warning edge creeping into her voice.

"We destroyed it," Gregson said. "Most of it, anyway. That was the mission. Only spent half of our ammo too, tore the place down like a bulldozer, and wasted everything we had for the M240. But we got unlucky; they had reinforcements nearby, and we had to make a run for it."

"What were you running from?" Keo asked.

"Technicals and rocket launchers. I mean, our armor could have survived a lot, but there were a lot of them, and who knows what else they had. Besides, our orders were to hit and run, then link back up with the rest of our forces. Failing that...well, it's been a while since we saw the beach. We knew they'd follow us here. Didn't think they'd send the skin meats, though."

"Skin meats?"

"Those ghouls. That's what some of us call them."

Keo raised an eyebrow. "You also call them ghouls?"

"Yeah. Why?"

"Where'd you get the name from?"

Gregson looked confused; either that, or he had another piece of information he thought was need-to-know. "It's just a name. Who cares?"

"Just curious," Keo said.

"How many people did you kill in the town?" Jordan asked.

Gregson didn't answer her.

"How many?" she asked again.

"I don't know; we didn't exactly get close enough to count," Gregson said. "A lot, I guess. I just drove. The others did the shooting. The mission was to leave just enough behind."

"'Just enough' for what?" Keo asked.

"So they can tell the others what happened."

"You want them to know. The other collaborators, in the other towns."

"Yeah," Gregson nodded. "To let everyone know there's something worse than the ghouls out here. *Us.* We killed just enough to make our point."

"Hundreds?" Jordan said. "Did you kill hundreds?"

"Maybe. It doesn't matter."

"Why doesn't it matter?"

"Because they're the enemy," Gregson said. "You're either with us, or you're against us. If you're against us, then you're the enemy, and the enemy doesn't deserve mercy. This is war, lady. We're trying to take back the planet." He looked to Keo. "You should understand that. How long have you been fighting these assholes out here?"

"You sonofabitch," Jordan said. "There are women and children in those towns!"

"Bullshit."

"Bullshit?" Jordan was almost screaming at him now. "What the *hell does that mean?*"

Gregson craned his head toward her, shouting back, "Bullshit, that's what that means! They stopped being women and children the moment they agreed to become food for the skin meats! They're just targets now!"

"You bastard..."

"Fuck off!"

Jordan reached for her gun as Gregson scrambled up from the ground, the two of them moving almost simultaneously. Keo beat them both to the punch by hitting Gregson in the side of the face with the stock of his M4, sending the tank driver collapsing back to the ground.

"Don't," Keo said, putting one hand over Jordan's arm as she aimed her Glock at Gregson.

"Why the hell not?" Jordan asked, almost spitting the words out.

Why the hell not? Keo thought, realizing he didn't really have a good answer for her. He had been worried he had just killed three U.S. Army soldiers earlier, but that turned out not to be the case. Gregson and his friends were something else entirely. Something that was either bad news or very bad news. He still hadn't decided yet.

He pushed Jordan's gun hand down. She resisted at first—he could see the defiance in her eyes, how badly she wanted to pull the trigger—but eventually relented.

"Why *not?*" she asked again, staring back at him. "You heard what he did. He killed God knows how many people back there. There are pregnant women and children in all those towns, Keo. He slaughtered *pregnant women.*"

"They were the enemy," Gregson said softly. He had pushed

himself back up to a sitting position against the tank and was wiping his bloody mouth with his shirt. "They made their choice, now they have to pay for it. This is just the beginning. If you thought yesterday was bloody, you haven't seen anything yet." He grinned at them; it was a grotesque sight with his teeth covered in blood. "Mercer's got plans. Big plans."

"What was it called?" Keo asked him.

"What?" Gregson said.

"The town you were assigned to attack."

"T-something. Benoit knew the exact name, but one town sounds the same as all the others to me. T-this, T-that."

"Was it T18?"

Gregson shrugged. "You'll have to ask Benoit." He glanced over at the first uniformed body Keo had shot. The man lay on his stomach among the blackened grass a few meters away, the back of his bald head reflecting the bright sun. "Oh, I guess you can't."

"I guess not," Keo said.

He drew his Glock a second time and shot Gregson in the right thigh.

"Shit!" Gregson shouted, falling sideways to the ground while clutching his leg. "What'd you do that for?"

Keo ignored him and looked at Jordan. She was staring at Gregson, the hate from a few seconds ago mostly gone from her face, replaced by something that looked almost like sympathy.

"Why didn't you let me shoot him?" she asked quietly.

"You're a good person, Jordan," Keo said. "I'm not."

◄━━ ━━►

GREGSON WASN'T LYING about the tank being out of fuel. It was bone dry. They had also burned through their entire armory yesterday, including the flamethrower, and were just left with small arms. Keo salvaged four AR-15 rifles and a can of ammo with 5.56 rounds, which would go a long way in backing up his M4's dwindling magazine, though he was more grateful to find MREs and water bottles tucked inside two storage compartments. There was a pile of civilian clothes in the back, but they were splattered with blood from the two tankers Keo had shot through the hatch.

He collected the rifles and stuffed the water and food into a couple of tactical backpacks when he saw the edge of a brown paper sticking out of a pants pocket on one of the dead man. Keo tugged it out, then unfolded it.

It was a map of Texas, with black markers circling towns around the southeast part of the state. Not the big cities like Sunport or Galveston, or even Houston, but the smaller, surrounding ones. There were red X's over some of them—about a dozen in all—but the rest were just circled.

"Shit," he said under his breath when he recognized one of the towns that had been circled.

Wilmont. Or, as he had come to know it the last few weeks, T18. *Gillian.* Pregnant *Gillian.*

He had left her behind with Jay because there was no other choice, and after the week he'd been through, he was convinced it was the right decision. But now…

Keo put everything down and concentrated on the map. One of the places with an X over it was marked as T22, and it was somewhere on the other side of Sunport.

What was that Gregson had said?

"We destroyed it. Most of it, anyway. That was the mission. Only spent half of our ammo too, tore the place down like a bulldozer, and wasted everything we had for the M240. But we got unlucky; they had reinforcements nearby, and we had to make a run for it."

So what did that mean for T18, which was missing an X? Maybe nothing, maybe everything. Or maybe as far as Gregson's crew knew, T18 wasn't their concern because it was someone else's job.

A lot of maybes, and most of them bad.

So what else is new?

Footsteps, just before Jordan's head appeared in the opening above him. "Find anything useful?"

"Just one," he said, and handed the map up to her.

Jordan sat on the turret, put the map in her lap, and looked at it for a moment. "What am I looking at? What do the X's stand for?"

"Targets."

"Oh." She paused for a moment, then, "They have T18 circled, but not X'ed out." She looked down through the opening at him. "Gillian."

"Yeah," he said, and climbed up with the rifles and backpacks.

He settled on the turret and glanced around him. The difference between the charred fields and the white sand of the beach on the other side was startling. Keo collected his thoughts and considered his options.

He had guns, ammo, and now, extra food and water. He could see himself spending a few more months down here in peace. Even if Lara never showed up with the *Trident*—and there was no reason for them to, without further contact from him—he could be satisfied. Even more so, if Jordan decided to stay behind, too.

It wouldn't be such a bad life—or however long he had left. Not bad at all.

"What about Gillian?" Jordan asked, bringing him back. "What if T18 is next on the list?"

He didn't answer her.

"Keo, we have to go back for her. She's our friend."

"I tried that, Jordan. *We* both tried that. Remember?"

"Things are different now. There are tanks rampaging through towns. Gillian doesn't know that. She stayed because she thought her baby would be safer in T18. Well, it's not. Not anymore."

It's not my problem, he thought, but didn't say it.

"Keo," Jordan said.

"She's still safer with Jay," he said. "Especially now that the towns know they're being hit. They'll take more precautions, put up proper defenses. Protecting their doctors will be top priority."

"You can't be sure of that."

"It's what I would do, and I'm just a shooter. The guys running these places are smarter than me. You saw the setup they had back there. It's like that everywhere."

Jordan didn't say anything. He wasn't sure if she believed him, or if she had given up trying to convince him. She looked past him instead, at the ocean on the other side of the burnt field. Wind blew her short blonde hair into her eyes, and she had to brush it aside.

They sat in silence for the longest time, but of course, it didn't last.

"So when you are going back for her?" Jordan finally asked.

He sighed, staring out at the impossibly blue Gulf of Mexico. "As soon as I find a working vehicle."

He didn't see it, but he thought he could feel her smiling triumphantly behind him.

"Shut up," he said.

"I didn't say anything," she said.

"Uh huh."

He was trying to convince himself that he wasn't the world's biggest idiot (maybe just Texas's), when a small black dot appeared against the water's surface in the distance. He stared at it for a moment, wondering if he was seeing things, but that couldn't have been it, because the object was definitely getting bigger...as it got closer.

"Is that...?" Jordan said.

"Yeah," he nodded, reaching for a rifle. "That's a boat heading this way."

CHAPTER 16

LARA

"YOU LOOK LIKE shit, Keo," Maddie said. "I mean, no offense, but compared to when we last saw you, it looked like you got caught in a combine."

"He was definitely handsomer the last time we saw him," Bonnie chimed in.

"I don't know, scars give a man character."

"Yeah? Then Keo went and got himself a big ass load of character."

Keo smirked at the two women. "Nice to see you guys, too. Especially you, Bonnie."

Bonnie rolled her eyes at him. "Give it a rest. I gave you plenty of chances when you were on the *Trident*."

"What can I say. I'm an idiot."

"Won't get any arguments from me."

Bonnie glanced past Keo to the woman standing on the road behind him. She was holding a rifle, with another one slung over her back, and looked as if she was waiting for some kind of signal that everything was okay. Keo did that now, turning and waving, then slung his own weapon. The woman nodded back but didn't come over.

"Is that her?" Bonnie asked. "The one you kept turning me

down for?"

"That's Jordan," Keo said. "Things didn't work out with Gillian. Long story."

"Must be."

"What did happen to your face?" Lara asked.

"That's part of the long story."

"I guess we're going to be here awhile," Maddie said. She looked over at Lara. "Where do you want us, boss?"

"Stay close," Lara said. When Maddie had started back toward the boat they had arrived ashore in, she said to Bonnie, "Keo's friend has the right idea. We don't want anyone sneaking up on us. Coming here was risky enough; let's not push our luck."

Bonnie nodded, then said to Keo, "Don't be a stranger," before heading up the beach with her M4.

Lara noticed that the ex-model walked a bit wobbly at first and was slowly adjusting with every step. The result of living on the *Trident* for so long, she thought; they had all become used to the boat's movements. She wondered if she looked that odd. Maddie, on the other hand, seemed to have no problems re-familiarizing herself with walking on land.

She glanced around them again, unable to fully shake the paranoia. The place had looked deserted when they were on approach, but after last night, she wasn't willing to just accept anything at face value. These days, ambushes were easy to come by and harder to spot from a distance, and God knew you could hear a motor coming for miles if you had ears.

"Yachting accident?" Keo asked, looking at her bandaged arm.

"Something like that."

With Bonnie now watching the road, Keo's friend walked down the beach toward them. She was pretty, with short blonde hair, and younger than Lara by at least a few years.

The woman stuck out her hand. "You must be Lara. Keo has told me a lot about you."

Lara shook her hand. "All good, I hope."

"Eh."

They exchanged a brief, easy smile.

"We were afraid you might have left when I didn't radio in yesterday," Keo said.

"I should have, especially after the fireworks show last night. You wanna fill me in on what happened? I guess I should have known you would be right in the middle of it."

"Long story."

"Of course it is."

"Where's the tugboat?"

"It's out there somewhere."

"Who's captaining it?"

"Blaine."

"What happened to *el capitan?*"

"He's been dealt with."

"Hunh."

"Yeah."

He fixed her with a long look. She couldn't tell if he was impressed or disturbed. Keo had never been particularly easy to read, and the weeks they'd spent on the *Trident* together hadn't helped her understand him any better. Then again, it wasn't like she didn't have a lot on her mind at the time. Or still did.

"Didn't think you had it in you," he said.

"He didn't give me much of a choice." Then, because she didn't want him to ask any more questions about Gage, "So, where is it? The last time I saw one in person, it was in a museum and I was ten."

"You know about that?"

"Impossible not to. Woke me up from this," she said, holding up her left arm.

"This way." Keo turned around, and with Jordan, led her up the beach.

"Was it them?" Lara asked.

"Depends on who you mean by 'them,'" Keo said.

"The U.S. Army."

"Then no."

"Dammit."

"You were hoping, too?" Jordan asked, looking back at her.

Lara nodded and told her about Beecher, a colonel who was in charge of a few thousand soldiers and civilians somewhere in Colorado. "That's the only remnants of the U.S. Army I know of, and I got the sense they were barely surviving up there."

"What about the Navy?"

"We haven't run across them the entire time we've been in the Gulf."

She saw the disappointment on Jordan's face before the other woman turned back around as they stepped onto the road. Bonnie had moved further inland, her M4 cradled alertly in front of her, watching the other direction. Lara thought she could see some kind of domed buildings blinking in the distance.

She looked back at Keo. "You wanna tell me what was so important I had to drop everything and meet you down here?"

"I wanted you to meet someone," Keo said. "But he's not here right now. We got separated two nights ago."

"Who was it?"

"Let's call him Frank."

Lara caught Jordan sneaking a look at Keo and saw him shaking his head back in reply. Both movements had been very slight and were hardly noticeable—except they were walking right in front of her, and she was staring at them.

Now what was that about?

"Why did you want me to meet him?" she asked instead.

"He had information about the ghouls," Keo said.

"Like what?"

"How they operate, their chain of command, all the nitty-gritty stuff." Then, he added, almost as an afterthought, "He also said he knew how to beat them."

She perked up. "How?"

"He didn't say."

"He didn't *say?* How does he not say, and how do you not force him to tell you something like that, Keo?"

Keo hesitated, and she thought he was picking his words very carefully when he said, "It's complicated, but he would only talk to you."

"Why me?"

"I don't know."

"Keo…"

"I don't know, Lara. Frank's not the most talkative type. You can ask him all the questions you want when you meet him."

They were moving through the field beyond the beach now, tall brown grass slapping at her legs. She thought she could smell something burning, like someone had left a stove on, but it was mostly obfuscated by the breeze coming from the nearby ocean.

"Tell me something," Lara said.

"If I can…" Keo said.

"Do you trust this guy?"

"I do," he said without hesitation.

"Why?"

"He saved my life. Three times now."

"Mine, too," Jordan said.

"What is he, some kind of collaborator?" Lara asked.

"Sort of," Keo said.

"Sort of?"

"It's hard to explain."

"That seems to be a common theme with you today."

"Yeah, sorry about that," he said. "Trust me when I say this wasn't how it was supposed to go down. Things…got complicated."

She had more questions—so many more questions—but the sight of the grass around them turning from brown and green to almost entirely charred black, with large swaths that had been burned completely away leaving behind only blackened dirt, caught her by surprise. The air had also begun to shift noticeably from bearable to almost suffocating.

"Here," Keo said, holding out a small T-shirt to her.

She took it gratefully and pushed it against her mouth and nose. In front of her, Jordan did the same thing with another shirt, but

Keo seemed to be fine with the air. Maybe he had just gotten used to it, though she couldn't understand how.

She forgot about everything else when she saw the tank sitting in the fields in front of them. It was so out of place and impossible to miss, especially the cannon jutting out from it. The tan-colored vehicle was surrounded by large swaths of charred earth and what looked like the carcasses of two-story houses that had been toppled like dominoes, except for a few that still, somehow, remained standing. She almost lost her balance when a crater that shouldn't be there popped up in front of her.

"Watch your step," Keo said.

She thought he was talking about the craters until she heard the *crunch*. Lara looked down at the remains of an arm—the radius was missing, but half of the ulna was still intact—as it crumbled under her boot. The fingers were all there, but the thumb had been blown off. She stepped over it, then around a small pile of bones—then another. They were scattered everywhere amongst the scorched ground, their numbers increasing exponentially the closer she got to the tank. Every step she took produced a loud *crunch* that made her wince.

The carnage was spread out, as if the battle had dragged from one side of the field to the other, leaving death everywhere. There was no blood, but she didn't expect to find any because the ghouls bled a different kind of blood that evaporated against sunlight. Even though she couldn't smell most of the acidic stench that still lingered in the air thanks to Keo's T-shirt, she could smell enough that she wished she were already on the *Trident* again, or at least back on the beach.

She focused on the tank instead, hoping that would take her mind off everything else. "How many tanks?"

"Just the one," Keo said.

"And you're sure it's not U.S. Army?"

"It may have belonged to Uncle Sam once upon a time, but not anymore."

The *crack* of a bone snapping under her boots made her flinch, but she willed herself not to look down.

"Did you find out who they were?" she asked.

Keo pointed at a twenty-something man sitting against the tank's wheels. He was only wearing an undershirt and khaki shorts, and one of his thighs was bandaged. His face was pale under the bright sun, and he didn't look like he could keep his eyes open as he watched them approach.

"His name's Gregson," Keo said. "Had to kill the rest of his crew."

"'Had to?'" she said.

"One of them went for their gun and, well, shit went downhill from there."

"Doesn't it always with you?"

"That wasn't a compliment."

"Depends on who you ask."

Gregson blinked up at her as they stopped in front of him. He looked paler and much weaker up close, and there was a thick clump of blood underneath him. Lara had seen enough people bleeding to last a lifetime and knew without a doubt this man wasn't going to survive the day unless someone treated his wound.

"What's with you and shooting people in the leg?" she asked Keo.

"I'm developing bad habits," he said. "Used to be I'd just shoot them in the head." He said to Gregson, "Tell her what you told us. Everything, including what you were using this bad boy for." He banged on the tank, producing dull *thuds*. "Don't leave out any details."

"I need medical attention," Gregson said. His voice was weak and his lips were cracked.

"You'll get it after we go over it again," Keo said.

Gregson squinted at Keo, as if trying to gauge his trustworthiness.

Good luck with that, she wanted to tell him. She had known Keo longer, and even she couldn't tell if he had meant what he just promised.

"We had a mission…" Gregson began.

SHE LISTENED TO Gregson talking in a slow, almost uninterested drawl. He spoke in such a matter-of-fact monotone that she had to remind herself she was standing in the middle of a warzone surrounded by the bones of ghouls and not in a park somewhere discussing the weather.

Jesus Christ. What's going on out here?

When he was done, Gregson lowered his head and stared down at the ground. That was, if his eyes were even still open, which she couldn't tell for sure. He seemed to have so little energy left after talking that he might have even forgotten to demand that medical attention Keo had promised.

She looked over at Keo, standing on top of the tank behind Gregson, looking back in the direction of the domed buildings she had glimpsed earlier. Jordan was turned the other way, back toward the beach with the shirt pressed against half of her face. They had heard Gregson's story already and might not even have noticed he had stopped talking.

"How many towns have they attacked so far?" she asked Keo.

He shrugged. "Apparently they were at it all day yesterday. That was the plan. Shock and awe. Hit hard and hit fast, before the collaborators could mount a proper defense. Sounds like they've been planning it for months."

He took a folded map out of his pocket and tossed it down to her. She opened it and stared at the circled locations. There were dozens of them.

"What am I looking at?" she asked.

"The circles are collaborator towns in Texas."

"I didn't know there were so many…"

"I don't think that's all of them, just the ones Mercer's people know about. Scouted in advance of yesterday."

There had to be at least two, possibly closer to three, dozen circles in all, and all of them concentrated in the southeast. Did that mean there weren't more in other parts of the state, or were these the only ones Mercer's people had "scouted"? Each one was marked with a T, followed by a number. About a dozen of the towns had large red X's scratched across them. One in particular was somewhere between the towns of Hellion and Starch.

Oh, dammit.

"I was at T18 last week," Jordan said, walking over. She pulled the shirt down just long enough to talk. "Gillian's there."

"Your Gillian?" Lara asked Keo.

He nodded. "Long story."

"Of course it is," she said. Then, "I've never been to any of these places, but from what I hear, there are supposed to be a lot of people in these towns."

"Hundreds, sometimes thousands," Keo said.

"T18 had around 4,000 the last time I was there," Jordan said. "A lot of the women are pregnant."

"Enemies of the state," Gregson said. His voice came out of nowhere and he still looked (and sounded) sapped of energy. "Take them out, and you starve the enemy."

"'Starve the enemy'?" Lara repeated.

"He means killing the collaborators," Keo said. "They're trying to take away what the ghouls prize most—the people in those towns."

"It's barbaric," Jordan said. She stared daggers at Gregson, daring him to challenge her, but he'd already looked back down at the ground. "I would rather die than give blood to those things, but slaughtering them …" She shook her head. "The man who came up with that plan should be hung for war crimes."

"They're the enemy," Gregson muttered to himself. "You're with us, or you're against us…"

"Apparently that's the slogan," Keo said. There wasn't any trace of humor in his voice, and he was looking out at the ocean across the charred field. "By the way, where's the Ranger? I expected to see him make the trip, not you."

"I sent him, Gaby, and Nate to Starch," she said. "That was a few days ago, before you got in touch. We're supposed to be in Port Arthur now, waiting to pick them back up."

"What's in Starch?" Jordan asked.

"An underground facility built by a man named Harold Campbell. We sealed it months ago before we left for Louisiana. It has supplies, ammo, guns, and something else Will and I have always talked about retrieving, just in case."

"Must be important for you to send them back out here," Keo said.

I thought it was, but now I'm not so sure, she thought, but nodded and said, "Lights."

"Lights?"

"UV lights."

Keo looked confused, maybe even doubtful. "Lara, you can go into any store and trip over all the UV lights you can carry. You didn't have to send the ex-Ranger and the girl to Starch for that."

"Those lights aren't like the ones in Starch," she said.

◄■■▮ ▮■■►

"THEY WORK," LARA said. "I've seen it with my own eyes. Ghouls turn to ash against them, the way they do against sunlight."

"That's a hell of a weapon," Keo said.

"It is," she nodded.

"And you're only trying to retrieve these lights now?"

"We didn't need them before. We had the island."

"And now?"

"After you left, we talked about needing an extra layer of security, just in case. I don't know what Harold Campbell's people did to those lights—or what they're actually made of—but we haven't been able to replicate them. Danny, Gaby, and I had a long talk, and we decided sending an expedition to Starch was worth the risk. If I knew there was even a remote possibility they would be walking into the middle of a warzone…" She shook her head. "Shit, Keo, if anything happens to them…"

"You didn't know," Keo said. "Neither did we, until last night. It's a big state, Lara."

"I know," she said, and looked past him at Bonnie, standing guard on the road with Jordan. The two women looked like they were in the middle of a conversation. She was grateful for the cool wind whipping in from the Gulf of Mexico, because they kept her from smelling the lingering fumes from the fields.

"What now?" Keo asked.

"My primary concern is keeping the *Trident* and everyone on it safe. And that's what I'm going to do while we head back to Port Arthur to wait for Danny to make contact."

"How long has it been?"

"Yesterday morning. His last position was outside a town called Hellion. Close enough to Starch that the next time he radioed in, I expected him to be doing it from inside Harold Campbell's facility."

"Did you say Hellion and Starch?"

She nodded somberly. "I saw them on the map."

"He could have gone around it. The Ranger's resourceful, bad jokes notwithstanding. And the girl's good."

"Gaby."

"Yeah, her. I'm not sure about the kid with the Mohawk, though."

She managed a smile. "He's a good kid."

"Yeah, but that haircut…"

"I know."

She looked off into the ocean, in the direction where she knew Blaine and the *Trident* were waiting for them right now. She couldn't see the yacht from here, which made her feel relieved. The last thing she needed was to have to fight off collaborators on the ocean, too.

"We're dealing with a Ranger here," Keo was saying. "I've crossed a few of them in my time, so don't press the panic button just yet. At least not for another day, and maybe not even then."

She wanted badly to agree with him, but the doubts made that impossible.

Would you have done it, Will? Or would you have been satisfied with staying on the Trident?

God, where are you when I need you most?

"What about Gillian and T18?" she asked. "How are you going to handle that one?"

"It's tricky."

"When is it not tricky with you?"

He grunted before glancing back at Jordan, on the road behind them with Bonnie. The two women still looked like they were in the middle of conversation.

"You got extra room for her?" he asked.

"If you're not coming, I have a feeling she won't, either."

"Why wouldn't she?"

Lara gave him an almost pitying look. "For a smart guy, you can be amazingly dense at times, Keo."

"When are people going to stop overestimating me? I keep telling everyone I'm just a guy with a gun."

"Right," she smiled. "You're just a guy with a gun."

CHAPTER 17

GABY

"HOW MANY, YOU think?" Nate asked.

She shook her head. "It's hard to tell. God knows how many more are buried underneath all that."

"It looks worse than I thought it would be."

"It's kind of what I expected."

"Really?"

"Mostly."

"I guess you have a better imagination than me."

"Well, this looks familiar," Danny said, climbing up the rubble behind them. He walked the short distance over and crouched next to her and looked out at the airfield. "Plan Z," he said quietly.

"What?" she said.

"Just thinking out loud. Don't mind me."

She followed his gaze back out to the world beyond the hangar. Or what was left of it. If she didn't already know she was looking at an airfield, she wouldn't have been able to guess from the remains. The ground had taken a lot of punishment, the slabs of asphalt and concrete that made up the runway scattered across the surrounding area. The group of administrative buildings on the other side was practically invisible against the widespread destruction.

Bleached white bones poked out of the discombobulated green, brown, and gray of the obliterated field like furless prairie dogs playing hide and seek with the sun. Dead *(again?)* ghouls. So many that she could have started counting and never finished before nightfall, and those were just the ones she could see from her perch. How many more were hidden underneath all that loosened earth and man-made material? What about behind them right now? Or among the scorched trees that flanked the airfield?

"Cluster bombs," Danny had said when Nate told him about the small parachutes he'd seen falling from the sky last night.

There was just enough wind to disperse most of the lingering stench of vaporized ghoul flesh, otherwise it would have been unbearable against so much unnatural death. Even so, she pulled her shirt up over half of her face, Danny and Nate doing the same next to her. Her eyes stung, a combination of the acrid smell of the dead and the scorched foliage from the woods around them.

They were crouched on a section of the hangar's front wall that was still standing, the top half blown off by one of the blasts from last night. Pieces of the caved-in roof provided a ladder of sorts, with just enough hand and footholds to crawl up its length. The only thing left now was to hop the ten feet down to the sturdy ground below, where most of the bombs had fallen short. Or maybe the pilots had hit exactly what they were supposed to and the hangar wasn't one of them.

Pilots. Because there was more than one plane last night. How many? Maybe it didn't matter. One or two, or ten of those Warthogs would still have changed everything. The bloody mess at T29 was proof of that.

"Well?" a voice said from behind them, from inside the hangar. "What's the verdict?"

Gaby looked back and down at Mason, standing at the bottom of the incline they had climbed up earlier, shielding his eyes in their direction. The sun glinted off the bloodied weapon in his right hand; his way of warning them that he was ready should they try anything.

"Climb up and find out for yourself," Danny said.

"No thanks," Mason said. "I'm going to let you go out there

first, then I'll follow later. Go our separate ways after that. No muss, no fuss."

"What about your friends?"

"What about them? After last night, they can go fuck themselves. And as far as I'm concerned, the three of you never existed." His eyes fell on her when he added, "Especially you. No offense, but you're some bad luck, kid. Josh figured that out too late, unfortunately for him."

She gritted her teeth at the comment but managed to stop herself from responding. There was no point. Mason wasn't worth wasting her breath on.

Danny, next to her, snorted. "And they say friendship among thieves gets a bad rap." He nodded to her and Nate. "Let's find out if anything survived last night's jamboree. Also, I don't wanna be walking around with just our sticks and berries to throw if his friends come back looking for him."

"We'll be lucky if we can find a bullet in all that," Nate said.

"How are we getting down?" Gaby asked.

"Jump," Danny said.

"Jump?"

"Just pretend you're a really big bunny," Danny said, before taking a step toward the edge and, saluting them, jumped down.

"ANYTHING?" GABY ASKED as she rolled a two-by-two chunk of concrete off a rifle stock, only to find the pulverized rest on the other side.

Twisted metal rebar stuck out of the blocks, sharp edges scraping against her palms. She let go and moved on. The last thing she needed right now was to get gashed in the arms or legs because she wasn't paying attention.

"Dick Butkus," Danny said from a few yards away. He turned over a piece of landing strip and finding nothing useful, straightened up with a heavy grunt. "Less than dick. Right now, I'd settle for a tiny bit of dick." Then, he added quickly, "Don't tell Carly I said that."

Despite everything, she managed a small smile anyway.

They had been moving steadily up the airfield, hoping to find something they could use as a weapon, always wary of the remains of the buildings up ahead. An hour and a lot of physical labor later, they still had nothing to show for it, and hour two was creeping up on them fast. Nate, having spread out to their right side, had come up just as empty-handed.

Gaby spent almost as much time not falling into holes that hadn't been there yesterday as she did trying not to roll rubble onto her feet or leg. Thank God she was still wearing boots, pants, and a long-sleeve shirt, or all the gathered dust from last night's explosive booby traps and concentrated bombing would have covered her from head to toe. Even so, she still had to keep her shirt over most of her face to spare her senses from not just the stench of evaporated ghoul flesh, but other harmful elements still clinging to the air.

A saying of her father's came to mind—as much as he hated his office job, at least he wasn't "digging ditches." She felt like she was digging ditches right now…with her bare hands.

There, something on the ground.

She crouched next to a gun barrel jutting out between a skeletal chest and a block of half-buried concrete. It wasn't much, but it was about a foot long and heavy enough to make a decent blunting weapon. She pulled it out and put it into her back pocket and continued on.

The closer they got to the buildings, the more pieces of guns and shredded black uniforms they stumbled across. Most of the collaborators from last night had stayed behind at the structures, but not all of them. Not that it mattered. Out here or over there, they were still sitting ducks when the Warthogs swooped in. She tried to imagine the terror of hearing that awful bellowing noise. Did they even know what it was? It was strange to say, but she would have preferred not to know.

"Are we going to talk about it?" she said after a while.

"Talk about what?" Danny said.

"You know what. Last night. That creature… It protected us, Danny."

"Was that what it was doing?"

"Wasn't it?"

He shrugged and tossed away the broken remains of a rifle's magazine he had picked up. "Maybe it was greedy, wanted us all for itself."

"You know that's bullshit," she said, stepping over a terribly deformed head buried in the rubble, wide-open blue eyes staring up at her. She didn't know where the rest of the man's body was, or if it was even still attached to him underneath his asphalt tomb.

"Do I?" Danny said.

"It saved us, Danny."

"I have no idea what happened last night. Willie boy was always the brains of the operation. If he was here, he'd probably have come up with a dozen theories for you by now. Unfortunately for us, I'm less theory-inclined. Or capable."

"So you didn't spend all of last night and most of this morning replaying what happened in your mind?"

"I didn't say *that*. But I am telling you I didn't come up with anything that even remotely makes any lick of sense." He glanced over. "You?"

"Same."

"So there you go. What's that old saying about keeping your trap shut if you don't know anything?"

"That's never stopped you before."

"Touché," Danny said. He glanced over at Nate, who had expanded his area further to their right. "Found any gold in them thar hills, Nate-o-rama?"

Nate looked over and shook his head.

"Guess the grass ain't any greener on the other side," Danny said. Then, a few seconds later, "Hey-yo." He bent down and picked something up from the ground. "Eureka."

He turned a knife over in his hand. It was a Ka-Bar and it looked mostly intact, though the grip and a part of the serrated section was blackened by fire.

"Lucky you," Gaby said.

"Mommy did always say I had the bestest luck. You know what they used to call me in college?"

"Lucky Danny?"

"Best Luck Danny. Now that I think about it, Lucky Danny would have been preferable." He grinned and slipped the knife into his back pocket, then rubbed his hands together. "Now, let's see what we can do about getting Lucky Danny an M4. Big money, big money…"

◄━━▌ ▌━━►

"WHAT TIME IS it?" Nate asked.

"Time for you to get your own damn watch," Danny said.

"I had one, but some assholes took it."

"Excuses, excuses." Danny glanced down at his watch. "Two hours till noon. That hot date's going to have to wait."

"Shhh, Gaby's here."

Gaby ignored them and said, "I didn't know we've been searching for that long."

"Long enough for Mason to finally poke his head out of the ground and see what all the fuss is about," Danny said, looking back across the airfield at the hangar on the other side.

It was the only structure still standing (if barely) and was hard to miss. Mason was crouched on the same spot she and the others had been earlier this morning. She waited for him to move, but he didn't; he seemed content to sit up there like some gargoyle, biding his time.

"Are we really just going to let him go?" Nate asked. He shielded his eyes as he looked back at Mason.

"You want to take him out?" Danny asked.

"We could take him. Shank or not."

She glanced over at Nate, surprised to hear him making the suggestion and not Danny. Nate was always the idealist, the easygoing guy who turned the other cheek when he could. It was one of the reasons why she liked him, because a part of her was afraid she had gone too far over the edge. Nate, in so many ways, balanced her out.

It was T29, she thought. It had affected her, but it had altered Nate even more.

"Fuck him, he's not worth the trouble," Danny said. "One or a dozen more collaborators running around out here won't make any difference, but we do need to get the hell gone before more show up with something other than a knife the size of their dicks in their hands."

Gaby stood up from the remaining half of a large oak desk she had been resting on. It stuck out of the ground from what she assumed was the main administrative building, surrounded by charred furniture and toppled walls, some with holes larger than her fists in them. Her boots had been resting on a deflated tire, the rest of the vehicle hidden somewhere in the rubble.

"Where do we go from here?" Nate asked.

"Starch," Danny said. "We still have a mission to accomplish."

"How far off course are we?" she asked.

"Sixty miles. More or less."

She sighed. "Sixty miles, more or less, is a lot of walking, Danny."

"It'll be good exercise," he said before pulling his shirt back up over his mouth and nose. "Come on; let's split this joint. All this death and destruction is really bringing me down."

She followed him and Nate, stepping over a small section of still-standing wall and around a half-burned American flag jutting out from a pile of bricks. A blood-smeared arm, its owner invisible somewhere underneath the stack, waved to her as she passed.

Gaby shot another glance across the field and at the hangar. Mason, still on the wall, little more than a stick figure in the distance. She wondered if he was watching them back, waiting for them to disappear before making his move.

"Hey," Nate said from in front of her.

She looked over as he took a charred but still-in-one-piece bottle of water out of a pants pocket and held it out to her. There was some water sloshing around inside, just enough to make her lips suddenly wet.

Gaby took it gratefully. "Nice find."

"Don't tell Danny," he smiled.

"Don't tell Danny what?" Danny said from further in front of them.

"That your jokes suck," Nate said.

"Hey, I don't take critique from people with monkey haircuts."

They followed Danny out of the ruins and toward a winding road. The trees flanking it were scorched and blackened, their leaves stripped bare from last night's fire blast. The entrance looked almost foreboding, like a mouth with teeth waiting to swallow her up.

Gaby took out the gun barrel from her back pocket and gripped it tightly. It wasn't much of a weapon, but it was better than nothing.

SHE SHOULD HAVE been afraid of the dark parts of the woods, but she wasn't. She couldn't explain why, exactly, but maybe it had a little something to do with how Mercer's people had so thoroughly devastated the area that there was still gray ash lingering over the two-lane road as they walked over it.

She stopped fearing the woods and concentrated on other potential dangers instead. They were flanked by guardrails, and a sign they had passed a few minutes back confirmed they had been in Larkin Airport. There was no housing in the area, just miles of woods as far as she could tell. She hadn't seen anything that indicated the presence of the town of Larkin itself, but if the airport was here, it stood to reason the town couldn't be further down the road.

There was a lot of shade, which made the December weather even chillier than it had been in the airfield, where they were standing directly under the sun without protection. She hadn't realized how many extra layers the assault vest had given her until she didn't have it anymore. Minus her equipment and weapons, she felt naked and

THE SPEARS OF LACONIA   223

exposed, though the sounds of birds chirping among the trees helped to alleviate some of her wariness.

"You know where we're going, right?" Nate asked after a while.

Danny, walking about ten yards in front of them, nodded. "Mercer showed me his map. Starch is west."

"But we're going east."

"I noticed that. We'll look for a vehicle inside Larkin, re-gear as best we can, and then start west."

"Ah."

"Is that approval I hear?"

"Eh," Nate shrugged.

"Tough road," Danny said.

Gaby smiled. Danny and Nate bickering like an old married couple helped convince her they weren't screwed, that they could still make it out of Texas alive. She hadn't realized how much she missed having the constant moving waves of the Gulf of Mexico under her until they were gone. Of course, there was also the food, the company, and the safety of the *Trident*. She missed all those things even more—

"Car!" Danny hissed in front of them, just before he darted right.

Gaby didn't know why, but she went left. She hopped the guardrail and slipped behind the trunk of a large tree, Nate doing the same with another tree two feet over. She had been afraid he had gone right with Danny and was glad to see him hugging the trunk next to her.

She looked across the road at Danny, nearly invisible behind another gnarled tree on the other side.

"Someone asked for a ride?" Nate whispered.

It was a beat-up red pickup truck. A Chevy, by the emblem on the front grill. Like the vehicle itself, the engine had seen a lot of wear and tear, and Gaby got the impression getting it started was half the battle, and keeping it running was the other. She spotted a figure behind the wheel, wearing a cap, but the man was still too far up the road for her to make out any details.

The truck was slow, moving at barely twenty miles per hour. She couldn't tell if that was because the Chevy couldn't go any faster or if the driver wasn't certain his vehicle could handle any more speed. Either way, it seemed to take the truck forever to rumble up the road toward them. She realized now that they could have taken their time hiding and would still not have been spotted.

"Damn, that thing's slow," Nate whispered. "I think I can get out and push it down here faster."

"Give it a try," she smiled back.

"Nah, I don't feel like getting run over."

"It's moving way too slow to run anyone over."

"Yeah, but why take the chance? This tree is so nice and com-fy…"

Eventually the pickup finally reached them, and as it was passing them by, she looked into the front passenger door at the side profile of the driver. He was leaning into the steering wheel, concentrating on the road ahead. She knew now why Danny had gone right—so he would be closer to the driver side.

Ping! as something struck the other side of the truck.

The driver instinctively jammed on the brake, and even as the tires squealed against the road, Gaby caught a flash of movement as Danny bounded over the guardrail behind the vehicle and leaped into the truck bed. Gaby didn't even know Danny had the ability to move that fast. Where the hell had he been hiding that kind of speed all this time?

Before she knew what she was doing, Gaby had slipped out from behind the tree and was running back to the road.

"Gaby!" Nate hissed behind her, somehow managing to shout and whisper at the same time.

She didn't stop, because she couldn't. Danny was out there, exposed.

She leaped over the guardrail, and, ducking to lower her profile, ran toward the passenger-side door just as the driver climbed out on the other side, his door creaking loudly as he pried it open. Gaby caught a glimpse of a rifle over the top of the cab, and the driver, visible from the neck down through the windows, was already turning toward the back where Danny was.

"Hey!" she shouted.

The driver seemed to freeze momentarily, as if unsure of where to point his weapon. It was just enough of a distraction for Danny to jump out of the truck bed, the vehicle dipping and rising slightly as he did so.

A loud *bang!* as the driver fired, and Gaby thought, *Oh no, oh no,* and raced around the front hood and to the other side—

The driver was on the road, the rifle still clutched in his right hand but pointed away from Danny, who was straddling the man's chest. Danny had the sharp edge of his fire-kissed Ka-Bar pressed up against the truck driver's exposed skin. The man was gasping, the round eyes underneath the cap's brim impossibly wide.

It was a girl.

She couldn't have been more than fifteen, with long auburn hair spilling out from under the weathered cap. She was grimacing up at Danny, simultaneously trying not to swallow for fear of the knife pressed against her throat and wanting desperately to swing the rifle up and shoot him.

"Gaby," Danny said.

She hurried over and reached for the rifle, making the girl's eyes flicker over to her in alarm while her fingers tightened on the weapon.

"Oh, come on," Danny said, almost exasperated. "I hate to be chauvinistic about this, but I'm clearly on top here."

The driver sighed, and Gaby wrestled the weapon from her. She stepped back and glanced up and down the road, listening for signs of another vehicle. There had been hundreds of collaborators at the airfield last night, all of them buried under the rubble this morning. But that didn't mean there weren't more still in the area that could have heard the girl's gunshot.

"Oh shit, you're bleeding," Nate said as he rounded the back of the truck.

Gaby thought he was talking to her, but no, it was Danny. Blood dripped from the bottom of his right ear, where the bullet had creased him.

Danny wiped at the scratch. "You shot me."

"You threw something at my car!" the girl shouted back.

"It was just a rock. Relax."

Gaby noticed a large dent in the driver-side door.

"A couple swings with a hammer, and it's good as new," Danny said. "You got insurance, right?"

"You can't take my truck!" the girl shouted (too loudly).

"Afraid I can, and I must."

"You can't!"

"Yes, I can." Danny stood up, taking the knife away with him. "What're you doing out here, anyway?"

The girl didn't answer him. She stood up, stumbling a bit and cradling her left arm. Her elbow was scraped and bloodied, and she kept looking back at the vehicle.

"What's inside?" Gaby asked.

The girl gave her a quick, scared glance. Gaby wondered if she ever looked that young, even before the world ended.

"We're going to take the truck," Gaby said. "If you have something in there that you want to keep, speak up now."

"Aren't you generous," Danny said.

"We're already taking her truck; might as well let her keep whatever we don't need."

"We should hurry up and go, guys," Nate said, walking over to them. "No telling who might have heard that gunshot."

"Alice," the girl said.

"Alice?" Danny repeated.

"Alice, come out," the girl said. She wasn't talking to them.

Danny backed up as the driver-side passenger door opened and a small figure scrambled out in jeans and boots. Both articles of clothing looked about a couple of sizes too large for her, but they were cinched in place by a belt. She had big brown eyes and looked nervously from Danny to Gaby before running over and grabbing the bigger girl around the waist.

"Well, damn," Danny sighed.

CHAPTER 18

KEO

"YOU THINK SHE bought it?" Jordan asked, watching the boat as it faded into the distance. In a few seconds, they wouldn't be able to tell there were three heavily-armed women in a tender out there in the endless expanse of the Gulf of Mexico.

You should be on that boat too, pal. So why aren't you?

"Bought what?" he said.

"About Frank."

"It's the truth."

"But not the *whole* truth."

He shrugged. "Close enough."

"I thought she'd, I don't know, press you more on him."

"She's got a lot on her mind, and when you've been through as much as she has, you learn to prioritize. The better question is, why aren't you on that boat with Lara heading back to the *Trident?*"

"Are we going through this again?"

She sounded exasperated, though he couldn't understand why. He had offered her a chance at probably the best thing that was going to come around in a long time—space on the *Trident*, out there somewhere, safe from all this madness—and she'd turned it down.

Just like you did. So who's the bigger idiot?

Probably a tie...

"Gillian's my friend," Jordan said. "I have a lot of friends back in T18. I'm not going to stand by and watch them get massacred by Mercer. Not if I can do something about it."

"I'm just going back for Gillian and no one else, Jordan."

"There's nothing that says we have to stay tied at the hips when we get there. You go do your thing, and I'll do mine." She turned around and began walking up the beach, back to the road. "You coming?"

He sighed, then turned to follow her. "What about Tobias?"

"What about him?"

"You know where he is right now?"

"The backup location. He should still be there, unless something's happened." She glanced back at him. "You want to ask him for help," she added. It wasn't a question.

He nodded. "Unless he's still licking his wounds, then we could use a few more guns. Or a dozen."

"So it's 'we' now?"

"If you insist on sticking around, we should at least do this together. Strength in numbers, and all that. Will he help?"

She thought about it for a moment before nodding. "I think he will. I can't see him sitting by and letting Mercer's people run a tank through T18. Not after everything he—*we*—went through to save them."

"We'll need a vehicle. Can't walk all the way back to League City. Well, we can, but I'd prefer not to."

"Too bad the tank's out of fuel. Maybe you can push it and I'll steer."

"What am I, the Hulk?"

"I thought you didn't read comic books."

"I don't, but everyone knows the Hulk. Big green guy with ripped short-shorts."

"Close," she chuckled. "Anyway, if you don't wanna push me, maybe you can carry me. Let me ride piggyback."

"Only if we take turns."

She gave him a brief smile, and he returned it.

"I like this better," she said.

"What's that?"

"When you're not being an asshole."

"When was I ever an asshole?"

"About half the time you open your mouth."

He snorted and got another grin from her.

"You really think he's still out there?" Jordan asked as they stepped up onto the road. She didn't have to say who "he" was. "Tell me the truth."

"I don't know."

"You sounded pretty confident with Lara. I almost believed you."

"I guess I'm getting better at lying."

"How was it supposed to work, anyway? You were just going to introduce Frank to her? 'Hey, Lara, this is Frank. Frank, this is Lara. You kids chat.' And what, she wouldn't ask any of the obvious questions, like why she's talking to a ghoul?"

"Funny, that's what I asked him the last time we were together in Sunport."

"What did he say?"

Keo shrugged. "I got the sense he hadn't thought that far ahead. Or if he had, he didn't feel like telling me."

THERE WERE TWO trucks, both Ford F-150s, which at this point Keo was sure was as ubiquitous to Texas as dickheads with guns trying to kill him. The vehicles were white and tan, both covered in dirt and mud, looking well-used. They were moving on large tires that chewed up the highway at a steady pace toward the beach.

He was expecting some kind of military hardware on display, but no, there were just two guys in the back of each truck, with two more inside. He couldn't make out faces at this distance, even looking through a pair of binoculars he'd gotten from Gregson's tank, but he could see just enough to know they were wearing black long-sleeve uniforms.

Collaborators.

He lay flat on his stomach in the fields, ten meters from the road. This part of the beach still had tall, swaying grass that was untouched by the tank's flamethrower. Somewhere on the other side of the two-lane road was Jordan, waiting for his signal.

"Full-auto," he said into the radio now, not bothering to whisper because the trucks were still too far away to overhear. The radios, like the binoculars and the spare ammo he had on him, were salvaged from the tank.

"Spray and pray?" Jordan said through the radio. He thought he detected a hint of amusement in her voice.

"Hopefully throw a little aiming in there, too. I'll take the first truck, and you concentrate on the second one. Shoot anything that moves."

She didn't answer that time.

"Jordan," he said. "Shoot anything that moves. We only need one working vehicle. Take out the two in the back first. Don't stop shooting until they both go down. Then focus on the ones inside. Got it?"

"Got it," she said.

"You good?"

"Yeah."

"Jordan…"

"This isn't my first rodeo, Keo," she said, sounding slightly annoyed. "I was outside T18, running around with Tobias for months before you showed up. I can handle this."

"I know you can," he said, hoping it was at least convincing.

The collaborators charging toward him now had already seen the Abrams parked out there under the sun behind him. It was hard to miss, surrounded by barren earth charred black by fire. The trucks hadn't left the road yet, so he guessed they were approaching the situation with caution, maybe a little bit afraid that cannon was still operational. Playing back what Gregson had said in his mind, Keo wondered if these incoming threats were part of the group that had fought with the tank yesterday and were just now showing up to finish what their ghoul allies had failed to do last night.

"We overshot our mark yesterday," Gregson had said, *"ended up having to fight it out with those collaborator assholes."*

He lowered the binoculars and laid it next to his pack, which had begun to tremble slightly as the vehicles neared. The four in the truck beds were peeking over the cabs, but they clearly only had eyes for the tank parked out there in the field, which was exactly what he was hoping for.

He picked up the M4 and focused on the first truck—the white one—as it sped toward him.

Fifty meters…

Forty…

He could make out the two figures inside the cab now. Both men—one had a bright red beard and the other looked bald.

Thirty meters…

The two in the back looked nervous. Both men. Twenties. The lack of a machine gun mounted in front of them did wonders for Keo's confidence. The last thing he wanted was to go head-to-head with a technical.

Twenty meters…

He smelled overworked tires and leaking fluid, both indications the vehicles had been on the road for some time now. He wondered how many other collaborators were running around out there, trying to deal with Mercer's encroachment.

Ten meters!

Keo shoved every other thought away, popped up onto one knee, and looked through the red dot sight at the front windshield of the white truck. He pulled the trigger and stitched the glass from right to left, starting with the driver before picking up the front passenger, and didn't stop shooting until the truck swerved as the man behind the steering wheel did exactly what Keo expected—he slammed on the brake instead of trying to drive through the gunfire.

The first F-150 was already skidding when Keo heard the *pop-pop-pop* of Jordan's rifle from the other side of the road. Keo concentrated on his target as it came to a stop, presenting its backside to him—along with the two uniformed men scrambling around in the truck bed. They were picking themselves up, having tumbled off their feet sometime during the chaos.

Keo flicked his fire selector to semi-auto and shot the first soldier in the chest as he was rising, an AK-47 clutched clumsily in one hand. The man disappeared behind the closed tailgate, while the second one—younger than Keo had first thought; he couldn't have been more than eighteen—was spinning around, face frozen in shock, just before Keo put two rounds into the largest part of him.

Meanwhile, the tan truck had done the exact same thing as the white one—its driver had hit the brakes when he saw the lead vehicle skidding in front of him. It always amazed Keo how poorly civilians reacted to being shot at.

He was already on his feet and racing through the grass, while at the same time angling his way back toward the highway. Jordan had continued firing, her rifle slamming round after round toward the second truck. Keo had a fresh magazine in his M4 before he was within sight of the driver, who was still alive and had spotted Keo as he stepped onto the road.

Keo put two fresh bullets into the windshield, directly over the spot where the driver was. The man twitched and must have stepped on the gas, because the truck lurched forward and barreled through the fields and kept going for a good thirty meters before finally slowing down on the other side.

He ignored the runaway truck and focused on the tan one still parked on the road in front of him. Fresh blood was splashed across the windshield, blocking his view of the passenger, but he could see the other driver just fine. The man had already opened his car door and was standing outside with his rifle, shooting over the truck bed at Jordan's position.

Keo jogged up the road, and he was within thirty meters before the man finally heard his approach and turned around. Keo shot him through the open driver-side door window and watched the man drop to the pavement.

The man was still alive when Keo reached him, though he had dropped his rifle and was in the process of reaching for his sidearm. Keo shot him in the chest, and the man stopped moving.

"Jordan!" he shouted.

"I'm good!" she shouted back.

He hurried to the back and looked into the truck bed. There was just one body—a young woman with a blonde ponytail—lying on her back in a pool of blood, staring up at him. She was clutching her stomach with both hands, blood pumping through dirt-covered fingers as she struggled to keep breathing. For a moment he thought it was Gaby, but the cheekbones were too sharp and the nose a little too flat.

Another body lay on the highway behind the vehicle where it had fallen. A man in his thirties, his face pressed into the hot pavement.

"Clear!" Keo shouted.

Jordan picked herself up and jogged over. "You okay?" she asked.

"I'm good," he said. "You?"

"I told you, this isn't my first rodeo."

"Noted."

When she reached the truck, Jordan looked into the back and saw the girl, and her face paled. Maybe this wasn't her first rodeo, but seeing your victim up close was a different animal than shooting them from a distance while looking from behind a rifle.

"Check the other truck, just in case," Keo said.

She looked up at him, opened her mouth to say something, but didn't. Instead, she gave the girl another look, then turned and hurried over to the white Ford parked in the grass halfway to the beach.

Keo turned back to the woman. She was still alive, if just barely. The bullet had hit her in the stomach and it didn't matter how hard she held on; the blood wasn't going to stop pouring out of her.

"Sorry," Keo said, and slung his rifle and reached for his sidearm, but by the time he looked back up, the girl had stopped moving completely. She continued staring, wide-eyed, at the bright morning sun above her.

Keo put the handgun away and checked his watch: 10:16 A.M.

He glanced up the road, back at Sunport's industrial buildings in the distance.

On the other side was T18...and Gillian.

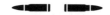

"WHAT ABOUT GREGSON?" Jordan asked when they were back on the road in the tan Ford F-150, with the beach fading in the rearview mirror.

There was blood in the front passenger seat where Jordan had shot out the window the same time she killed the man next to it. To avoid sitting in the mess she had made, Jordan was in the backseat with the rest of their supplies, including the AR-15s he'd taken from the tank and everything they had managed to salvage from the other truck.

The driver of the vehicle had somehow managed to escape Jordan's initial volley unscathed, until Keo killed him outside on the road, so Keo had the luxury of not sitting in someone's blood as he drove. Not that he hadn't done something like it before and had a feeling he'd have to do it again in the future.

"What about him?" Keo said.

"Even after everything he's done, I don't like the idea of leaving him out there."

"You wanna go back and put him out of his misery?"

"That's not what I meant."

"What did you mean?"

"I don't like leaving him out there, hurt."

"He's getting what he's got coming."

"A lot of people can say the same about you."

"And they'd be right."

She was watching him curiously in the rearview mirror. "You really believe that?"

"Yeah," he said without hesitation.

"I don't."

"That's because you're a good and decent human being, Jordan."

"When did that become a bad thing?"

"About the same time the world ended."

She didn't answer, and instead looked out her window at the outskirts of Sunport rolling by. He couldn't even begin to guess what was going through her mind at the moment. Maybe it was still Gregson, or the girl she had shot. Maybe both. Or she could be wishing she had left with Lara, like he had told her to.

"Any idea who's taken over T18 after Steve didn't come back from Santa Marie Island?" he asked.

Jordan thought about it for a moment. Then, "A few people come to mind, but no one stands out. Steve had that place on a pretty tight leash. I would have said Jack, but he's dead, too."

"What's the protocol when one of the leaders get taken out?"

"I have no idea. I don't even know how Steve got chosen in the first place."

"Tobias never talked about it? Steve told me they used to be co-leaders."

She shook her head. "He never did."

"What about Gillian?"

"What about her?"

He grinned. "How do you think she's going to react when I show back up there again?"

Jordan smiled back at him. "Gillian loves you, Keo."

"She has a strange way of showing it."

"Don't blame her for what happened with Jay. We thought you were dead. It was worse for her. There were times when I didn't think she'd make it. Not because she couldn't physically, but because she didn't want to."

Keo didn't know how to respond to that, so he kept quiet.

"In a lot of ways, that baby saved her life," Jordan continued. "Don't hate me, but she made the right decision. I don't mean sleeping with Jay; I don't know why she did that. I mean deciding to stay behind, even after you finally showed up."

"I know," he said.

And he did, which was why he was fully prepared to move on. The truth hurt, but it was undeniable. Gillian, in her current state, would have struggled to survive out here. Maybe if he had gotten her to the *Trident*, where Zoe could have helped with the pregnancy, but there was a lot of space between T18 and the Gulf of Mexico.

Besides, who was he kidding? Happy endings were for other people, not someone like him. He had come to accept that long ago, even though, for a short time there, he had almost managed to convince himself that he deserved one, too.

What an idiot. I guess we know better now, don't we?

CHAPTER 19

LARA

"I CAN'T BELIEVE he didn't come back with you," Carly said, even before Lara had completely stepped inside the bridge of the *Trident*. "And after dragging our asses down here, too. You should have given him a swift kick in the balls for wasting our time."

"He has his reasons," Lara said.

"He always has his reasons. What were they this time?"

"He had someone with him named Frank that he wanted me to meet. Or this Frank wanted to meet me. I'm not sure which."

"Frank?" Carly said. "What a stupid name. Sounds like an out of work porno actor."

"You know a lot about that?" Blaine asked from his usual position behind the yacht's controls.

"Hey, I had cable TV, just like everyone else. Scrambled, sure, but you can still see stuff if you look at it at just the right angles."

"Makes sense to me," Blaine said. He glanced back at Lara: "Maybe this Frank heard one of your radio messages and wanted to meet the woman behind it. Like it or not, you're pretty popular these days."

"Maybe," she said, though she didn't believe that could even be remotely true. Nothing Keo had told her about this Frank made him sound like a "fan." Besides, just the thought of someone out there going through all this trouble just to "meet" her was…unsettling.

What was that Keo had said about Frank?

"He had information about the ghouls. How they operate, their chain of command, all the nitty-gritty stuff. He also said he knew how to beat them."

She looked at Carly and Blaine, then at the wide-open and calm ocean outside the windshield behind them. What good was Frank's information to her, even if it was true? Or to Vera and Elise, and all the others onboard the *Trident* at the moment? She couldn't think of a single thing.

We should have gone straight to the Bengal Islands, Will. You would have taken us there, wouldn't you? You would have done the right thing. The smart thing. You always did.

"It's a moot point anyway, because he wasn't there," Lara said. "They got separated two nights ago. Keo says he's still alive, but I'm not sure he actually believes it."

"So that's why he didn't radio in," Carly said. "A lot of people are losing their radios these days…"

Lara put a hand on Carly's arm and they exchanged a brief, private smile. It was a rare occasion to see Carly so somber, and Lara thought she needed the support, even if it was just a simple touch. God knew Carly had done so much more for her over the last few weeks.

"So what *did* happen over there last night?" Blaine asked. He was, thankfully, oblivious to the private moment taking place behind him. "If Keo was on that beach, that means he was either involved or he saw what went down."

"A little of both," Lara said.

"Why am I not surprised?" Carly said.

Lara told them about Gregson and Mercer, about the tank, the destruction it had caused including the scorched fields and the cemetery of bones, and what Gregson and Keo had told her was happening out there in the rest of Texas.

"Damn," Carly said when Lara was done. "Sounds like a party I'm glad no one invited me to." She might have even shivered a bit. "They have that kind of firepower?"

"I saw the tank with my own eyes," Lara said. "I don't have any reason to disbelieve this Gregson."

"People lie, Lara."

"I don't think Gregson was lying. He didn't have any reasons to at the time."

"But they're definitely not the U.S. Army?" Blaine asked.

"No," Lara said. "Far from it. They're dangerous. That's why we should steer as far away from them as we can. And that means staying the hell away from the coast unless we absolutely have to."

"I won't argue with that."

"So what about Keo?" Carly asked. "He's gone for good this time?"

"I think so, yeah," Lara nodded.

"Too bad. Carrie was really looking forward to having him back onboard. You told her yet?"

"I didn't see her on my way here, but Bonnie said she'd talk to her. Were they ever involved? Keo and Carrie?"

"I don't think so. From what she's told me, he was stuck on this Gillian chick twenty-four seven. But not anymore, I take it."

"I guess it's complicated."

"It's Keo, so why wouldn't it be?"

"There was another woman on the beach with him. Her name was Jordan."

"That guy works fast," Blaine chuckled.

"Let the man have his distractions," Carly said. "I'm a little—okay, a *lot*—annoyed with him for bringing us down here, but the guy's done a lot for us. He deserves a little tail."

Lara smiled, remembering how clueless Keo had been when she mentioned that Jordan probably wouldn't be leaving with her. Then, later, when Jordan confirmed it, the numbers still didn't seemed to have computed for Keo.

I guess he really is still stuck on Gillian, she remembered thinking.

"So what's the order, boss?" Blaine asked.

"How are we for fuel?" Lara asked.

Blaine glanced down at the monitor in front of him. "I'm not gonna lie; we're running low. We'll be running on reserves soon, but it's enough to get us back to Port Arthur and hit another one of the refueling depots on Gage's list."

Carly looked at Lara, and she was almost pleading. "Tell me we're going back."

"We are," Lara said. To Blaine: "Pull up anchor and take us back."

"Thank Jesus Lord," Carly said, not even trying to hide the relief on her face.

"What about the fuel situation?" Blaine asked.

"One problem at a time," Lara said.

Carly walked over and casually draped one arm over Blaine's shoulder. "Boss lady's spoken. Port Arthur or bust, *el chauffeuro*. Is that how you say chauffeur in Spanish?"

Blaine grunted. "Close enough."

◀━▌ ▐━▶

"TOO BAD ABOUT Keo," Carly said as she walked Lara back to her cabin. "We could have really used him, especially now with stupid Danny still running around out there, refusing to pick up my phone calls."

"He'll be fine," Lara said. "He's got Gaby and Nate to watch his back."

"Gaby, yes. Nate? I'm not so sure."

"Is it the haircut?"

"What else? I gotta get Gaby to convince him to cut it. She could tell that boy to jump into the ocean and wrestle a shark, and he'd do it."

"Guys will do anything for a pretty girl, I guess."

"How do you think I'd been paying the bills before the world went kaput?"

"No details, please."

"Your loss."

They entered her cabin and Lara unclasped her gun belt and

tossed it on the small bed, then went to a small fridge in the corner and took out a bottle of water. She walked over to her bed and sat down, opened the nightstand, and took out one of Zoe's bottles. She shook out two of the painkillers and downed them with the water.

"Arm giving you trouble?" Carly asked.

"It's manageable."

"You sure?"

"It itches more than it hurts."

"I guess that's good."

"The pills help."

Carly caressed one side of her neck. "At least some dumb bitch didn't shoot you in the neck."

Lara smiled. "I was lucky. Gage could have done a lot more damage."

"It's funny," Carly said.

"What's that?"

"I think he actually thought we'd forget about all the shit he'd done, or was planning to do to the island." Carly looked thoughtful while staring across the room at the window. "Funny the things people manage to convince themselves."

"Danny will come back, Carly," Lara said. "He'll contact us when he gets the chance."

"But…"

"But nothing."

Carly narrowed her eyes at her. "What aren't you telling me?"

"I told you everything."

"No, you haven't." She didn't take her eyes away. "Tell me, Lara. What did you learn out there that you're not telling me now?"

Lara sighed. "Mercer."

"What about him?"

"I told you his people are attacking the towns."

Carly nodded.

"One of them was a place called T29," Lara continued. "It's between Hellion and Starch."

"Hellion," Carly said. "That's where Danny and Gaby were the day before their last call-in. The place where they ran into some trouble."

"Yeah."

Carly paused, maybe processing the information, or maybe she already knew and was too afraid to know more.

"Tell me the rest," her friend said anyway.

"There's a chance the expedition might have run across T29 on their way to Starch. I don't know. But it's Danny…"

"Yeah, it's Danny," Carly said quietly.

"He'll be fine, Carly."

"I know," the redhead said, smiling back at her. "Besides, he promised me he'd come back and he knows I'd kick his ass if he didn't keep it."

Lara gave her friend a pursed smile, wondering to herself how many times she had told herself that exact same thing about Will…

◄━━▌ ▌━━►

HER RADIO ON the nightstand squawked sometime later. When she opened her eyes, it was still daylight and there were no signs of Carly, who had stayed behind for another hour to talk and who was still talking when the pills kicked in and Lara drifted off to sleep.

"Lara, you awake?" Blaine said through the radio.

She rolled over and snatched the radio, then pressed the transmit lever.

Is it Will? she wanted to say, but instead, the words that came out were, "Is it Danny?"

"No, sorry," Blaine said.

Goddammit, Danny. First Will, now you. You goddamn Rangers.

"What's going on?" she asked, sitting up on the bed. Her head was pounding and she made a mental note to talk to Zoe about switching meds to something less…torturous.

"We need you on the bridge."

"Are we there already?"

"We're not even close. There's something else."

"I'm on my way," she said, and climbed out of bed, grimacing when she accidentally reached down to push up with her left arm without thinking.

She grabbed her gun belt and clasped it into place. With the radio in hand, she headed out into the hallway. Turned right and walked the short distance to the bridge on the other end.

The door was open and Carly and Blaine were already inside, surrounded by sunlight. She was surprised to see that it was still afternoon, which meant she hadn't slept more than a few hours at the most.

Carly looked over. "Hey, sleepyhead."

"Sorry about dozing off on you."

"Eh, I liked talking to myself better anyway."

"How long was I asleep?"

"Four hours, give or take."

"You should have woken me sooner."

"No point, until now."

She looked out the front windshield, expecting to see something that didn't belong, but there was just the familiar blue waters staring back at her. "What am I looking at?"

"Someone wants you," Carly said, and pressed one of the many buttons along the curved boat console.

Lara didn't know what the button did until she heard a young woman's voice slowly rising through the bridge's speakers. It was slightly distorted—until Carly pressed something else and the voice cleared up.

"The scanner picked it up about thirty minutes ago," Blaine said. "Normally I wouldn't bother with the radio, but it can get pretty lonely up here by myself."

Lara focused on the voice. "Is she live?"

"Oh yeah," Carly said. "Poor girl's been saying the same thing over and over since I showed up."

Carly pressed the same button a few more times and the volume increased, the voice becoming clearer:

"...goes out to Lara. If you're hearing this, it's urgent you make contact. We desperately need your help."

There was a brief pause, then the woman (*girl*) continued, this time from the beginning:

"This message goes out to Lara. If you're hearing this, it's urgent you make contact. We desperately need your help."

Carly turned down the volume until Lara could barely hear the voice. Not that she really needed to. The girl was simply reading the same three sentences over and over.

"How do you know I'm the 'Lara' she's looking for?" Lara asked.

Carly rolled her eyes. "Is there more than one Lara spreading the news on the radio that no one told me about? It's you, girl."

"She's been repeating the same message for thirty minutes?"

"She took a break about ten minutes ago," Blaine said. "Then she changed channel and repeated it. I wonder where she got that idea."

"Yeah, we're trailblazers, all right," Carly said. "All the young'uns are following in our footsteps." Carly smiled at her. "You're *mucho* popular these days, kiddo. The first celebrity in the apocalypse, if you will. First, some guy gets Keo to call us down here just for a meet and greet, now there are people actually *calling* you on the radio. I'm kinda jealous."

"They're pretty smart," Blaine said. "Whoever the 'we' is with her. They know we're still broadcasting, so we're likely to also be monitoring the frequencies."

"Good for her," Carly said, "but we're not going to answer, are we?"

"She says they need our help. *Your* help, Lara. Desperately, apparently. Do we just ignore that?"

"Yes," Carly said. She looked at Blaine, then at Lara. "Guys, come on. Did we forget what happened with Song Island? What that Karen bitch almost did to us? *We don't answer strange calls over the radio.*"

"If we didn't, we wouldn't know about Beecher," Blaine said. "Or that kid in Japan. Those guys in New York, Alaska...on and on."

"But none of those people wanted something from us." She focused on Lara. "This is a very bad idea. You have to see that."

"She's got a point," Lara said.

Blaine nodded. "I guess."

"Don't guess, *know*," Carly said. "We need to go back to Port Arthur. We should never have left in the first place, but I'll accept it, because it's Keo and God knows we owe K-pop like crazy. But we have to go back now. Tell me we're going to ignore this and go back for Danny and Gaby. That's what Will would do. You know that, Lara. He'd take care of his own first."

Lara pursed her lips into a half-smile. Apparently she wasn't the only one who was asking herself *What would Will do?* a lot these days.

"Lara?" Carly said.

"We keep going to Port Arthur, as planned," Lara said. "We'll pick up Danny and Gaby, refuel and resupply, and then we head south to the Bengal Islands."

"Thank you," Carly said.

"I should have done it a month ago. I'm sorry I waited so long."

"Hey, better late than never." Carly sighed with relief and hugged her (maybe a bit too tightly, and Lara winced a bit from a jolt of pain along her left arm), and whispered, "Thank you. Thank you, thank you, *thank you*."

"You're welcome," she whispered back.

Despite the radio's lowered volume, Lara could still hear the girl's voice coming through the bridge's speakers, talking to her, asking her to make contact, desperately seeking her help. She did her best to shut it out and concentrated on the shifting waters of the Gulf of Mexico outside the window instead.

Somewhere out there was Danny, Gaby, and Nate, waiting for her to come pick them up, hoping they hadn't been abandoned. She was the one who had sent them out there, and she'd be damned if she was going to leave them behind.

Not again. Not again…

CHAPTER 20

GABY

THE GIRL'S NAME was Taylor, and she was fifteen. Her sister, Alice, was eleven and reminded Gaby of Elise and Vera, but unlike those two, Alice was malnourished and her clothes hung off her body. Her big sister didn't look any more well-fed, but that could have just been the large man's overalls and bad haircut. Which was to say, she probably cut her own hair and Alice's in the year since the end of the world.

If Alice hadn't come out of the truck, Gaby was pretty sure she, Danny, and Nate would have been on the road to Starch by now. Or maybe they would have even reached the town already. It was only sixty miles to the west of them, after all. Though with the collaborators likely on high alert after yesterday, maybe she was being too generous.

Instead, they were somewhere in the woods surrounding Larkin, waiting in the living room of a small cottage as Taylor carried a pile of rifles out from a back room while Alice dragged a raggedy backpack along the wooden floor after her.

"Someone must have been real nice, because I think Christmas just came early," Danny said.

"You'd be surprised what you can find out there, just sitting around," Taylor said. "You can take whatever you want. I don't even know how to use most of them, and I'm a little scared to even try."

She laid the weapons down on the heavily chipped wooden kitchen counter, and Gaby, Nate, and Danny walked over and formed a semicircle around it.

"That thing's bigger than you," Danny said to Alice.

The girl grunted back at him. Danny grinned and took the backpack from her and opened it, then pulled out unopened boxes of bullets and three handguns—two automatics, including a Glock, and a six-shot revolver.

"God bless Texas," Danny said, and laid the handguns down next to the pile. "Dig in, kids."

"You don't want to keep any of these?" Nate asked Taylor.

The teenager shook her head. "I already have the hunting rifle."

"She won't let me have one," Alice frowned.

"You're too young."

"Not anymore."

Taylor rolled her eyes. "I'm not talking about this again."

The younger sibling had a point, Gaby thought. They had all grown up fast these days. You had to, or you didn't at all.

"Where'd you find them?" Nate asked.

"Mostly around town," Taylor said. "We haven't really strayed too far from Larkin. There are fish in the pond out back, so we've been able to keep going with the supplies we took from homes and stores nearby. There's just the two of us, and we don't really need a lot."

"Last night must have been scary," Gaby said.

Taylor nodded. "It was like listening to World War III out there. Every time those planes went by, it sounded like they were right on top of us."

"They were flying low," Danny said. "Warthogs do their best work at close range."

"It helped that the collaborators didn't show up with anti-aircraft guns," Nate added. "I guess they didn't know what they were dealing with."

"They do now. Which means we have to be more careful on the

roads. They're going to be shooting first and fuck the questions." He glanced quickly at Alice. "I mean, forget the questions."

Alice smiled back. "I've heard worse."

"I bet you have."

"Come on," Taylor said, and the girls drifted over to the other side of the kitchen, where Taylor opened a can of pineapple for the younger girl using a manual can opener. Alice's mouth was already watering before Taylor even got the lid all the way off.

In the year since The Purge, Gaby could see that the two sisters had made a decent life for themselves out here. The cottage itself was located in a wooded area with a small pond behind them. The girls had no idea how to fish twelve months ago, but Taylor had learned pretty fast.

"There's no refrigeration, so we pretty much cook and eat them the same day after I catch them," Taylor had explained.

Adapt or perish, right, Lara?

The cottage had faded yellow walls and dirt-covered floors, with two bedrooms in the back and a shack for supplies outside. It was out of the way, with no actual roads leading to its front doors, which was how the sisters had managed to avoid detection from both humans and ghouls. She hadn't asked if this was their place or if they had just stumbled across it; the fact was, those things just didn't matter anymore.

Gaby looked back at the weapons on the counter between her, Danny, and Nate. There were three hunting rifles, a pump-action shotgun, and two AR-15s in the pile. Danny snatched up one of the rifles—it was tanned and looked well-worn, with chips along the sides and stock. He pulled out the magazine, found it empty, and began reloading it with rounds from one of the ammo boxes.

Nate picked up the other rifle and offered it to her across the counter.

"And it's not even my birthday," she smiled at him.

"Just remember that when I actually forget your birthday," Nate said.

"Charming."

"Just trying to score bonus points for future screwups."

"Oh, you said screw*ups*," Danny said. "I thought you said something else."

"Not in front of the kids," Gaby smirked.

The rifle was matte black, and unlike the one Danny was turning over in his hands, hers looked almost new. It had a collapsible stock, which she thought was a nice touch. Both had simple red dot sights unlike the hunting rifles, which were equipped with very long scopes. They were good for long-distance shooting, but she'd learned to appreciate the semi-automatic capabilities of an AR. The ability to send a lot of rounds downrange in a short amount of time, she'd found, couldn't be beat in a gunfight.

Gaby looked over at Taylor. "You've never used any of these?"

The girl shook her head. "Those things are too complicated. The one I have is easier. Just pull that thingie back and shoot."

Gaby smiled. Was she ever that innocent when it came to weapons?

"So there wasn't anything there?" Taylor asked. "Back at the airfield?"

"Just a lot of rubble," Gaby said. "What were you hoping to find?"

"Anything useful. I thought about waiting a couple of days, but I guess I was too curious about last night."

"You know what they say," Danny said, "curiosity killed the kid in the cottage."

"Now you tell me," Taylor said.

Gaby liked the girl. She would have been pretty if she let her hair grow out; or, at least, stopped cutting it herself. The fact that Taylor had managed to keep her little sister alive out here all by herself made her even more impressive.

"We'll be heading back this way when we're done with our thing," Gaby said. "If you want, we can pick you two up, take you back to the *Trident* with us."

"You mean, and live on a boat?" Taylor said doubtfully.

"It's not as bad as it sounds. In fact, it's pretty great."

"It'd be cool to live on the ocean," Alice said wistfully between mouthfuls of pineapple.

Gaby's mouth watered just looking at the syrup dripping down the girl's chin. When was the last time she had some of that? It was probably before that mess at Mercy Hospital, back in Louisiana. It seemed like a lifetime ago now.

"I'm just giving you the option," she said to Taylor. "It's up to you, but you don't have to decide now."

Taylor nodded. "We'll think about it. When will you guys be back?"

Gaby glanced at Danny.

He shrugged. "As early as a day, as late as a week."

"Basically, whenever," Nate said.

"What I said."

"Not really."

"Close enough."

"We don't know for sure," Gaby said, seeing the confusion on Taylor's face. "But it shouldn't be more than a few days."

"Is it safer out there?" Taylor asked.

"On the *Trident*? Yes. Out there, on the ocean, you don't have worry about people—or other things—showing up at your front door."

"Or bad men on the road trying to steal your ride," Danny added.

"And that, too."

Taylor didn't say anything. Gaby could see the indecision on her face, that struggle between burgeoning hope and trying to stamp it down because hope was a hard thing to embrace these days. She'd learned that the hard way, too. There was a time when she hoped Will would finally contact them, to tell Lara that he was okay, and come back.

I should have known better. Even Will can't survive out here by himself.

"When you come back, we'll know for sure," Taylor said. She sounded certain; either that, or she was putting on a very good front.

"You wouldn't happen to have a ham radio, would you, kid?"

Danny asked her.

"I don't even know what that is."

"It's definitely *not* a radio made out of ham."

"Is there a Radio Shack or electronic store in town?" Nate asked. "They might carry one."

"I don't really remember," Taylor said. "There's a couple of strip malls, but I don't remember a place that sells just radios."

"Should we look anyway?" Gaby asked Danny. "We need to let the *Trident* know we're still alive. They must be crazy with worry right now."

Danny shook his head. "Starch is sixty miles from here. We can get there in a few hours even using just the smaller roads. All we have to do is stay out of trouble until then."

"That's the trick, isn't it?" Nate said.

"Indeed it is, Nate-ometer. The facility will have everything we need. Best part: no poking around Hicksville, USA, for them." He slung the AR-15 and looked back at Taylor. "This everything, kid?"

"That's all I found," Taylor said. "What, you want more?"

"Normally this would be enough, but after what we've seen? Hells yeah. I'll take whatever else you got."

"That's it, sorry."

"No grenades?"

"Grenades? Um, no."

"Hey, couldn't hurt to ask." Danny started to go, but stopped and turned back to the counter and picked up the pump-action shotgun. "Just in case…"

WITH ONLY SIXTY miles between them and Starch, a mostly serviceable ride, and now armed, they felt good enough about their situation that they decided to eat first before taking off. They didn't want to dig further into the sisters' stash, so Danny and Nate spent a few minutes outside at the pond with a pair of fishing poles, catching a dozen fish in less than ten minutes. A year's worth of spawning, with only the two girls to cut into the inventory, meant fish were attacking the plastic lures as soon as they hit the water.

Like shooting fish in a barrel, she thought.

They were in the beat-up truck and back on the road by midday, with more than five hours left to reach Harold Campbell's facility. More than enough time, unless they encountered obstacles along the road, which after yesterday was a very real possibility. It wasn't just collaborators they had to worry about, though; it was Mercer's men, too. Texas had become impossibly deadlier since the last time they set foot on it, something she didn't think she would ever say a year ago.

We should have stayed on the Trident. *I wonder if Lara is saying the same thing to herself right now?*

"Tough kids," Nate was saying from the backseat. "Did we ever ask them if that was their place?"

"No," Gaby said.

"I guess it doesn't matter."

Nate was looking out the rear window, even though the cottage had long disappeared behind a wall of trees. Danny picked their way through the unpaved dirt trails, eventually locating a stretch of empty country road that, according to a sign, would take them away from Larkin and westward. The idea was to avoid the main highways completely.

As they headed back toward civilization, Gaby found herself listening for the telltale signs of approaching warplanes from above.

"Warthogs do their best work at close range," Danny had said.

She had seen that for herself yesterday, and just the memory of it made her shiver unwittingly. She hoped the men in the truck with her hadn't noticed, and when neither one of them said anything—especially Nate behind her—she guessed she was safe.

Nate had one of the bolt-action hunting rifles in his lap, the backpack with the extra ammo next to him, and they each had one of the handguns. She had the Glock in her front waistband (what she wouldn't have given for a tactical gun belt at the moment), Nate liked the Smith & Wesson revolver, while Danny had chosen the Sig

Sauer. She wasn't going to complain about the extra weapon or the spare magazines, but the fact was, if they had to rely on them today, it meant her hope of a smooth sailing to Starch had been dashed.

If the truck was visually unimpressive on the outside, it sounded worse inside. No wonder they had heard the vehicle coming back at the airport. The pickup made too much noise, and she swore the tires squeaked every time they found a pothole or went over something as minor as a hill of dirt, which given the countrified nature of the road, was often.

She didn't say anything for the longest time, and neither did Nate or Danny. She didn't know what was going through their minds at the moment, but she kept expecting uniformed men to come out of hiding in front of them, springing an ambush the way they had done to poor Taylor this morning. The only question was whether those men would be wearing tan or black uniforms. Either way, the thought made her grip the AR-15 just a little bit tighter, her right forefinger rubbing against the trigger.

After about half an hour of driving in silence, with nothing but the trees and woods for company and the wind whistling in their ears, Gaby finally said, "Are we going to talk about it?"

"Talk about what?" Danny said.

"Mercer."

"What about him?"

"This war of his."

"What about it?"

"They're killing people, Danny. Civilians. If it was just the soldiers, I wouldn't care. But they're being indiscriminate."

"I don't know what you want me to say," Danny said.

"Do we just look the other way?" she asked.

"You're assuming we can do something about it."

"Can't we?"

"The three of us? Not a chance in hell. Mercer's got an army. We just saw a small part of it back there at the airfield. He's got moving pieces all across the state. The man has been planning this for months now. Hell, he might have been cooking it up since the

night everything went to shit, for all I know. A guy like that..."
Danny shook his head. "It's going to take more than just the three of
us to stop him."

He was right, and the worst part was, she'd known for a while
now, but knowing and accepting weren't the same thing. The idea of
not doing anything at all made her shift in her seat.

"We have to worry about the *Trident* right now," Danny continued. "And the people on it. Carly, Vera and Elise, the others. What
happens in Texas isn't our problem. Mercer's right about one thing:
The people in those towns made their choice."

"They didn't ask to be bombed from the air," she said.

"No, they didn't. But there's nothing we can do about that.
We're outgunned six ways to Sunday." He sighed, his voice growing
more somber, and for a moment she could almost imagine Will
talking, and not Danny. "We'll get what we came for, and then we'll
go home. We'll swing by on our way and get the sisters, and we'll call
that a victory. As for everything else, let God sort them out. It's time
he earned his pay, anyway."

◄━━▮ ▮━━►

STARCH, TEXAS, WAS exactly how she had pictured it: a small town
of a few thousand people (or it used to be, anyway) along a main
highway, and no one would have realized it even existed if not for
Lake Livingston somewhere behind it. That lake was why an
eccentric millionaire had built an underground facility designed to
withstand just about any calamity. To hear Lara tell it, the place had
done exactly that, until one night when everything came undone.

After an hour of driving through barren streets, over railroad
tracks, and down spur roads that never seemed to end, they finally
hit the road to hell that would take them to the end of their jour-
ney—the reason they had come back to Texas in the first place.

She didn't need to ask Danny what time it was; she could keep
track of the sun by looking out her window. By her count, it was
around 3:00. Soon, very soon, it would be dark again, but they had

made good time and she was feeling buoyed by their progress.

Too bad the road to Harold Campbell's facility was doing its damnedest to ruin her good mood. The massive walls of trees to the left and right of them didn't help, either. They were so thick that Gaby couldn't see past them, and they cast such an imposing shadow over everything she could almost believe they were driving through a tunnel instead of a country road.

The craters under them weren't accidents of nature, but put there by Campbell to deter people from doing exactly what they were doing at the moment. After about ten minutes of struggling to hold onto her seat and not throwing up, she had to grudgingly admit that Campbell might have known what he was doing. After all, he had access to a helicopter and would never have had to use the road himself. She wasn't so lucky.

If she thought there was a possibility Taylor's truck might not survive the sixty-mile trip from Larkin to Starch, she was now almost certain it wouldn't survive the three kilometer-long hike up this pothole-infested hell. Gaby swore she could hear pieces of the vehicle *crunching* and *clanging* off the undercarriage with every bump they hit.

"This is nuts!" she shouted.

"Which part of eccentric millionaire didn't you understand?" Danny shouted back.

"Crazy assholes with money!" Nate shouted behind them.

"How much further"—she started to ask, when the road suddenly smoothed out and she could hear herself just fine again—"to go?"

"There. We've survived the Trip of Doom," Danny said. "Which means the facility should be up ahead."

"'Should be'?"

"It's definitely up ahead."

"I think I'm going to throw up," Nate said quietly from the backseat.

"Out the window, so you don't get it on the upholstery," Danny said. "This thing's a classic, after all."

"This thing's a piece of junk," Nate said.

"Same difference."

She turned around in her seat and smiled at Nate. He returned it, looking boyish and handsome back there by himself, one hand holding his stomach and his Mohawk flopping too much to one side.

"You okay?" she asked.

"Good," he said. "You?"

"Hanging in there."

"I'm fine too, thanks for asking," Danny said.

"You okay, Danny?" she asked.

"Great, thanks for asking," he said.

She turned back around and picked her rifle up from the floor, then focused on the road ahead. "Almost there?"

"Almost there," Danny said.

"I don't see anything."

"Almost *almost* there."

Now that the road was even again and she wasn't bouncing in her seat, it was easier to pay attention to the dancing shadows and overly chilly air around them. She wished she could see what was hiding in the woods to the left and right of the road, but it was just one continuous black wall. She thought she might have seen something moving inside—something *fast*—but Danny had picked up speed and they were past it before she could be sure.

"What's wrong?" Nate said, leaning forward between the two front seats.

She shook her head. "Nothing."

"You sure?"

"I thought I saw something…"

"Where?"

"In the woods."

He looked out his side window.

"Back down the road," she said. Then, hoping it was at least convincing, "It was probably nothing."

"Eyes forward, kids," Danny said.

She looked out the front windshield as they came up to an opening—a wide field carved out of the woods. They passed what look like the remains of a front gate, with an old guard shack on Danny's side. A wild jungle had grown since the last time anyone was here, and they had to stop the truck about twenty yards past the nonexistent gate.

Danny put the vehicle in park and leaned forward against the steering wheel. He had clearly seen something that disturbed him when he said, "Hunh."

"What?" she said.

"Those weren't here last time."

She followed his gaze out the windshield and across the field.

They were impossible to miss: a small cluster of vehicles, all yellow, sitting in the open. One had a scooper-type arm, and she was pretty sure another one was some kind of bulldozer. Grass had grown around their heavy tires, a clear indication they had been brought here and abandoned a while ago.

"Construction equipment," Nate said, leaning between the two front seats again. "Looks like diggers."

"Diggers?" she said.

"For digging."

"Of course," she said, feeling stupid.

"Which begs the question: What were they digging out here?"

Danny reached for his rifle, said, "Eyes wide, ears open, and weapons hot at all times, got it?" and climbed out.

She and Nate followed his example on the other side of the truck, their rifles gripped tightly in front of them. The grass was taller than it had looked from inside their vehicle, and if they had kept going, they might have become stuck in another twenty to thirty yards.

"Danny?" she said across the warm hood at him.

He was peering at the construction equipment, as if he could see something she and Nate couldn't. "Stay frosty," he said, before starting forward. "Shoot anything that moves that isn't us."

Gaby exchanged a quick look with Nate, who shrugged.

She flicked the safety off her AR-15 and followed Danny into the weeds. Grass slapped at her legs, prompting her to think about what things might be lurking inside all the unseen parts of the field at the moment. Not ghouls, of course; it was still daylight—

She glanced up instinctively at the still-high sun. Still time.

But not a lot.

Danny had stopped in front of them and was looking down at something.

"Danny," she said. "What is it?"

He shook his head but didn't say anything. She walked over and looked down at what he had been staring at.

It was a big, gaping rectangular hole in the ground, surrounded by obliterated gray and black chunks of something that, once upon a time, had been big enough to cover the opening. Now, there were only piles of the object scattered about the grass, some as small as her fist and others as big (if not bigger) than a desk.

She had noticed the difference under her boots a few yards back, where the soft dirt ended and the hard, even concrete floor began. The construction around the "door" was still intact, but everything else—anything standing more than a few feet above the ground—had been demolished months ago, leaving behind divots and giant clawlike markings that could only have been put there by one of the construction vehicles.

"Oh man, this isn't good, is it?" Nate said, as he stopped next to her and looked down.

Like the two of them, she was transfixed by the hole in the ground. It was massive and framed by gray concrete walls. Sunlight illuminated some of the stairs leading down, but not enough, and most of what was on the bottom was lost in a thick pool of darkness. She could see the shape of some kind of lightbulb just beyond the light, but there was no telling how long it had been out.

Then the darkness *shifted and moved*, and all three of them took a quick step back and lifted their weapons instinctively.

"Whoa," Nate breathed next to her.

"Don't sweat it; they're more scared of you than you are of them," Danny said.

"You think?"

"Absolutely not."

Danny lowered his rifle and wrinkled his nose, as if he had an itch he couldn't get to. Then he turned and walked away, stopping about ten yards later. He stomped down on something buried in the ground, producing a loud metallic *clang!*

"What is it?" Gaby asked.

"The titanium door that was supposed to be over that opening," Danny said. "We were pretty sure it could withstand a nuke." He looked in the direction of the construction equipment. "But why use a nuke when you could just pry it open with the right can openers."

"Collaborators," Nate said.

"Unless the ghouls have mastered driving a stick, then probably, yeah."

"So we came all the way out here for nothing?" Nate asked, unable to hide his disappointment.

"It would appear so." Danny sighed and let his rifle hang at his side. "I guess it was too much to hope the little bastards would leave the facility alone after we left. This'll teach me to be optimistic."

Gaby wasn't entirely sure why she wasn't more angry, or at least as visibly disappointed as Nate and Danny were. But she wasn't. Maybe it was everything they had seen and been through since arriving back in Texas. The events of Hellion, T29, even Larkin. After all those things, coming here and finding Starch empty was...anti-climactic.

At least no one died here, unlike the 400 people in T29. Or the poor bastards in Hellion.

She walked over to Danny. "We should go. It'll be dark soon."

Danny nodded, then took a moment to look around at the clearing. "We cleaned out Starch pretty good when we were here. Spent a lot of time searching for silver in every nook and cranny."

"Did you guys happen to stash some silver bullets in town?"

"Afraid not."

"What about the facility?" Nate asked.

They looked back at him.

"What about it?" Danny said.

"Maybe if we can lure them out…"

Danny gave him an almost pitying look before grinning at Gaby, though she could tell he didn't quite have his heart in it this time. "Captain Optimism, this guy," Danny said. "Thinks we can lure them out into the open when there are probably a few thousand of them squeezed in there. This, with two hours until nightfall, and no way to close the door."

"Guess not," Nate said.

"Facility's gone, along with everything inside it. We officially came all the way here for nothing. I'm sorry, kids. Maybe next time."

"You don't have to be sorry," Gaby said. "We knew the risks when we volunteered." She glanced at Nate, and he nodded and smiled back at her. "So the question is, what's our next move?"

"It's too late to go back to Larkin, so we'll hole up in Starch," Danny said. "I know Lara and Carly. Even without contact from us, they'll wait at Port Arthur for as long as possible. They're not going anywhere until someone shows them our dead bodies."

"Ugh, not the best choice of words there," Nate grunted.

"Sorry about that."

"You're certain of that?" she asked. "That they'll wait for us?"

"Sure as Pauly Shore."

"I don't know who that is."

"Damn kids," Danny said, and started walking back to the truck. Under his breath, she heard him muttering, "Texas is really starting to *piss* me off."

Gaby and Nate turned and followed him in silence. She took a moment to glance up at the sun just to assure herself it was still up there. Was it her imagination, or did the sky look darker since the last time she—

Something flickered in the corner of her eye, some kind of *figure*, and she stopped and looked toward the woods across the clearing.

She saw trees—a lot of trees.

"What is it?" Nate asked. He had kept walking a few steps before realizing she had stopped and turned back around.

"I don't know," Gaby said quietly, as if afraid someone might overhear her.

"You saw something?"

"I'm not sure."

"Like back at the road?"

Yes, she thought, but said instead, "It's this place. It's spooky."

Nate gave her a reassuring smile. "*Trident* or bust, right?"

She smiled back. Or tried to, anyway. "*Trident* or bust."

They walked the rest of the way to the truck, where Danny was already waiting for them.

Something moved in the corner of her left eye, but Gaby ignored it.

There's nothing out there, she told herself. *It's just your imagination.*

BOOK THREE

OF MONSTERS AND MEN

CHAPTER 21

KEO

"GET THE GIRL. Lose her. Go back for the girl."

It wasn't exactly the best plan in the world, but then things had a bad habit of going sideways these days. Surviving The Purge had been a crapshoot, but the year afterward had become one big blur of gunfights and near misses. He supposed when he really thought about it, riding back to Gillian, a woman who had already spurned him once (or was that twice now?), was about par for the course.

It wasn't like anything else had worked out these last few months. He would have been perfectly happy to hop back onto the *Trident* and ride the waves to the Bengal Islands with Lara and the others. Carrie would be there, and of all the women on the yacht, she was always the best reason not to go look for Gillian. And there was also Bonnie...

He must have sighed out loud, because Jordan said, "That's a pretty big sigh right there, mister."

"Just thinking," he said.

"Uh oh."

"Yeah."

Jordan was watching him while leaning against the front passenger door of the truck. After about ten minutes with a T-shirt between her and the bloody stains on the seat, she had gotten over being squeamish. At the moment, there was nothing but undeveloped land rushing by outside the open window behind her.

"What?" he said.

"I'm just trying to figure you out," she said.

"You're trying too hard."

"You're more than you let on."

"Like I told Lara, I'm just a guy with a gun. It's not that complicated."

"I don't believe that. Bonnie doesn't believe it, either. We had a little talk back at the beach. Are you curious what she said?"

"No."

"Oh, I don't believe that."

He sighed. "What did she say?"

"Sorry, private conversation."

He flashed her an annoyed glance, but she just smiled back at him.

They drove on for a few more minutes in silence, the cool wind blasting against his face through the windowless driver-side door. December in Texas was so unlike anything he had experienced in other parts of the world, and he still hadn't decided if he liked it or was disturbed by it. Maybe a little of both.

They had left Sunport behind a while ago, and there was just empty farmland around them now. A red barn popped up every now and then, along with fenced off property devoid of cows or other livestock. Texas State Highway 288 was a low-to-the-ground two-lane road that connected Sunport and Angleton, and they were on the northwest-bound lane with the southeast-bound thirty meters over to the left. Both long, gray stretches of pavement were barren, with no other vehicle within sight.

"How close are we to the turn-off?" he finally asked.

Jordan took out the same map he had liberated from Gregson's tank and unfolded it in her lap, then traced the route with her forefinger. "We're closing in on Angleton. About five more miles. From there, take State Highway 35. That should take us to Alvin, then I-45 after that."

"You sure he's going to be there?"

"I'm sure. The question is, will he welcome you back?"

"I don't know what you're talking about; I think I made a pretty good first impression."

She might have rolled her eyes when she said, "You tried to kill him."

"I was *sent* to kill him, but I didn't. Big difference."

"Let's hope he makes that distinction."

"I'm sure he will. Question is, do you think Captain America will help us?"

She thought about it for a moment before nodding. "I think he will once I explain what's happening out here. The Tobias I know wouldn't be able to sit by while Mercer's people are butchering civilians. It's not how he's wired."

"What about the others? Would they come along, too?"

"I don't know about the rest, but Reese will. He looks up to Tobias. There's a good chance the rest will follow, too. The ones that can still fight, anyway. They were pretty banged up the last time we saw them."

"So, at least two more guns," Keo nodded. "Four against an army. A *mobilized* army on high alert, waiting for an impending attack."

"Doesn't sound quite as good when you say it out loud."

"Are you kidding me? Those are the best odds I've had in months."

She gave him an unconvinced glance.

"If I'm lying, I'm dying," he grinned back at her.

"I can't tell if you're serious."

"Like a stroke," he said, when he saw it a second later and thought, *Oh, fuck me.*

He didn't hear it, but he imagined it was there somewhere outside the vehicle—the telltale *swoosh!*—as the sun glinted off the dull olive green of the rocket-propelled grenade as it flashed across the windshield, entering the periphery of his vision from the right and disappearing out of the left.

Keo didn't have time—didn't waste time—tracking the rocket's trajectory as it missed the truck by a few feet and kept going. A civilian might have slammed on the brake in shock, but Keo wasn't a civilian. He floored the gas pedal and the Ford F-150 lurched forward, gaining even more speed as it went.

"Keo!" Jordan shouted as her body was thrown back against her seat by the sudden acceleration.

"Hold on!" he shouted back.

He had both hands on the steering wheel to make sure the truck didn't do anything he didn't want it to. His eyes shot left then right, to the rearview mirror and forward, always moving, even as he willed the truck to go faster, faster, *faster.*

They had been moving at forty miles an hour before, but he was already up to sixty—

—seventy—

—*ninety*—

"Keo!" Jordan shouted again, clutching to the handhold over her door with one hand, the other gripping her M4 by the barrel.

"Ambush!" he shouted back. "Hold on!"

He zeroed in on the rearview mirror as a man-sized lump—no, *two*—stood up to the right of the highway, where they had been hiding among the sunburnt fields. They were wearing dark-colored uniforms.

Collaborators?

He expected pursuit at any moment—vehicles to burst out of the grass like some wild animal—but each time he stole a quick glance at the rearview mirror the road behind him remained empty, and even the two that had stood up were just looking after them—

A loud *boom!* shattered his eardrums, and a second later the steering wheel was fighting his control and the truck was, impossibly, starting to turn sideways. Then he went from looking at the gray stretch of pavement out the windshield to staring at the cloudless sky to seeing the sun-bleached grass twirling in front of his eyes.

They were flying. The *Ford* was flying through the air.

But not for long. They came back down to earth, and there was an earsplitting blast as the glass around him shattered, drowning out

Jordan's screams. The cacophony of natural and unnatural sounds was followed by the loud *crunch!* of metal as the car smashed, rolled, and smashed again into the abandoned farmland.

The engine was still turning when he opened his eyes, very aware of the seatbelt strap pinning him to his seat. He pushed past the thrum of pain and concentrated instead on the heavy *tap-tap* of footsteps in the background. Something wet streaked across his forehead and into his hair and *drip-drip-dripped* down to…the ceiling?

Combat boots appeared outside the shattered front windshield before he could unlatch himself from the seat belt and reach for his weapon. The legs were upside down for a reason. Oh, right, because *he* and the truck were overturned.

"Holy shit, they're still alive," someone said.

"Not for long," a second voice said.

The familiar sting of cold metal pressing into the side of his temple was enough to make Keo forget about the pain. He couldn't quite turn his head all the way around, so he couldn't see who was crouching just outside the driver-side door.

"Close enough for ya, Tanner?" the first voice asked with a laugh.

"Just about," the second man, Tanner, said, followed by the very clear *click* of a gun hammer being pulled back.

"Well, do it already, before she—"

A loud squawking noise cut him off, followed by a muffled female voice. "What's the body count?"

"—too late," the first voice finished.

"Sonofabitch," Tanner said, and Keo felt the barrel depress slightly against his temple.

"Give me a sitrep," the female voice said.

He heard another *click* as someone keyed a radio's transmit lever. "They're still alive," the first man said.

"I'm on my way. Don't do anything until then."

"Tanner wants to—"

"I said, *don't do anything* until I get there."

"Yes, ma'am," the man said, though Keo detected obvious derision and wondered if he had transmitted that last part or said it to empty air. "You heard her; don't pop them yet."

"Fuck," Tanner said.

Rough hands grabbed and pulled him out of the overturned Ford and deposited him on the ground on his back, allowing him a great view of the wide-open skies above. It was a very bright afternoon, the kind that would have looked perfect from the aft of the *Trident*.

Shoulda, woulda, coulda, pal.

"Look at that face," the man named Tanner said. "Shit, man, looks like you've been through the wringer. Made you real pretty."

"Girl looks pretty good, though," the other one said.

"She still alive?"

"I think so. She's moving. I'll go check…"

Footsteps, fading.

Then Tanner's voice again, somewhere in the background. "How'd you dodge that first rocket?"

Rocket? What—Oh. That rocket.

"You must be the luckiest sonofabitch I know," Tanner said when Keo didn't answer. "Harry never misses. That guy's like a savant with an M72. Good thing Doug was a better shot, or you'd still be hauling ass down the road. Too bad for you, chum."

An M72 LAW rocket launcher. Uncle Sam's version of an anti-tank weapon that apparently was just as good against a moving truck going, what, ninety miles an hour? He tried to imagine what the F-150 must have looked like when it was hit. The round probably struck the back first, which accounted for the *booming* sound, before sending the Ford shooting forward and upward like a launching missile. He would have approved of the sight if he wasn't the one inside the target at the time.

A new pair of footsteps approached before a familiar female voice (this time unmuffled) said, "He's not wearing a uniform."

The same woman who had ordered Tanner not to kill him through the radio. His savior. In the flesh, she had a just barely-there Hispanic accent.

"No, but that's definitely one of our trucks," Tanner said. "Goran and Paul took two of them out to track down that tank from yesterday."

"Sunport?"

"Yeah."

A brief moment of silence.

"We should finish them off," Tanner said, slightly agitated. "Look at the blood inside. That's not new. They killed Goran and Paul, and who knows how many, for their vehicle."

The woman still didn't say anything.

"We should—" Tanner pressed.

"No," she cut him off.

"Why the fuck not?"

"If they came from Sunport, then they might know something about who's launching these attacks," the woman said. "I wouldn't be surprised if they were in the tank. My guess is it's run out of fuel and they had to commandeer Goran and Paul's truck. Right now, we need intel more than we need two more dead bodies. Go and bring the truck over."

"I'm telling you, Marcy, this is the wrong move—"

"And I *said,* go and bring the goddamn truck over," Marcy snapped.

I guess we know who wears the pants in this family, Keo thought, wishing he could see the woman's face.

Footsteps leaving. Tanner, huffing and puffing as he went, probably.

Dumb bastard. Pushed around by a girl.

"You got a name?" the woman asked.

Was she talking to him?

The crimp in his neck had lessened, the throbbing pain starting to numb, and he was finally able to turn his head slightly to the left, just enough to see a woman with curly black hair staring down at him. She was in her thirties, wearing a black uniform with a patch of Texas over one shoulder. The name "Marcy" was stenciled across a name tag, and a pair of binoculars hung loosely off a long neck.

Collaborators. Just my luck.

Brown eyes peered back at him. "Name. You got one?"

"Keo," he said.

"Keo," she repeated. "What kind of name is that?"

"José was taken."

She narrowed her eyes. "Funny, you don't look Hispanic."

"It's my disguise."

Pale lips curved into a smile, but there was no genuine trace of humor. "All right, funny guy. Let's find out what you know. Then I'll decide if I'll do you a favor and kill you and your friend fast, or take my time."

THEY DIDN'T HAVE to carry him very far because the truck was parked nearby. He was put into the back, his ankles and arms zip tied, but at least they didn't blindfold him, which allowed him to keep an eye on the amazingly bright sky. Of course, some of that great view was marred by a man in a black uniform manning a machine gun standing above him. The welding that connected the MG's tripod to the cab looked rushed, which made him wonder if they had put the technical together only recently, possibly in response to Mercer's attacks yesterday.

He turned his head until he could see Jordan's unconscious body next to him. She was also bound, strays of short blonde hair matted to her forehead by small clumps of blood. She looked okay—or as okay as you could look after getting tossed off the road by a rocket strike, anyway.

The back of the truck closed with a *bang!*, and then they were back on the road.

The soldier manning the machine gun was alert, swiveling the weapon around as they moved. It looked like an older model squad automatic weapon, but even an aging piece was still dangerous when you could throw a few hundred rounds a minute downrange without having to reload.

Why was he so surprised the collaborators were all over the highway? Maybe he had expected them to remain around the towns to protect the inhabitants instead of spreading out into the countryside. How many other groups were out there between him and Gillian, waiting to ambush whoever was stupid enough *(like us)* to be driving out in the open?

Of course, he wouldn't be in this position if it wasn't for Mercer. Hell, he'd probably be on the *Trident* right now, maybe even watching Bonnie and Carrie swimming in bikinis at the back of the anchored boat. Wouldn't that be nice?

Coulda, woulda, but didn'ta, pal.

The soldier standing near his head shuffled his feet, the dried dirt caking his boots flaking off with every movement.

"Hey," Keo said.

The man ignored him.

"Hey," Keo said again.

The man looked down. He was wearing dark shades and Keo got a quick glimpse of himself in the reflective lens, lying on the truck bed. There was blood along the side of his face and in his hair, but he concluded that they looked worse than they actually were, since it certainly didn't feel as if he was bleeding to death at the moment. Probably.

"What?" the man said.

"Where we going?"

"Base," the man said, and returned his attention to the road.

"Angleton?"

"Angleton's dead," the man said. "Been dead for a year now."

"So where's base?"

"You'll find out when we get there."

Keo hadn't been able to glimpse the man's name tag, with the soldier's back to him most of the entire time. "You got a name?" he asked.

"Yeah," the man said.

Keo smiled. A man after his own heart. "I'm Keo."

"Good for you. Now shut up."

"Just trying to pass the time. Seen any tanks lately?"

That got the reaction Keo was looking for, and the soldier stared down at him for three very long seconds. "Keep it up. I got a shit-stained rag in my back pocket that's looking for a mouth to call home."

"Fair enough." Keo glanced at Jordan instead. "Jordan."

She didn't move.

"Jordan," he said again, louder this time.

She finally opened her eyes and grimaced up at the sun for a moment.

"Over here," he said.

She turned her head slowly and blinked at him. There was a cut along her right temple, but it looked minor next to the contusion in the middle of her forehead. "This is not good," she said, her words slightly slurred.

"Hey, we've been in worse situations. Remember Santa Marie Island? Or yesterday? Or all of this week?"

"I'm trying not to," she frowned.

"How's your head?"

"Like someone's hitting me with a sledgehammer. Repeatedly." Her eyes darted upward, toward the collaborator hovering over them. Then, after a moment, "Is there something sitting on my forehead?"

"Looks like you hit it on something during the crash."

"I don't know how that's possible. That seat belt almost cut me in half."

"We flipped."

"We flipped?"

"The truck. It flipped."

She stared at him in disbelief.

"They hit us with a LAW," he said.

"Law?"

"Light Anti-Tank Weapon. I guess they came fully prepared to take out a tank. Can't say I blame them."

"Oh."

"We're lucky," he said.

She frowned again. "One of these days we need to sit down and have a really long talk about your definition of lucky, Keo."

THEY DROVE FOR another ten minutes or so before the vehicle abandoned the smooth, paved highway and turned right onto a dirt road. Dust enveloped the truck, making him cough. The machine gunner, well-prepared for this part of the trip, pulled a handkerchief that was wrapped around his neck over the lower half of his face. Keo could only close his mouth and try not to breathe in the swirling dust. Jordan did the same next to him, squinting her eyes like she was gagging.

The loud squeal of brakes as the truck, and the ones behind and in front of it, stopped. Doors squeaked open and heavy boots pounded the ground.

The soldier behind the machine gun pulled off his handkerchief and looked down at Keo. "Welcome to base."

"I call first dibs on the Jacuzzi," Keo said.

The man grinned, but said nothing. He stepped over Keo, and the truck dipped slightly before rising again as he leaped down the back without bothering with the tailgate.

Keo turned his head and found Jordan looking back at him.

"Another opportunity for that golden tongue of yours to get us out of trouble," she said. "Start wagging."

"I'll do my best."

"Don't let me down."

"When have I ever?"

She sighed. "God, you're going to get us both killed."

"Thanks for the vote of confidence."

BUT THEY DIDN'T give him a chance to talk his way out of it.

Instead, a pair of armed men led Jordan and Keo from the truck and across the large front yard of a farmhouse. They were surrounded by technicals, and armed men stood guard on the rooftops of a two-story white house on one side and the bright red barn in front of them. The highway was somewhere to his right, but Keo couldn't spy even a tiny glimpse of it at the moment.

The farm was surrounded by vast fields of sun-bleached land, and if something had been growing out there once upon a time, they were long dead, replaced by empty stretches of brown earth. He could probably scream all day and no one would hear, or care, if they heard.

The zip ties around their legs had been removed so they could walk, but the ones around their wrists remained in place. Not that Keo had any intentions of making a run for it. There were too many men in black uniforms with guns, and the ones on top of the barn were watching them like hawks. There were no signs of Marcy, the obvious leader of the pack, and the men walking them didn't seem interested in conversation.

Keo spotted a dozen vehicles, including the three that had returned from the ambush, before they were escorted through the barn's open doors and his entire universe suddenly boiled down to rotting wood and the aroma of stale feed and hay, overlapped with old urine and manure stains.

Jordan made a face. "Jesus…"

"Never been inside a barn before?" he asked.

"No. You?"

"Once or twice."

"Do they all smell like this?"

"This one's special. A year's worth of abandonment."

"I feel so privileged."

There was no one inside the barn but them, which he guessed made sense; who wanted to spend all their time in here, with the smells? Their escorts led them to their destination: a metal cage at the back. It looked like some kind of kennel, about ten feet high and just as wide.

One of the men used a key on the cage's padlock, then pulled the door open. "Inside."

Keo and Jordan stepped through, crunching year-old hay (and other things he'd rather not think too much about) as they did so. The door *clanged* shut and the collaborator slipped the lock back through the latch, snapped it closed, then pocketed the key.

"Hands," the man said.

Keo squeezed his bound hands through the bars, and the man took out a pair of pliers and snipped the restraints. He did the same to Jordan's zip ties.

"We could use some medical attention too," Keo said, rubbing at his wrists.

"Tough nuts," the man said.

"Maybe later, but just the medical attention for now."

The man grunted. "If it was up to me, I'd keep the both of you hog-tied and rolling around in there." Then he turned and walked off.

Keo leaned against the cage, feeling like a prisoner in a bad movie, and watched his guards leave. They didn't go far, though, and stood guard in front of the open barn doors underneath the bright sun. Well, it was bright for now, but it wasn't going to last forever, which was the problem.

"I thought you were going to talk us out of this?" Jordan said.

"I didn't exactly get an opportunity."

"Excuses."

"Maybe when Marcy shows up…"

"Who's Marcy?"

"The one running the show."

"When did you two become buddies?"

"While you were unconscious."

"Figures," Jordan said. "I close my eyes for one moment, and you're already chatting up a new girl."

Sunlight streamed in around them, through the holes and boards that made up the barn's walls, and Keo's eyes were drawn to the ceiling, where he could hear the slight *creak* each time one of the two collaborators up there moved around, which was about once every thirty seconds or so.

Nervous in the service, boys?

He focused on the bars, then gripped them and tried pulling. They didn't budge, of course, especially with one end buried in concrete. The individual metal rods themselves were too close together to slide through and he could just barely get his entire arm out, never mind the rest of him.

"What is this thing?" Jordan asked, pulling on the bars on another side of the cage.

"Probably a kennel for wild animals," Keo said. "Or two innocent travelers, in this case."

"Innocent, huh?"

"Innocent-ish." He glanced at the sentries above them again. "Looks like they're on high alert."

"Mercer."

"Yeah. I don't think I've ever seen nine technicals in the same place before. Combine that with the LAWs, and it looks like we just stumbled into the middle of a full-fledged war. What they have going on out here with Mercer's people is going to make what you and Tobias had to deal with back at T18 look like child's play."

"Wow, why is it every time you open your mouth, I feel less and less like we're going to survive this?"

"Sorry."

Jordan leaned against the bars next to him and tried to get a better look at the open doors to their left. "How's your leg?"

"Still attached."

"You know what I mean."

"It's fine."

"Is that you being a tough guy?"

"Yup."

"Okay, tough guy, so what do we do now?"

"We wait."

"For what?"

"They kept us alive to find out what we know. Marcy's deduced that we're a part of Gregson's tank crew, trying to go incognito."

"'Deduced'?" Jordan said with a wry smile.

"She figured," he shrugged.

"So, what do we know?"

"Hopefully enough to convince them to keep us alive, at least long enough to make our play."

"Which would be?"

"I don't know yet."

"That doesn't sound very reassuring." She walked to the back of the cage and sat down on a pile of old hay. "I should have taken Lara's offer. The *Trident*'s looking pretty good right about now."

He smiled to himself. How many times had he said *that* in the last few weeks?

"I don't want to say I told you so," he said, "but I told you so."

"Yeah, yeah."

She was suddenly very quiet, and Keo looked back at her. "Jordan…"

"What?" she said.

"Jordan," he said again.

She looked up and stared back at him. "What, Keo?"

"We'll be okay."

"Bullshit."

"I promise."

She didn't say anything, and he wasn't sure if she believed him. Hell, he wasn't certain if *he* believed him.

"Okay," she finally said, and leaned back against the bars and closed her eyes.

He turned back around and glanced toward the open barn doors, wondering how exactly he was going to make good on that promise.

CHAPTER 22

GABY

DIDN'T WE JUST do this?

Nate sat across from her in the pitch darkness, Danny's still form to her right. The ex-Army Ranger was asleep and snoring lightly, his head tilted to one side, the carbine he had gotten from Taylor's stash lying across his lap. Nate was wide awake and looking back at her. Or she thought he was, anyway. It was hard to tell, because she couldn't quite make out the blue of his eyes despite there only being five feet or so of open space between them.

It wasn't fear that moved through her at the moment. Or, at least, not the familiar paralyzing effects that usually accompanied the onset of terror. She could breathe just fine, clench and unclench her fingers against her rifle without difficulty, and she had no problems feeling the slight vibrations that ran through the rotting wooden floor underneath the stained carpet as they moved around below her.

Tap-tap-tap.

Nate had heard it too, because his outline went suddenly rigid.

Tap-tap-tap.

They were traveling across the same places she, Nate, and Danny had less than an hour ago. There was no mistaking the patter of their bare feet moving over dirt-stained slate tiles, the *clicks* and *clacks* as they randomly bumped into items hanging off shelves or that had toppled in the year since customers stopped coming.

She slid one hand along the length of her AR-15 and slipped her forefinger into the trigger guard. The weapon felt overly bulky, but she knew that was only because she wasn't used to it yet.

There wasn't a lot of space in the attic, and most of it was already taken up with crates of plumbing fixtures, empty water cooler bottles, and unopened boxes of cheap plastic Christmas trees. The only thing they had found to be any use when they had searched it earlier, back when there was still enough light to see with, were two stacks of duct tape. And you could never have too much duct tape—

Concentrate!

The creatures were smart, but they could be fooled. Which was why they had parked Taylor's truck six buildings down the street, then walked to the hardware store and climbed up to its attic. She would never have known the room existed if Danny hadn't remembered it from all those months ago when he had raided the place for supplies with Will.

The *bang!* of the store's front glass door slamming, followed by silence.

Five seconds became ten…then twenty…but she didn't let herself relax until a full minute had gone by without the familiar *tap-tap-tap* coming from directly below her.

Close one. Real close one.

The sound of rustling clothes as Nate got up and slipped from one side of the attic to the other before sitting down next to her on her left.

"Sounds like we're in the clear," he whispered.

"Sounds like it," she nodded back.

"Tired?"

"Aren't you?"

"Just a little bit." He leaned around her to look at Danny. "Is he really asleep?"

She nodded. "Like a rock."

"A snoring rock."

She managed a smile.

"You should go to sleep, too," he said. "I'll stay up, and you can relieve me around midnight."

She glanced over at Danny, still snoring lightly to her right. He looked amazingly at peace, as if he were back on the *Trident* and not trapped in Starch waiting for sunlight as ghouls flooded the streets and buildings around them.

"Wake me up at midnight," she said.

He nodded.

"I mean it," she said. "Don't pull any of that chivalrous crap on me."

"Midnight. Got it."

"Nate…"

"Hey, I want to get some sleep, too, okay?"

She narrowed her eyes at him. "Promise?"

"Cross my heart and hope to die."

"Hopefully it won't come to that."

She leaned over and kissed him on the mouth. He tasted of sweat and dirt, but somehow, still sweet at the same time.

When she pulled back, he was smiling at her.

"What?" she said.

"I wish we were back on the *Trident*…"

She rolled her eyes. "They'll be plenty of time for that later, lover boy."

"Have you talked to Lara? About getting us our own cabin?"

"We're not the only two people on the yacht, Nate. Everyone has to share."

"There's that room behind the engine…"

"The one we're holding Gage in?"

"It's about time we throw that guy into the ocean anyway." She must have been unable to hide her surprise, because he added, "Being out here, with all that's going on, it's given me a new perspective."

"I'll talk to Lara."

"Good. Now, go to sleep. And if you don't mind, I'm going to think about all those other sexy times while you're doing that."

"You have my permission," she smiled, and laid her rifle across her lap, before leaning against Nate's shoulder.

For whatever reason, the steady rise and fall of his heartbeat to her left and Danny's impossibly calm breathing to her right lulled her into a strange sense of serenity. Her bones ached and her muscles were sore, and she didn't realize just how emotionally and physically draining the last few days had been until she closed her eyes and didn't want to open them again.

◀━▮ ▮━▶

"*GABY.*"

She was asleep, but also awake at the same time. Like floating in a bathtub filled with warm milk, bubbles caressing the bottom of her chin. Soothing and calming, but at the same time dangerous, with the threat of drowning hovering over her head.

"*Wake up.*"

There was something familiar about the voice, but she couldn't quite put her finger on it. Like a faded echo, tempting her closer to the surface.

"*Gaby.*"

She opened her eyes to darkness and Nate's outline in front of her. He was crouched on one knee, his arm extended forward and shaking her awake.

"What—" she started to say *(Too loud!)*, when Nate's hand clasped over her mouth.

His other hand was already gripping his rifle and he lifted it now, pointing it across his body at the attic door. She had to look past Danny, still snoring quietly next to her, his head lolled to one side. He looked as if he might fall down at any second, but somehow remained upright despite the odds.

She didn't dare move a single muscle as she listened while staring at the long rectangular-shaped trapdoor. Maybe she was still groggy and her senses weren't up to full speed yet, but she couldn't hear anything.

She glanced back at Nate for confirmation. He must have read the doubt on her face, because he gave her a slight nod.

"Are you sure?" she mouthed.

"Yes," he mouthed back. *"Downstairs."*

She reached down and picked up her AR-15 with one hand and pushed Danny with the other. His eyes snapped open almost as soon as she touched him, and they darted in the direction of the attic door before swiveling over to her.

"They found us," she mouthed.

His lips moved as he began to mouth something back, but he hadn't managed to form a single soundless word yet when there was a *crash!* from below, like a gunshot against the deathly silent night, but not quite as thunderous.

Danny snatched up his carbine and turned toward the door while Nate took up position in front of it with his bolt-action rifle. Gaby crab-walked backward, keeping as quiet as possible even though every step sounded like mini-explosions to her ears. She had always been thin, but the end of the world had excised any fat she might have had held onto from high school. Despite that, she was convinced she was moving with all the grace of a bloated whale as the three of them spread out to give each other as much room as possible in the already cramped attic space.

She didn't stop backing up until she bumped into the boxes of Christmas trees, thankful there were no decorations inside to jingle or clink on contact. She positioned the rifle in front of her, and out of pure habit reached down with a finger to make sure the fire selector wasn't stuck on safe.

Danny glanced over his shoulder and flashed her a wry smile. She saw it easily in the semidarkness, so maybe her eyes had finally adjusted to the conditions after all.

She nodded back at him, as if to say, *"I'm fine,"* but of course he knew better.

Danny returned her nod anyway before turning back to the door. "Hey, Nate Archibald," he whispered.

Nate looked over, and matching his pitch, "What?"

"Switch places."

"Why?"

Danny held up his rifle. "I got more firepower."

"Oh."

Nate scooted back while Danny went forward to take his place. They were incredibly quiet for two people moving around in heavy combat boots while slightly hunched over. Danny was settling in front of the door when he froze in place.

Shit, she thought, when the very loud *clump-clump* of heavy boots moving around in the store below reached them clear as day. If the creatures hadn't been able to conceal their presence while moving on bare feet, there was no chance at all whoever was down there could while stomping around in boots.

Voices drifted through the floorboards, but they were muffled for some reason, and she could barely make out the words. She did know with absolute certainty there was more than one person moving around *(very loudly)* below them. It could have been collaborators or some of Mercer's people, though she guessed it was more likely the former. Only collaborators would so nonchalantly walk around at night these days.

Danny had moved again while she wasn't paying attention and was now crouched on the far side of the attic door. He laid his rifle down and slowly, very slowly, flattened himself against the floor, pressing his ear against the dirty carpeting.

The voices from below were getting louder—but not necessarily clearer—as they drew closer. She wondered what Danny was hearing at the moment. Maybe he could actually discern what the men down there were saying.

Cla-ching!

She recognized the sound without having to think about it, because she had spent an entire summer behind one of them. That was a cash register opening.

"Dude, really?" someone said below them. It was a man's slightly high-pitched voice and it was very clear that time. "What exactly is your dumb ass gonna do with all that cash?"

"I always wanted a new car," someone else said, chuckling. "I should have enough to buy the whole thing cash on the barrelhead by the end of the night."

"Leave that shit alone," a third voice snapped. Another male voice, this one filled with authority. For a moment she thought it might have been Mason *(Nate's right; we should have dealt with that prick when we had the chance)*, but no, this voice was much deeper.

"I'm just fucking around," the second voice said.

"Do it on your own time," the leader said. "Clear the store. We're running out of night."

"We're never going to run out of night, man," the first man said. "Always gonna be another one tomorrow, and the day after that, and day after that…"

"No, but I'm running out of patience, so get the fuck back on the clock. This ain't no fucking vacation. You forgot about what happened yesterday?"

Gaby recalled the layout of the store when they were moving through it earlier, doing their very best not to touch anything. They'd even left the door unlocked and the windows uncovered, because the creatures knew if you moved something. She didn't know how, but somehow they just knew.

Dead, not stupid, right, Will?

The store had a simple floor plan, with the front door opening onto four aisles of products. The cash register was at the very end, behind a counter, and the attic entrance, also behind the counter, was five feet from the register. She guessed that was so only employees could access it. The upstairs room was as long as the employee area below, and they were safe up here as long as no one spotted the outline of the door against the ceiling, even though Danny had made sure to bring up the pull rope.

She listened to the *clump-clump* of boots moving around below them, then the loud *crash* of a door being kicked in. That would be the bathroom door in a hallway to their left. More voices, once again garbled by distance and…something else.

Nate, in front of her, hadn't moved, and neither had Danny

across the room. The ex-Ranger still had his ear pressed into the carpeting, doing a very good job of ignoring the smell and filth that clung to every fiber of the rug. She hadn't noticed it before, but it was cold enough inside the attic that she could see mists forming in front of her lips as she breathed in and out, in and out.

More garbled voices, mingling with the *clump-clump* of footsteps as the men below them started to drift into the background. Moving away, possibly toward the front door, but definitely away from them.

That's right, go. There's nothing here. Just keep going. Search the next building.

Keep going…

As if reading her mind, Nate glanced over his shoulder and smiled. The blue of his eyes was like a beacon drawing her in and calming her nerves. She guessed that he knew it, too, and was doing this for her benefit.

She returned his smile and thought about his request to get them their own cabin on the *Trident*. It was something she'd been thinking about too, especially since spending time with him meant sneaking around when everyone else was occupied elsewhere. But if Lara finally dealt with Gage, then that would open up an extra room below deck. She could even learn to live with all the engine noise.

"Almost home free," Nate mouthed to her now, except he was only halfway through "free" when there was a *bang!*, and the floorboard an inch from his body splintered and a bullet *zipped* through and punched a hole into the ceiling above him.

A small sliver of moonlight spilled through the hole instantaneously, highlighting a part of Nate's suddenly pale face as he scrambled away from the spot even as the *pop-pop-pop!* of someone letting loose with a three-round burst from below shattered the silence.

"Fuck!" Nate shouted, launching himself away from the exploding floor with wild abandon. Splintered wood flooded the attic as he hugged the wall, pieces of shredded carpeting billowing around him like insects.

The first shooter hadn't even stopped firing when someone else joined in. The second shooter strafed the ceiling, clearly trying to cover as much ground as possible, maybe somehow even tracking Nate's footsteps. God knew Nate wasn't exactly being quiet about his movements as he dodged the chasing bullets.

"Shit!" Nate shouted again.

Gaby scooted slightly forward, took aim with her rifle, and fired into the floor. She grouped her shots around the visible bullet holes in the carpeting, hoping to hit whoever was down there even as they continued firing up at them. She pulled the trigger again and again, the hammering of her gunshots like thunderbolts in the closed confines, each empty brass casing flickering and disappearing into the jungle of carpet strands. The crush of each discharge *boomed* inside her ears, but after a while they became little more than a buzzing noise in the background.

She was still shooting, spacing her shots across the floorboards, when there was a sudden flood of cold air. She looked up just in time to see the attic door swinging up, then a figure lunging toward the opening.

Danny!

He was there one second and gone the next, disappearing through the rectangular slot before she could even form his name in her head, never mind actually calling it out loud.

Danny's disappearance was followed by a single *pop!* from below, then two more shots—*pop! pop!*—coming in such quick succession that all three rounds had to have been fired in the space of less than two seconds.

Then...nothing, except for her own ragged breathing to fill the silence. She kept waiting for more shooting, noises—*anything.*

Nate had pushed off the wall and was trying to peer through the dozen or so holes that the shooters below had created and she had added to. She couldn't tell if he could make out anything despite the streams of moonlight pouring through from the bullet holes below and above them.

"Anything?" she whispered.

He shook his head. "Can't see shit."

"Danny's down there."

"I know."

Two more quick shots, followed by the very obvious *clatter* of a rifle skidding against the tiled floor below.

Danny!

Gaby scooted forward and spent a second trying to look through the bullet holes in the floor the same way Nate had done earlier, but the carpeting was too thick and they still covered up too much for her to spy anything on the other side.

When she looked up, Nate was already at the door looking down. He glanced over, saw the question on her face, and shook his head. "It's too dark," he whispered.

She hurried over to him, no longer caring about making too much noise. At this point, everyone *(everything)* who was in the area already knew where they were. She looked down the opening, realizing that Danny had never unfurled the ladder before he took the plunge. He had simply jumped down like an idiot, not knowing what was waiting for him down there.

Carly's going to kick your ass if you die, Danny.

The silence inside the store below her had lengthened to thirty seconds...

...forty...

"Danny," she whispered.

There was no reply.

She exchanged a look with Nate.

He didn't say anything, but nodded back as if reading her thoughts and saying, without actually saying the words, *"Go for it."*

She smiled back at him, reveling in the fact that they could have a conversation without having to say a word. The last few weeks on the *Trident* had been some of the best nights of her life, even if they did have to sneak around most of the time. Not because the adults didn't already know, but because there were also a lot of kids on the boat.

Looking at him now, his blue eyes calm and understanding despite the harrowing last few minutes when it probably felt like every bullet in the world was trying to kill him, gave her a flush of pride.

She returned her focus to the opening, to the sea of black on the other side.

Nate put a hand on her shoulder. The feel of his skin against hers, even through the thermal clothing, was warm and soothing, and a silent promise that he would be there, no matter what awaited them on the other side.

She took a deep breath and jumped down.

CHAPTER 23

KEO

"HOW'S THE FACE?" Keo asked.

"I don't know," Jordan said. "Is there still an 800-pound gorilla sitting on my forehead?"

"Not that I can see."

"Then I guess it's better than the last time you asked. Which reminds me: stop asking."

"I'm just worried about you."

"Hey, it's nice that you care, but once every hour is enough, don't you think? Especially since we're not going anywhere anytime soon. If we ever get out of here at all, which in this case is looking unlikely."

"There you go, being all positive again."

She gave him a wry smile. "I try."

"Try harder."

"Whatever."

Keo pressed against the cold metal bars and glanced toward the closed front doors, their rectangular frames illuminated by the dipping sun on the other side. They had sealed off the barn an hour ago, followed by a flurry of activity outside. He had heard more than a few of the vehicles roaring to life before taking off.

"It'll be dark soon," he said, glancing down at his watch:

4:24 P.M.

"How long have we been in here?" Jordan asked from the other side of the small cage.

"Three hours and change."

"It feels longer." She paused for a moment, then added, "What do you think they're doing out there? Why hasn't anyone come in to talk to us yet? I thought they were going to interrogate us for information."

"I don't know," he said, and looked up at the ceiling. He could just barely make out the lone, silhouetted form through the wooden slabs. He wasn't sure where the other one had gone, or when.

"I wish they'd get it over with," Jordan said. "The wait's killing me." Then, "Sorry, wrong choice of words."

"You're right; they should have started in with the cattle prods by now. The fact that they're leaving…" *Is worrying,* he thought, but said instead, "…doesn't make any sense."

"Cattle prods? They use that for interrogation?"

"Among other things."

"Have you?"

"Among other things."

"Jesus, Keo."

"Yeah."

"Remember how I was curious about what you used to do before all of this?"

"Uh huh."

"I changed my mind."

"Smart."

She went quiet for a moment. Then, "Maybe they know we're not who they thought we were. Maybe they found out about what you did at T18."

He shook his head. "I doubt it. Communication isn't what it used to be. Nothing's instantaneous anymore. You don't realize how futuristic we had things back in the good ol' days, until it's gone. Remember when they switched out textbooks for tablets in schools?"

"You kidding? I was ecstatic. No more lugging around five text-books that weighed more than me combined across campus."

He glanced back at her, leaning against the bars with her eyes slightly closed. She looked almost content—that is, if he didn't know any better. Sometimes he forgot how young Jordan was. Like everyone he'd met on the road, she'd had to grow up too fast.

He turned away just as she opened her eyes.

"You think he's still alive?" she asked. "Gregson?"

"I stopped giving a shit about his well-being the second he closed his mouth."

"You're all heart, Keo."

"It's my weakness."

"Remind me never to get on your bad side."

"That's easy."

"Yeah?"

"Just don't try to shoot me."

"That's all it takes, huh?"

"Yup."

"Good to…" she said, but didn't finish.

He glanced back and saw her leaning a little bit too much to the right, as if she might have fallen asleep in the middle of her sentence. He hurried across the cage and crouched in front of her, then held her chin with one hand and righted her head.

"The hell?" she said as her eyes flew open. "What are you do-ing?"

"I thought you might have lost consciousness," he said, letting go of her chin. "You okay?"

"Didn't we already talk about that?"

"Are you?" he pressed.

"I'm fine. The head's pounding just a little bit. Okay, a lot." She kneaded her forehead with both hands. "You said the truck flew after it got hit?"

"It flew, rolled, and crashed."

"Yeah, I remember the crashing part. Well, not really remember it, but I can definitely still feel it…"

He put his hand on her forehead and felt the bump. It was more pronounced than last time, which meant there was a very good chance of a concussion. He pulled the strip of cloth he still had inside his back pocket, spat on it, and scraped at some dried blood clinging to the side of her temple.

"Ugh," she said.

"Sit still."

"It stinks."

"It's just spit."

"I know, and it stinks. Did you brush your teeth this morning?"

"No, but I used mouthwash."

"Really."

"No."

"Right."

She stopped talking and stared back at him as he cleaned her. Maybe it was the lack of light inside the barn, but the brown of her eyes was surprisingly lively.

"What?" he said.

"Nothing," she said. "You about done?"

"Close."

"Hurry up."

"Yes, ma'am."

She smiled.

"What?" he said again.

"Nothing," she said, but he noticed she hadn't stopped smiling.

◄━━▌ ▐━━►

NIGHT CAME EARLY in winter, and by 5:30 P.M. there was just the moonlight sneaking through the cracks along the wall and roof to keep Keo and Jordan from completely sitting in darkness. It took a few minutes before his eyes assimilated to the new environment and he was able to make out Jordan next to him, their backs pressed against the cage with the barn wall on the other side. Cold wind seeped through the rotting wood, and though he listened for it, Keo couldn't *(yet)* hear the sound of bare feet against the empty earth outside.

He found himself eyeballing the distance separating the bars of their cage again. Five inches, give or take. Five whole inches. Was that enough for a creature of skin and bones to squeeze its way through? Maybe. Of course, he and Jordan wouldn't exactly be standing by, mouth agape like slack-jawed morons, as the creatures assaulted the cage.

How much force would it take to cave in a deformed skull? He had a feeling he was going to find out sooner rather than—

Creaaaak! as the barn doors were pushed open.

Keo shot up to his feet and moved to the front of the cage, Jordan keeping pace beside him. The large twin doors had swung open, and a lone silhouetted figure walked purposefully, as if it had all the time in the world, toward them.

He recognized wide hips and the gait of a woman, and he guessed Marcy *(And so it begins)* before she actually revealed herself in a pool of moonlight about ten steps later. She stopped on the other side of the cage, bundled up inside a black leather jacket that had a patch of Texas on the shoulder. She was holding a dirty white plastic bag in one hand.

"Hungry?" Marcy asked.

"I thought you'd never ask," Keo said. "I don't wanna be one of those guys, but service in this place is lacking."

Marcy smirked and pulled something out from her back pocket. His titanium spork. She tossed it into the cage, and the heavy utensil clattered loudly across the concrete floor to the other side.

"Thought you might want this back," Marcy said.

"Couldn't you have just handed it to me?" Keo asked.

"No," Marcy said, and reached into the bag and pulled out an unlabeled metal can.

This time, she did aim it at him, and Keo caught it. Behind him, Jordan had picked up the spork and was cleaning it off using her shirt.

"You know there are two of us, right?" Keo asked, holding the lone can up.

"I'm being generous giving you the spork back," Marcy said.

"Scork, actually."

"Whatever."

"Yeah, I'm not a fan of the word, either."

The can had a pull tab, so he didn't need the spork to open it. Jordan was practically drooling by the time he tossed the lid away, revealing mushy tuna inside. The smell was indescribable, and Keo couldn't decide if that was good or bad. It did overwhelm most of the aroma in the place, so that was a plus.

He handed it to Jordan. "Split it with you?"

She grinned, then took the can and dug in with the spork.

Keo looked back at Marcy, watching them from the other side of the cage. "Thanks," he said. "For the utensil, too."

"It's your last meal," Marcy said. "Thought you deserved to eat it with some dignity, even after what you did to our guys at the beach."

Shit, Keo thought, but he said, "What is it that you think we did?"

"I know what you did. We found the other guy, too. The one next to the tank."

Gregson.

Marcy's face was stoic, lacking anything that he could have interpreted as either happiness or sadness. "He's been dealt with, in case you're wondering. And you will be, too, tonight."

"I thought you wanted to ask us questions," Jordan said between mouthfuls of tuna.

"Change of plans." Marcy's eyes focused on Keo. "Want some advice?"

"Does it involve us getting out of here?" he asked.

She shook her head.

"Gee, how about some advice, Marcy?" Keo said in the flattest voice he could manage.

"Don't resist," the collaborator said. "Answer every question you're asked, and don't lie. Because they'll know." She pressed her forefinger against her own temple. "They can get inside. You don't want them rummaging around in there, because once you open the door and let them in, there's no way to close it. They're inside for good and it can get a little…maddening at times. I've seen…" She stopped.

"What?" Keo said.

"You don't want them in there for too long, that's all," Marcy said. "So don't fight it. Just don't fight it."

They watched Marcy turn around and walk back to the doors.

"Marcy," Keo said after her. When she didn't respond or stop, "Marcy, where are you going? Where's everyone going?"

The woman kept walking before stepping outside through the doors. Two men in jackets pushed the doors closed with a solid *thunk.*

"What was she talking about?" Jordan asked.

"Hell if I know," he said.

"Here," Jordan said, and scooped some tuna and held it out to him.

It was too salty and covered in a thick film of something that he preferred not to think too much about, but most of it was lost in the metallic taste of the spork anyway. But like Jordan, he was hungry and swallowed it down despite the rank smell.

"Not bad," he said.

She gave him a wry smile. "It tastes like donkey shit, but at least it's food."

"Yeah, that too."

They spent the next few minutes eating in silence. He held the can while Jordan sporked the food between them. Despite the strange liquid that covered the tuna, he was dying for something to drink when they were done. They kept their eyes on the barn doors the entire time, expecting them to open at any moment.

"Don't resist," Marcy had said. *"Answer every question you're asked, and don't lie. Because they'll know."*

"They"? Who was "they"?

Jordan scooped the last piece of tuna and held it out to him.

"Finish it," he said.

"I've eaten more of it than you have."

"Jordan…"

"Shut up and open your mouth."

"How am I supposed to do that?" he grinned.

"Just do it," she snapped.

He opened his mouth and had to force himself to swallow down the last piece of tuna. "Thanks."

"You're welcome."

He flicked the empty can through the bars and watched it vanish into the shadows along the far wall.

"Your spork," Jordan said, holding up the utensil. "You think she forgot it on purpose?"

"Doubt it. It's a little ol' spork, and they have guns. They're probably not too worried about us feeding them tuna to death, though given how bad it tastes, that might actually be worse than getting shot."

He took the titanium spork from her and cleaned it against his pant legs, then put it back into one of his pockets.

"How's your head?" he asked.

"Like someone's piping *Für Elise* directly into my brain, and it's not nearly as soothing as it used to be when I was younger."

He put his hand on her forehead again. The good news was, the bump seemed to have lessened in the last few hours, but there was a definite hard-to-miss bruise in its place.

"Can I tell you something?" she asked.

"What?"

"I like it when you touch me."

He raised both eyebrows. "It's official; you're delirious."

"I'm really not."

"No?"

"No," she said, and leaned forward and wrapped both arms around his neck and kissed him.

It caught him by surprise—he saw her coming, the purposeful look in her eyes, but didn't process what was about to happen until he tasted her lips against his. He kissed her back because he didn't know what else to do, and because *he was a man.*

But then she pulled away, her breath slightly ragged. "Jesus."

"No, just Keo," he said.

She rolled her eyes. "I meant the tuna."

"Tuna?"

"I can still taste tuna on you, and it reeks."

"Gee, thanks."

"Yeah, yeah. Sit down."

"What?"

"Sit down."

"Why—"

"Just do it," she snapped.

He slid along the bars until he was sitting down on the hard concrete floor. "Jordan," he got out in the half-second before her mouth covered his again, and he forgot what he was going to say next.

She sat down in his lap, legs wrapping around his waist, and her kiss grew in intensity, her mouth so warm and her lips so soft and welcoming that he couldn't have resisted even if he wanted to.

And he certainly didn't want to. Christ, he didn't want to.

He wrapped his arms around her waist and pulled her body tighter against his. She groaned against his mouth and he inhaled her scent, which made it easier to ignore the strong odor of old hay and spoiled feed and mold, not to mention the stink of the bad tuna both of them had just eaten.

For some reason, she pulled back a second time—causing him to groan in annoyance—but like last time, she was still so close he could have kissed her again without barely moving. She looked strangely sad, but her brown eyes were bright in the semidarkness and he couldn't turn away.

"Keo," she whispered.

"What?" he said, suddenly aware of his own slightly labored breathing, mirroring hers.

"What are we doing?"

"I don't know."

"What about Gillian?"

"What about her?"

"Do you still love her?"

"I don't know."

"Maybe we should stop until you do know."

"Maybe."

She sighed. "But we're probably going to die in here."

"Probably," he nodded.

"Soon."

"Yeah."

"I don't want to regret not doing this. Even here, in this stinking barn. I've been wanting to do this for a while now, but with every-thing that's happened…"

"Gillian."

"Yeah. Gillian."

She started to get up, but he tightened his grip around her waist and didn't let her.

"Keo," she said softly.

"No."

"We should wait."

"Why?"

"For some place better. Less…disgusting." She glanced toward the other side of the cage. "There are people outside the building."

"Screw them."

"Pun intended?"

He grinned. "You're right; we're probably going to die soon."

"Probably."

"So…"

"So…" she whispered.

She leaned forward and kissed him again.

He didn't bother with her shirt and reached for her belt.

"Keo," she whispered against his mouth. "Keo, Keo, Keo…"

THERE WAS SOMETHING different about the barn, something not

quite right in the way the air smelled or even flowed. The change wasn't just inside the cage, either. He became aware of the strange shift even as he sat against the bars, Jordan's body curled up in his lap, his jacket and hers covering her in a makeshift blanket.

He opened his eyes. "Who the fuck are you?"

"You don't need to know my name, meat," it said from the darkness. No, it didn't say—it *hissed.* "You don't deserve to know."

It looked like Frank, but it wasn't. He knew that from the sound of its voice—similar to Frank's, but there was a noticeable difference. This was what Frank looked like underneath that trench coat and that hoodie he always kept on, as if afraid someone might notice he was no longer human.

Keo should have been afraid—even terrified—but for some reason he wasn't. He felt a strange calmness that he couldn't explain.

What the hell is wrong with me?

It was nude, pruned black flesh gleaming against a spill of moonlight. Its legs carried it out of the shadows with that same preternatural gait that always made him stare for just a half-second too long every single time, trying to decide if it was real or a figment of his imagination. It moved with its back slightly arched, its blue eyes *(like Frank's)* throbbing against the blackness that seemed to shift around its form as if seeking to avoid it.

He thought about waking Jordan up, but she was snoring lightly in his lap with just that ghost of a smile on her lips. He decided to let her sleep through this. It wasn't as if the both of them being awake was going to make a damn bit of difference. He'd seen Frank tear apart a marina full of soldiers, seen him hold back an ocean of black-eyed ghouls. If this blue-eyed monster was anything like Frank, then there was absolutely nothing Keo could do at the moment, with just his hands and feet, and year-old hay scattered around him, to keep them alive.

It stopped at the bars, long arms (much too long) hanging at its sides. He expected to see the ebony eyes emerge out of the blackness in the background, revealing themselves after having somehow sneaked into the barn while he wasn't looking, while he was asleep. How the hell had this thing managed to slip inside without him noticing, anyway?

"I can smell him on you," the creature hissed. "Is he there right now? Looking through your eyes?"

'He'?

"Call him," the creature said.

"Who?" Keo said.

It smiled. Or tried to. Thin lips, like purple drawn-in lines, creased into something that resembled almost a smile. Almost.

"Call him," it hissed, louder this time.

Jordan stirred and shivered in his lap. Something about its voice must have dug all the way into her subconscious. Keo stroked her hair to calm her. If they were going to die tonight, he'd rather she didn't see it coming. He wished he could have taken that option himself.

Hell, he was wishing for a lot of things at the moment. Though, for some reason he still couldn't explain, *he wasn't afraid.*

"I don't know who you're talking about," he said to the creature.

The blue-eyed ghoul cocked its head to one side. Reading him? Maybe trying to gauge if he was lying. The "smile" had vanished in the meantime.

"No," it said. "You don't know, do you? Because he's spared you." It might have laughed; it was an unnatural and choked sound that could, in the right circumstances, be mistaken for laughter. "He's still trying to hold onto his humanity, trying to deny his real nature. But that doesn't mean I can't still use you to bring him to us, meat."

Frank. It's talking about Frank.

Maybe he was still alive out there after all. Why was he so surprised? He had seen Frank survive a lot of things. What was one more impossible situation?

Frank. You out there, pal? I could really use your help right now.

But it wasn't Frank who was gripping one of the cage bars in front of him. Keo could actually hear its bony fingers tightening against the metal—just before it gave a swift pull and the padlock broke off, and the door swung open.

"I won't be nearly as gentle," it hissed as it stepped inside the cage.

CHAPTER 24

FRANK

HE'D TRACKED THEM from the hangar and into the woods, then to a cottage with two girls sleeping inside, and finally back here, where, in so many ways, his old life found its real purpose. The trees were just as thick as he remembered; the ground as unruly; and there, on the other side of the woods, the bitter wetness of lake water against his tongue. They were using an old truck, and it had been leaking motor oil and a variety of other fluids all the way from Larkin.

As he sat perched on a tree, hidden in a fold of darkness, he could smell them all around him. The woods were teeming with them. Thousands. Tens of thousands. The canopies so thick and high they sheltered them from the sunlight even in the daytime.

He jumped down now and picked his way through the shadows, slipping and hiding when necessary. He knew where it was. The town. He'd been through it so many times with Danny in the past. It was just as deserted now as when they'd first found it almost a year ago. Even the surrounding areas had been raided, the few survivors plucked from their holes and basements and fed to Mabry's machinations.

He moved cautiously through the heart of Starch, darting between homes and buildings and apartments, picking his way around the shadows and alleyways and always staying one step ahead—or behind—the black eyes. They were out there, searching among the town, beyond it; all across the state. He could sense the anxiousness in them, in the voices that echoed inside his head.

"Find them, kill them," the voices said. *"These humans have to be taught a lesson. This is our world now."*

The man named Mercer had done that. He and his army of silver-armed killers. His attacks yesterday had been unexpected, the first time Mabry was ever caught off guard. It was less the destruction, the deaths, and the waste of resources that had bothered Mabry; it was that he hadn't seen it coming. They'd had it so easy this last year. The humans were cooperating, the towns were thriving, and the blood was flowing freely.

And then, and then, a wrench in the cog named Mercer.

"You're grasping at straws," Mabry had said to him.

Perhaps not. Perhaps not, after all...

He had to be very careful because there were blue eyes in the area. Not in Starch, but close enough. He could feel their close proximity in the way the air shifted. They could easily converge if he was exposed, so he couldn't be seen.

Then something else—a new smell. Sweat against dirty skin. *Humans.*

He paused to listen in the shadows. They couldn't see him, because human senses were limited. They were bundles of nervous energy tonight, their hands slicked with perspiration even in the cold weather. The months had been too good to them, and they had reverted to their old selves—fat, lazy, and privileged—and they were no longer used to being in the darkness at the same time as the black eyes.

They turned their heads too fast and kept their voices low as they talked amongst each other, as if afraid of being overhead. Their words were muffled by the various-shaped gas masks snapped too tightly over their faces. Why the masks? Because they were told to, in order to make it easier on the black eyes to tell the difference between the uniforms, because Mercer's people wore uniforms too, and the black eyes were easily fooled.

"*Stay away,*" the voices had said. "*Stay away from the soldiers with masks.*"

They were searching the buildings along Main Street, yet another part of the town he was familiar with. He had gone into every building and checked every room with Danny and the others. A long time ago now. Was this where Danny had gone? He had lost their track somewhere in a parking lot a few streets back, where they had abandoned the leaking vehicle.

Beams from flashlights sliced across the endless waves of darkness. The crackle of radios back and forth, the loud *crunch* of heavy boots. And every now and then, nervous conversation between the small group. He was so close to them he could have reached out and snapped their necks. It was tempting. So, so tempting.

"The airfield," one of them was saying. "Shit, it was a fucking massacre. Everyone's fucking dead."

"How many?" someone asked.

"Hundreds. I lost count. We didn't even bother to pull out the bodies."

"You're shitting me."

"No, man, I'm telling you, the whole airfield was just gone. Bodies everywhere under all that mess. I think they rigged the ground with bombs or something."

"Jesus," someone else said.

"Maybe we're on the wrong side," the second one said, dropping his voice to barely a hushed whisper.

The first one laughed softly. Or tried to. It came out choked and desperate to be convincing. "Look around you. It doesn't matter how many tanks or planes they have, or how many bombs they drop. They're never going to beat this. Trust me: we chose the right side."

"Yeah, you're right," the second one said. He had a bit of confidence that time. "The planet's theirs. Nothing we can do about it now."

"How's Rachel coming along?"

"Good, good. Two more months and she's gonna pop that kid right out."

A brief exchange of nervous laughter before they moved on, entering a new building as a group. Quick and efficient movements, clear signs they had practiced this. He was almost impressed.

A *bang!* tore through the street, so loud he would have heard it from across the city.

The soldiers that had gone into the building rushed out, their heavy boots pounding against the pavement like explosions.

"What was that? Who fired?" someone shouted. "Where'd that shot come from?"

The squawk of a radio, but by then he was already pushing up the side of a brick apartment and blocking out the voices. He reached the edge, pulled himself up, then raced across the rooftop.

The air around him shifted as the black eyes, somewhere in the outskirts of the city, reacted to the sound.

More gunshots, like rolling thunder, poured up the street one after another. Automatic rifles.

There, a hardware store in a strip mall. It looked familiar...

The gunshots got louder as he neared. One after another, after another. Like a ringing dinner bell to every set of black eyes in the area. The blue eyes had noticed too, but they hadn't converged. Why not? Because random gunfire wasn't something they concerned themselves with. Besides, the humans were here. They'd take care of it. And if they couldn't, the black eyes would.

Good. That would give him some time.

He flung himself off the roof and landed in the parking lot, then raced toward the store. Silhouetted figures moved on the other side of the windows, the staccato flashes of discharging weapons blinking on and off inside the darkened building.

A blast of warm air as he entered the store and skipped over a rotating rack that had fallen, spilling cheap trinkets across the floor. One of the three figures turned around, sensing him. Wide eyes attempted to focus on his moving form as he slipped between two aisles. The man was confused by his presence—or maybe the trench coat that fluttered around him, or possibly the sight of the hoodie draped over his head—and didn't know whether to shoot or welcome him.

Before the collaborator could decide, three shots exploded behind him. One after another. Evenly spaced, clearly from the hands of an expert.

The sounds of crumpling bodies followed by...silence.

"Fuck me on a stick," a voice whispered.

Danny.

Boots squeaked as Danny turned, trying to track him with a rifle. All it would take was a single headshot. Danny was good, and fully capable.

He swerved around the racks, but Danny didn't shoot. Not yet. He wouldn't commit until he had a target—

Bang!

His left ear disappeared against the bullet, but he kept moving.

A second shot. This one sailed harmlessly past him while he was in midair.

Faster!

He landed on top of Danny, grabbed the rifle by the barrel, and threw it away. Danny let out a startled gasp, but that didn't last, and his right hand reached down for the handgun stuffed into his front waistband.

He grabbed Danny's wrist and pinned it to the floor. An unceremonious grunt, but no screaming. Not from Danny, whose own blue eyes glared up at him, daring him. But these blue eyes were filled with life and humanity, unlike his own.

Danny swung, hitting him in the side of the face with a balled fist. He barely felt it the first time, the second time, or the third time.

"Stop it," he hissed.

Danny stopped punching him. He stopped moving completely.

He could see it in those very human blue eyes—the confusion, the realization that once again everything he thought he knew about the universe had changed.

"They're coming," he hissed. "The uniforms and gas masks. Put them on. Let them see you. It's the only way."

More confusion swept across Danny's face.

"It'll work," he hissed, hating the sound that came out of his mouth, the *unnaturalness* of every word.

He wrestled the gun out of Danny's hand and climbed off, bounding over the counter. He dropped the gun on the floor as he went and pushed through the door.

Cold air attacked him at the same time as the jungle of arms and legs and teeth. He'd misjudged their distance. The black eyes had been much closer and converged much, much faster than he had anticipated.

"There you are." Mabry's voice, echoing triumphantly inside his head. *"I told you, sooner or later I'd find you."*

He fought through the limbs collapsing all around him, but there were too many. They climbed over him and dragged him down to the street, pummeling him to the pavement with their sheer numbers.

"I always do."

He grabbed the closest creature and snapped its neck, then detached the head from the spinal cord with a soft *pop!* He dug two fingers into its eye sockets and swung it like a bowling ball. A head cratered, another jerked out of his path, but still they scrambled over him, biting and clawing and holding on.

"Haven't you tired of running yet?"

He swung and punched and kicked. Clumps of black blood erupted and savaged the air, covering him. He drove his fist through a sunken chest, the resistance like flimsy plastic wrap, and speared flesh and bone with his sharp elbows.

"You can't save them. You can't even save yourself."

The skull in his hand turned brittle and fell apart. He let it go and grabbed two of the black eyes and whipped them right and left, then forward, before pushing, pushing with both feet and for all he was worth.

"All your plans. Your Plan Z's. What good are they now?"

Push. Don't stop. Push. Push! *Push!*

"Look at you. You're pathetic."

Finally! He was out of the pile and racing up the street. Except they were everywhere, reaching for his arms and legs and head. They were doing whatever they could to stall him until the blue eyes could arrive. And they were coming. He could feel their drawing presence in the air.

"*Why do you keep fighting me?*"

Fingers cut into his flesh, and bone cracked against him as he leapt onto a vehicle, the roof caving under him as he landed. He didn't stop, didn't hesitate, and immediately jumped again and grappled onto the streetlight above. He had momentum on his side and flung himself up toward the edge of a nearby rooftop. Reached out—and almost missed the edge!

"*Why won't you admit the truth?*"

He pulled himself up, the loud patter of footsteps around him like thunderbolts. They were already inside the building and racing up the stairs. There were even more climbing up the wall below him.

"*You can't win. You could never win.*"

He didn't look down the side of the building to see how many of them were coming up. The answer would be too many. There were always too many. So he ran instead.

"*There are no second chances. No happy endings.*"

He ran faster. *Faster. Faster!*

"*Not for you.*"

Another leap of faith, the wind brushing against his face, the flaps of the trench coat fluttering behind him as he cut through the night air like a spear, unencumbered by all the things that used to make him human, that once limited what he could do.

"*Wherever you go, however far, I will always be there. Always...*"

He closed his eyes and plummeted headfirst into the dark woods. He could already sense them below—an ocean of black eyes—waiting for him with open arms.

CHAPTER 25

KEO

"SHIBAL," KEO MUTTERED under his breath.

It stopped for a moment—a brief half-a-heartbeat, anyway—to let what he had said sink in, but apparently deciding it wasn't important enough to dwell on, the creature resumed stepping inside the cage.

Keo scrambled back, managing a single step *(Too slow, pal!)* before it was standing directly in front of him. The speed with which it had moved left him breathless, and Keo was still trying to grapple with the physics of it when cold, bony fingers slithered around his neck and, perhaps just as a demonstration that it was in full control, pulled him slightly forward only to shove him back against the bars. The metal rods had been cold all day and were even colder now that night had fallen, but it was nothing against the wicked surge of temperatures flooding Keo's senses like wildfire.

Frank hadn't been this cold. Then again, Frank had worn that ugly trench coat and kept that hoodie over his head almost the entire time they were traveling together. Maybe that wool fabric did more to absorb his natural *(Ha! "Natural.")* body temperature than Keo had realized. He wondered if Ol' Blue Eyes had done that for his benefit or its own. He guessed he would never find out the answer to that one, among other things he'd never get to do again.

The one bright spot he could see—while the blue-eyed ghoul tightened its grip around his throat, threatening to crush his windpipe with a simple flick of its wrist—was that Jordan was still asleep. She lay on the floor where he had left her, warm underneath a pile of their jackets. She was curled up into a ball, just the top half of her face visible under his coat. She looked peaceful and beautiful, and he regretted all those nights when he never realized it.

"I can smell his scent on you," it hissed, razorblade lips forming a sneer as it sniffed the air between them. "It lingers like a disease. Is he nearby? Tell me, meat, is he coming to rescue you right now?"

It was referring to Frank again. The *other* blue-eyed ghoul in Keo's life. The thought made him want to laugh—if only he could at the moment.

I went looking for a girl, and all I got were blue-eyed monsters. Daebak.

Of course there was nothing awesome about this, with the metal bars against his back. He had to exert every ounce of strength just to suck in enough air to keep breathing, and that was probably because the creature still wanted to keep him alive…for now.

It cocked its head to one side, long neck flexing with a grace that shouldn't have been possible for something so unnatural. It looked him up and down, as if trying to figure out what made him tick, or special. Keo could have told it there was absolutely nothing unique about him, though he got the impression the monster wouldn't have believed him anyway.

"Call him for me," it said, caressing Keo's face in a plume of hot and cold breath, "so I can take him home, where he belongs."

'Call him'? I would if I could, pal. I'd call him to come here and kick your ass. Or at least tear your head off. I've seen him do it…

"You're running out of time," the creature said. It turned its head to look at Jordan's sleeping form. "Both of you."

Leave her alone, you fuck.

"I can smell her all over you, too," it hissed, that bad attempt at a smile again. "Lovers rutting in a barn. How animal of you."

Better than dead, assfuck.

"I wonder if she'll scream for me, too," it asked.

He clenched his teeth and managed to wheeze out a sound. It wasn't nearly as dramatic as he had planned it in his head. But then, it was taking everything he had just to keep breathing, to suck air into his lungs.

The creature turned its gaze back to him, eyes like a siren's call drawing him in. Goose bumps raced up and down Keo's flesh.

"We'll keep her alive for a while," it hissed. "We'll have fun with her. Play our little games. And when we're bored, we'll put her out of her misery. But until then, she'll wish she was dead. Now *call him*."

Keo shook his head. Or tried to. He mostly just wiggled it left, then right, then left again. He wanted to shout, *'I have no fucking idea how, you piece of shit!'* but he couldn't.

God, why was it so hard to just *breathe?*

Then, unexpectedly, the creature's fingers (he swore he could feel every single joint in the thing's hand) unfurled slightly. Not enough for Keo to convince himself that he might survive tonight, but just enough that he could suck in a lungful of precious air.

"I...don't...know...*how*," he managed to gasp out.

The creature cocked its head to the other side, pulsating blue eyes watching him closely. It was reading him, trying to gauge his truthfulness.

"It's...truth..." he croaked out.

The taut flesh over its improbably smooth domed head seemed to wrinkle in response. "No, you can't, can you?"

Did it just sound...disappointed?

Tough nuts, pal.

"But he's left his imprint on you," the creature said. "He'll be able to find you...eventually. And when he does, we'll be there waiting. You'll still prove useful after all, meat."

Hey, use away, as long as you keep me alive, Keo thought, but could only get out, "Ack."

"What was that?" it said, lips forming something that could almost be mistaken for a smile if viewed at just the right angles. "I can't hear you. Speak louder."

"Ack," Keo said again.

"What was that?" It leaned forward, then turned its head, presenting a useless stump that used to be an ear to him. "Louder, meat. Convince me I should let you keep all your limbs. After all, I don't need *all* of you, do I?"

Closer.

Its eyes bored into him like twin moons. "Did you say something?"

I said closer...

"I can't hear you," it hissed. "Speak up."

There. That's close enough.

He tightened his grip around the metal handle of the spork, the same one that Marcy had given back to him to eat the tuna with. The thing that was technically a scork, but he hated that name. He had palmed the utensil as the creature entered the cage, wasting a precious second when it couldn't see where his hands were, hidden under the jacket covering Jordan's body. He hadn't used it yet because it was too far, and because it would have taken him at least a second to swing his arm up, then left toward his target: the creature's head.

"They're smarter than the rest," Danny had said. *"If you see them, run the other way, Obi-Wan Keobi. Or shoot them in the head. That seems to work pretty well."*

Shoot them in the head. Right. If only I had a gun, and it was standing perfectly still.

But at least I have a scork. Ugh, I hate that word.

He almost laughed, because it was that absurd. He was going to die trying to stab this blue-eyed freak in the head with an eating utensil. The combination fork/spoon/can opener was titanium and strong as hell, so at least there was that. All he'd have to do was punch hard enough to break skin and get it through the bone. Of course, before he could do that, he had to make sure it didn't see him striking.

Yeah, no sweat—

"Oh, shit," a breathless voice said, before he could finish his thought.

The creature, just as surprised by the voice as Keo, twisted its head to find Jordan scrambling up from the dirty barn floor, the coats falling off her. She stumbled backward until she bumped against the bars on the other side of the cage. She had gone the wrong direction, Keo saw; if she had gone right instead of back, she could have easily escaped through the open door.

If she was still groggy from sleep, she was wide awake now, and her eyes snapped from the ghoul to him, where they remained.

"Go!" he croaked. "The door!"

Her eyes flashed from him to the creature, then to the open door. There was nothing to stand in her way. It couldn't grab her and keep its hold on him at the same time. The question was: Which one of them did it want to keep inside the cage more? Of course, he already knew the answer to that one.

"But he's left his imprint on you," it had said. *"He'll be able to find you…eventually. And when he does, we'll be there waiting."*

It didn't need her, except as leverage against him. And right now—

"Go, goddammit!" he managed to get out. It wasn't nearly as forceful as he had intended, but it was all he could muster with the creature's fingers still wrapped around his throat like a metal glove.

But for whatever reason, Jordan didn't move toward the door. She had seen it, and she was smart enough to know there was no way the creature could stop her. So why hadn't she moved, for God's sake?

"Jordan!" he said again, the effort of shouting (or trying to) making every inch of him tremble with pain. "Get out of here!"

Instead of running for the door, Jordan stood where she was, as if her feet were planted to the concrete floor. Then she did something he hadn't expected—or wanted, for that matter. *She ran right at them.*

No, not at them, but *at the creature.*

Oh hell, Jordan, he thought as the ghoul's ghost-thin lips slithered into a mock smile. It held him steady against the bars with one hand and began lifting the other one—

Keo pulled out his right hand, the one with the spork, out from behind his back.

Go for the head! Go for the head!

But even as he told himself what he had to do, his mind judged the speed and distance and what it would take—a wide, exaggerated arc from bottom to top, right to left, because there wasn't any other way to get it from behind his back and to the creature's temple where it had to go, because anywhere else was pointless.

Not enough time. Not nearly enough time.

What was the lesson he'd been taught in school? Oh, right. The fastest path to a target was a straight line. Like a bullet. Or, in this case, a goddamn spork.

So Keo jerked the titanium utensil upward and toward the ghoul's exposed chin instead.

He felt a flush of triumph at the sight of the spork's teeth breaking flesh, could feel the resistance from its jawbone on the other end, but he kept pushing and pushing, putting everything he had into it, until finally *(Eureka!)* the tines broke through bone.

It let him go then, and even as it did so, Keo pulled the spork back out, the *slurp* as thick black blood splashed on the ground, leaving a trail as the creature stumbled backward. Keo couldn't tell if he had hurt it or if it was just shocked. Either way, he was free and he could breathe again, and Keo took the next few seconds to gasp for breath like a drowning man.

"Oh, Jesus!" Jordan shouted. She had frozen halfway to them.

The blue-eyed ghoul was touching its chin, thin trickles of blood oozing through its fingers. Keo couldn't figure out if that flicker of something on its face was hurt or anger (or curiosity?), and he didn't waste another breath thinking about it.

Air filled his lungs, and he felt renewed strength as he launched himself forward and smashed into the creature, catching it full in the chest. It was like hitting a sack of flour, and Keo couldn't reconcile its unnatural strength with how weak its body was pushing back against him. He drove it back, back, until there was a satisfying *clang!* as the monster's rail-thin form collided with the metal bars.

Keo pulled back slightly and shoved his forearm against its throat. Its neck was slick because it was covered in its own blood, but he ignored the nausea-inducing sensation and pressed harder. He pinned it to the cage with his left hand while cocking back his right, tightening his grip on the handle of the spork, just before sending it flying forward for the killing blow—

No!, his mind screamed as the creature snatched his right hand by the forearm and grabbed him by the shirt collar with its other hand and, as if it were dealing with a petulant child, threw him back. He crashed into the metal bars, felt rather than heard the entire cage rattling on impact, just like what every bone in his body was doing.

He stumbled forward, but his legs were wobbly and he couldn't focus. He did managed to see the floor rushing toward him just in time to somehow stick his hands out before he hit the hard pavement, saving his face from a painful collision.

Get up! The voice inside his head screamed. *Get up, get up, get* up.

He pushed himself up from the floor, every inch of his body screaming with pain, begging him for rest. His arms had doubled in weight for some reason. Keo managed to turn his head, looking up as the creature hovered over him.

"Human," it hissed, the act of talking *(hissing),* of moving its jaw up and down, sending black blood dripping to the floor a few feet from Keo's head. "You're only human."

So close. So goddamn close.

It ran its ice-cold fingers through his hair, got a firm grip, then dragged him up. Keo let out an excruciating howl as his scalp burned and threatened to tear from his head, and it was all he could do to scramble to get his feet under him and stand up so he wouldn't be completely at the creature's mercy.

"I've decided," the creature hissed, "that you don't need your arms."

It pushed him back into the bars, and Keo only managed to get out a grunt even as the ghoul let go of his hair and grabbed both of his arms and grinned at him.

God, that grin. For as long as he lived—however short—he

would never forget—

The spork.

Shit, he'd lost the spork. It wasn't in his hand anymore, and Keo didn't remember when he had dropped it. Probably somewhere between being thrown around the cage like a monkey and having his hair yanked like he was someone's bitch. Not that it would have mattered anyway, because the ghoul was tightening its fingers around both his forearms, and there was no way in hell it was going to let go this time.

It leaned forward until it was so close it could have stuck out its tongue and slipped it into his mouth. Keo almost retched at the imagery.

"This is going to hurt," it hissed. "But don't worry. You won't die. We have ways to stave off death. You'll thank me."

It cocked its head, and again, that goddamn grin. He hated the *fuck* out of that goddamn grin.

"Or not," it hissed.

Then the blue-eyed ghoul did an odd thing. It was pulling back—to get into a better position to render his arms from their sockets, he assumed—when its eyes suddenly abandoned Keo's face and snapped left—

And Keo thought, *Wait, where's Jordan?*

There was a dull *thunk!* from somewhere in the cage, and the ghoul released both his arms. The sudden absence of its impossibly strong grip was so swift that Keo was sinking to the floor *(Again? Jesus, I can't stay off this floor.)* before he could wrap his mind around what had happened, what *was* happening, and why both his arms were flopping uselessly to his sides instead of lying on the cage floor in a pool of blood.

Fortunately, he was staring forward the entire time, even as he was dropping to his knees. Keo saw the ghoul let out something that sounded almost like a guttural squeal before it vanished out of his peripheral vision. There was another loud *clanging!* as something bounced against the cage bars yet again. Except this time, thankfully, it wasn't him.

Keo found the strength to turn his head until it settled on the ghoul, which was sitting on the floor with its back against the rods. Its eyes were wide open and staring forward, as if it was still trying to focus on something and having a difficult time. But of course it wasn't, because there was a metal object sticking out of the center of its forehead between its eyes.

So that's where the spork went.

The shiny metal had gone in deep, its handle buried halfway in the creature's skull after having penetrated not just bone, but whatever was still back there. Small rivulets of blood poked through the point of impact and dripped along the titanium eating utensil.

A figure was crouching on the other side of him—Jordan, her face flushed with worry, brown eyes focused entirely on him. "Keo..."

"Shit, Jordan," he said. Or croaked. Or coughed the words. One of those.

"You dropped the spork," she said, barely managing a smile, even though he could see her lips quivering and her hands were shaking uncontrollably as she stroked his cheeks.

He smiled back at her before he saw it. The cage door. It was wide open, and the padlock was lost somewhere in the darkness of the barn.

Darkness. The barn. Night.

"Jordan," he said.

"Shhh," she said, peering at him. "I can't even tell what color your neck is at the moment. Did it—"

He shook his head. "Outside. The barn. Night. Remember?"

It took a second—just a second—before she understood. Her eyes flew open, and she glanced back at the open cage door. "Oh, God. What do we do?"

"Danny told me a story," he said, looking at the dead ghoul. "It's about a farmhouse in Louisiana..."

THEY DIDN'T HAVE ropes or duct tape to tie the creature up, but its bony arms and legs were pliable enough for them to shove the limbs through the bars and pull and prod them into position, at least enough to keep it in place. For something that had been unfathomably strong, its body was light enough that Jordan did most of the carrying, while he helped out the best he could with arms that had all the strength of spaghetti strings.

If it were only his arms or aching body, he would have been happy. His throat throbbed too, the windpipe bruised, and God knew what other damage he had suffered. He took some comfort in the fact he could still breathe, so at least he wasn't wheezing anymore.

"You think they're out there?" Jordan asked.

She sat next to him at the back of the cage, both of them wearing their jackets. She had helped him put his on, Keo flinching with pain the entire time. The spot gave them a perfect view of the dead *(again?)* blue-eyed ghoul's malformed ass and back. Its head was tilted to one side, the way it had done more than once during its interrogation of him. It almost looked as if it were embracing the cage, arms and legs wrapped around the bars, refusing to let go.

"Willie boy cut off their heads and stuck them on pikes," Danny had told him. *"I don't know why, but they responded to it. The black eyes. They stayed away from the farmhouse all night."*

Gaby had confirmed Danny's story. Not that Keo ever doubted it, though he had to admit that sometimes the ex-Ranger had a tendency to exaggerate. He hadn't, that time.

"This is crazy," Jordan said. "Why would they stay away just because we killed him? *It.* Whatever."

He glanced down at his watch. 10:11 P.M. It wasn't even midnight yet. There were still nine hours before sunrise.

Goddamn Texas winters.

Jordan moved closer so they could share their body heat. "It wanted him, didn't it? Frank."

He nodded.

"Does that mean he's still alive?" she asked.

"Maybe," he said softly.

"Hopefully?"

"Maybe that, too."

You out there, Frank? You still alive, buddy?

Can you hear me now?

He smiled.

"What?" Jordan said. When he gave her a questioning look: "You had a stupid grin on your face."

He shook his head. "Just thinking of a joke—"

Tap-tap-tap.

He stopped in mid-sentence.

The sounds had come from above them. From the roof.

They both looked up in time to see a pair of figures flitting across the cracks, temporarily blocking the streams of moonlight. Next to him, Jordan's body went rigid before she reached down and picked up the spork from the floor. Blood, like mud, caked the stumpy tines.

Tap-tap-tap.

That came from outside the barn.

Tap-tap-tap.

From all around them.

Tap-tap-tap…

He and Jordan sat in silence and waited. He could hear her accelerated heartbeat, the sound of her fingers tightening around the spork's handle.

Saved by a spork, he thought. Never in a million years did he ever think he'd have to rely on an eating utensil to survive the end of the world.

They waited and waited, but the creatures never made any attempts to enter the barn, though he could hear them easily enough through the rotting barn walls. They sounded agitated and restless, and yet they *never tried to come inside*. Maybe they could see through the cracks and saw the dead blue-eyed ghoul hanging off the cage door. Or maybe they just, somehow, *knew*.

After a while, he noticed the ones on the roof above them had simply…left.

"This is freaky," Jordan whispered.

Better than dead.

"I don't think they're coming in," she added, just a trace of barely restrained hope in her voice. "God, I can't believe we're going to survive this. Jesus, Keo, Jesus…"

He looked over and was surprised to see her crying silently next to him. He reached over and brushed the wet drops off her cheeks, even though doing so made his entire arm feel like it was going to fall off at the socket.

She gave him a pursed smile and shook her head. "I'm ten years old again," she said, alternating between choking back tears and laughing.

He smiled and put his arm around her, grimacing with pain, and pulled her to him. She came willingly, leaning her head against his shoulder. It hurt like a sonofabitch, but he didn't let her know that.

In the semidarkness, with little to do and even less to hear, he found himself thinking about the last few weeks. It was funny how things had worked out. He had come to Texas to find Gillian, but had found Jordan instead.

He had to admit, it wasn't an entirely bad trade. Not bad at all.

CHAPTER 26

GABY

SHE LANDED ON the tiled floor with a loud *thump!* and, in a crouch, immediately sprang up. The suffocating blackness was the first thing she noticed, followed by the two figures lying on the floor in front of her, their outlines visible in what little moonlight had managed to punch through the front windows of the hardware store. Her forefinger tightened against the trigger and she almost pulled it but stopped herself just in time because neither body was moving.

She hadn't stood up for more than a second before there was another *thump!* behind her. Nate, falling through the attic door after her. He was so close as he landed that he probably had to do some fancy maneuvering at the last second to avoid crashing into her. It was her fault; she had forgotten to move out of his way.

She did that now, taking a step forward, the rifle in front of her. She swung it left, then right, scanning the darkness.

Christ, it was dark.

"Danny!" she hissed.

"That's my name, don't wear it out," a voice said, just before a lone shadow appeared from around one of the many shelves that separated the back of the store from the front. If she hadn't heard his voice first, Gaby might have fired because she could only see a dark specter blanketed in shadows, moving toward her.

"Jesus, Danny," she said.

"No, just Danny." He stopped and crouched before reaching her.

"What are you doing?"

"Those other two—start stripping them."

"What?"

"Their clothes. Grab them quick, before they come back."

"Before who comes back?" Nate said behind her.

"Spider-Man and his amazing friends, who else?"

She glanced back at Nate, who was slowly lowering his rifle. She could just barely make out his soft blue eyes in the darkened store.

He met her gaze and shrugged. "I should have known he was too stupid to die."

"I heard that," Danny said.

"You were supposed to."

The dead man closest to her was lying on his stomach, his head turned to one side so that the protruding breathing apparatus of a gas mask over his face was easy to make out. He had on a brown jacket, and a rifle lay next to him, within reach of his extended fingers. Gleaming brass casings surrounded him like a police chalk outline.

When she turned the dead man over onto his back, he had on a black uniform underneath. There was a name tag, but she didn't waste the second it would have taken trying to squint out the letters. He was a collaborator—a dead one—and that was all she needed to know.

Nate moved past her and toward the second body. He crouched and pulled off the man's jacket to get at the uniform underneath. He glanced back at her before the two of them looked over the counter at Danny on the other side. He was already unbuckling the third dead man's gun belt while keeping one eye on the front door.

She followed his gaze, but couldn't see anything out there.

"Danny," she said.

"Less talk, more stripping," he said.

"Is this going to work? The uniforms?"

He didn't answer her.

"Danny…"

"Sure," he said, his grin just barely visible in the semidarkness. "Put everything on. Uniform, gun belt, and gas mask—the works."

She wasn't sure if she believed him, or if *he* even believed it himself, but she turned back to her man anyway. Her fingers were trembling slightly as she pulled down the jacket's zipper.

The collaborator was younger up close, probably in his midtwenties, with short black hair and hazel eyes. There was a hole in the middle of his forehead, where blood pooled. His face looked frozen in a state of shock.

Better you than me, she thought, and pulled off his jacket.

THE PANTS AND shirt were a size too big for her, but she fixed both at the same time by tucking the hem of the shirt into her waistband and tightening the gun belt another notch. There was surprisingly little blood on the clothes. At least, in the darkness of the hardware store. It would probably look different in the morning.

If she was still alive to see morning.

Nate hadn't been quite as lucky. His man had bled out so much he made a face the whole time he was pulling the shirt on, then zipped up a jacket over it. He picked up a gas mask from the floor next. "Is this really going to work?"

"I don't—" she started to say.

Danny interrupted her, snapping, "Put them on *now*," from the other side of the counter.

She glanced over, surprised by the edge in his voice, but something else drew her eyes past him, and she saw the silhouetted figures moving outside the store on the sidewalk, their emaciated forms like dancing shadows against the moonlight.

Ghouls.

She sucked in a large breath and pulled her gas mask on, then grabbed the dead soldier's M4 she had laid on the counter. The ammo pouches around her waist were full again after combining the leftover magazines with the ones she had been carrying since this morning. She touched the butt of her Glock, just to make sure it was still in the holster along her hip.

Nate had wandered over to stand next to her, clutching his own stolen M4. His appearance, with his lengthening Mohawk sticking out above his gas-masked face, made for a menacing sight, like something out of a bad post-apocalyptic movie.

"Stay here," Danny said, taking a step forward.

"Where are you going?" she asked, wondering if her voice sounded as odd as his did through the gas mask.

"Gotta let them know we're in here, so they don't come in for a closer look."

"Danny…"

"Trust me."

She sighed and clutched the rifle tighter, watching Danny walk toward the front of the store to stand about five feet from the windows. He had stopped in a pool of moonlight, as if presenting himself to the swarm of undead things outside.

God, Danny, I hope you know what you're doing.

His presence didn't go unnoticed, and the creatures surged toward the store seconds later. The sight of them rushing forward made her catch her breath, and it took everything Gaby had to fight the instinct to retreat. She didn't, because there was nowhere to go. The only escape was up, back into the attic—and then what? Could they really survive up there all night?

"I think it's working," Nate whispered next to her.

The ghouls were pressing themselves against the glass panes, some sliding their bodies back and forth, leaving thick clumps of thick liquid in their wake. A bony elbow *tap-tapped* against another section of window, though she wasn't sure if the creature was doing that on purpose or if it just couldn't help itself because of its mangled arm. They hadn't made any attempts to enter the store through the lone door yet, which was the best indication Nate could be right, that this might actually be working—

One of the creatures glared past Danny and straight at her.

Her legs might have wobbled slightly, and when her hands showed signs it might follow suit, she tightened her grip around the rifle to keep them busy. The sight of them rubbing themselves against the glass and peering in at Danny (and her) made her skin crawl. She willed the rest of her body to remain still, and slowly, very slowly, they obeyed.

Then, one by one, the creatures pried themselves from the windows and raced off up the street. The sight of them, simply pulling back and disappearing one by one by one, leaving thick films of brown and white (and yellow?) liquids behind to mark their presence, made her breath quicken even more so than when they were staring in at her.

"Sonofabitch," Nate said breathlessly next to her.

Danny turned around and began walking back to them. He looked calm, as if he hadn't just been playing who-will-blink-first with a swarm of ghouls, with just a thin wall of glass between them a few seconds ago.

"I can't believe that worked," Nate said.

"Oh, ye of little faith," Danny said.

"It must be the uniforms and gas masks. They're using them as some kind of identifying markers. Like dogs."

"Like dogs?" she said.

"That's what they are, when you get down to it. Just animals. Not any smarter or dumber. And it's pretty easy to trick an animal, even one that runs on two feet."

Danny finally reached them and pulled off his gas mask.

"I never doubted you for a second," she smiled at him.

"Not even a second?" he smiled back.

"Okay, maybe just a pinch," she said, pinching her fingers in front of her.

Danny grinned, and from the look on his face, he probably had a clever comeback ready, but he was interrupted by a loud squawk that blared across the store, followed by a muffled voice from somewhere in the darkness.

"Come in, Perkins," the muffled voice said. "You still there?"

"That's a radio!" Nate said, dropping his voice to almost a whisper for some reason.

"Find it!" Danny said.

Nate searched behind the counter while she looked on the other side, and Danny went through the aisles, scanning the floor.

"Anything?" Danny called.

"Nothing," she called back.

"It's not back here," Nate said.

"Keep looking!" Danny said.

Another squawk from somewhere in the darkened store, followed by, "Perkins, come in."

The voice sounded clearer (and closer!) this time, and she hurried toward a corner, feeling like a blind man groping for a clue.

There!

She snatched it up from the floor, said, "Got it!"

Nate and Danny hurried over as the radio squawked again, and this time a new voice said, "If they're not answering, it means they're dead."

"All of them?" the first voice asked.

"What do you think, genius? If the others are still around, they'd answer, wouldn't they?"

"What now?" a third voice asked. "Do we go in after them?"

"We don't even know where they were when the shooting started," the second man answered.

"Somewhere in the middle of town," the first said, though he didn't sound entirely convinced.

She knew leaders when she heard it, and there wasn't one among the three they were listening to now. There was too much doubt in their voices and too little certainty. You couldn't hope to lead men with that kind of wavering. She had learned that much just watching Will at work.

"Can't go in there now, not with all that activity," the second voice said. "Nightcrawlers are all over the place like fucking cockroaches in heat. They must be chasing something big. I don't wanna get in the middle of that."

"So what, just leave them in there?" the first one asked.

"It's risky, that's all I'm saying."

"We should wait till morning," the third man said. He was trying to sound confident, and failing. "We'll get reinforcements then. That's assuming whoever's in there is still alive after tonight. That's a big if."

"Yeah, I like that idea even better," one of the other two said. She was losing track of who was who; there was a mechanical distortion through the handheld radio that made the voices start to blur together.

"Tomorrow," someone else said, clearly relieved.

They waited to hear more conversation, but the radio remained quiet.

After a while, Danny grinned at her and Nate and said, "See? Told you. Easy peasy."

Then he let out a big sigh.

◄━━▌ ▐━━►

JUST IN CASE the dead soldiers' friends decided to risk entering the town anyway, they dragged the third body behind the counter and deposited it in a pile with the other two. They left the attic door open with the rope connected to the ladder dangling down, in case they needed it in a hurry. She didn't like the idea of being cornered up there again—the brief but hellacious gun battle from earlier still fresh in her mind—but it was preferable to facing the snake pit of ghouls gathered outside the store at the moment. She could still see them occasionally moving back and forth across the store's glass walls.

Danny had locked the front door just to be safe, not that any of them thought it was going to do a hell of a lot of good if the creatures decided to assault the building anyway. The glass windows weren't going to hold for very long, at least not between now and morning. The lock was more for the benefit of any humans that might be poking around. If nothing else, it would provide them with an early warning.

They crouched behind the counter with the bodies a few feet behind Gaby. She did her best to ignore their presence, which was difficult because it seemed like her boots squeaked on their blood or she kicked a stray brass casing whenever she moved. Nate was on the other side of the back counter, and Danny had taken up position in the middle. Danny sat against the back wall now, another one of the dead soldiers' M4s in his lap. His recently acquired jacket was zipped up all the way to his neck, and he looked like a turtle with its head stuck out of the opening.

They had all removed their gas masks for the sake of comfort, though at the moment, with the stink of the bodies nearby, she was having second thoughts.

"What happened?" she asked Danny. She wasn't quite whispering, but she kept her voice low enough that she could be heard and still hear anything approaching the store.

Danny looked over. "When?"

"After you jumped down."

"I shot them."

"All three?"

"I got lucky. It was dark and they were preoccupied with trying to pinpoint where you and Nate Dogg were up in the attic. That, and they probably didn't expect me to jump down the way I did. You know, all idiot-like."

"You fired two more times after that. What were those for?"

Danny's face changed slightly, from relaxed to something she hadn't seen in a while, not even when they had discovered that their expedition to Harold Campbell's facility was for nothing.

It looked like...uncertainty.

"Danny..."

He shook his head. "I don't think you'd believe me if I told you, kid."

"After all we've been through? After last night in the hangar?"

He grinned, though she could tell he didn't quite have his heart in it.

"What was it, Danny?" she pressed.

"Remember back at the farmhouse?"

"What about it?"

"The blue-eyed ghouls?"

"Wanna play?" the creature had asked her, the sound of its voice burying itself so deep into her soul that she would never be able to forget it for as long as she lived.

"What about them?" she asked.

"One of them was here tonight. Earlier."

Nate's shadowed outline stiffened at the other end of the counter. She should have reacted the same way, but she was surprisingly...calm. Maybe it was the last few days, or last night back in the hangar at the Larkin airfield, but for some reason she couldn't quite summon the fear that should have been natural when told there had been *a blue-eyed ghoul inside the store with them earlier tonight.*

"What happened?" she asked.

"I can't explain it," Danny said.

"Try."

"It told me to put on the uniform and gas mask. Told me they would work to keep the ghouls out."

She didn't reply. Neither did Nate. How do you respond to something like *that?*

"Jesus, Danny," was all she could manage.

"I told you you wouldn't believe me," Danny chuckled. "Hell, I still don't believe it, and I actually lived through it. Unless, of course, this is all one big dream, in which case where are the bikini-clad girls? In my dreams only, you understand, so don't be running off half-cocked and blabbing that last part to Carly without proper context."

"You said it *told* you the uniforms would work?" Nate asked.

"Uh huh."

"Why would it do that?"

"I haven't a clue, kid. Not a clue." He paused, then added, "There was something weird about it..."

"You mean besides the fact that it was a blue-eyed ghoul and it was *talking* to you, while simultaneously *not* trying to kill you?"

He grinned. "Yeah, that too."

"What was it?"

"I don't know. Something…" He shook his head again. "I don't know how to explain it. Hell, I might have just imagined the whole thing. It was pretty danky up there in the attic with you two. Lots of bad BO going around."

Despite the jokes, she could see it on his face: Danny was at a loss for words, something she couldn't say with any regularity. But whatever had happened before she and Nate came down the attic, it had struck him speechless. More than that, it had left him confused and unsure of himself.

"I'm still not convinced this isn't a dream," Danny said.

"It's not," Gaby said.

"You sure?"

"Pretty sure."

"Ditto," Nate said.

"Well, shit," Danny said, "if I can't trust you, who can I trust, Nathaniel Ramsey? You are, after all, a war hero."

"I still don't know who that is," Nate said.

"You should pick up a book sometime. Books, in case you crazy kids and your wacky Internets don't know, are these heavy things made of paper and bound into a big boxlike object that you can also employ as a rat beater. Very useful."

"Did it, uh, say anything else?" Nate asked. "This…*thing?*"

"Nope. It said to put on the uniforms and gas masks, then to show myself to the looky-loos outside." He shrugged, and Gaby thought he might have reached down instinctively to clutch the M4 in his lap just to be sure it was still there. "Figured, what the hell. The damn thing had me by the balls and it tells me how to save myself, then just runs off? Didn't think I had much to lose after that."

"Jesus Christ, Danny," she said again, unable to think of anything else to say.

"Yeah," he said, and stared into the darkness again.

She wondered if he was replaying the moment with the blue-eyed ghoul over and over in his head, still unsure of everything he had seen or heard even now, long after the creature had gone. God knew her own encounter with one of those things had been traumatic enough, and hers only wanted to kill her. This one wanted to...*save* them?

And here she thought things were finally starting to make some sense. Returning to Texas had completely undermined that belief. First, there was the insanity at the airport hangar, and now this. Whatever "this" was. She still wasn't entirely sure, and judging by the continued confused expression on Danny's face, neither did the ex-Ranger.

We should have stayed away. We should have stayed out of Texas. God, why did we ever come back? For lights?

They didn't say anything after that for the entire night. No one knew what to say. Not Danny, not her, and not Nate. Instead, they sat in silence and watched the shadows with suspicion, and waited for an attack that never came.

In the morning, it was a different story.

CHAPTER 27

KEO

HEY, FRANK, YOU out there? Someone was looking for you last night. Give me a call back when you get this, pal. We gotta have a nice, long talk.

"You're looking thoughtful," Jordan said.

"Do I?" he said.

"I'm guessing you're either thinking about Gillian or Frank."

"It's not Gillian."

"No?"

He shook his head. "I haven't thought about Gillian all night."

"Was it something I said?"

"Something you did."

"Ah," she said, and he thought she looked pleased with his answer.

"You did it very well," he said.

"I've had practice. Though probably not nearly as much as you."

"Are you calling me a whore?"

"Adventurous," she smiled.

"Sounds better," he smiled back.

"The arms?"

"Like a fat man's sitting on them."

"Try not to move them."

"Sound advice," he said, peering through the half-an-inch of viewing space between the door and the side of the barn.

He could see just enough of the farmhouse's front yard to know that all the vehicles that were still capable of moving had done just that last night, taking along with them any visible signs of soldiers on the premises. There also wasn't any of the familiar aroma of vaporized flesh outside, unlike behind him and Jordan at the moment.

They had opened their eyes to the sight of the blue-eyed ghoul, still fastened over the cage door, slowly turning to ash as morning sunlight claimed it. The creature had simply wasted away, leaving just bleached white limbs to continue clinging to the bars.

A few minutes after that and they were running through the barn, trying to figure out how they were going to fight their way through men with guns who already thought they were a part of Mercer's murderous brigand. Except they didn't have to, because the collaborators really had abandoned the place last night, which was probably also why Marcy had never come back for the spork.

"Don't resist," she had said last night. *"Answer every question you're asked, and don't lie. Because they'll know."*

Keo got the feeling Marcy didn't expect to ever see him again after last night. He didn't blame her; he wasn't even sure how he had survived himself. But all he had to do was look across the barn doors at Jordan, leaning across from him and peering out at the empty front yard, for his answer.

"What?" Jordan said.

"Just thinking—"

"Uh oh."

"—how you saved my life last night."

"Oh," she said. Then, "What did you come up with?"

"I'm glad you were here."

She chuckled. "Because I saved your life?"

"Yeah, that too."

She rolled her eyes. "Are we talking about the sex again?"

"It was very good sex."

"Save it for later, Romeo."

"The sex, or talking about it?"

"Both. For now, what are our options?"

"What options? I just see one. They're not out there right now, but that doesn't mean they won't come back."

"You think they're coming back?"

"I don't see why they'd just abandon this place."

"I don't, either." She paused for a moment, then, "Are you sure you can do this in your condition?"

"I'm fine," he lied. He reached into his back pocket and produced the spork. "Besides, I'm in possession of a very lethal weapon."

"Watch where you're pointing that thing."

"Are you talking about the spork?"

"Cute." She looked back at the door. "Ready?"

"On five?"

"On five," she said.

He faced the door and began silently counting down from *five*. On *one* he pushed his door open, Jordan doing the same to hers.

He had put on a game face when Jordan asked if he was all right, but pressing his shoulder into the door made him wonder if the blue-eyed bastard hadn't actually broken every single bone in his body last night, given the relentless throbbing and wobbly knees that suddenly made their presence known. He grunted through the pulsing pain and kept pushing, until the warmth of the sun surrounded him and he blinked up at the wide-open skies.

He had the spork gripped tightly in one hand and ready to fight, as if it was going to do a damn bit of good if someone with a gun was standing outside waiting for them. Then again, he bet the *dead* blue-eyed ghoul probably hadn't thought the eating utensil was much of a weapon, either, but it had since learned otherwise.

Fortunately for both of them, the farmhouse was just as deserted as it had appeared from inside the barn. The only reminder that there had been men and women here yesterday was a white pickup truck parked at the edge of the wide clearing. Keo hurried over to it, but he already knew what he'd find—or not—before he even reached it.

There was no convenient car key dangling from the steering

wheel, and when he opened the hood, there was no battery. He lowered the hood back down, careful not to let it slam, just in case there were people in the area. Sound traveled these days.

"Can we use it?" Jordan called from the front porch of the main house. She had been peering through the windows but hadn't tried to go in yet.

"They abandoned it for a reason. Anything over there?"

"It's too dark inside, but I'm pretty sure I saw something moving in the back hallway. Maybe we should risk it. There might be weapons, food…"

"Move on. It's too risky."

She gave one of the windows another quick glance before hopping off the porch and walking back to him.

Keo had climbed into the pickup, in search of something, anything, he could use. He found a rusty tire iron on the floor and pulled it outside with him. It wasn't a gun or a knife, but he wasn't going to complain about a melee weapon. If nothing else, it had better reach than the spork.

"Whatcha got there?" Jordan asked.

He tossed the tire iron over to her.

"Ah, you shouldn't have," she said, catching and turning the rusted object over in her hands, before wiping some (though not all, by any means) of the rust off on her pants. "Could be a little cleaner."

"Could be a gun, too, but we can't always get what we want."

"No kidding. I was hoping to wake up on a nice comfy bed this morning."

"Such an optimist."

"And someone with less scars on his face."

"Sorry about that."

"Eh, I'll live." She smiled at him, before her eyes dropped to his feet. "What's that?"

"What?"

She pointed and Keo looked down at a white piece of paper, about half the size of normal writing paper, trapped under one of his boots. He took a step back and picked it up. It would have been pristine if not for his boot print, and there was lettering on it in big, blocky capital letters, as if it had been cranked out by a printer.

Jordan leaned in to get a better look. "What's it say?"

It read, in three separate rows:

JOIN THE FIGHT TO TAKE BACK TEXAS
WAR IS HERE PICK A SIDE
THIS IS ONLY THE BEGINNING

Keo read it out loud, then handed her the paper. Jordan peered at it, as if she could see more than what was printed on the page. He walked over and glanced into the back of the pickup and saw two more identical pieces of paper inside.

He scooped them up and walked back to her. "Saw them back there earlier, but I thought they were just litter."

"Mercer?" Jordan said.

"I'd bet my spork on it."

"So, what, they're driving around throwing these things out of their car windows? I hope they're getting good gas mileage, because it's a big state."

"They wouldn't need to hit the entire state; just the areas where they've struck. Remember the map from Gregson's tank? The towns they were attacking were almost entirely clustered around the southeast." He glanced up at the clear skies. "Besides, maybe they have a better delivery system."

"Planes?"

"It would take a lot to hide planes from the collaborators for all this time, but they managed exactly that with the tanks and themselves, so maybe…"

Jordan turned the paper over, but it was blank on the other side. "So this is some kind of propaganda?"

"Gregson did say Mercer has a plan. I guess this is part of it."

"What's that? Bomb the shit out of people, then ask them to join you?" She stared at the paper. "It says to 'pick a side,' but doesn't say how, or where to go."

"Maybe if we're lucky, we'll run into more of Mercer's people between here and T18, and you can ask them for all the details."

"Again with the warped definition of luck." She crumpled the flyer and flung it across the yard with everything she could muster. "So what do you think?"

"About?"

"'Pick a side.' What happens if we don't?"

He didn't answer right away. Keo had never had any problems choosing sides—it was usually the people who paid him the most. But that kind of no-brainer decision wasn't going to work anymore. Which was too bad; he liked it better when things were simpler.

"We might not have a choice," he said. "The people who get hurt the most in a war are usually the ones caught in the middle."

"Like the civilians in the towns. Like Gillian."

He nodded.

"There's some sense to it, I guess," Jordan said. "What Mercer's doing. The townspeople would have heard about what had happened to the other places by now. Even if the ones in charge of the towns managed to stick all the survivors from the attacks into a dark room somewhere, there's still the soldiers. They wouldn't be able to stop blabbing about it. That's how it is in T18, and I'm guessing in the other settlements, too: the soldiers are just civilians with uniforms. Most of them are married or living with someone. You're encouraged to, because being a couple means getting out of the dorms and into your own house."

"Coupling plus sex plus babies?"

"Pretty much. Anyway, you can't hide something like this. This kind of news will spread like wildfire." She paused, then, "What was that Gregson said? Something about letting everyone know there were other things out there scarier than the ghouls? He was talking about them. Mercer's troops."

"Sounds like it."

"So what do you think?"

"About what?"

"About everything. Mercer. This plan of his. The war with the collaborators. All of it."

Keo shook his head. "I think this Mercer guy knows exactly what he's doing. Either that, or he's fucking insane."

"Can't it be both?" Jordan asked.

He chuckled. "Definitely."

HIS INSTINCTS WERE to leave as quickly as possible, just in case Marcy and the others did return, but there was still too much of the place left to explore for potential weapons. The optimism in him was hoping to find something useful the collaborators might have forgotten or left behind, maybe either because they were in a hurry or were just clueless. He was, after all, just dealing with, when you got right down to it, conscripted soldiers.

They spent half an hour searching the parts of the farmhouse that they could be sure didn't have any ghouls hiding inside, including a storage shack in one corner of the property. Inside, Keo found a lot of tools, an old tractor that might have still worked if there were gas, and enough parts to probably make two more of the machine. He also discovered an old, rusted over machete on a shelf near some piles of lug nuts and spare tires.

"Got a knife," he said when he came back out of the shack.

"Looks more like a sword," Jordan said.

"Technically a machete."

"Can you even cut anything with that?"

"Sure, if you hit them hard and often enough," he said, and switched the machete for her tire iron.

"Aw, you get me all the bestest gifts, Keo."

"I like to show my appreciation when a woman does me the honor of boinking me in a barn."

"If I knew boinking guys in barns would get me this much gratitude, I'd have done it throughout college."

"I have a feeling you didn't have a lot of problems getting guys to do what you wanted in college, Jordan."

She smiled at him. "You don't have to kiss my ass anymore. You already got in my pants, remember?"

"It never hurts to lube up."

"Sounds like the prelude to something painful."

He chuckled. "We'll see."

"Promises, promises."

She gave the machete the once-over, then put it through a few practice swings. In the sunlight, the blade was more rusted over than it had looked inside the building, but it was still a decent weapon. Even if that edge couldn't cut as well as it used to, it was nevertheless going to hurt coming down on an arm or a leg.

"Not bad," she said when she was done. "If I can't kill someone with this thing, I can at least give them tetanus."

"That's the spirit."

"So," she said, fixing him with a serious look. He could tell she had been thinking about it ever since they woke up this morning, and even more since. "After everything we've seen—Gregson, those collaborators yesterday, that blue-eyed thing last night—what are the chances we're going to even make it to Gillian alive, much less actually be in a position to save her when we get there?"

Good question, he thought, and looked around at their surroundings.

It was the same now as the last time he had checked: A flat and open land, and somewhere out there was the highway. The problem wasn't finding it—just follow the dirt road connected to the house. It was the very long road (and when you were moving on foot, everything took too long) between here and T18 that was going to be a problem.

Marcy and her collaborators were on high alert, if all the firepower he had seen yesterday was any indication. Besides the technicals, they were carrying around LAWs, no doubt as a response to Mercer's tanks. What were the chances he and Jordan could make it to Tobias, and then Gillian, without ever running across another group of well-armed men with itchy trigger fingers?

You just walked right back into a warzone, pal. Congratulations.

He sighed out loud.

"I take it the chances are pretty piss poor," Jordan said.

"I've been in worse situations," he said. "Come on; let's find the highway."

"There are people with guns and rocket launchers on the highway, remember? Maybe we should stay out of the open as much as possible."

"Look at you, being all tactical."

She smirked. "I just don't wanna get blown up again."

"Yeah, that wasn't very fun, was it?" He glanced in the direction of the highway. "I guess we start walking."

"That's your big plan?"

"We'll figure it out between here and there, wherever 'there' ends up being for now."

"I could have come up with that plan," Jordan said.

"Yup," he said, and started off.

Jordan followed behind him, and they didn't say anything for a while. He was hoping it would stay that way, but of course he should have known better.

Less than thirty seconds later, Jordan said, "What are you going to tell Gillian?"

"About what?"

"You and me. *Is* there a you and me?"

"After last night, you still have to ask?"

"Yes."

He stopped and looked back at her. "I gave up on Gillian a week ago."

"Just like that?"

"Yes," he lied.

He wasn't entirely sure if she believed him, but she gave him a pursed smile anyway. "I should tell you something."

"What's that?"

"I expect a promise ring."

He chuckled. "Will you settle for my letterman jacket?"

"Depends. What did you letter in?"

"Pure badassness."

"Impressive."

He smiled and turned around and continued walking. She followed, picking up her pace until she was walking beside him stride for stride.

"It's going to be a long walk," she said.

"Uh huh."

"Maybe we'll get lucky and find a working car on the road."

"Ever the optimist."

"Of course. How do you think I finally landed you?" she said, and smiled at nothing in particular.

CHAPTER 28

GABY

"I SEE TWO vehicles," Nate said. "How many do you see?"

"Two, too," she said.

He chuckled.

"This isn't funny, Nate. We're probably going to die in the next few minutes."

"Sorry."

She was crouched beside one of the windows at the front of the hardware store watching the vehicles coming up the street. Nate mirrored her pose on the other side of the building, his breath fogging up the glass surface in front of him. She flexed her fingers around the pistol grip under the barrel of the M4 to keep it from going numb. The weapon had a red dot sight, which was more than good enough for daylight fighting. The dead collaborator she had taken it off had been carrying two extra magazines, and counting the two she already had for the AR-15, gave her a total of five. She'd had to make do with much less.

"Maybe they'll pass us by," Nate said.

"Maybe," she said, though she didn't believe it for one second.

They were close enough that she could have heard him (and vice versa) even if he were whispering, which he wasn't because he didn't have to. The soldiers were still a good hundred yards down the street, and they didn't seem to be in any hurry.

She paid very close attention to the four figures moving on foot as they peeked into windows and kicked in doors on both sides of the street. The vehicles stopped each time they made entry, then resumed when they re-emerged. At this rate, she didn't think they would reach her and Nate for another half an hour.

They don't have to rush, because the night belongs to them. They can take all day if they want to.

There was a lone woman among the soldiers, and Gaby watched her breaking a window with the stock of her rifle before peeking inside. It wasn't much of a search on her part, but she seemed satisfied with it and jogged over to rejoin the others. Gaby didn't blame her for wanting to stick as close to the weaponized trucks as possible.

"Technicals," Danny and Will called them. The ones she was looking at were blue and red, and both had machine guns mounted in the back, each one manned by a soldier. They weren't wearing gas masks, but she could see the breathing apparatuses hanging from their belts as they moved about. She guessed they didn't need them in daylight, without the ghouls around to mistake them for the enemy.

She was glad to be rid of the mask herself. It sat somewhere on the counter behind her now, along with the uniform of the dead man she had put on last night. All three of them had swapped back into their old clothes, though they had kept everything else, including the rifles, gun belts, and supply pouches. It was more than they'd had even after the trip to Taylor's cottage outside of Larkin.

"We should have brought lunch," Nate said.

"I never asked, but can you cook?"

"Hell no. What about you?"

"Why? Because I'm a woman I should know how to cook?"

"Well, yeah."

She smirked, and he chuckled.

"They sure are taking their sweet time, though," Nate said, focusing back on the street.

She wasn't at all concerned with the deliberate speed of the soldiers. It was those machine guns that made her wary. She had seen
what kind of damage those things could do up close. Bonnie had
become very good with the M240 they had onboard the *Trident,* and
she'd seen the ex-model obliterating targets in the water with one
pull of the trigger.

The soldiers were less than fifty yards when she said, "Get
ready."

"Danny?" Nate said.

"Soon."

"When?"

"He didn't say. But soon. Just be ready."

Nate stood up, his body sliding against the wall next to the glass
window, and stretched his legs. She did the same thing on her side,
extending first her right leg, then her left. Her hands had numbed a
bit while waiting, and she forced blood to circulate along the rest of
her limbs now.

She zeroed in on the men inside the two vehicles. Only the blue
one had another soldier in the front passenger seat besides the
driver, and that man was talking into a radio. When he was done, he
put it on the dashboard and said something to the man behind the
steering wheel. The fact that she hadn't heard the radio clipped to
her hip squawk when the man was using his told her they had,
smartly, switched channels after last night.

There were nine of them that she could see—"could see" being
the operative phrase. Who knew how many more were further up
the street or in other parts of Starch? How many were waiting on the
outskirts of town right now, ready to swarm once these nine located
their targets? How many were the collaborators committing to
flushing them out? Or maybe the better question was, how many
could they *afford* to commit, with Mercer's people still running
around out there?

Even if this was it, nine was still a lot for them to kill. For *her* to
kill. And they'd have to do exactly that to get out of Starch alive. The
Trident was waiting for them somewhere out there. They'd never

leave until they had exhausted every effort to find them. Danny was right about that. She had seen how long Lara was willing to wait for Will; her friend would never just abandon them after a few days. A few weeks from now might be another story, though.

"Holy shit, is that…" Nate said from across the store.

She turned to him and was about to ask what "that" was when she heard it, too.

It was a slight *buzzing* sound that came out of nowhere and gradually increased, until she knew exactly where it was coming from: Outside, but more importantly, *from above.*

Gaby glanced out at the street and saw the soldiers jumping up the sidewalks and seeking shelter against building storefronts. Their heads were upturned and following the object as it glided across the open skies. It was hard to miss, because it was the only unnatural thing up there.

It was a plane.

Round and fat and gray as it moved high above them.

Gaby's first instincts were similar to the collaborators: Run and hide. She was already hiding, but how much cover would the hardware store provide when that plane started dropping bombs? Or, if it was anything like the Thunderbolts that had laid waste to T29 and the Larkin airfield, started its strafing runs? Anyone outside would be most vulnerable—

Danny.

He was out there, in the open, and was a sitting duck to any type of aerial bombardment. She looked anxiously up at the ceiling, wondering if he had come to the same conclusion as she had, and waited to hear him scrambling around up there, where he had taken up position ever since sunrise filled out Starch.

Except the plane didn't shoot, even if it did seem to be dropping something out of its belly. White…something was falling in long, jagged lines down to earth from the craft. More than a few of them landed on the rooftops in front of her, some on the streets. One fluttered almost majestically to the sidewalk—

Crack!

The shot had come from above her, from the hardware store's rooftop.

Danny!

She almost smiled. Of course the ex-Ranger would be the only one to realize the perfect opportunity to strike, while everyone (including her and Nate) were distracted by the appearance of the plane.

She focused back on the street just in time to see the soldier standing behind the machine gun on the blue technical collapse into the truck bed. The weapon he had been manning swiveled as he released it, the muzzle aiming harmlessly up at the cloudless sky.

"Now, Nate, now!" she shouted.

She stepped away from the wall and lifted the M4, lining up the red dot with the soldier standing in the back of the red truck. He was in the process of taking aim at the rooftop of the hardware store with his weapon and was crouching slightly to get a better angle.

Forty yards. Easy shot with a carbine.

She fired, the bullet smashing the window in front of her, and a split-second later the machine gunner disappear out of her scope.

Then Nate was firing to her left, unloading downrange with three-round bursts. Gaby blocked out his shots and zeroed in on the driver of the red truck. The man had slammed on the gas because the vehicle started lurching forward, picking up speed as it went. Her second bullet drilled through the windshield, spiderwebbing it, and—*missed!*

Shit!

She scrambled to line up the sight, but before she could squeeze off a frantic make-up shot, the truck's windshield spiderwebbed again, but this time directly in front of the driver. The man slumped forward into the steering wheel and a loud blaring sound—the horn—filled the air. She waited for the vehicle to stop, but instead it kept coming—*straight at her.*

"Nate!" she shouted, trying to be heard over his three-round bursts. "Incoming!"

He pulled his eye away from his scope just in time to see the truck. She was already moving even before he did and had to be satisfied with the knowledge that Nate was too smart to stand there and gawk at the technical as it barreled its way up the street at them. She hoped, anyway.

She gripped her rifle with both hands as she swerved around the aisles until, finally, saw the counter at the back. She thought about grabbing the attic door and going up, but there wasn't going to be enough time. She could already hear the loud roar of the truck's engine (was it revving?) as it approached the front windows—

The massive *crash!* she had been waiting for, as the vehicle's front fender took out the remainder of the glass curtain wall that she and Nate hadn't already obliterated, along with the door. Her ears rang, even as she heard the continued *pop-pop-pop* of automatic gunfire coming from above her, from Danny as he continued raining fire on the soldiers in the street.

Now, now, now!

She dropped and slid the last few feet along the dirty floor, flinching at the gross image of leftover blood from last night that she was soaking up with her clothes like a sponge. Her slide was true, and she disappeared through the entrance of the back counter at the same time all hell broke loose behind her. Her forward momentum carried her past the counter and she tucked her body into a ball, the rifle clutched against her stomach, and careened into the wall with the back of her neck.

As she unfurled, she found herself with a perfect vantage point to see Nate as he was hopping over another part of the counter in some kind of parkour move she had only seen in the movies. She wasn't prepared for that. She always knew Nate was athletic and in excellent shape, but she didn't know he could do *that*.

Nate landed facefirst, somehow managing to stick out his hands in time before impact, but his rifle wasn't so lucky, and it clattered loudly as it struck the floor and skidded away. He scrambled to get as far under the countertop as he could manage as glass shards and nails slammed into the wall and fell around them. She thought he had the right idea and scooted forward to be next to him.

He glanced over as the last few items inside the hardware store settled around them, and grinned. She returned it, but their moment was short-lived because gunshots were still ringing out from the street as well as above them, where Danny was still perched—which meant the truck crashing into the building hadn't brought down the roof.

Thank you, Jesus.

She scrambled up to her knees and looked over the debris-strewn counter. The red technical was buried halfway into the building, tossing shelves and all the abandoned tools on them everywhere. The driver had finally taken his foot off the gas and was nowhere to be found.

"Danny?" Nate said.

She craned her neck as two shots *boomed* above them, as if on cue.

"Still kicking," she said, and got up and ran back through the store, skirting around the vehicle that had claimed a large piece of the interior. The *crunch-crunch* of objects under her boots and from behind her sounded as Nate followed on her heels.

There wasn't anything left of the storefront, a fact that occurred to her just as she slid to a stop, about the same time a bullet *buzzed!* past her head and *pinged!* off the tailgate of the truck behind her. She was standing out in the open with absolutely nothing to hide behind, like an idiot, and Gaby would have dived to the floor for cover if it weren't covered with sharp chunks of brick and mortar and an ungodly amount of broken glass.

Instead, she turned around as—*ping!*—another bullet nearly took her head off, but hit and ricocheted off the truck a second time instead.

Pop-pop! from the other side of the truck as Nate opened fire into the street.

She smiled to herself *(He's covering my retreat. God, I think I love this man.)* as she ran back to the driver-side door and opened it. A body fell through and slumped on the floor at her feet, but she ignored it and moved behind the broken window. On the other side, Nate had slowed his shots now that she was safe.

She spied a figure moving behind the blue technical still parked in the middle of the street. There were bullet holes in the front windshield, either Danny's or Nate's doing, but no signs of the driver. The figure stuck its head out from the back bumper. It was the woman Gaby had seen earlier, and she was lining up a shot at Nate.

Gaby fired twice in the woman's direction, both rounds hitting the side of the truck, one smashing the back lights. It was enough to drive the woman behind cover before she could pull her own trigger.

The *crunk!* of a car door opening as Nate followed her example on the other side of the useless vehicle. She looked across the bloody front seats as he slapped a fresh magazine into his M4.

"You okay?" she asked.

He glanced over. "Yeah. You?"

"One piece, thanks to you."

"Just don't let it happen again."

She smiled. "I'll do what I can."

When she looked back, the street outside had grown eerily quiet, though she might have heard faded scratching from above her. Danny, maybe moving around for a better shot. He had the high ground because Danny was smart and this was what he did. She couldn't imagine what it would have been like to have to face him *and* Will at the same time.

She focused out the smashed front wall of the hardware store and concentrated on the two bodies next to the blue truck—one was on the sidewalk; the other lay almost perfectly in the middle of the two-lane road. Two bodies that she could see, but more that she couldn't. She knew for a fact there was one body in the back of the red truck she was hiding behind at the moment, and another one at her feet.

Two plus two made four collaborators accounted for.

Then there was the blue truck's driver and the dead machine gunner in the back.

Two plus four made six.

"Take out the machine gunners first," Danny had said this morning. *"Those bad boys are going to chew us up and spit us out in little vomit chunks if we let them get going."*

So she had waited for Danny to take out his man before she targeted hers while Nate sprayed the street to sow confusion. One of those bodies on the streets might have been his—not that any of them were going to be taking a tally after this.

That left them with three live bodies to account for, including the woman. Unless the passenger of the blue technical was already dead and somewhere on the floor of the vehicle. Then that would leave two. Two or three.

She had to admit, she liked those odds.

Gaby watched and waited. What were the remaining two (or three) going to do now? If they were smart, they'd stay right where they were and radio for backup. Which meant…

She looked into the truck and saw the two-way, covered in blood, on the front passenger seat. She waited for it to squawk, for the soldiers outside to radio for help, because there *had* to be other collaborators outside Starch at this moment, right? These nine couldn't possibly be all there were. Maybe—

A flicker of movement out of the corner of her eye, and she turned around in time to see a figure—a man—leaping up the back of the blue truck. He was going for the machine gun. That was the plan, anyway, but the man hadn't finished throwing his other leg over the tailgate before a shot rang out and he stopped his forward momentum. A second later, he collapsed and disappeared over the back.

"So much for that idea," Nate said. "One left?"

"Maybe two."

"You saw two?"

"No, there might be two, but definitely one more. The woman."

"What's she going to do now?"

"The smart thing would be to call for help." Gaby glanced back at the silent radio again.

"You're assuming they're sm—" Nate started to say, but he ended up shouting "Shit!" instead as two figures made a run for it on the street.

She stepped sideways, away from the door, and tracked them. She ended up filling her optic with the back of the woman, and fired—and *missed again!* Her bullet went high, and the woman ducked and turned left—toward the mouth of an alley.

Gaby took her time and fired a second bullet and saw the woman spin in mid-stride.

Gotcha!

Next to her, Nate was shooting, his bullets raking the wall behind the woman, who was still moving despite her wound. A second later the figure disappeared from the sidewalk.

Or not, she thought when there was a single *crack!* from above them, and the man who had taken off at the same time as the woman stumbled and dropped to the opposite sidewalk, about eighty yards up the street.

"Gaby!" Danny shouted from above them. "Secure Speed Racer!"

Gaby raced out of the building. Nate, as always, was right behind her.

She jogged up the street, waiting for the man to make a move, but he never did. He must have known he wouldn't have gotten far even if he managed to pick himself up. Gaby peeked at the alleyway where the woman had disappeared just as she ran past it. Splashes of blood on the sidewalk, but no signs of the collaborator.

Pieces of paper, the objects she had seen falling out of the plane earlier, reflected back the sunlight around her, littering the streets, but she didn't have time to stop and pick one up.

"I got the alley!" Nate shouted behind her.

She continued on toward the wounded soldier alone.

He was lying on the pavement on his back, clutching his right leg. Danny's shot had gone through his thigh and the collaborator was grimacing in pain. His teeth were clenched, and Gaby wasn't sure if he was going to curse her or scream for help when she finally reached him. A pool of blood gleamed under him.

"Fancy meeting you here, beautiful," the man said. "I should have known it'd be you and your little friends running around out here causing trouble again."

Mason.

Of course he was still alive. The man really was like a cockroach, showing up whenever they least expected him.

"You're looking well," he said as she picked up his rifle lying a few feet away. He held his hands up in surrender as she pulled his handgun out of its holster and stepped back.

"Clear!" she shouted.

She took a moment to scan the streets. There was no way someone within miles of them hadn't heard those back-and-forth volleys. If there were more collaborators around, they would be here within minutes. The fact that they hadn't shown up yet put her slightly at ease. Maybe Mercer's attacks had spread them out thinner than she had imagined.

Footsteps behind her, followed by Nate's voice. "The woman's gone. You got her good, though. She bled all the way to the back of the alley where she went over a fence."

"I guess I should have gone left instead of right, huh?" Mason said.

"Guess so," Nate said. Then, recognizing the man, "Sonofabitch. You again."

"I'm like Steven Seagal. Hard to kill, even though I've been marked for death, under sieged, and have stood on deadly ground many a times before. Get it?"

"Get what?"

"Never mind," Mason sighed.

More footsteps behind her, then Danny's voice: "How was my shot?"

"True," she said.

"That's how I likes 'em. The other bird?"

"Flew the coop," Nate said.

"Well, that's disappointing. I guess it's true what they say: You want someone dead, you gotta shoot them yourself."

"What do we do with him?" Gaby asked.

"Good question," Mason said.

"Shut up."

"Yes, ma'am."

"Blue truck's still good," Danny said. "We'll grab Doogie Howser, M.D. here and boogie before more of his friends show up. Nate, salvage what you can."

Gaby hadn't looked away from Mason. A part of her thought he might vanish if she turned away for even a second. He had struggled to sit up and was still clutching his leg.

"Why?" Gaby asked.

"Why what?" Mason said.

"I wasn't talking to you." She looked back at Danny. "Why are we wasting our time dragging this piece of trash along with us?"

"Hey, come on now, no need for that kind of language," Mason said.

"Shut the hell up," she said, and pointed her rifle at him.

He stared defiantly back at her. She could almost believe he wasn't frightened, but she knew better. He was putting on a good front, but men like Mason didn't want to die.

"Because he's still got friends out there," Danny said. "What are the chances we're going to get around all of them? Unlikely, and you know how optimistic I can be. But I bet our new friend here's willing to point out all the ambush spots so we can go around them."

"And why would I do that?" Mason asked.

"Because if we get caught, you're going to be the first to go. And I ain't talkin' about the bathroom, short stuff. You *comprehende* my bad *Spanishe?*"

Mason grinned widely. "Well, you do make a persuasive argument."

"See? We're practically BFFs. That's how I am. I live and let live. There's even a word for that."

"Magnanimous?" Mason said.

"No thanks, I just ate."

Gaby sighed. She didn't like it. The thought of having to spend another minute around Mason made her queasy, but Danny was right. They needed to get home, which meant making their way back to Port Arthur. There was a lot of highway between them, and with Mercer out there, more dangerous than when they had first traveled the same miles.

Her eyes drifted to the road around them, at the white pieces of paper strewn about, as if someone had dumped their office trash out of a second-floor window. "Danny. The plane. They were dropping paper."

Danny snatched one up. "You guys littering now?" he asked Mason.

"Not us," Mason said.

There were large, blocky capital letters on the paper in Danny's hand, but she couldn't make out the words over his shoulder.

"What's it say?" she asked.

He skimmed it, then handed it to her. It looked like some kind of advertising flyer, about half the size of the paper she was used to back in school. The letters were clearly generated by a printer, and they read:

> JOIN THE FIGHT TO TAKE BACK TEXAS
> WAR IS HERE PICK A SIDE
> THIS IS ONLY THE BEGINNING

She returned her gaze to Mason, still sitting on the pavement, either too hurt to try to get up or too afraid of being shot.

"Mercer," she said.

"Would be my guess," the man nodded.

"Looks like we got ourselves a regular Hatfields and McCoys situation," Danny said. "Hide the relatives and pass the ammo. Me personally, I like to stay out of other people's civil wars." He looked back at Mason. "So the question of the moment is, how many more of your pals are out there beyond the town limits?"

"This is it," Mason said.

"I don't believe you."

"Believe what you want." He nodded at the flyer in Gaby's hand.

"We got bigger problems right now. They sent us back here just to see what happened to their friends."

"Sent you?" Gaby said. "You used to be in charge of a whole town."

Mason sighed almost wistfully. "Things change, blondie. We're not in Louisiana anymore. New job, new position. That whole Song Island fiasco messed up my cred with the bosses. I guess you could say I'm back in the mail room."

"So we won't run into more of you out there?" Danny asked.

"I didn't say that. The towns may be on lockdown, but the guys in charge aren't just going to sit back and wait. It's the Wild West out there—multiple kill teams running around shooting each other. Theirs and ours. Lucky for you, I know where our guys will be. I know their movements."

"And Mercer's peeps?"

Mason shrugged. "Your guess is as good as mine."

"Danny," Gaby said. "He's too dangerous. We can't trust him."

"We have to," Danny said. "He gives us a better chance of getting home." Danny tapped his Sig Sauer for effect when he added, "Of course, for someone with a ten-year-old girl's body, he's got a nice big juicy head. I bet I could plug that thing from fifty yards using this here handgun, easy."

Mason swallowed, but smartly didn't say anything.

Danny looked over at her. "Let's go home, kid."

"What if he's lying, and he leads us right into a trap?" she asked.

"Then we'll kill them, along with anyone else who gets in our way," Danny said, and turned to go.

CHAPTER 29

KEO

THEY HAD BEEN walking north for the last hour, keeping parallel to the highway about fifty yards to their right while staying out of the open. Unfortunately, that meant traveling across fields of farmland and grass that at times went all the way up to their knees. Fortunately, the land wasn't fenced off, which saved them the trouble of having to go around each individual property. The extra precaution didn't make them completely hidden from the road, but it was better than just walking around out there exposed, the way they had done in the truck yesterday. They'd eaten a rocket for that little bout of stupidity.

"Remember what that guy said about Angleton?" Keo said.

"Something about it being dead," Jordan said. "For a year now. Why?"

"Might be worth looking for supplies there."

"You really think they'll be something useful after all this time?"

"Won't know until we look."

"But wouldn't your friend Marcy and her pals have already raided it by now? I got the sense they were based around here."

"My 'friend' Marcy?"

"She did give you back the spork."

"She gave *us* back the spork. And as I recall, she threw it into the cage."

"Probably her idea of foreplay."

Keo glanced over, not sure if all of this was her way of teasing him or—

She was grinning.

Right. Teasing. Walked right into that one, didn'tcha?

"I'm just messing with you, Keo," she said. "Have to keep myself entertained somehow."

"Good to know."

She shooed away a bug that had launched from one of the sunburnt blades of grass around them and landed on her forehead. "How long have we been walking, anyway?"

"An hour."

"You sure? It feels like more. By the way, I'm hungry."

"Too bad, because there's nothing to eat."

"Can't you go, I don't know, make a trap out of some twigs and catch us a rabbit or something?"

He wished there were something in the endless acres of untended farmland spread out to the left, right, forward, and back of them. He would have settled for a fruit or two. Jordan wasn't the only one starving this morning.

"What am I, your servant?" he said instead.

"Aren't you?"

"No."

"Well that's disappointing. What kind of relationship can we possibly have if you won't even go out there and hunt down food for me?"

He chuckled and whirled the tire iron in the air, listening to the *whoosh-whoosh* it made, the only sound other than their tired footsteps for miles around. The lack of anything made him wonder who the farmhouse they had escaped from belonged to, and why the people had come all the way out here, so far from another living human being.

"Jesus, where is everyone?" Jordan said after a while.

"We're in the boondocks."

"This isn't the boondocks, Keo. This is Mars. Only drier."

He looked toward the highway. It was flat and empty and cut across the fields, the only stubborn hint of civilization having even reached this far out into the countryside. Like Jordan, he wondered where Marcy and her collaborators had gone to. Was there a city nearby that he didn't know about or hadn't seen on the map when they still had one? It would make sense, assuming the machine gunner wasn't lying when he told Keo Angleton was "dead."

"I'm hungry," Jordan said next to him.

"You already said that."

"I'm starving."

"I got the gist when you said you were hungry."

She sighed. "Do something, Keo. Go find a cow and beat it over the head with that tire iron and cook me something to eat."

He smiled. He would, if he could, but there was nothing around them but unfettered tall grass swaying in the morning breeze. What were the chances there was an animal or two hiding among them? Towns like T18 had their share, but they were far from T18 at the moment.

"*Car!*" Jordan half-shouted and half-whispered.

He went into a crouch even before Jordan had finished saying the word. She did the same next to him, clutching the machete, the dull brown-colored blade so rusted over he was afraid it might fall apart if she moved it too fast. He changed up his grip on the tire iron, but like the last hour, still found it incredibly lacking.

What's that old saying? "Don't bring a tire iron to a gunfight."
Or something like that.

It was a white Ford truck, overturned in the ditch on the other side of the road, about forty meters in front of them. Its wheels were sticking out just above the grass line, sunlight glinting off their rims. He scanned the empty acres around them but came up as empty now as the last dozen or so times he'd searched for clues of humanity.

He glanced at Jordan. "I'll go first. Don't move until you see me reach the other side."

He expected an argument, a variation of "If you can do it, I can too" girl power nonsense, but Jordan just nodded back.

He must have looked surprised, because she said, "What?"

"Keep an eye out around us, just in case," he said, then got up and jogged forward, angling right as he went.

He bent over at the waist to lessen his profile as much as possible, but he knew it wouldn't be nearly enough if someone was out there watching him. The fact that he was wearing dark clothes and moving through a mostly tan/brown sun-scorched field likely didn't help. He stuck out like the proverbial sore thumb.

Keo breathed easier (though not by much) when he finally reached the ditch on their side. He snapped a glance up, then down the road, saw pieces of glass, metal, and aluminum spread across the pavement, and burnt tire tracks. Sections of the truck had broken loose as the vehicle skidded off the road before finally landing on its roof on the other side. He sniffed freshly spilled gasoline and leaked motor oil, so whatever had happened hadn't been all that long ago. Maybe even this morning.

He took a breath, then climbed out of the ditch and darted across the road, still keeping himself as low as possible. He waited for gunshots, but they never came. He finally reached the other side and hopped down, breathing with relief when he flattened his back against the cold dirt wall, because no one had fired a shot yet.

He started up the ditch, *crunching* glass hidden among the thick weeds. There were still no signs of people or blood in the ditch or on the road to his left, and he wasn't entirely sure if that was a good or bad sign. Cars didn't drive themselves, and they certainly didn't lose control and overturn without a reason.

Keo stopped for a moment and peeked over the top of the ditch to see Jordan moving steadily from the fields and toward the other side. She finally got there and hopped into the ditch, then peered up and across at him. They exchanged a brief nod.

He continued toward the truck, trying to see as much of the vehicle as possible, but the angle was all wrong and he ended up staring at the bent back bumper and a Texas license plate hanging on by just one remaining screw. He was fully prepared to break someone's head open with the tire iron should they lunge out at him from the wreckage, but he didn't have to, no matter how much noise he was making with all the *crunching* glass under his boots.

When he finally reached the damaged vehicle, Keo sneaked a quick look into the shattered back passenger window by exposing his head for a brief half second before pulling it back and waited for the gunshots that never came.

Breathing easier now, he crouched and took a longer look this time. There was no one inside the back or the front seats. Shredded upholstery, more broken glass, and splashes of blood covered the driver's seat and front passenger's. He figured out where most of that blood came from when he spotted the two spiderwebbed bullet holes in the front windshield. There was plenty of evidence that whoever was in the vehicle when it ran off course hadn't left unscathed, but there were no signs of the people themselves.

Keo stood up and looked around him again. This was the first time he had gotten a good view at the open land on this side of the highway, not that there was much of a difference; it looked just as brown and sun-bleached on this side as it had on the other.

He swept the immediate area around the truck, trying to find traces of where the driver and passenger had gone. There was a lot of blood in the grass around him, but no clear indications the men (or women) had been pulled out and then dragged away.

So where the hell were the bodies?

He turned back to the highway. "Clear," he said, just loud enough for Jordan to hear.

She climbed out of the ditch. "Bodies?"

"They must have either been thrown clear or taken."

"Who would take them?"

"I don't know. But they bled all over the place."

"I'll see if they're back there," she said. "They might have things we can use, like real weapons."

"Good luck."

Keo watched her walking down the highway for a moment before crouching again and pulling open the back driver-side door and crawling inside. He had to pick his way through two dozen or so stray cartridges scattered along the ceiling just to find a couple of empty MRE bags. He could still smell their contents—lasagna in one, mashed potatoes and turkey in the other. His stomach growled at the aroma. Close, but no cigar.

There wasn't much in the front except some empty water bottles and candy bar wrappers. He spotted more abandoned 5.56 rounds, but no hints of the weapons they were meant to load. The fact that he couldn't find a single spent shell casing told him the truck's owners hadn't fired back when they were ambushed.

And this was definitely an ambush. The only thing that didn't make any sense was the bodies. Where the hell were the bodies?

"There's nothing back there," Jordan said when he crawled back outside the vehicle. She was perched on the highway behind him. "Anything useful?"

"Not a thing."

"Food?"

"See first answer."

"Bummer."

"Yeah."

"Well, I didn't completely come back empty-handed," she said, holding out a familiar piece of white paper—more of the flyers they had found back at the farmhouse, except this one had fresh tire tracks over it. "They're going to get such a stern talking to when Texas finds out they're littering out here."

The white sheet had the same blocky capital letters as the others, and read:

> JOIN THE FIGHT TO TAKE BACK TEXAS
> WAR IS HERE PICK A SIDE
> THIS IS ONLY THE BEGINNING

Keo climbed up from the ditch and stood on the highway. Jordan stretched next to him, then folded the piece of paper and slipped it into her back pocket.

"Are you collecting them now?" he asked.

"I'm going to take a look at them again later."

"Why?"

She shrugged. "There might be a secret code or something we're just not seeing."

"Seriously?"

She smiled. "It'll give me something to do. Better than staring at your ugly face all the time."

"Damn," he said.

"Just kidding. Your face is beautiful. Even with all those unsightly things on it."

She flicked some dirt off his forehead and leaned in and kissed him. She tasted of sun and day-old tuna, but that didn't stop him from kissing her back. She rubbed her hands playfully against his butt, and he might have thrown her to the highway and had his way with her right then and there if she didn't pull away, laughing as she did so.

"Let's make a promise," she said.

"What's that?"

"Next time, it has to be on a bed."

"Not a lot of beds around here, Jordan…"

"So when we finally find one, it'll be even more spectacular."

"'Spectacular'?" he smiled. "Don't make promises you can't keep."

"I never do," she said, and gave him a quick kiss on the lips before looking back down at the truck in the ditch. "So what happened to it?"

He smiled, amused she could switch topics so easily when they were just making out like teenagers a moment ago.

"Bullet holes in the front windshield took out the driver and his passenger," he said. "Or maybe just the driver, who lost control of the car and ended up there. Same difference."

"So where are the bodies?"

"That's a good question."

"Maybe the animals took them?"

"That's assuming there are still wild animals out here."

"There has to be, right? There was that dog back at the beach outside of Sunport. Anyway, who do you think they were?"

"Don't know, don't care." He glanced up at the sun and shielded his eyes. "Angleton's close by. We should hit it before nightfall, then figure out our next move after that."

"So you're saying we should be angling toward Angleton?"

She was smiling triumphantly as she said it, and Keo hated himself for not having noticed much, much earlier what a beautiful woman Jordan was. Or maybe he always knew? He remembered really liking her when they had first met outside of Earl's cabin many months ago, but Gillian had been there at the time. Gillian was still around now, but it wasn't the same.

He smiled back at her. "Been saving that one up, huh?"

"Just a wee bit," she said, pinching her fingers together.

He exaggerated an eye roll. "Let's get going before I throw you more softballs."

"I love your softballs, Keo. But then, I've always had small hands."

He groaned. "Seriously?"

She laughed. "Hey, a girl's gotta do what a girl's gotta do to amuse herself. It's really, really boring out here."

"Can I at least be in on the joke, too?"

"I'll think about it," she said, and turned back up the highway.

She took one step, then two, when there was a loud, ear-shattering *crack!* and Jordan crumpled like a marionette with its strings cut. The painful *thump!* as her head hit the pavement at the same time he dropped to one knee and grabbed at, and caught, her limp body, the gunshot still echoing all around him—

A second *crack!* and a bullet *zipped!* past his head, so close that he swore his left ear was left flaming hot in the aftermath of the near miss.

He should be running, heading for cover, anything to *get out of the open,* but instead he dropped the tire iron and frantically slipped both hands under Jordan's armpits and began dragging her sagging body backward. His body screamed with pain, and both arms threatened to fall off again. It seemed to take forever (Jesus Christ, how long was this goddamn road?) before he finally reached the other side, and he deposited both of them into the ditch, gasping for breath as he landed on the cold soft dirt, Jordan's body *twumping* next to his.

He crawled over and grabbed her, suddenly aware that his clothes were clinging to his chest and sticky with blood. Was he bleeding? No. It wasn't his. It was Jordan's. It was all Jordan's. She was struggling to breathe, her eyes blinking uncontrollably, fading brown eyes snapping frantically all around until they finally found his face.

He smiled down at her. Or tried to. "You'll be all right. Gotta find the wound and patch you up. Give me a second, okay?"

She didn't answer, even though her lips were quivering, as if constantly on the verge of making a sound but never succeeding. Her face was impossibly pale, every inch of her body trembling in his lap.

He couldn't find the bullet hole in her jacket through all the blood, so he had to unzip it and pull it off her. There, the source of all the bleeding, just over her left breast. The bullet was still in there somewhere, pumping blood out through the single wound.

There was so much blood. Jesus, why was there so much blood?

Keo picked her jacket back up and pushed it against her chest. She seemed to seize up, maybe from the pressure he was putting on her, but he didn't ease up because the bleeding needed to be stopped at all cost.

"Shoot for center mass. Then take out the brain to make sure."

Everyone knew that, from the cops to the military grunts to guys like him. You always shot for center mass—the chest—to get the target down, then you finished him off with a head shot. It was SOP. Whoever was out there—whoever had taken the shot—had done exactly that.

Jordan continued to blink up at him, and there was a hollowness to her eyes that didn't belong. The Jordan he knew—who had kept her friends alive after the end of the world, who had saved his miserable life last night—was full of life. But he didn't see that right now. There was only sadness looking back up at him.

"You'll be fine," he said. "I've stopped the bleeding. No one boinks me in a barn and gets to just run away."

Her eyes widened, that familiar Jordan life coming back, if just for a split second, and her lips somehow managed to form a smile.

He returned it, or thought he did. He focused on her eyes, on her pained face, and forgot (and didn't care) to react to the pounding footsteps crossing the highway, just a few seconds before a figure leaped into the ditch in front of him.

He heard similar sounds behind him and knew another one was back there.

"Shit, got one," a voice said. Male. Young. Keo could practically feel the giddiness dripping from his every word.

He tore his eyes away from Jordan's paling face and looked up as a man *(boy)* moved cautiously toward him. He had black, brown, and green paint over his face and was wearing some kind of Ghillie suit stuffed with brown straw and grass. He was cradling an AR-15 with a large scope on top, the weapon covered in the same camo pattern as his face. A gun belt, with a holstered sidearm, stuck out of his right hip.

"Don't fucking move," the man said. He was trying to sound menacing and doing a poor job of it. Despite the face paint, he couldn't have been more than twenty.

Behind Keo, the second ambusher shuffled closer, too.

Keo looked back down at Jordan, at the thin smile frozen on her lips. There was a peaceful expression on her face, belying the fact she had just been shot in the chest and had bled enough for both of them.

The man in front of him leaned forward and peeked down at Jordan. "Dead center, Bill. Nice shot."

Bill, the man behind Keo, said, "Told you. And yours went wide."

"Not my fault; he dropped on me."

"What's that, two for me and one for you?"

"Sounds right."

"You see a uniform on them?"

"Nope," the one in front of him said. "Civilian?"

"Don't take any chances. These collaborators can be sneaky."

They're Mercer's men, Keo thought as he listened to their back and forth.

But even as his mind processed that information, he couldn't take his eyes off Jordan, lying in his lap. Her body had gone completely still, but her face remained serene as he stroked her cheeks and brushed at strings of tears falling from the corners of her eyes. There was blood on her lips, and he thumbed them away gently.

He sighed and closed his eyes. Just for a brief second.

When he opened them again, he focused on his surroundings. The young one in front of him, the older-sounding one behind him. The soft wind blowing through the fields around all three of them, causing the grass to sway to his left and skirting across the highway to his right, picking up some of the debris from the crash. But most of all, the bright red of Jordan's blood on his hands, sticking to his fingers.

"The flyer," Keo said.

"What?" the young one said.

"The flyer," he said again, pulling the piece of paper out of Jordan's back pocket and holding it up. It was wet with her blood.

The one in front of him took two steps forward and snatched the paper out of Keo's hand. He flicked it open, glanced at it once, then looked past Keo at Bill. "It's one of ours."

"'Join the fight to take back Texas,'" Keo said. "'War is here. Pick a side.' That's what we did. We picked a side."

"The fuck is he saying, Luke?" Bill asked.

"It's from the flyer," the man named Luke said, holding the paper, covered in Jordan's blood and tire tracks, up for the other man to see. "I guess he's saying he came looking for us, to sign up?"

"Bullshit. It's a trick."

Luke had let both arms drop to his sides, including the right hand with the AR-15. "But that's why we dropped them in the first place, right? To get recruits?"

"They didn't say anything about bringing in recruits," Bill said. "That's not our job."

Keo wondered how much older Bill was compared to Luke. Maybe he should interject, say something to help push Luke along. He had a feeling whether he lived or died was going to be decided in the next few seconds, and Luke was going to play a very big part of it.

"Yeah, but the flyer," Luke said, holding it up again.

Bill sighed. "Shit." Then, clearly annoyed, "You checked him for weapons?"

"He only had that tire iron, and he dropped it back on the road." He looked down at Keo. "So, you wanna join up, huh?"

Keo ignored his question, and said instead, "I need help with her."

"What for? She's dead."

"She's still alive."

"No way." Luke leaned in to get a better look. He was close enough Keo could smell dirt and sweat on his body underneath the Ghillie suit. "You sure?"

"She's still alive," Keo said, looking up at him. "I stopped the bleeding, but I need to dress the wound. The bullet missed vital organs, from what I can tell. You got a first-aid kit?"

"Damn," Luke said, and slung his rifle.

"What are you doing?" Bill asked, alarmed.

"Relax; I told you, he's unarmed," Luke said. "I was watching him the whole time, remember?"

"Be careful."

"Yeah, yeah." The young man knelt in front of Keo and reached into one of the pouches along his belt. He leaned in closer to get a better look at Jordan at the same time. "You sure she's even breathing, man?"

"Dammit, kid, don't get too close," Bill said.

Luke might have been on the verge of saying something back, but he never got the chance because Keo brought out his right hand, the one with the spork, and jammed it into the side of Luke's neck.

"Fuck!" Bill shouted.

Keo lunged forward while simultaneously pulling Luke toward him, using the handle of the lodged spork as leverage. He jerked his legs out from under Jordan's limp form and slid behind Luke.

"Fuck!" Bill shouted again.

Keo slid one arm around Luke's neck, clamping his struggling body against his own, while his right hand dropped to Luke's hip, blood-covered fingers searching out the young man's holstered gun among the grass and straws.

"Let him go!" Bill shouted.

Bill had lifted his rifle—another AR-15—and was shuffling his feet less than two meters away. Keo hadn't realized how close the man had been to him. Bill was wearing a Ghillie suit that was almost identical to Luke's, and his face was covered in the same camo pattern. He clutched and unclutched his rifle even as he swayed left and right, trying to line up a shot on Keo.

But Bill didn't shoot, because Keo was using Luke as a shield and doing everything possible not to expose his head for a clear shot. Luke's body spasmed uncontrollably in front of him, the younger man's hands groping for the spork sticking out of the side of his throat like some cancerous appendage.

By the time Bill realized what Keo was doing, Keo already had Luke's gun out of its holster. Bill finally fired—*and struck Luke in the stomach*. Keo didn't give him the chance to pull the trigger again and shot Bill in the chest with the handgun. He didn't stop shooting until Bill had collapsed to the ditch floor on his face.

Keo finally allowed himself to breathe again, the gun still pointed, and watched Bill's body the entire time, in case the guy was wearing some kind of bulletproof vest underneath his suit and tried to get back up.

A second, then two—before Keo shot Bill in the top of his exposed head just to make sure.

Satisfied now that Bill wasn't getting back up, Keo sat down and pushed Luke off him with one of his boots. The body careened forward and landed on its stomach, mirroring Bill's posture in front of them. Keo lay down and stared up at the sun, and inhaled in and exhaled out the chilly winter air in silence.

He didn't know how long he stayed down, blinking up at the clear skies. It could have been a few seconds, or a few minutes, or possibly a few hours.

Finally, he sat back up, then crawled over to Jordan and knelt next to her. She still had that strangely contented look on her face, and if not for all the blood and the balled up jacket crushed against her chest, he might have been able to convince himself she was just asleep.

He stole a quick look up at the sun again. He had plenty of hours left, but it wouldn't last.

Nothing ever did, these days.

◄━▌ ▐━►

HE LEFT LUKE and Bill in the ditch and carried Jordan into the fields about fifty meters from the highway before digging a shallow grave using two Ka-Bar knives he'd salvaged from the dead men. It took longer than expected, and his palms were raw and blistered by the time he was done. He buried Jordan and covered her up to keep any animals that might still be roaming around out there from getting to her, then sat down next to her grave for about half an hour, with just the silence and the wind to keep him company.

Afterward, he walked back to the bodies and went through their pockets. They were carrying identical AR-15s, each one mounted with a large scope for long-distance shooting. He slung Bill's rifle, then threw Luke's as far into the grass as he could. He had a feeling he had a long walk ahead of him, and each rifle was already at least seven pounds of extra weight. He slapped on a gun belt, then put the Sig Sauer he had taken from Luke in the holster. Keo pulled the spork out of Luke's neck and wiped off the blood, then pocketed it. The damn thing had saved his life twice now; the least he could do was keep it around.

He couldn't find any tactical packs on either men, which meant

THE SPEARS OF LACONIA ✦ 371

they had left them behind somewhere. Keo climbed back up to the highway and reoriented himself, remembering where he and Jordan had been standing when the shots came. Then he backtracked the source of the gunshots into the endless fields and kept walking until he found two camouflage packs among the grass about 150 meters away.

He unzipped them one by one, pulling out MREs, canned beans, and extra magazines. They were both too heavy to take, so he tossed most of the canned goods and extra ammo and kept just the MREs and the spare magazines he could carry without overburdening himself. The load was still too heavy, but he figured it'd get lighter as he used up the supplies along the way. If not, he'd just eject what he didn't need, as needed.

He spent another hour looking for Luke and Bill's vehicle. He was sure it was out there somewhere, like their packs. They couldn't have humped all the way out here on foot, could they? It was possible, but where would they have stayed last night? He was obviously dealing with a two-man kill team. He wouldn't have been surprised to learn there were identical squads crawling all over Texas at the moment, making life miserable for the collaborators.

But despite his confidence, he didn't find a vehicle anywhere in the vicinity. Either the men had hidden it too well, or they really had been dropped off. Both were possible, and neither one did him any good at the moment. He considered expanding his search range, but that would have taken much too long, and time was, as always, not on his side.

Keo walked about a mile up the highway, sticking to the ditch alongside it to stay mostly hidden, before finally stopping when his stomach growled again. He took a break and opened one of the cans, devouring the beans inside using the spork. He noticed there was still blood along one of the tines but ignored it.

He opened one of the pouches around his waist and took out the map he had spotted earlier while removing the belt from Luke. It was heavily marked, with collaborator towns circled in red ink, including T18 just outside of League City. The new map was almost identical to the one he had taken from Gregson, but with a few notable additions. One had a rough drawing of a star within a circle next to a town called Larkin, Texas. A second star-within-a-circle marked Lochlyn, about twenty miles northwest of his current location. As far as he could tell, Lochlyn was a small place in the middle of nowhere. Both new locations had crude drawings of planes next to them.

Airfields. That's how they're getting in and out of Texas. Using private, isolated airfields hidden in the countryside.

He glanced up at the sky, then down at his watch. Five hours of sunlight left. If he didn't stop to rest again, he could easily make Lochlyn before nightfall.

And then what?

He had limited options, but one of them was to continue on to T18 and try to rescue Gillian, which would mean fighting his way back into a town he had already barely survived the first time. But she was in there, and she was in danger, and goddammit, he owed it to her and Jordan to get her out before Mercer's people attacked again.

What was the alternative?

Go to Lochlyn, find Mercer, and kill him.

If the man was even there, and *if* putting a bullet between Mercer's eyes stopped this—whatever "this" was. But then again, what was a snake without its head? If killing Mercer stopped the war, then Gillian would be safe. Her and the baby and *(Fuck you)* Jay.

Two possibilities. Two directions. They weren't much, but there it was.

Lochlyn was closer, but what were the odds Mercer was even there? Fifty-fifty? Ten-ninety, against? Maybe he'd get to Lochlyn and there wouldn't be anyone there at all. Those plane markers, for all he knew, could have just been doodling, Luke's way of passing the time.

The odds that Mercer was even there, that killing him would change anything, was slim. On the other hand, getting back into T18—even with Tobias's help—and rescuing Gillian while the town was on lockdown was going to be a hell of a feat.

Shit. It was bad odds either way.

But he'd had worse.

He checked his watch again.

Keo got up, tossed away the empty can of beans, and climbed out of the ditch, jogging across the highway.

Fuck it, he thought as he headed northwest.

EPILOGUE

"IRONY"?

Was that the word? Sometimes he had difficulty grasping the easiest things. He blamed it on having too many voices inhabiting the same space inside his head, an unending tide of chatter, almost like being stuck in a small box with a few million other people, but maybe the answer was simpler. A lack of focus on things that didn't matter, that was pushed into the background, because everything else in the forefront was crucial to his survival.

Maybe the word he was looking for was "poetic."

Or "tragic."

It had to be one of those. Sooner or later, it would come to him. It always did.

Just like how they had led him here. He hadn't expected it, but here he was. He'd killed the two blue eyes outside of Starch, decapitated them in the woods and left their bodies to be found far, far from this place. It hadn't been easy, and they had gotten their shots in, but he was always good at surviving.

Adapt or perish, someone once said.

The night had dragged on, and through the seemingly endless throng of black eyes, he had arrived—hurt, bleeding, and badly in need of extra nights of healing. So what else was new? It seemed like that was all he did these days: fight, survive, and rest, in order to do it all over again.

He had abandoned his mission, left Keo and the woman to fend for themselves somewhere out there in the world. There hadn't been any choice, because Danny was in danger. He and Gaby, and the boy, Nate. But Keo was still alive. He could feel him out there, somewhere. The connection wasn't as strong as it could have been, but it was good enough.

And there was Mercer. Once a potential ally in possession of an army, with airpower and armor at his disposal. A plan months in the plotting *("You're with us, or you're against us.")*. Except Mercer wasn't the answer he had been hoping for. No, Mercer was dangerous. Too dangerous to trust her with.

She was still out there, maybe still waiting for him. He wouldn't blame her if she had given up. It had been days. Weeks? Months? It might have been months. It was sometimes difficult to keep track of the days and nights, because the days tended to blur by when all he could see whenever he opened his eyes was darkness.

But he had arrived at this place, where all the answers he had been searching for were waiting for him. The blue eyes had given it away. They thought they were hunting him, when in truth it was the other way around. Oh, they hadn't wanted to, and they fought tooth and nail, but there were ways around that.

This was where it had all started, with that night in the dilapidated apartment building where he found salvation in a pair of silver crosses, just as he needed them the most. A sign from God, or just coincidence? He still didn't know. Did God even exist? If the devil did, then shouldn't God, too?

He slid carefully along the rooftop and lowered himself to the edge. The hulking shape of the highway, flat gray in the moonlight, impeded his vision. Metal, plastic, and aluminum carcasses of objects that no longer had any uses covered the mighty structure from end to end. And there, in the background, all the familiar buildings, the skyscrapers, the homes and offices of people who once called this place home.

Ironic.

That was the word he was searching for. It was ironic that he would end up back here, after all the months of running away from it.

Here, back at the heart of the infestation.

Back here, where the longest night of his life occurred, where he and Danny fought for hours to escape the hordes of undead.

Here. In this city. He was in there, somewhere.

Mabry.

The streets and highways and buildings were crammed with them. He was far enough beyond their reach that they couldn't see or sense or smell him, but he would never be able to get any closer than he was now. They would guard Mabry with their lives, keep him from prying eyes night and day. The blue eyes were in there, too. He couldn't fight them all, even if he was at full strength.

At least, not alone.

He could already feel Mabry stirring, sensing his nearness. How did he know? Because he was everywhere, and nowhere. Except that wasn't true anymore. Mabry *was* somewhere. He was *here.*

He turned and fled, leaping across rooftops, avoiding the black eyes below. All it would take was for one of them to look up and see him, and they'd swarm. He would never make it out alive.

Two rooftops, three…and the voices remained silent inside his head, a good sign he was still undiscovered. Faster and further. He had to keep going. Keep moving. It wasn't safe here, not this close to Mabry.

He was bleeding again, the constant motion draining him, slowing him down with every step, every jump, every rooftop. He couldn't allow that. Weakness lowered his guard, and he needed the mental walls even more now to keep back the voices, to stay beyond Mabry's reach.

Rest. He needed to rest, and sleep, and heal.

He slowed only after he had left the world of brick and concrete behind and could feel soft earth under his feet. Gray gave way to green as he went deeper, and deeper still, into the woods.

Rest. He needed to rest.

And heal…

"WHY DO YOU fight?"

Mabry. Calling out to him, trying to get him to reveal himself. He maintained the wall, but there was no denying Mabry's voice. It burrowed deep, despite all his best attempts to drown it in memories of his old life, of her...

"You must know by now. There's no point."

He concentrated on the worms crawling over his arms and legs. Slippery things. Wet. Once upon a time, he would have been disgusted. Now, they were his daily companion.

"She'll never accept you. None of them will."

His eyes snapped open. Footsteps—a flood of bare feet—directly above him. Mabry's scouts, spreading out into the darkness of the woods. Had Mabry sensed his closeness after all? Was he exposed? Something that might have been panic (or maybe just memories of what panic was) flooded his senses.

"But Kate was right about you."

No, it was just a false alarm. The black eyes had continued into the woods, the tremors across the ground signaling their passing. It took a while because there were so many of them, but eventually, eventually they faded, until there was just the peace and quiet again.

"Your knack for survival is uncanny."

He closed his eyes and raised extra mental defenses. He could feel Mabry groping at the corners of his mind. Close, so close, but still searching blind.

"You won't give up, will you?"

Sleep. Rest. Heal.

"You'll never give up."

Soon, very soon, he would come face-to-face with the monster, and he would either slay him or be slayed by him. Soon, very soon, the end would come, and he would either rise victorious or fall. But he had to try. Because too many lives were at stake, especially hers. He would do anything—*everything*—to protect her, even if he couldn't stand side by side with her when it was over.

"You'll fight as long as there's a breath in your body."

Mabry was becoming agitated, scouring the connections between the brood with renewed intensity. Because Mabry was the constant voice, the hand that guided them *(me)* and soothed their worries. Without him, they *(we)* would be mindless things. Husks.

"You would have been such a worthy successor."

Mabry was the beginning, and the end.

"Someone to carry on my legacy."

The everything, and the nothing.

"Alas, alas…"

He was everywhere, and nowhere.

But that last part wasn't true anymore, because he knew exactly where Mabry was now. The dying blue eyes had led him right to his doorstep.

Here, back in Houston, where it had begun almost a year ago.

Mabry was in there, somewhere.

Sleeping.

Hiding.

And very, very vulnerable…

31191802R00242

Made in the USA
Middletown, DE
21 April 2016